Mercy

JUSSI ADLER-OLSEN

Translated by Lisa Hartford

PENGUIN BOOKS

PENGUIN BOOKS

Published by the Penguin Group
Penguin Books Ltd, 80 Strand, London WC2R ORL, England
Penguin Group (USA) Inc., 375 Hudson Street, New York, New York 10014, USA
Penguin Group (Canada), 90 Eglinton Avenue East, Suite 700, Toronto, Ontario, Canada M4P 2Y3
(a division of Pearson Penguin Canada Inc.)
Penguin Ireland, 25 St Stephen's Green, Dublin 2, Ireland (a division of Penguin Books Ltd)
Penguin Group (Australia), 707 Collins Street, Melbourne, Victoria 3008, Australia
(a division of Pearson Australia Group Pty Ltd)
Penguin Books India Pvt Ltd, 11 Community Centre, Panchsheel Park, New Delhi – 110 017, India
Penguin Group (NZ), 67 Apollo Drive, Rosedale, Auckland 0632, New Zealand
(a division of Pearson New Zealand Ltd)
Penguin Books (South Africa) (Pty) Ltd, Block D, Rosebank Office Park,
181 Jan Smuts Avenue, Parktown North, Gauteng 2193, South Africa

Penguin Books Ltd, Registered Offices: 80 Strand, London WC2R ORL, England

www.penguin.com

First published in Danish as *Kvinden i buret* by Politikens Forlag 2008
This translation first published in Great Britain by Penguin Books 2011
This edition published 2013

002

Copyright © Jussi Adler-Olsen, 2008
Translation copyright © Lisa Hartford, 2011

The moral right of the author and translator has been asserted

All rights reserved
Without limiting the rights under copyright
reserved above, no part of this publication may be
reproduced, stored in or introduced into a retrieval system,
or transmitted, in any form or by any means (electronic, mechanical,
photocopying, recording or otherwise), without the prior
written permission of both the copyright owner and
the above publisher of this book

Set in 12.5/14.75pt Garamond MT Std
Typeset by Jouve (UK), Milton Keynes
Printed in Great Britain by Clays Ltd, St Ives plc

A CIP catalogue record for this book is available from the British Library

PAPERBACK ISBN: 978-1-405-91265-5
OM PAPERBACK ISBN: 978-1-405-91321-8

www.greenpenguin.co.uk

Laois County Library
Leabharlann Chontae Laoise

Acc. No. ...... 16/3902......

Class No. .... F ....

Inv. No. 13496

...mmitted to a sustainable
...ess, our readers and our planet.
...rom Forest Stewardship
...paper.

Dedicated to Hanne Adler-Olsen.
Without her, the well would run dry.

Prologue

She scratched her fingertips on the smooth walls until they bled, and pounded her fists on the thick panes until she could no longer feel her hands. At least ten times she had fumbled her way to the steel door and stuck her fingernails in the crack to try to pry it open, but the door could not be budged, and the edge was sharp.

Finally, when her nails started pulling away from the flesh of her fingers, she tumbled back on to the ice-cold floor, breathing hard. For a moment she stared into the thundering darkness, her eyes open wide and her heart hammering. Then she screamed. Screamed until her ears were ringing and her voice gave out.

She leaned her head back and again felt the fresh air streaming down from the ceiling. Maybe she could jump up there if she got a running start and then grabbed hold of something. Maybe then something would happen.

Yes, then maybe those bastards outside would have to come in.

And if she stuck out her fingers and aimed for their eyes, maybe she could blind them. If she was fast enough and didn't hesitate, maybe she could. And then perhaps she could escape.

For a moment she sucked on her bleeding fingers, then pressed them against the floor and sat up.

Blindly she stared up at the ceiling. Maybe it was too far

to jump. Maybe there was nothing for her to grab. But she had to give it a try. What else could she do?

She took off her jacket and carefully placed it in a corner so she wouldn't trip over it. Then in one bound she leaped off the floor, stretching her arms in the air as high as she could, but she touched nothing. She did it a couple more times before retreating to the far wall, where she paused for a moment to collect herself. Then she took a running start, and with all her might jumped into the darkness, her arms flailing after hope. When she crashed back down, her foot slipped on the smooth floor and her body landed on its side. She gasped loudly as her shoulder struck the concrete, and she screamed when her head smashed against the wall, slamming her brain full of flashes of light.

For a long time she lay very still, wanting only to cry. But she didn't. If her prison guards heard her, they'd take it the wrong way. They would think she was on the verge of giving up, but she wasn't. On the contrary.

She was going to look after herself. For them she was the woman in the cage, but she was the one who decided how far apart the bars would be. She would think thoughts that opened out on to the world and kept madness at bay. They would never break her. That's what she decided as she lay there on the floor, her shoulder throbbing fiercely and the swelling around her eye forcing it closed.

Someday she would get out of here.

I

2007

Carl took a step towards the mirror and ran one finger along his temple where the bullet had grazed his head. The wound had healed, but the scar was clearly visible under his hair, if anyone cared to look.

But who the hell would want to do that? he thought as he studied his face.

It was obvious now that he had changed. The furrows around his mouth were deeper, the shadows under his eyes were darker, and his expression showed a profound indifference. Carl Mørck was no longer himself, the experienced criminal detective who lived and breathed for his work. No longer the tall, elegant man from Jutland who caused eyebrows to raise and lips to part. And what the hell did it matter anyway?

He buttoned his shirt, put on his jacket, tossed down the last dregs of his coffee and slammed the front door behind him, so that the other residents of the house would realize it was time to haul themselves out of bed. His gaze fell to the nameplate on the door. It was about time he changed it. It had been a long time since Vigga moved out. Even though they weren't yet divorced, it was definitely over.

He turned around and set off for Hestestien. If he caught the train in twenty minutes, he'd be able to spend a good half-hour with Hardy at the hospital before he had to head over to police headquarters.

He saw the red-brick church tower looming above the bare trees and tried to remind himself how lucky he'd been, in spite of everything. Only an inch to the right and Anker would still be alive. Only half an inch to the left, and he himself would have been killed. Capricious inches that had spared him a trip along the green fields to the cold graves a few hundred yards in front of him.

Carl had tried to understand, but it wasn't easy. He didn't know much about death. Only that it could be as unpredictable as a lightning bolt and infinitely quiet after it arrived.

On the other hand, he knew everything about how violent and pointless it could be to die. That much he really did know.

He was only a couple of weeks out of the police academy when the sight of his first murder victim had been burned permanently on to Carl's retina. A small, slight woman who had been strangled by her husband and ended up lying on the floor with dull eyes and an expression that had left Carl feeling sick for weeks afterwards. Since then, scores of cases had followed. Each morning he had prepared himself to face it all. The bloody clothes, the waxen faces, the frozen photos. Every day he'd listened to people's lies and excuses. Every day a crime in a new guise, gradually making less and less of an impact on him. Twenty-five years on the police force and ten in the homicide division had hardened him.

That's how things had gone until the day when a murder case pierced his armour.

*

They had sent him and Anker and Hardy out to a decrepit barracks on a worn, dirt road where a corpse was waiting to tell its own unique story.

As so often before, it had been the stench that prompted a neighbour to react. The victim was just a recluse who had lain down peacefully in his own filth and exhaled his last alcoholic fumes. Or so they thought, until they discovered the nail from a nail gun lodged halfway in his skull. That was the reason the homicide division had been called in.

On that particular day it was Carl's team's turn to respond, which was OK with him and his two assistants, even though Carl griped as usual about being overworked and how the other teams were slacking off. But who could have known how fateful this call would turn out to be? Or that only five minutes would pass from the time they entered the room with the reeking corpse until Anker lay on the floor in a pool of blood, Hardy had taken his last steps, and the fire inside Carl had been extinguished – the flame that was absolutely essential for a detective in the homicide division of the Copenhagen Police.

2

2002

The tabloids loved everything about the Democrats' vice-chairperson, Merete Lynggaard, and everything she stood for. Her sharp comments at the podium in the Folketing, the Danish parliament. Her lack of respect for the prime minister and his yes-men. Her feminine attributes, mischievous eyes and seductive dimples. They loved her for her youth and success, but above all they loved her for the fodder she gave to speculations about why such a talented and beautiful woman had still not appeared in public with a man.

Merete Lynggaard sold a hell of a lot of newspapers. Lesbian or not, she was truly great material.

And Merete was fully aware of this.

'Why don't you go out with Tage Baggesen?' her secretary urged, as they headed for Merete's small blue Audi, avoiding the puddles forming in the Christiansborg car park, which was reserved for members of parliament. 'I know there are plenty of men who'd like to take you out on the town, but he's completely crazy about you. How many times has he tried to ask you out? Have you even counted how many messages he's left on your desk? In fact, he left one today. Just give him a chance, Merete.'

'Why don't *you* date him?' Merete glanced down as she dumped a pile of folders on to the back seat of her car.

'What am I supposed to do with someone who's chair of the Traffic Committee and also a member of the Radical Centre Party? Can you tell me that, Marianne? What am I? Some sort of traffic roundabout in the provinces?'

Merete raised her eyes to look over at the Royal Arsenal Museum, where a man in a white trench coat was photographing the building. Did he just snap a picture of her? She shook her head. The feeling of being watched had begun to annoy her. Of course it was sheer paranoia. She really needed to relax.

'Tage Baggesen is thirty-five years old and he's fucking gorgeous,' said Marianne. 'Well, OK, maybe he could stand to lose a few pounds, but on the other hand he owns a country house in Vejby. Plus a couple of others over in Jutland, I think. What more could you want?'

Merete shook her head sceptically. 'Right. He's thirty-five years old and lives with his mother. You know what, Marianne? You should take him yourself. You've been acting really strange lately. Take him. Be my guest!'

She grabbed all the folders her secretary was holding and flung them on to the seat with the others. The time on the dashboard clock was 17:30. She was already late.

'Your voice will be missed in the Folketing this evening, Merete.'

'I suppose,' she said with a shrug. Ever since she'd entered politics, there had been a firm agreement between herself and the chairman of the Democrats that after six p.m., her time was her own, unless it was a matter of crucial committee work or a vote. 'Not a problem,' he'd told her back then, fully aware of how many votes she pulled in. So it shouldn't be a problem now, either.

7

'Come on, Merete. Tell me what you've got planned.' Her secretary tilted her head. 'What's his name?'

Merete gave her a quick smile and slammed the door. It was about time she found a replacement for Marianne Koch.

3

2007

Homicide chief Marcus Jacobsen was a slob when it came to keeping his office in order, but that didn't bother him. The mess was just an external phenomenon; on the inside he was meticulously organized. There, in his shrewd mind, everything was neatly arranged. He never lost sight of the details. They were still razor sharp ten years later.

It was only in situations like the one that had just occurred, when the room was crammed with super-attentive colleagues who had been forced to sidle around worn-out document carts and heaps of case materials, that he regarded the ragnarok of his office with a certain dismay.

He raised his chipped Sherlock Holmes mug and took a big gulp of cold coffee as he thought for the tenth time that morning about the half pack of cigarettes in his jacket pocket. It was no longer even permitted to take a damned smoke break out in the courtyard. Fucking directives.

'OK, now listen up!' Marcus Jacobsen turned to look at his deputy, Lars Bjørn, whom he'd asked to stay behind after the general briefing was over. 'The case of the murdered cyclist in Valby Park is going to drain all our resources if we don't watch out,' he said.

Lars Bjørn nodded. 'Then this is a hell of a time for Carl Mørck to rejoin the team and monopolize four of

9

our very best detectives. People are complaining about him, and who do you think they're complaining to?' He jabbed at his chest, as if he were the only one who had to listen to people's shit.

'He shows up hours late,' he went on. 'Rides his staff hard, rummages around with the cases, and refuses to return phone calls. His office is utter chaos, and you won't believe this, but they called from the forensics lab to bitch about a phone conversation with him. The boys from forensics – can you believe it? It takes a lot to aggravate those guys. We need to do something about Carl, Marcus, regardless of what he's been through. Otherwise I don't know how the department is going to function.'

Marcus raised his eyebrows. He pictured Carl in his mind. He actually liked the man, but those eternally sceptical eyes and caustic remarks could piss anybody off; he was well aware of that. 'Yeah, you're right. Hardy and Anker were probably the only ones who could stand working with him. But they were kind of strange too.'

'Marcus. Nobody's coming right out and saying so, but the man is a total pain in the butt, and actually always has been. He's not suited to working here; we're too dependent on each other. Carl was hopeless as a colleague from day one. Why did you ever bring him downtown from Bellahøj?'

Marcus fixed his eyes on Bjørn. 'He was and is an outstanding detective, Lars. That's why.'

'OK, OK. I know we can't just throw him out, especially not in this situation, but we've got to find some other solution, Marcus.'

'He's only been back from sick leave for about a week,

so why don't we give him a chance? Maybe we should try going easy on him for a while.'

'Are you sure? In the last few weeks we've had more cases dumped on us than we can handle. Some of them are major ones, too, as you well know. The fire fatality out on Amerikavej – was it arson or not? The bank robbery on Tomsgårdsvej, where a customer was killed. The rape in Tårnby, where the girl died; the gang stabbing out in Sydhavnen; the murder of the cyclist in Valby Park. Need I say more? Not to mention all the old cases. We haven't even made a dent in several of those. And then we've got a team leader like Mørck. Indolent, surly, morose, always bitching, and he treats his colleagues like crap, so the team is about to fall apart. He's a thorn in our side, Marcus. Send Carl packing and let's bring in some fresh blood. I know it's harsh, but that's my opinion.'

The homicide chief nodded. He'd noticed his colleagues' behaviour during the briefing that had just ended. Silent and sullen and worn out. Of course they didn't want someone dumping on them.

Marcus's deputy went over to the window and looked out at the buildings across the way. 'I think I have a solution to the problem. We might get some flack from the union, but I don't think so.'

'Damn it, Lars. I haven't got the energy to go head-to-head with the union. If you're thinking of demoting him, they'll be on our backs in an instant.'

'No, we'll kick him upstairs!'

'Hmm.' This was where Marcus needed to be careful. His deputy was a damned good detective with tons of experience and plenty of solved cases to his credit, but he still had a lot to learn when it came to managing personnel. Here, at headquarters, you couldn't just kick someone up or down the ranks without a good reason. 'You're suggesting we promote him, is that what you're saying? How? And who were you expecting to make room for him?'

'I know you've been up almost all night,' Lars Bjørn replied. 'And you've been busy this morning with that damned murder out in Valby, so you probably haven't been keeping up with the news. But haven't you heard what happened in parliament this morning?'

The homicide chief shook his head. It was true that he'd had too much on his plate ever since the murder of the cyclist in Valby Park had taken a new turn. Until last night they'd had a good witness, a reliable witness, and she had more to tell them – that much was very clear. They were sure they were close to a breakthrough. But then the witness had suddenly clammed up. It was obvious that someone in her circle of friends had been threatened. The police had questioned her until she was completely exhausted; they had talked to her daughters and her mother, but no one had anything to say. The whole family was terrified. No, Marcus hadn't got much sleep. So apart from seeing the headlines of the morning papers, he was out of the loop.

'Is it the Denmark Party again?' he asked.

'Exactly. Their legal spokesperson has presented the proposal again, as an amendment to the police-bill compromise, and this time there'll be a majority in favour. It's going to pass, Marcus. Piv Vestergård is going to get her way.'

'You're kidding!'

'She stood at the podium and ranted for a good twenty minutes, and the parties in the government supported her, of course, even though the Conservatives were probably squirming.'

'And?'

'Well, what do you think? She brought up four examples of ugly cases that had been shelved. In her opinion, it's not in the best interests of the public for such cases to remain unsolved. And that wasn't all she had in her goodie bag, let me tell you.'

'Jesus Christ! Does she think the crime squad puts cases on ice for the fun of it?'

'She insinuated that might actually be what happens with certain types of cases.'

'That's bullshit! What sort of cases?'

'She mentioned cases in which members of the Denmark Party and Liberal Party have been victims of a crime. We're talking about cases nationwide.'

'The bitch is off her rocker!'

The deputy shook his head. 'You think so? Well, she was just getting warmed up. After that, of course she also mentioned cases involving children who had disappeared and ones in which political organizations have been subjected to terrorist-type attacks. Cases that are especially bestial.'

'OK, OK, she's fishing for votes, that's what she's doing.'

'Yeah, of course she is, otherwise she would have handled it outside the Folketing chamber. But they're all fishing, because right now all the parties are in negotiations over at the Justice Ministry. The documents will be in the hands of the Finance Committee in no time. We'll have a decision within two weeks, if you ask me.'

'And what, exactly, will be the gist of it?'

'A new department will be established within the criminal police. She herself suggested it be called "Q", since that's the designation of the Denmark Party on the ballot. I don't know whether that was meant to be a joke, but it's sure going to end up as one.' He gave a sarcastic laugh.

'And what's the objective? Still the same?'

'Yes. The sole purpose is simply to handle what they're calling "cases deserving special scrutiny".'

'"To handle cases deserving special scrutiny."' Marcus nodded. 'That's a typical Piv Vestergård expression. Sounds very impressive. And who's supposed to decide which cases warrant such a label? Did she mention that too?'

The deputy shrugged.

'OK, she's asking us to do what we're already doing. So what? What does it have to do with us?'

'The department will come under the auspices of the National Police Commission, but administratively there is every reason to believe it will be under the homicide division of the Copenhagen Police.'

At this, Marcus's mouth fell open. 'You've got to be joking! What do you mean by administratively?'

'We plan the budgets and keep the account books. We provide the office staff. And the office space.'

'I don't understand. You mean now the Copenhagen Police are also going to have to solve ancient cases that are under the jurisdiction of police districts way out in the sticks? The regional districts will never go along with that.

They're going to demand to have representatives in the department here.'

'Not necessarily. It's going to be presented as a way of taking some of the burden off the districts. Not as an extra workload.'

'You realize what you're saying, don't you? That now our department is also going to have to provide a flying squad for hopeless cases. With my staff providing backup. No way, damn it, no! You can't be serious.'

'Marcus, try and listen to me. It's only a matter of a couple of hours here and there for just a few staff members. It's nothing.'

'It doesn't sound like nothing.'

'OK, then let me come right out and tell you how I see it. Are you listening?'

The homicide chief rubbed his forehead. Did he have a choice?

'Marcus, there's money attached to this.' He paused for a moment as he fixed his eyes on his boss. 'Not a lot, but enough to keep one man on salary and at the same time pump a couple of million kroner into our own department. It's an extra appropriation that's not meant to displace anything else.'

'A couple of million?' He nodded appreciatively. 'OK, now you're talking!'

'Brilliant, isn't it? We can set up the department in no time, Marcus. They're expecting us to dig in our heels, but we won't. We'll give them an accommodating response and propose a budget that avoids earmarking any specific tasks. And we make Carl Mørck the head of the new department, but there's not going to be much to be in change of, because he'll be on his own. And at a safe distance from everyone else, I can promise you that.'

'Carl Mørck as head of Department Q!' The homicide chief could just picture it. A department like that could be easily run on a budget of less than a million kroner a year, including travel expenses and lab tests and everything else. If the police requested five million a year for the new department, there'd be enough left over for a couple more investigative teams in the homicide division. Then they could concentrate mainly on older cases. Maybe not Department Q cases, but something along that line. Fluid boundaries, that was the key to the whole thing. Brilliant, yes. Nothing short of brilliant.

4

2007

Hardy Henningsen was the tallest person who had ever worked at police headquarters. His military records reported his height as six feet, nine and a half inches. Whenever they made an arrest, it was always Hardy who spoke, so that the perps had to lean their heads way back while their rights were read to them. That sort of thing made a lasting impression on most people.

Right now Hardy's height was not an advantage. As far as Carl could tell, his long, paralysed legs never got stretched out full length. Carl had suggested to the nurse that they cut the footboard off the bed, but apparently that was not within her realm of expertise.

Hardy never said a word about anything. His TV was on 24/7, and people kept coming and going in his room, but he didn't react. He just lay there in the Hornbæk Clinic for Spinal Cord Injuries, trying to survive. Attempting to chew his food, to move his shoulder a bit, since that was the only part south of his neck over which he had any control, and otherwise allowing the nurses to wrestle with his unwieldy body. He merely stared up at the ceiling as they washed his groin, stuck needles in him, emptied the bag collecting his waste products. No, Hardy didn't have much to say any more.

'I'm back at headquarters again, Hardy,' said Carl, straightening the bedclothes. 'They're working full blast on the case. They haven't discovered anything yet, but I know they're going to find out who shot us.'

Hardy's heavy eyelids didn't even flicker. He didn't bother to glance at Carl or at the TV news programme on Channel 2 that was filling airtime with a hyped-up report about the eviction of the kids squatting at the Youth House. He seemed indifferent to everything. Not even anger remained. Carl understood him better than anyone else. Even though he wasn't about to show it to Hardy, he didn't give a fuck about anything either. It was completely irrelevant who'd shot them. What good would it do to find out? If it wasn't one person, then it was somebody else. There were plenty of arseholes like that running around.

He nodded curtly to the nurse who came in with a fresh IV drip. The last time he'd been here, she had asked him to step outside while she tended to Hardy. She didn't get the response she was expecting, and it was clear that she hadn't forgotten.

'So, you're here again?' she said sullenly, glancing at her watch.

'This is a better time for me, before I go to work. Is that a problem?'

Again she looked at her watch. Yeah, so what if he showed up for work later than most people?

The nurse extended Hardy's arm and inspected the IV attached to the back of his hand. Then the door to the corridor opened, and the first physiotherapist of the day came in. She had hard work ahead of her.

Carl patted the sheet where the contour of Hardy's right arm was visible. 'These harpies want to have you all

18

to themselves, so I'm going to take off now, Hardy. I'll come back a little earlier tomorrow so we can have a talk. Keep smiling, man.'

The smell of medicine followed him out in the corridor, where he stopped to lean against the wall. His shirt was sticking to his back, and the sweat stains under his arms were ploughing their way further down his shirt. After the shooting incident, it didn't take much.

Hardy, Carl and Anker, as was their custom, had arrived at the murder scene in the suburb of Amager ahead of the others, and they were already wearing the white disposable coveralls, masks, gloves and hairnets that procedures prescribed. It was only half an hour since the old man had been found with the nail in his head. The drive from police headquarters took no time at all.

That day they had plenty of time before the body would be examined. As far as they knew, the homicide chief was at some sort of reorganization meeting with the police commissioner, but there was no doubt that he would arrive as soon as he could, along with the medical examiner. No office hassles were going to keep Marcus Jacobsen away from a crime scene.

'There's not much outside the house for the crime-scene techs to go on,' said Anker, jabbing his foot at the ground, which was soft and sludgy after the rain the night before.

Carl looked around. Aside from the marks left by the neighbour's wooden clogs, there weren't many footprints around the barracks building, which was one of those that the military had sold off in the sixties. Back then the barracks had all probably looked great, but by now, for this particular building at any rate, those days were over. The rafters had fallen in, the tar paper on the roof was riddled with holes, not a single plank on the facade was still in one piece, and the dampness had done its job. Even the sign, on which the name 'Georg Madsen' had been printed with a black marker, was half rotted off. And then there was the stench of the dead man, seeping out through the cracks. All in all, a real shithouse.

'I'll go and talk to the neighbour,' said Anker, turning towards the man who had been waiting half an hour. It was no more than five yards to the porch of his small cottage. Once the barracks were knocked down, his view was guaranteed to improve significantly.

Hardy was good at tolerating the stench of corpses. Maybe because he was taller and towered over the worst of it, or maybe because his sense of smell was decidedly less acute than most people's. This time the odour was especially bad.

'Damn, what a stink,' grunted Carl, as they stood in the hallway, pulling on the blue plastic booties.

'I'll open a window,' said Hardy, stepping into the room next to the claustrophobic entrance.

Carl went over to the doorway leading to the small living room. Not much light was coming through the blind that had been pulled down, but there was enough to see the figure sitting in the corner with the greyish-green skin and deep fissures in the blisters that covered most of his face. Reddish fluid trickled from his nose, and the buttons of his shirt were threatening to pop off from the pressure of the swollen torso. His eyes were like wax.

'The nail was fired into the head with a Paslode pneumatic framing nailer,' said Hardy from behind. 'It's lying on the table in the next room. There's also a power screwdriver, and it's still charged. Remind me that we need to find out how long it can lie around before it needs recharging.'

They'd been standing there surveying the scene for only a moment when Anker joined them.

'The neighbour has lived out here since the 16th of January,' he said. 'So that's ten days, and he hasn't seen the deceased come out of the house even once.' He pointed to the body and looked around the room. 'The neighbour was sitting outside on his porch, enjoying the global warming, and that's when he noticed the smell. He's really shaken up, the poor man. Maybe we should get the medical officer to take a look at him after he examines the body.'

Later Carl was only able to provide a very sketchy description of what happened next, and the top brass would just have to make do with that. According to most people, he hadn't been fully conscious anyway. But that wasn't true. He actually remembered all too well what occurred. He just didn't feel like going into detail.

He'd heard someone come in the kitchen door, but he hadn't reacted. Maybe it was the stench, maybe he thought it was the crime-scene techs arriving.

A few seconds later, out of the corner of his eye, he registered a figure wearing a red-checked shirt who launched himself forwards into the room. Carl thought that he should draw his weapon, but didn't. His reflexes failed him. On the other hand, he did notice the shock waves when the first shot struck Hardy in the back so that he fell, pulling Carl down and trapping him underneath. The enormous pressure of Hardy's bullet-pierced body wrenched Carl's spine hard to one side and jammed his knee.

Then came the shots that struck Anker in the chest and Carl in the temple. He recalled with great clarity how he lay there with a frantically hyperventilating Hardy on top of him, and how Hardy's blood seeped out through the coverall to mix with his own on the floor beneath them. And as the perpetrators' legs moved past him, he kept thinking he better get hold of his gun.

Behind him, Anker was lying on the floor, trying to wriggle his body around as the assailants talked to each other in the small room beyond the entrance. Only a few seconds passed before they were back in the living room. Carl heard Anker ordering them to halt. Later he found out that Anker had drawn his gun.

The reply to Anker's command was yet another shot, which shook the floor and struck Anker right in the heart.

That's all the time it took. The shooters slipped out the kitchen door, and Carl didn't move. He lay there totally motionless. Not even when the ME arrived did he give any sign of life. Later both the ME and the homicide chief said that at first they thought Carl was dead.

Carl lay there a long time, as if he'd fainted, with his head full of desperate thoughts. They took his pulse and then drove off with him and his two partners. Only at the hospital did he open his eyes. They told him that his eyes had a dead look to them.

They thought it was the shock, but it was from shame.

*

'Can I help you with something?' asked a man in his mid-thirties wearing a white coat.

Carl stopped leaning on the wall. 'I've just been in to see Hardy Henningsen.'

'Hardy, yes. Are you a family member?'

'No, I'm his colleague. I was Hardy's team leader in the homicide division.'

'I see.'

'What's Hardy's prognosis? Will he be able to walk again?'

The young doctor made a barely perceptible move away. The answer was clear. The state of his patient's health was none of Carl's business. 'I'm afraid I can't give out information to anyone other than his family. I'm sure you understand.'

Carl grabbed the doctor's sleeve. 'I was with him when it happened, do you understand that? I was shot, too. One of our colleagues was killed. We were in it together, so that's why I'd like to know. Is he going to be able to walk again? Can you tell me that?'

'I'm sorry.' He brushed off Carl's hand. 'I can't give you that information, but in your line of work I'm sure you'll be able to find out. Each of us has to do our job as we see fit.'

That little note of authority acquired by all physicians, the measured enunciation of vowels on the tip of the tongue, and the slightly raised eyebrows were all to be expected, but they still felt like petrol poured over Carl's process of spontaneous ignition. He could have knocked the doctor upside the head, but instead he chose to seize him by the collar and yank him forwards. 'Do our job?' he

23

snarled. 'You'd better watch that smarmy suburban mug of yours before you get too full of yourself, pal. Get it?' He tightened his grip on the man's collar, and the doctor started to look frantic. 'When your daughter doesn't come home at ten o'clock, we're the ones who go out looking for her; and when your wife is raped or your shitty beige-coloured BMW is missing from the car park, we're the ones you call. We show up every time, even if it's only to offer consolation. Get it, you arsehole? So I'm going to ask you one more time: Will Hardy be able to walk again?'

The doctor breathed in big gulps of air when Carl let go of his collar. 'I drive a Mercedes,' he said, 'and I'm not married.' Mørck could see it in the white-coat man's eyes. He thought he'd figured out the state Carl was in. Presumably something he'd learned on a psychology course that he'd squeezed in between anatomy lectures. 'A smattering of humour usually defuses the situation,' was what he'd apparently been taught, but it didn't work on Carl.

'Why don't you toddle off to the minister of health and learn what real arrogance is like, you little shit,' said Carl as he shoved the doctor aside. 'You're just a novice.'

They were waiting for him in his office, both Marcus Jacobsen, the chief of homicide, and that idiot Lars Bjørn. An unsettling sign that the doctor's cries for help had already been heard outside the thick walls of the clinic. Carl studied the two men for a moment. No, it looked instead as if some lunatic impulse had invaded their bureaucratic brains. He caught them exchanging glances. Or did the situation smell more of some sort of crisis

24

intervention? Was he once again going to be forced to talk with a psychologist about how to understand and combat post-traumatic stress? Could he expect yet another man with deep-set eyes to appear and try to force his way into Carl's dark nooks and crannies, so he could unveil what had been told and what had not? They might as well stop wasting their time, because Carl knew better. It was impossible to talk his way out of this problem. It had been coming on for a long time, but the incident out on Amager had pushed him over the edge.

They could all kiss his arse.

'Well, Carl,' said Jacobsen, motioning with his head towards his empty chair. 'Lars and I have been discussing your situation, and in many respects we think we've arrived at a parting of ways.'

Now it sounded like he was going to be fired. Carl began drumming his fingernails on the edge of the desk as he stared over his boss's head. They wanted to fire him? Well, he wasn't going to make it easy for them.

Carl looked beyond Tivoli Gardens, up at the clouds that were gathering and threatening the city. If they fired him, he would leave before the rain started pissing down. He wouldn't bother chasing after the union rep. He would go straight over to the union office on H. C. Andersen Boulevard. Fire a good colleague a mere week after he returned from sick leave and only a few weeks after he was shot and lost two good teammates? They couldn't do that to him. The world's oldest police union was just going to have to show that it was worthy in its old age.

'I realize that this is a bit sudden for you, Carl. But we've decided to give you a slight change of air, and in a manner that will allow us to make better use of your excellent abilities as a detective. To put it simply, we're going to promote you to department head of a new division, Department Q. Its goal will be to investigate cases that have been shelved, but are of particular interest to the public welfare. Cases deserving special scrutiny, you might say.'

I'll be damned, thought Carl, tilting his chair back.

'You're going to have to run the department alone, but who would be better at it than you?'

'Just about anybody,' he replied, staring at the wall.

'Now listen here, Carl. You've been through a tough time, and this job is custom-made for you,' said the deputy.

What the hell do you know about it, you bugger? thought Carl.

'You'll be running the show entirely on your own. We'll select a number of cases in consultation with various district police commissioners, and then you can prioritise how to handle them and what procedures to use. You'll have an expense account for travel; we just need a monthly report,' added his boss.

Carl frowned. 'District police commissioners? Is that what you said?'

'Yes, this is a nationwide jurisdiction. Which is why you can no longer be on the same team with your former colleagues. We've set up a new department here at headquarters, but it will be a separate entity. Your office is being furnished at this very moment.'

Clever move. Now they won't have to listen to my bitching any more, thought Carl. But what he said was: 'Is that right? And where is this office located, if I may ask? Are you thinking of giving me yours?'

Now his boss's smile looked a bit embarrassed. 'Where your office is located? Well, for the time being it's in the basement, but we may be able to change that later on. Let's see how things go first. If the percentage of cases you solve is even halfway decent, who knows what might happen.'

Carl once again turned his gaze to the clouds. In the basement, they said. So that was the plan. They were going to wear him down. They would toss him a few bones, freeze him out, isolate him, and make sure he was depressed. As if it made any difference whether that was done up here or down below. He was still going to do exactly what he wanted to. Which was, as much as possible, absolutely nothing.

'How is Hardy doing, by the way?' asked Jacobsen after a suitable pause.

Carl shifted his gaze back to his boss. It was the first time he'd ever asked that question.

5

2002

In the evening Merete Lynggaard was her real self. With every white line that whipped beneath her car on the way home, she discarded a part of herself that didn't fit in with life behind the yew trees in Magleby. She felt transformed the instant she turned towards the sleepy expanses of Stevns and crossed the bridge over the Tryggevælde River.

Uffe was sitting there as usual, a cup of cold tea on the edge of the coffee table in front of him, bathed in the light from the TV, with the volume turned up full blast. After she parked the car in the garage and walked around to the back door, she could clearly see him through the windows facing the courtyard. Always the same Uffe. Silent and motionless.

She kicked off her high heels in the utility room, dumped her briefcase on top of the furnace, hung up her coat in the entrance hall, and left all her papers in her office. Then she took off her Filippa K. trouser suit, placed it on the chair next to the washing machine, took down her dressing gown from its hook, and put on her slippers. Everything was exactly as it should be. She wasn't the type who needed to wash off the day under the shower as soon as she stepped in the door.

Then she rummaged in the plastic bag and found the

Hopjes sweets at the bottom. Only when the candy lay on her tongue and raised her blood sugar was she ready to turn her attention to the living room.

It wasn't until then that she shouted: 'Hi, Uffe! I'm home now.' Always the same ritual. She knew that Uffe had seen the headlights of her car the second she drove up the hill, but neither of them had a need for contact until the time was right.

She sat down in front of him, trying to catch his eye. 'Hey there, mister, are you sitting here watching TV and mooning over that cute newscaster Trine Sick?'

He scrunched up his face so his crow's feet reached his hairline, but his eyes never left the screen.

'You're a real rascal, you know that?' Then she took his hand. It was warm and soft, as always. 'But you like Lotte Mejlhede better. Do you think I haven't noticed?'

Now she saw his lips slowly widen into a grin. Contact was established. Oh yes, Uffe was still inside there. And Uffe knew full well what he wanted in life.

She turned to look at the TV screen and listened to the last two reports on the evening news. The first had to do with the Nutrition Council's appeal to institute a ban on industrially manufactured trans-fatty acids; the second was about the hopeless marketing campaign conducted by the Danish Poultry Association with government financing. She was only too familiar with the issues. They had resulted in two long nights of intense work.

She turned to Uffe and ruffled his hair so that the big scar on his scalp became visible. 'Come on, lazybones, let's see about getting ourselves some dinner.' With her free hand she grabbed one of the sofa cushions and slapped it against the back of his neck until he started shrieking with joy and flailing his arms and legs. Then she let go of his hair, leaped like a mountain goat over the sofa, through the living room and out to the stairwell. It never failed. Hooting and chuckling with glee and stifled energy, Uffe followed close on her heels. Like a couple of train carriages connected by spring steel, they raced upstairs, down again, outside to the front of the garage, back to the living room, and finally out to the kitchen. Soon they would sit down in front of the TV to eat the food that the home help had cooked for them. Yesterday they had watched *Mr Bean*. The day before it was Chaplin. Today it would be *Mr Bean* again. The video collection that Merete and Uffe owned included only what Uffe enjoyed watching. He usually lasted half an hour before he fell asleep. Then she would spread a blanket over him and let him sleep on the sofa. Later in the night he would find his own way upstairs to the bedroom. There he would take her hand and grunt a bit before falling asleep beside her in the double bed. When he was finally sound asleep, making soft whistling noises, she would turn on the light and start getting ready for the next day.

That was how the evenings and nights unfolded. Because that was how Uffe loved things to be – her sweet, innocent little brother. Sweet, silent Uffe.

6

2007

It was true that a brass plate on the door was engraved with the words 'Department Q', but the door itself had been lifted off its hinges and was now leaning against a bunch of hot-water pipes that stretched all the way down the long basement corridor. Ten buckets, half filled and giving off paint fumes, still stood inside the room that was supposed to be his office. From the ceiling hung four fluorescent lights, the type that after a while would provoke a splitting headache. But the walls were fine – except for the colour. It was hard not to make a comparison with hospitals in Eastern Europe.

'Viva Marcus Jacobsen,' grumbled Carl, trying to get a grip on the situation.

For the last hundred yards along the basement corridor he hadn't seen a soul. In his end of the basement there were no people, there was no daylight, air, or anything else that might distinguish the place from the Gulag Archipelago. Nothing was more natural than to compare his domain with the fourth circle of hell.

He looked down at his two spanking-new computers and the bundle of wires attached to them. Apparently the information superhighway had been split up so that the intranet was linked to one computer and the rest of the world to the other. He patted computer number two. Here he could sit for hours and surf the Net to his heart's content. No pesky rules about secure surfing and safe-guarding the central servers; at least that was something. He looked around for an ashtray and tapped a cigarette out of the pack. 'Smoking is extremely hazardous to you and those around you', it said on the label. He glanced around. The few termites that might thrive down here could probably handle it. He lit the cigarette and took a deep drag. There was definitely a certain advantage to being head of his own department.

'We'll send the cases down to you,' Marcus Jacobsen had said, but there wasn't so much as a single sheet of A5 paper on the desk, and all the shelves were empty. They must have thought he needed time to settle into the place. But Carl didn't mind; he wasn't about to work on anything until the spirit happened to move him.

He shoved the chair sideways over to the desk, sat down, and propped his feet up on the corner. That was how he'd sat for most of the time he'd been off on sick leave. During the first few weeks at home he'd simply stared into space, smoking cigarettes and trying not to think about the weight of Hardy's heavy, paralysed body or the rattling sound that Anker had made before he died. After that he'd surfed the Internet. Aimlessly, without any sort of plan, just trying to numb his mind. That was exactly what he intended to do now. He looked at his watch. He had just about five hours to kill before he could go home.

Carl lived in Allerød, which had been his wife's choice. They'd moved there a couple of years before she walked out on him and moved into a cottage in an allotment garden in Islev. She'd looked at a map of Zealand and quickly worked out that if you wanted to have it all, you needed plenty of dough in the bank – or else you could move to Allerød. Nice little town on the S-train line, surrounded by fields, with forested land 'within walking distance', as they say. It had lots of pleasant shops, a cinema, theatre, social groups, and, to top it all, the house was located in the Rønneholt Park development. His wife had been ecstatic. For a reasonable price they could buy a semi-detached house made from stacked-up breeze blocks with plenty of room for both of them, as well as her son. They would even have access to tennis courts, an indoor swimming pool and a community centre, all in the proximity of fields of grain, a marsh, and a hell of a lot of good neighbours. Because she'd read that in Rønneholt Park everyone cared about each other. Back then that hadn't been a plus as far as Carl was concerned, because who the hell believed that sort of crap anyway? But later on it had turned out to be important. Without his friends in Rønneholt Park, Carl would have fallen flat on his arse. Both metaphorically and literally. First his wife took off. Then she decided she didn't want a divorce, but instead took up residence in the allotment garden. Next she went through a whole series of young lovers, and she had the bad habit of ringing Carl to tell him all about them. Then her son refused to keep living with her in the garden cottage, and in the full throes of puberty had moved back in with Carl. And finally there was the shooting out in Amager, which brought to a screeching halt everything that Carl had been clinging to: a solid purpose in life and a couple of good colleagues who didn't give a damn whether he'd got out of bed on the wrong side or not. No, if it hadn't been for Rønneholt Park and the people who lived there, he would have really been up shit creek.

When Carl got home, he leaned his bicycle against the shed outside the kitchen, noting that the other two occupants of the house were both there. As usual, his lodger, Morten Holland, had turned the volume all the way up as he listened to opera in the basement, while his stepson's downloaded blowtorch heavy metal was blasting out of a window upstairs. A less compatible collage of sounds was not to be found anywhere else on the planet.

He forced his way inside the inferno and stomped a couple of times on the floor. Down in the basement *Rigoletto* was instantly wrapped up in cotton wool. It wasn't that simple with the boy upstairs. Carl took the stairs in three bounds and didn't bother to knock on the door.

'Jesper, for God's sake! The sound waves have shattered two windows down on Pinjevangen. And you're the one who's going to pay for them!' he shouted as loud as he could.

The boy had heard the same story before, so he didn't move a muscle as he hunched over the computer keyboard.

'Hey!' yelled Carl, right in his ear. 'Turn it down or I'll cut the ADSL cable.'

That got a reaction.

Downstairs in the kitchen, Morten had already set plates on the table. Someone in the neighbourhood had once labelled him the surrogate mother at number 73, but that wasn't right. Morten was not a surrogate; he was a real housewife and the best that Carl had ever encountered. He took care of the grocery shopping and laundry, the cooking and cleaning, while opera arias trilled from his sensitive lips. And to cap it all, he even paid rent.

'Did you go to the university today?' asked Carl, knowing what the answer would be. Morten was thirty-three years old, and he'd spent the past thirteen of those years diligently studying all kinds of subjects other than the ones having any direct bearing on the three degree programmes in which he was officially enrolled. The result was an overwhelming knowledge about everything except the subjects for which he was receiving financial support and which in the future would presumably earn him a living.

Morten turned his heavy, corpulent back to Carl and stared down the bubbling mass in the pot on the stove. 'I've decided to study political science.'

He'd mentioned that before; it was just a matter of time before he tried that subject, too. 'Jesus, Morten, don't you think you should finish your economics degree first?' Carl couldn't help asking.

Morten tossed some salt into the pot and began stirring. 'Almost everybody in economics votes for the government parties, and that's just not me.'

'How the hell do you know that? You never even go to class, Morten.'

'I was there yesterday. I told my fellow students a joke about Karina Jensen.'

'A joke about a politician who started out as an extreme left-winger and ended up joining the Liberal Party? Shouldn't be hard to make a joke about that.'

'"She's an example of how to hide a Neanderthal behind a high-brow," I said. And nobody laughed.'

Morten was different. An overgrown adolescent and androgynous virgin whose personal relationships consisted of remarks exchanged with random supermarket customers about what they were buying. A little chat by the freezer section about whether spinach was best with or without cream sauce.

'What does it matter if nobody laughed, Morten? There could be lots of reasons for that. I didn't laugh either, and I don't vote for the government parties, in case you'd like to know.' Carl shook his head. He knew it was no use. But as long as Morten kept on making a good salary at the video store, it really didn't matter what the hell he studied or didn't study. 'Political science, eh? Sounds deadly boring.'

Morten shrugged as he sliced a couple of carrots and added them to what was cooking in the pot. He didn't say anything for a moment, which was unusual for him. Carl knew what was coming.

'Vigga phoned,' said Morten at last with a hint of concern in his voice. In this situation he normally added in English: 'Don't shoot me. I'm just the piano player.' But this time he didn't say it.

Carl didn't reply. If Vigga wanted something from him, she could wait to call until he got home.

'I think she's freezing over there in that garden cottage,' Morten ventured as he shoved the spoon around in the pot.

Carl turned to face him. It smelled damned good, whatever Morten was cooking on the stove. It had been a long time since he'd had such an appetite. 'She's freezing?

36

Maybe she should stuff a couple of her well-fed lovers into the woodstove.'

'What are you guys talking about?' said a voice in the doorway. Behind Jesper, the cacophony from upstairs was again blasting from his room, making the walls in the hallway vibrate.

It was a miracle they could hear each other at all.

Carl spent three days staring alternately at Google and at the walls in the basement room. He'd made himself familiar ad nauseam with the walk down the hall to the toilet, and realized he felt more rested than ever before. Then he counted off the four hundred and fifty-two paces up to the homicide division on the third floor, which was the domain of his former colleagues. He was going to demand that the workmen finish what they were doing in the basement and hang the door back on its hinges so he would at least have something to slam if he was so inclined. And then he would circumspectly remind them that he hadn't yet received the promised case files. Not because there was any rush, but he had no intention of losing his job before he'd even started.

Maybe he'd expected his former colleagues to stare at him with curiosity when he entered the homicide premises. Was he on the verge of a breakdown? Had his face lost all colour after his sojourn in the eternal gloom? He'd expected inquisitive and also scornful looks, but not that everyone would simultaneously slip inside their offices with such a well-orchestrated closing of doors.

'What's going on here?' he asked a man he'd never seen before who was unpacking removal boxes in the first office.

The man held out his hand. 'Peter Vestervig. I'm from City Station. I'm going to be part of Viggo's team.'

'Viggo's team? Viggo Brink?' Carl asked. A team leader? Viggo? He must have been appointed the day before.

'That's right. And you are?' the man asked.

Carl managed a brief handshake and then glanced around the office without replying. There were two other faces he didn't recognize. 'They're on Viggo's team too?'

'Not the one over by the window.'

'New furniture, I see.'

'Yes, they just brought it up. Aren't you Carl Mørck?'

'I used to be,' he said and then walked the rest of the way over to Marcus Jacobsen's office.

The door was ajar, but even a closed door wouldn't have stopped Carl from barging in. 'So you're bringing in more staff, Marcus?' he said without preamble, interrupting a meeting.

The homicide chief's face took on a resigned expression as he glanced at his deputy and one of the office girls. 'OK, Carl Mørck has emerged from the depths. We'll continue in half an hour,' he said, stacking up his papers.

Carl gave Jacobsen's deputy a surly smile as the man went out the door; the smile he got in return was equally scathing. Vice-Superintendent Lars Bjørn had always known just how to keep the icy feelings between them warm.

'So, how are things going down there, Carl? Are you getting a handle on how to prioritise the cases?'

'You might say that. At least with regard to the ones I've received so far.' He pointed behind him. 'What's happening out there?'

'You might well ask.' Marcus raised his eyebrows and

straightened the Leaning Tower of Pisa, as everyone called the pile of newly received cases on his desk. 'Due to the overwhelming case load, we've had to put together two more investigative teams.'

'To replace mine?' Carl smiled wryly.

'Yes, plus two others.'

Carl frowned. 'Four teams? How the hell are you going to pay for them?'

'A special appropriation. Allocated as a result of the police reform, as you know.'

'I do? Well, I'll be damned.'

'Was there anything specific you wanted, Carl?'

'Yes, but I think it can wait. I need to look into something first. I'll be back in a while.'

It was common knowledge that plenty of the members of the Conservative Party were business people who hobnobbed with each other and did whatever the trade organizations asked them to do. But Denmark's slickest party had always attracted police officers and military personnel as well – only the gods knew why. Right now Carl knew that at least two of the former type were members of parliament, voted in by the Conservatives. One was a real prole who had pushed his way up through the police hierarchy only to find just as swift an exit; but the other was a nice old deputy police commissioner whom Carl knew from his days in Randers over in Jutland. He wasn't particularly conservative, but the constituency included his home district, and the job was undoubtedly well paid. So Kurt Hansen from Randers became a member of parliament, representing the Conservatives, and a member of the Judicial

Committee. He was Carl's best source for any information of a political nature. Kurt wouldn't discuss everything, but it was easy to get him started if the issue in question was at all interesting. Carl wasn't sure whether his would qualify.

'Mr Deputy Commissioner Kurt Hansen, I presume,' he said as soon as the man answered the phone.

His words prompted a deep and genial burst of laughter. 'Well, what do you know? It's been a long time, Carl. Great to hear your voice. I heard you got shot.'

'It was nothing. I'm OK, Kurt.'

'Didn't go so well for two of your colleagues, though. Any progress in the case?'

'It's moving forwards.'

'I'm glad to hear that. Really, I am. Right now we're working on legislation that will expand the sentencing parameters by fifty per cent for assaults on civil servants while on the job. That ought to help matters. We need to support you guys who are out on the barricades.'

'Sounds good, Kurt. I hear that you've also decided to support the homicide division in Copenhagen with a special appropriation.'

'No, I don't think we've done anything like that.'

'Well, maybe not the homicide division, but something else over here at police headquarters. It's not a secret, is it?'

'Do we have any secrets here when it comes to funding appropriations?' asked Kurt, laughing heartily, as only a man with a big fat pension could do.

'So what exactly have you decided to fund, if I might ask? Does it come under the National Police?'

'Yes, the department actually comes under the auspices

of the Danish Criminal Investigation Centre, but we didn't want the same people to be investigating the same cases all over again, so it was decided to establish an independent department, administered by the homicide division. It's going to handle cases deserving "special scrutiny". But you know all about that.'

'Are you talking about Department Q?'

'Is that what you're calling it over there? That's an excellent name for it.'

'How much funding was allocated?'

'Don't quote me on the exact figure, but it's somewhere between six and eight million kroner annually for the next ten years.'

Carl looked around at the pale green walls of his basement office. OK, now he understood why Jacobsen and Bjørn were so intent on exiling him to this no-man's-land. Between six and eight million, he'd said. Straight into the pockets of the homicide division.

This was damned well going to cost them.

The homicide chief gave Carl a second look before taking off his reading glasses. It was the same expression he wore whenever he was studying a crime scene and the clues were indecipherable. 'You say you want your own car? Need I remind you that the Copenhagen Police Force doesn't provide vehicles assigned to specific individuals? You'll have to get in touch with the motor-pool office and request a car whenever you need one. Just like everybody else, Carl. That's the way it is.'

'I don't work for the Copenhagen Police. You're just acting as the administrator for my department.'

'Carl, you know full well that the officers up here are going to raise a real stink if we give you that sort of preferential treatment. And you say you want six men for your department? Are you crazy?'

'I'm just trying to build up Department Q so it will function according to its mandate. Isn't that what I'm supposed to be doing? It's a big job to take all of Denmark under my wings; I'm sure you understand that. So you won't give me six men?'

'No, damn it.'

'Four? Three?'

The homicide chief shook his head.

'So I'm the one who's going to do all the work?'

He nodded.

'Well, then I'm sure you realize I'm going to need a vehicle at my disposal at all times. What if I have to go to Aalborg or Næstved? And I'm a busy man. I don't even know how many cases are going to end up on my desk, do I?' He sat down across from his boss and poured coffee into the cup left behind by the deputy. 'But no matter what, I'm going to need to have an assistant down there, a jack of all trades. Somebody with a driver's licence who can take care of things for me. Send faxes and stuff like that. Do the cleaning. I've got too much to do, Marcus. And we need to show results, right? The Folketing wants value for its money, don't you think? Was it eight million kroner? That's a hell of a lot of money.'

7

2002

No calendar was big enough to hold all the appointments for the vice-chair of the Democrats' parliamentary group. From seven in the morning until five in the afternoon Merete Lynggaard had fourteen meetings with special-interest groups. At least forty new people would be introduced to her in her position as chairperson of the Health Committee, and most of them would expect her to know their backgrounds and positions, their hopes for the future, and their professional support base. If she'd still had Marianne to provide assistance, she would have had a reasonable chance of managing it all, but her new secretary, Søs Norup, wasn't as sharp. On the other hand, she was discreet. Not once over the course of the past month since Søs had been hired as secretary had she broached any subject of a personal nature. She was a born robot, although lacking in RAM memory.

The organization representatives now sitting in front of Merete had been making the rounds. First with the ruling parties and after that with the largest of the opposition parties, which meant it was Merete's turn. The reps seemed pretty desperate, and rightfully so, since not many in the government were concerned with anything other than the scandal in Farum and the mayor's diatribe against various ministers.

The delegation did its utmost to inform Merete about

the possible negative health effects of nanoparticles, magnetic guidance of particle transport in the body, immune defences, tracking molecules, and placenta studies. The latter, in particular, was their key issue.

'We're fully aware of the ethical questions that need to be addressed,' said the head of the delegation. 'For that reason we also know that the government parties represent population groups that are particularly opposed to wholesale collection of placentas, but we still need to discuss the matter.' The spokesperson was an elegant man who had long since earned millions in the field. He was the founder of the renowned pharmaceutical company Basic-Gen, which primarily conducted basic research for other, larger pharmaceutical corporations. Every time he had a new idea, he appeared at the offices of the Health Committee. Merete didn't know the rest of the delegates, but she noticed a young man standing behind the spokesman, staring at her. He wasn't supplying his boss with very much data, so maybe he was merely there to observe.

'Oh yes, this is Daniel Hale, our best collaborative partner on the laboratory front. His name may sound English, but Daniel is Danish, through and through,' said the spokesman afterwards, as Merete greeted each delegate in turn.

She shook Hale's hand, noticing at once the blazing heat of his touch.

'Daniel Hale, is that right?' she asked.

He smiled. For a moment her gaze wavered. How embarrassing.

She glanced over at her secretary, a neutral entity in the office. If Marianne had been there, she would have hidden a gleeful smile behind the papers she was always holding. There was not a hint of a smile from the new secretary.

'You work in a laboratory?' Merete asked.

At that point the spokesman broke in. He needed to make use of the few precious seconds allocated to him. The next delegation was already waiting outside Merete Lynggaard's office, and no one ever knew when there'd be another chance. It was a matter of money and a costly investment of time.

'Daniel owns the finest little laboratory in all of Scandinavia. Well, it's not really little any more, since you acquired the new buildings,' he said, turning to speak to his colleague, who shook his head with a smile. It was a delicious smile. 'We'd like to be allowed to submit this report,' the spokesman continued, turning back to Merete. 'Perhaps as chair of the Health Committee you'd be willing to study it in depth when time permits. It's tremendously important for posterity that the issue be given the most serious consideration at once.'

She hadn't expected to see Daniel Hale down in the Snapstinget restaurant. She was even more surprised to see that he seemed to be waiting for her. On every other day of the week she ate lunch in her office, but each Friday over the past few years, she would join the chairpersons from the health committees of the Socialist and Radical Centre parties. All three of them were feisty women who could make the members of the Denmark Party see red. The mere fact that they so openly cultivated their coffee klatsch didn't sit well with a lot of people.

He was alone, half hidden behind a pillar, perched on the very edge of his Kasper Salto chair, with a cup of coffee in front of him. Their eyes met for a second as she came through the glass doors, and it was all Merete could think about the whole time she was there.

When the women got up after finishing their conversation, he came over to her.

She saw people looking at her and murmuring to each other, but she felt mesmerized by his gaze.

8

2007

Carl was more or less satisfied. The workmen had been busy all morning in the basement room, while he'd stood outside in the corridor, making coffee on one of the rolling tables and tapping one cigarette after another out of the pack. Now carpeting covered the floor of his so-called office in Department Q, and the paint cans and everything else had been tossed into gigantic plastic rubbish sacks. The door was back on its hinges, a flat-screen TV had been brought in, a whiteboard and a bulletin board had been hung up, and the bookshelves were filled with his old law books, which other people had thought they could commandeer. In his trouser pocket was the key to a dark blue Peugeot 607, recently decommissioned by the Intelligence Service because they didn't want their bodyguards riding behind the queen's royal vehicles in a car with scratches in the paint. The Peugeot had only forty-five thousand kilometres on it, and was now the sole property of Department Q. What a status symbol it was going to be in the car park on Magnolievangen. And no more than twenty yards from his bedroom window.

In a couple of days he'd have the assistant they'd promised him. Carl had got the workmen to clear out a small room directly across the corridor. The room had been used for storing the battered helmets and shields used by Civil Defence Forces during the riots that erupted over the closing down of the Youth House. Now the space held a desk and chair, a broom cupboard, and all the fluorescent tubes that Carl had thrown out of his own office. Marcus Jacobsen had taken Carl's request literally and hired a man to do the cleaning and any other necessary tasks, but Marcus required that his assistant clean the rest of the basement as well. This was something Carl was going to get changed at some later date, which Jacobsen was no doubt expecting. It was all part of a tug of war to decide who was going to handle what – and, more specifically, when it would all get done. No matter how one looked at it, it was Carl who was sitting in the dark depths of the basement while the others were upstairs with a view of Tivoli. There needed to be a series of trade-offs, in order to strike a balance.

At one o'clock in the afternoon that day, two secretaries from Admin finally arrived with the case files. They told Carl they contained only the general documents, and if he wanted more extensive background materials, he'd have to send in a requisition form. At least now he had two people from his old department that he could consult. Or at least one of the secretaries: Lis, a warm, fair-haired woman with provocative, slightly overlapping front teeth. With her he would have liked to exchange much more than ideas.

He asked the secretaries to set their stacks of folders on either end of the desk. 'Do I happen to see a twinkle in your eye, or do you always look so fantastic, Lis?' he asked the blonde.

The brunette gave her colleague a look that could have made even Einstein feel like a fool. It had probably been a long time since she herself had been the recipient of such a remark.

'Carl, dear,' said the fair-haired Lis, as she always did. 'The twinkle in my eye is reserved for my husband and children. When are you going to accept that?'

'I'll accept it the day the light vanishes and eternal darkness swallows me up along with the rest of the earth,' he replied, not exactly understanding his case.

Even before the two secretaries had turned down the corridor and headed for the stairs, the brunette was voicing her indignation.

For the first couple of hours Carl didn't even glance at the case files. But he did muster the energy to count the folders; that was a form of work, after all. There were at least forty, but he didn't open any of them. Plenty of time for that. At least another twenty years before retirement, he figured, as he played a couple more games of Spider Solitaire. If he won the next game, he'd consider taking a look at the pile of folders on his right.

After he made his way through at least two dozen games, his mobile rang. He looked at the display but didn't recognize the number: 3545-and-something. It was a Copenhagen number.

'Yeah,' he said, expecting to hear Vigga's overwrought voice. She was always able to find some sympathetic soul to lend her a mobile. 'Get your own phone, Mum!' Jesper was always saying. 'It's fucking annoying that I have to call your neighbours to get hold of you.'

'Yes, hello,' said the voice, and it sounded nothing like Vigga. 'This is Birte Martinsen. I'm a psychologist at the

Clinic for Spinal Cord Injuries. I'm just ringing to inform you that when one of the assistant nurses gave Hardy Henningsen some water this morning, he tried to suck it down into his lungs. He's OK, but very depressed, and he's been asking for you. Could you possibly come and visit? I think it would help him.'

Carl was allowed to be alone in the room with Hardy, even though the psychologist clearly would have liked to listen in on their conversation.

'So, did you just get sick and tired of it all, old boy?' he said, taking Hardy's hand. There was a tremor of life in it. Carl had noticed that before. Right now the tips of his middle and index fingers curled slightly, as if they wanted to beckon Carl closer.

'What is it, Hardy?' he said, bending his face down to his colleague's.

'Kill me, Carl,' he whispered.

Carl pulled away and looked him right in the eye. His tall partner had the bluest eyes in the world, and at that moment they were filled with sorrow and doubt and an urgent plea.

'For God's sake, Hardy,' he whispered. 'You know I can't do that. You need to get back on your feet. You need to get up and walk again. You've got a son who wants his father home. Don't you realize that, Hardy?'

'He's twenty years old. He'll be fine,' whispered Hardy.

That was just like him. He was perfectly lucid. And Hardy meant what he said.

'I can't do it, Hardy. You're going to have to tough it out. You're going to get well.'

'I'm paralysed, and that's how I'm going to stay. They gave me the prognosis today. No chance of recovery. Not a chance in hell.'

'I imagine that Hardy Henningsen probably asked you to help him take his own life,' said the psychologist, inviting Carl's confidence. Her professional demeanour required no reply. She was convinced she was right. She'd seen it before.

'No, he didn't!'

'Oh really? I was positive he would.'

'Hardy? No, that wasn't what he wanted.'

'I'd be most interested to hear what he did say to you, if you wouldn't mind telling me.'

'I could do that.' Carl pursed his lips and looked out the window at Havnevejen. Not a soul in sight. Damned strange.

'But you're not going to?'

'It would make you blush if you heard what he said. I can't repeat something like that to a lady.'

'You could try.'

'I don't think so.'

9

2002

Merete had often heard about the little café on Nansen-gade called Bankeråt, with the strange, stuffed animals, but until that evening she had never been inside.

There, amid the buzz of conversation, she was welcomed with a warm smile and a glass of ice-cold white wine. The evening was off to a promising start.

She had just finished saying that she would be going to Berlin with her brother on the following weekend. That they made the trip once a year, and they'd be staying close to the Zoo.

Then her mobile rang. 'Uffe was really upset,' the home help told her.

For a moment Merete sat motionless, her eyes closed, swallowing the bitter pill of what she'd just heard. It wasn't often that she allowed herself to go out on a date. Why did he have to ruin things?

In spite of the slippery roads she made it home in less than an hour.

Uffe had been shaking and crying almost all evening. That's what happened occasionally if Merete didn't come home at the usual time. Uffe didn't communicate in words, so it could be difficult to decipher what was going on with him. Sometimes it even felt like nobody was there, inside his body. But that wasn't true at all. Uffe was very much present.

Unfortunately, the home help was clearly distressed. Merete knew she wouldn't be able to count on her again.

Not until Merete persuaded Uffe to come upstairs to the bedroom and put on his beloved baseball cap did he stop crying, but he was still upset. His eyes looked worried. She tried to calm him down further by describing all the people in the restaurant and the peculiar stuffed animals mounted on the walls. She recounted everything she'd done and thought during the day, and she could see how her words began to soothe him. It was what she had always done in similar situations, ever since he was ten or eleven. Whenever Uffe cried, the sobs came from deep in his subconscious. At those moments, the past and the present became linked inside Uffe. As if he remembered his life before the accident, back when he was a perfectly normal boy. No, that wasn't right. Not normal. Back then he was an extraordinary boy with a brilliant mind filled with fabulous ideas, and excellent prospects for the future. He'd been an amazing boy. And then came the accident.

For the next couple of days Merete was tremendously busy. And even though her thoughts had a tendency to drift away much of the time, there was no one else who could do her work for her. She arrived at the office at six each morning, and after a hard day she would race along the highway to make it home by six in the evening. Not much time to sort everything out.

So it did nothing to improve her concentration when she found a big bouquet of flowers on her desk.

Her secretary was obviously annoyed. She came from the Danish Association of Lawyers and Economists, where people were evidently much better at drawing the line between work and their personal life. If Marianne had still been Merete's secretary, she would have swooned and hovered around the flowers as if they were the crown jewels.

No, Merete couldn't expect much support from this new secretary in terms of personal matters, but maybe that was for the best.

The following day she got a valentine telegram from TelegramsOnline. It was the first valentine card she'd ever received in her life, but it didn't really feel right since it was almost two weeks past 14 February. Pictured on the front was a pair of lips and the words 'Love & Kisses for Merete'. Her secretary looked indignant when she handed it over.

Inside the telegram it said: 'Need to talk to you!'

She sat there for a moment, shaking her head as she stared at the lips.

Then her thoughts shifted back to the evening at the Café Bankerât. Even though the memory stirred up a wonderful feeling inside her, she knew this just wasn't going to work. The only thing to do was to put a stop to the situation before anything really developed.

She spent some time formulating what she wanted to say, then punched in his number and waited for the voice-mail to pick up.

'Hi, this is Merete,' she said lightly. 'I've been giving things a lot of thought, but it's just no good. My work and my brother make too many demands on me, and I don't think that's ever going to change. I'm really sorry. Please forgive me!'

Then she picked up her appointment diary from the desk and crossed out his number in the phone section.

At that moment her secretary came in and stopped abruptly in front of the desk.

When Merete lifted her head, she saw the woman smiling in a way that she'd never seen before.

He was standing coatless outside on the steps in the courtyard of the parliament building, waiting. It was bitterly cold, and the colour of his face was not healthy. In spite of the greenhouse effect, February weather was not conducive to spending much time outdoors. He gave Merete a pleading look and didn't see the press photographer who had just come through the gate from the palace square.

She tried to pull him towards the courtyard entrance, but he was too big and too desperate.

'Merete,' he said, putting his hands on her shoulders. 'Don't do this. I'm totally devastated.'

'I'm sorry,' she said, shaking her head. She saw the sudden change in his expression. There it was again, that deep, insinuating look in his eyes that made her uneasy.

Behind him the press photographer had raised his camera to his cheek. Damn it. If there was one thing she didn't need right now it was a tabloid photographer taking their picture.

'I'm afraid I can't help you!' she shouted and ran towards her car. 'It's just not possible.'

Uffe had looked at her with wonderment when she started to cry as they ate dinner, but it didn't really affect him. He lifted his spoon as slowly as he always did and smiled every time he swallowed a mouthful. His eyes were fixed on her lips, but he remained far away.

'Damn it!' she sobbed, slamming her fist on the table and looking at Uffe with bitterness and frustration etched deep in her soul. Recently that feeling had begun to come over her more and more often. Unfortunately.

She awoke with the dream burned into her consciousness. So vivid, so cherished, so terrible.

That day had begun with a wonderful morning. A slight frost and a thin layer of snow, just enough to enhance the holiday season atmosphere. They were all so full of life. Merete was sixteen, Uffe thirteen. Her father and mother had spent a night together that made them cast dreamy glances at each other from the moment they loaded the car with packages until the moment it all ended. Christmas Eve morning – what an oddly linked and joyous chain of words that was. So filled with promise. Uffe had talked about getting a compact disc player; it was the last time in his life that he expressed any specific sort of wish.

Then they took off. They were happy, and she and Uffe were laughing. Everyone was expecting them at their destination.

Uffe had given her a shove on the back seat. He was more than forty pounds lighter than his sister, but as pushy as a wild little puppy, diving in among the rest of the litter to suckle. Merete shoved him back, taking off her Peruvian cap to use it to bat him on the head. It was then that things got out of hand.

As the car went around a curve in the woods, Uffe hit her again, and Merete grabbed hold of her brother to force him back on to the seat. He kicked and howled and shrieked with laughter, and Merete pushed him down harder. At that instant, as her father chuckled and reached back his hand to give them both a swat, Merete and Uffe looked up. Their car was in the middle of overtaking another vehicle. The red Ford Sierra right next to them had a grey spattering of salt on its side doors. A man and woman in their forties were sitting in front, staring straight ahead. On the back seat sat a boy and a girl, just like them, and Uffe and Merete smiled at the pair. The boy looked like he was a couple of years younger than Merete; his hair was cut short. He caught her gleeful glance as she knocked her father's arm aside and she laughed back at him, not noticing her father had lost control of the car until the boy's expression suddenly changed in the light flickering through the spruce trees. For a second the boy's terrified blue eyes were riveted on hers, and then he was gone.

The sound of metal grinding against metal coincided with the shattering of the side windows on the other vehicle. The children sitting on the back seat fell over just as Uffe toppled against Merete. Behind her, glass was breaking, and in front of her the windscreen was covered by dark shapes bumping against each other. She couldn't tell whether it was their car or the other vehicle that made the trees along the edge of the road come toppling down, but by then Uffe's body had twisted around and he was about to be strangled by the seat belt. Then came a deafening crash, first from the other car, then from theirs. The blood on the upholstery and front windscreen was mixed with dirt and snow from the forest floor, and a tree branch pierced the calf of Merete's leg. A broken tree trunk rammed the bottom of the vehicle and tossed them up in the air for a moment. The crash when they landed with the nose of the car on the road merged with the screeching sound of the Ford Sierra knocking over a tree. Then their car flipped over with a jolt and slid along on its side, into the thickets. Uffe's arms were sticking up in the air, and his legs were pressed against the back of their mother's seat, which had been wrenched from the floor. At no time did Merete see her mother or father. She saw only Uffe.

She woke with her heart pounding so hard in her chest that it hurt. She was ice-cold and clammy with sweat.

'Stop it, Merete,' she told herself out loud, taking as deep a breath as she could manage. She put her hand to her chest, as if physically trying to wipe away the memory. Only in her dreams did she see all the details with such terrifying clarity. At the time, she hadn't been able to take them all in – she'd comprehended only the general situation. The flashes of light, screams, blood and darkness, followed by more light.

She took another deep breath and looked down. Lying in the bed beside her was Uffe, breathing with a slight whistling sound. His face was calm. Outside, the rain was quietly trickling through the roof gutters.

She reached out her hand and cautiously stroked her brother's hair as she pressed her lips tight to hold back the sobs trying to force their way out.

Thank God it was ages since she'd last had that dream.

10

2007

'Hello, my name is Assad,' he said. The hairy mitt that he held out towards Carl looked as if it had tried a bit of everything.

Carl didn't immediately realize where he was or who was talking to him. It hadn't exactly been a scintillating morning. As a matter of fact, he'd actually fallen sound asleep with his feet propped up on the desk, the Sudoku magazine on his lap, and his chin tucked halfway down in the opening of his shirt, whose usually sharp creases on his shirt now resembled an ECG. His legs were half asleep as he took them down from the desk and stared at the short, dark man standing in front of him. There was no question that he was older than Carl, or that he hadn't been recruited from the same peasant kingdom that Carl called home.

'Assad. OK,' replied Carl sluggishly. But what the hell did this have to do with him?

'You are Carl Mørck, as it says outside on the door. I must want to help you, they say. Please, is that correct?'

Carl squinted a bit, weighing all the possible interpretations of what the man had just said. Help him?

'Yeah, I sure as hell hope so,' was Carl's reply.

He'd brought this all on himself, and now he was a victim of his own poorly thought-out demands. Unfortunately, he hadn't realized until now that having someone else in the office across the hall would create obligations. On the one hand, the man had to be kept busy; on the other hand, Carl also had to occupy himself, at least to a reasonable degree. No, he hadn't thought things through. He would no longer be able to drift through the day, now that he had that man staring at him. He'd thought it would make life easier, having an assistant. The man would have plenty to do while Carl kept busy counting off the hours behind his closed eyelids. The floor had to be washed, coffee had to be made, and documents needed to be added to the case files, which then had to be put away. There would be more than enough tasks to occupy him, he'd thought at first. But now, a little more than two hours later, the man was sitting there, staring at him with big eyes, and everything was nice and neat and tidy. Even the bookshelf behind Carl had been filled with reference books, arranged alphabetically, and the spines of all the ring binders had been numbered and were ready for use. In two and a half hours the man had completed all the work, and that was that.

As far as Carl was concerned, he might as well go home now.

'Do you have a driver's licence?' he asked Assad, hoping that Marcus Jacobsen had forgotten to take that detail into account. If so, the whole question of the man's employment could be taken up for discussion again.

'I drive a taxi and a car and a truck and a T-55 tank and also a T-62 and armoured cars and the motorcycles with and without sidecars.'

That was when Carl suggested that for the next couple of hours Assad should sit quietly in his chair and read some of the books on the shelf behind him. He turned around and grabbed the nearest volume, which he handed to his assistant. *Handbook for Crime Technicians* by Detective A. Haslund. Sure, why not? 'Pay attention to the sentence structure while you're reading, Assad. It can teach you a lot. Have you read much in Danish?'

'I have read all the newspapers and also the constitutions and everything else.'

'Everything else?' said Carl. This wasn't going to be easy. 'Do you like solving Sudoku puzzles, too?' he asked, handing Assad the magazine.

By the afternoon his back was aching from sitting up straight. Assad's coffee was an alarmingly potent experience, and Carl's sleep deprivation had now been given a jolt of caffeine. He had the annoying sensation of blood racing through his veins. That was why he had started leafing through the folders.

A couple of the cases he already knew inside and out, but most of them were from other police districts, and a couple were from before he joined the criminal investigation department. What all of them had in common was that they'd required a massive number of man-hours and had sparked enormous attention in the media. Several of the cases had involved citizens who were well-known public figures. But all of the cases had stranded at the stage where the leads had petered out.

If he sorted them into rough categories, there were three types of cases.

The first and largest category included ordinary homicides of all types in which plausible motives were found, but the perpetrator remained unknown.

The next type of case also involved homicides, but of a more complex nature. It was sometimes difficult to pinpoint a motive, and there could be more than one victim. A conviction may have been handed down, but only with regard to accessories to the crime; the ringleaders or primary perpetrators were never identified. The murder itself may have had a certain random quality to it, and in some instances the act could be designated a crime of passion. The solving of these types of cases could sometimes be aided by lucky coincidences. Witnesses who just happened to be passing by; vehicles that were used in the commission of some other crime; information acquired through other unrelated circumstances, and so on. They were cases that could prove difficult for the investigators unless accompanied by a certain amount of luck.

And then there was the third category, which was a hotchpotch of homicides or presumed homicides linked to kidnappings, rapes, arson, robberies with deadly consequences, certain types of financial crimes, and a number of cases with political undertones. They were all cases the police had failed to solve, and in certain instances the very concept of justice had suffered a serious blow. An infant that had vanished from a pram; a resident of a retirement community who was found strangled in his flat. A factory owner who was discovered murdered in a cemetery in Karup, or the case of the female diplomat at the zoo. Even though Carl hated to admit it, Piv Vestergård's officiousness, did have a certain value, even if it had been prompted by a desire to win votes. Because every one of these cases was bound to incense any cop worth his salt.

He lit another cigarette and glanced at Assad sitting across from him. A calm man, he thought. If Assad could keep himself occupied the way he was doing at the moment, maybe the situation would work out after all.

Carl put the three stacks of case files on the desk in front of him and looked at his watch. Another half-hour with his arms crossed and his eyes closed. Then they could both go home.

'What are these kinds of cases then, that you have there?'

Carl peered up at Assad's dark eyebrows through the slits of his eyelids, which refused to open any further. The man was bending over the desk, holding the *Handbook for Crime Technicians* in one hand. He'd stuck his finger inside as a bookmark, indicating that he'd made quite a bit of headway in his reading. Or maybe he was just looking at the pictures; that was what a lot of people did.

'You know what, Assad? You've interrupted my train of thought.' Carl suppressed a yawn. 'Oh well, what's done is done. OK, so these are the cases that we're going to be working on. Old cases that other people have given up on. You get it?'

Assad raised his eyebrows. 'It is very interesting,' he said, picking up the folder on top. 'Nobody knows anything about who did what, and like that?'

Carl stretched the muscles in his neck and looked at his watch. It wasn't even three o'clock. Then he took the folder from Assad and studied it. 'I'm not familiar with this case. It has something to do with the excavation on the island of Sprogø, when they were building the Great Belt Bridge between Zealand and Funen. They found a

63

body out there, but that's about as far as they got. The police in Slagelse handled the case. A bunch of slackers.'

'Slackers?' Assad nodded. 'And this comes first for you?'

Carl looked at him, uncomprehending. 'You're asking me if this is the first case we're going to work on? Is that what you mean?'

'Yes. Is this it then?'

Carl frowned. Too many questions at once. 'I need to study all of the files before I make up my mind.'

'Is this very secret?' Assad carefully placed the folder back on the stack.

'The case documents? Yes, it's likely that they contain information not meant for anyone else's eyes.'

The dark man was silent for a moment. He looked like a boy whose request for an ice-cream cone had been refused, but knows that if he stands there long enough, there's still a chance he might get one. They stared at each other for so long that Carl ended up feeling confused.

'What?' he asked. 'Is there something specific you want?'

'Since I am here and I promise to keep my lips sealed and locked and never say anything about what I read, can I look at the folders then?'

'That's not your job, Assad.'

'No, but what is my job right now? I've came just to page forty-five in the book, and now my head wants something different.'

'I see.' Carl looked around to find some other challenges, if not for Assad's head, then for his well-proportioned upper arms. He could see that there really wasn't much for Assad to do. 'Well, if you promise me on all you hold sacred that you won't talk with anyone else but me about what you read, then go ahead.' He pushed one of the stacks of folders a couple of inches towards Assad. 'There are three piles here, so don't get them mixed up. I've worked out an excellent system, which has taken me a long time to devise. And just remember: No talking to anyone else about these cases, Assad.' He turned to his computer. 'And one more thing, Assad. They're my cases, and I'm really busy; you can see for yourself how many there are. So you shouldn't expect me to discuss the cases with you. You've been hired to do the cleaning and make the coffee and drive me around. If you don't have any-thing to do, it's all right with me if you want to read the files. But that has nothing to do with your job. OK?'

'OK, yes.' He stood there a moment, staring at the centre pile of folders. 'It is some special cases that lie by themselves. I can understand it. I will take the top three folders. I will not get them mixed all up. I will keep them in the folders by themself over in my room. When you need them, then just shout, I then bring them again.'

Carl watched Assad leave the office with three folders under his arm, and the *Handbook for Crime Technicians* at the ready. It had him really worried.

No more than an hour later Assad was once again standing next to Carl's desk. In the meantime, Carl had been think-ing about Hardy. Poor Hardy, who had asked his colleague to kill him. But how could Carl do that? These were not the sort of thoughts that would lead to anything constructive.

Assad placed one of the folders in front of Carl. 'Here is the only case that I remember for myself. It happened exactly while I was taking Danish language lessons so we read about it in the newspapers. It was so very interesting. That was what I thought back then. Also now.'

He handed the document to Carl, who glanced at it. 'So you came to Denmark in 2002?'

'No, in '98. But I took Danish lessons in 2002. Were you working on that case then?'

'No, it was the Rapid Response Team's case, before the reorganization within the police force.'

'And the Rapid Response Team did it because it had to be fast?'

'No, because it was . . .' He studied Assad's alert face with the dancing eyebrows. 'Yes, that's right,' he corrected himself. Why should he encumber Assad, who had absolutely no background knowledge, with all the intricacies of police procedures?

'She was a pretty girl, that Merete Lynggaard, I think.' Assad gave his boss a crooked smile.

'Pretty?' Carl looked at the beautiful, vital woman in the photograph. 'Yes, she certainly was.'

II

2002

Over the next two days the messages began piling up. Merete's secretary tried to hide her annoyance and pretended to be amiable. Several times she sat and stared at Merete when she thought her boss wouldn't notice. She once asked if Merete would like to play squash with her on the weekend, but Merete declined. She had no desire for any sort of camaraderie with her staff.

After that the secretary resumed her usual morose and aloof demeanour.

On Friday Merete took home the last messages that her secretary had left on her desk. After reading through them several times, she tossed them in the wastebasket. Then she tied the strings of the bin liner in a knot and carried it out to the dustbin. She needed to put an end to this, once and for all.

And she felt mean and miserable.

The home help had left a casserole on the table. It was still lukewarm when Merete and Uffe were done dashing about the house. Next to the ovenproof dish was a little note on top of an envelope.

Oh no, she's going to quit, thought Merete and then read the note.

'A man brought this letter to the house. I suppose it has something to do with the ministry.'

Merete picked up the envelope and tore it open.

'Have a nice trip to Berlin,' was all it said.

Uffe was sitting next to her with an empty plate, smiling in anticipation as his nostrils quivered at the delicious aroma from the food. Merete pressed her lips together and scooped up some of the casserole for her brother as she tried not to cry.

The rushing of the east wind was getting louder, whipping up the waves so the foam splashed halfway up the sides of the ship. Uffe loved to stand outside on the sun deck and watch the wake form alongside the ship while the seagulls soared on outspread wings overhead. And Merete loved seeing Uffe happy. She was looking forward to their weekend. It was good that she'd decided they should go after all. Berlin was such a marvellous city.

Up ahead on the deck an elderly couple was looking in their direction; behind them a family sat at one of the tables close to the smokestack, with Thermoses and sandwiches that they'd brought along. The children had already finished eating, and Merete gave them a smile. The father looked at his watch and said something to his wife. Then they began packing up what was left of their lunch.

She remembered going on this sort of excursion with her parents. That was a long time ago. She turned around. People were already heading below deck to where their cars were parked. They would soon reach the harbour at Puttgarden; only ten more minutes, but not everybody was in a rush. Two men were standing over near the huge picture windows in the stern, with scarves wrapped snugly around their necks as they calmly gazed out to sea. One of them looked frail and gaunt. Merete estimated that they were standing at least six feet apart, so they probably weren't together.

A sudden impulse made her take the note out of her pocket and look at the six words again. Then she put it back in the envelope and held it up in the air, letting it flutter in the wind for a moment. Then she let it go. The envelope flew upwards and then dived down, slipping inside an opening in the side of the ship, underneath the sun deck. For a moment she thought they'd have to go downstairs and retrieve it, but then the note suddenly reappeared and began dancing over the waves. It spun around a few times and vanished into the white foam. Uffe laughed. He'd been watching the envelope the whole time. Then he gave a shriek, took off his baseball cap, and tossed it after the envelope.

'No, don't!' was all she managed to shout before the cap plunged into the sea.

It was a Christmas present and Uffe's most-beloved possession. The minute it was gone, he regretted what he'd done. It was clear that he was considering jumping after the cap, in an attempt to get it back.

'No, Uffe!' she yelled. 'You can't do that. It's gone!' But Uffe had already set one foot on the metal barrier of the railing. He stood there bellowing over the wooden rail, his body's centre of gravity far too high up.

'Stop it, Uffe! There's nothing you can do,' she shouted again, but Uffe was strong, much stronger than she was, and he was far away. His consciousness was down in the waves with the baseball cap that had been a Christmas present. It was a relic of his simple, godless life.

Then she slapped him hard in the face. She'd never done that before, and she instantly pulled back her hand in fright. Uffe couldn't understand what was happening. He forgot about his cap and touched his cheek. He was in shock. It was years since he'd felt pain like that. He didn't understand. Then he looked at her and struck back. He hit her harder than he'd ever done before.

12

2007

Homicide chief Marcus Jacobsen had spent yet another night without much sleep.

The witness in the case of the cyclist murdered in Valby Park had tried to kill herself with an overdose of sleeping pills. Jacobsen couldn't understand what the hell could have pushed her so far. She had children and a mother who loved her, after all. Who could have threatened a woman into taking such extreme measures? The police had offered her witness protection and everything else within their powers. She was under surveillance day and night. Where on earth had she got those pills?

'You should go home and get some sleep,' said his deputy when Marcus came back from his usual Friday-morning meeting with the police chief in the commissioner's conference room.

He nodded. 'Well, maybe just for a couple of hours. But you and Bak need to go out to the National Hospital and see what you can get out of that woman. And make sure to take her mother and children along, so she can see them. We need to try and bring her back to reality.'

'Uh-huh, or away from it,' said Lars Bjørn.

All phone calls were supposed to be redirected, but the phone rang anyway. 'Don't let anybody through except the queen or Prince Henrik,' he'd told his secretary. So it was probably his wife. 'Yeah?' he said, feeling suddenly more tired than ever.

'It's the police commissioner,' whispered Bjørn, holding his hand over the receiver.

He handed the phone to Marcus and tiptoed out of the room.

'Marcus,' said the commissioner in her distinctive voice. 'I'm calling to tell you that the justice minister and the committees have made fast work of things. So the extra allocation of funds has been approved.'

'That's good to hear,' replied Marcus, immediately trying to work out in his mind how the budget could be divided up.

'Yes, well, you know the chain of command. Today Piv Vestergård and the Judicial Committee of the Denmark Party met with the justice minister, so now all the wheels will start turning. The chief of police has asked the head of the National Police to find out if you've got the new department set up yet,' she said.

'Yes, I believe we have,' he said with a frown as he pictured Carl's weary face.

'That's good. I'll let them know. So what's the first case you're going to tackle?'

That was not exactly a question he found particularly energizing.

Carl was just getting ready to head home. The clock on the wall said 16:36, but his inner clock was several hours ahead. So it was undeniably a disappointment when Marcus Jacobsen rang to say that he'd be coming downstairs to pay Carl a visit. 'I need to report what you're working on.'

Carl looked with resignation at the blank bulletin board

and the row of used coffee cups standing on his little meeting table. 'Give me twenty minutes, Marcus. Then you're welcome to come down here. We're right in the middle of something at the moment.'

He put down the phone and puffed out his cheeks. Then he slowly exhaled as he stood up and went across the hall to the room where Assad had made himself at home.

On his abnormally small desk stood two framed photographs showing a big group of people. On the wall above the desk hung a poster with Arabic script and a lovely picture of an exotic building that Carl couldn't immediately identify. From a hook on the door hung a brown smock of the type that had gone out of fashion along with leg warmers. Assad had neatly arranged his cleaning implements in a row along the far wall: a bucket, mop, vacuum cleaner, and a sea of bottles containing caustic cleaning fluids. On the bookshelves were rubber gloves and a little transistor radio with a cassette player that was emitting muted sounds that were reminiscent of the bazaar in Sousse. Next to the radio lay a notebook, some paper, a pencil, a copy of the Koran, and a small selection of magazines with Arabic text. Spread out on the floor in front of the bookshelf was a multicoloured prayer rug that hardly looked big enough for Assad to kneel on. All in all, quite a picturesque scene.

'Assad,' said Carl. 'We're in a hurry. The homicide chief will be here in twenty minutes, and we've got to get things ready. When he arrives, I'd appreciate it if you could be washing the floor at the other end of the hall. It's going to mean a little overtime, but I hope that's OK.'

*

73

'I must say, I'm impressed, Carl,' said Marcus Jacobsen, nodding at the bulletin board with tired eyes. 'You've certainly got this place organized. Are you getting back on your feet?'

'Back on my feet? Yeah, well, I'm doing what I can. But you need to realize it's going to be a while before I'm up to speed.'

'Let me know if you need to have a talk with a crisis counsellor again. You shouldn't underestimate the amount of trauma that can result from the type of experience you've been through.'

'I don't think that's going to be necessary.'

'That's good, Carl. But don't hesitate to speak up.' Jacobsen turned to look at the far wall. 'I see you've got your flat-screen up,' he said, staring at the forty-inch image of the news programme on Channel 2.

'Yes, we have to keep up with events in the world,' said Carl, thinking gratefully of Assad. It had taken his assistant all of five minutes to set up the whole damn thing. Apparently that was something else he was good at.

'By the way, it was just reported that the witness in the case of the murdered cyclist tried to commit suicide,' Carl went on.

'What? For Christ's sake, how did that leak out already?' exclaimed the homicide chief, looking even more knackered.

Carl shrugged. After ten years as head of the homicide division, the man must be used to the game by now. 'I've divided up the cases into three categories,' he said, pointing at the piles of folders. 'They're big, complicated cases. I've spent days reading through the material. This is going to take a lot of time, Marcus.'

Jacobsen shifted his gaze away from the TV screen. 'Take however much time you need, Carl. Just as long as you produce results once in a while. Let me know if anyone upstairs can assist you.' He attempted a smile. 'So which case have you decided to work on first?'

'Well, er, I'm looking at several initially. But the Merete Lynggaard case will probably be the first.'

Jacobsen's face brightened. 'Oh yes, that was a strange one. The way she disappeared from the Rødby–Puttgarden ferry. One minute she was there, the next she was gone. And without a single eyewitness.'

'There are plenty of strange aspects to the case,' said Carl, trying to recall just one.

'I remember that her brother was accused of pushing her overboard, but the charge was later dropped. Is that a lead you might follow up?'

'Maybe. I don't know where he is now, so I'll have to track him down first. But there are also other lines of inquiry that spring to mind.'

'I seem to remember the documents saying the brother was committed to an institution in northern Zealand,' said Jacobsen.

'Oh, right. But he might not be there any more.' Carl tried to look pensive. Go on back to your office, Mr Homicide Chief, he thought. All these questions, and so far he'd spent only five minutes reading the case report.

'He is in something called Egely. In the town of Frederikssund.' The voice came from the doorway where Assad stood, leaning on his mop. He looked like someone from another planet, with his ivory smile and his green rubber gloves and a smock that reached to his ankles.

The homicide chief stared in bewilderment at this exotic being.

'Hafez el-Assad,' he said, holding out a rubber-gloved hand.

'Marcus Jacobsen,' said the homicide chief, shaking the man's hand. Then he turned to give Carl an inquiring look.

'This is our new assistant in the department. Assad has heard me talking about the case,' said Carl, giving Assad a look that he chose to ignore.

'I see,' said Jacobsen.

'Yes, my Deputy Police Inspector Mørck has really worked hard so. I have just helped a little here and so there, and where one can.' Assad smiled broadly. 'What I do not understand is then why Merete Lynggaard was never found in the water. In Syria, where I come from, there are tons of sharks in the water that eat the dead bodies. But if there are not so many sharks in the sea around Denmark, the bodies should probably be found at some point. The bodies get as big as balloons because of all the rotting from inside that blows them up.'

The homicide chief tried to smile. 'Yes, well. The waters around Denmark are deep and wide. It's not unusual that we fail to find the bodies of people who have drowned. In fact, it's quite common for someone to fall overboard from a passenger ship in those waters. And often the body is never found.'

'Assad,' said Carl, looking at his watch. 'You can go home now. I'll see you tomorrow.'

Assad nodded briefly and picked up the bucket from the floor. After some clattering across the hall, he reappeared in the doorway and said goodbye.

'Seems like a real character, that Hafez el-Assad,' said Jacobsen when the sound of the man's footsteps had died away.

13

2007

After the weekend Carl found a memo from the deputy chief on his computer.

I've informed Bak that you're working on the Merete Lynggaard case. Bak was assigned to the case as part of the Rapid Response Team during the final phase of the investigation, so he's familiar with the details. Right now he's slogging away on the cyclist homicide, but he's prepared to discuss the case with you, preferably as soon as possible.

Lars Bjørn

Carl snorted. 'Preferably as soon as possible.' Who the hell did Bak think he was, that sanctimonious son of a bitch? Self-righteous, self-important, self-promoting. A bureaucrat and yes-man all in one. His wife probably had to fill out a form in triplicate to apply for any erotic fondling below the belt.

So Bak had investigated a case that had *not* been solved. How nice. Carl almost felt motivated to try to untie the knots himself.

He picked up the case file from his desk and asked Assad to make him a cup of coffee. 'Not as strong as last time, Assad,' he requested, thinking about the distance to the toilet.

*

The Lynggaard case file was undoubtedly the most organized and comprehensive file that Carl had seen yet. It included copies of everything from reports on the health of the brother, Uffe, to transcripts of police interviews, clippings from the tabloids and gossip columns, a couple of videotapes of interviews with Merete Lynggaard, and detailed transcripts of statements from colleagues, as well as from passengers on the boat who had seen the brother and sister together on the sun deck. There were photos showing the deck and the railing and the distance down to the water. There were fingerprint analyses taken from the spot where she disappeared. There were addresses of countless passengers who had taken pictures on board the Scandline ferry. There was even a copy of the ship's log, which revealed how the captain had responded to the whole incident. But there was nothing that could give Carl a real lead.

I need to watch the videotapes, he thought after reading through the material. He cast a defeated look at the DVD player.

'I've got a job for you, Assad,' he said when the man returned with a steaming cup of coffee. 'Go up to the homicide division on the third floor, through the green doors and over to the red hallway until you come to a bulge where –'

Assad handed Carl the coffee mug, the smell of which from a distance already hinted at likely stomach troubles. 'A bulge?' he said with wrinkled brow.

'Yes, you know, where the red hallway gets wider. Go over to the blonde woman. Her name is Lis. She's OK. Tell her that you need a videotape player for Carl Mørck.

We're good friends, she and I.' He winked at Assad, who winked back.

'But if the dark-haired one is the only one there, just forget about it and come back.'

Assad nodded.

'And remember to bring back an adaptor,' he called after Assad as he ambled down the fluorescent-lit basement corridor.

'It was the dark-haired who just was up there,' said Assad when he returned. 'She gave me two video machines and said they do not want them back.' He smiled broadly. 'She was also beautiful.'

Carl shook his head. There must have been a change in personnel.

The first video was from a TV news programme that was broadcast on 21 December 2001, in which Merete Lynggaard commented on an informal health and climate conference she had attended in London. The interview dealt primarily with her discussions with a senator named Bruce Jansen regarding the American attitude towards the work of WHO and the Kyoto Protocol, which in Merete's opinion warranted great optimism for the future. I wonder if she's easy to fool, thought Carl. But aside from a certain naivety, which was no doubt attributable to her age, Merete Lynggaard seemed otherwise level-headed, professional and precise. She outshone by far the newly appointed interior and health minister, who was standing next to her, looking like a parody of a high-school teacher in a film from the sixties.

'A really elegant and pretty lady,' remarked Assad from the doorway.

The second video was from 20 February 2002. Talking on behalf of her party's environmental spokesperson, Merete Lynggaard offered comments on the conceited environmental sceptic Bjarke Ørnfelt's report to the Committee Pertaining to Scientific Deception.

What a name to give to a committee, thought Carl. To think that anything in Denmark could sound so Kafkaesque.

This time it was an entirely different Merete Lynggaard who appeared on the screen. More real, less of a politician.

'She is really, really so beautiful there,' said Assad.

Carl glanced at him. Apparently a woman's appearance was a particularly valuable factor in his assistant's worldview. But Carl agreed with him. There was a special aura about Merete during that interview. She exhibited a surplus of that incredibly strong appeal that almost all women are capable of emanating whenever things are going especially well for them. Very telling, but also confusing.

'Was she pregnant then?' asked Assad. Judging by a number of family members in his photos, it was a feminine condition with which he was quite familiar.

Carl lit a cigarette and leafed through the case file again. For obvious reasons, there was no autopsy report that might help him answer that question, since the body had never been found. And when he skimmed through the gossip columns, there were blatant hints that she wasn't particularly interested in men, although of course that didn't preclude her from getting pregnant. But when he took a closer look, he realized that she hadn't been seen in intimate contact with anyone at all, man or woman.

'She was probably only just fallen in love,' concluded Assad as he waved the cigarette smoke away. He had now moved so close to the screen that he was practically crawling inside it. 'That little patch of red on her cheek there. Look!'

Carl shook his head. 'I'll bet it was only two degrees Celsius that day. Outdoor interviews always make politicians look healthier, Assad. Why do you think they'd put up with them, otherwise?'

But Assad was right. There was a marked difference between the previous interview and this one. Something had happened to Merete in the meantime. There was no way that Bjarke Ørnfelt, a crackpot professional lobbyist who specialized in splitting facts about natural disasters into unrecognizable atoms, could have made Merete Lynggaard glow so tastily.

Carl stared into space for a moment. In every investigation there was always a moment when a detective fervently wished that he could have met the victim alive. This time it was happening earlier than usual.

'Assad. Phone that institution, Egely, where Merete Lynggaard's brother was placed, and make an appointment on behalf of Detective Inspector Mørck.'

'Detective Inspector Mørck? Who is that?'

Carl tapped his finger to his temple. Was the man just plain stupid? 'Who do you think?'

Assad shook his head. 'Well, inside my head I thought you were deputy police superintendent. Is that not what it is called now, since the new police reform?'

Carl took a deep breath. That fucking police reform. He didn't give a shit about it.

The director at Egely called back ten minutes later, not even trying to hide his curiosity about what this might concern. Evidently Assad had improvised a bit, but what the hell could Carl expect from an assistant with a doctoral degree in rubber gloves and plastic buckets? After all, everybody had to crawl before they could walk.

He glanced over at his assistant and gave him an encouraging nod when he looked up from his Sudoku puzzle.

It took only thirty seconds for Carl to explain things to the director, whose reply was swift and brief. Uffe Lynggaard never spoke a word, so the detective inspector would gain nothing by trying to talk to him. In addition, although Uffe was both mute and difficult to reach, he had not been placed under legal guardianship. And since Uffe Lynggaard had not given permission for anyone at the institution to speak on his behalf, *they* couldn't say anything either. It was a real Catch-22.

'I'm familiar with the procedures. Of course I'm not trying to commit a breach of confidentiality. But I'm investigating his sister's disappearance, so I think that Uffe might actually benefit a great deal from speaking to me.'

'But he doesn't talk. I just told you that.'

'Actually, a lot of people that we interview don't talk, but we manage all the same. We're good at deciphering non-verbal signals over here in Department Q.'

'Department Q?'

'Yes, we're an elite investigative team here at police headquarters. When can I come out to see him?'

Carl heard the man sigh. He wasn't stupid. He recognized a bulldog when he met one.

'Let me see what I can do. I'll get back to you,' he said then.

'What exactly did you tell that man when you called him up, Assad?' yelled Carl when he put down the receiver.

'That man? I told him that you would talk only to the chief and not to a director.'

'The director *is* the chief, Assad.'

Carl took a deep breath, got up, and went over to his assistant, looking him in the eye. 'Don't you know the word "director"? A director is a kind of boss.' They nodded to each other; all right then. 'Assad, tomorrow I want you to pick me up in Allerød, where I live. We're going to take a drive. Do you understand?'

He shrugged.

'And there's not going to be any problem with that when we're out driving around, is there?' Carl pointed at the prayer rug.

'I can roll it up.'

'All right. But how do you know which way Mecca is?'

Assad pointed to his head, as if he had a GPS system implanted in his temporal lobe. 'And if a person is still a little like he does not know where, then there is this.' He picked up one of the magazines from the bookshelf to reveal a compass underneath.

'Huh,' said Carl, staring at the massive conglomeration of metal pipes running along the ceiling. 'But that compass isn't going to work down here.'

Assad again pointed at his head.

'So, I suppose you just have a sense of where it is. And you don't have to be precise, is that it?'

'Allah is great. He has such wide shoulders.'

Carl stuck out his lower lip in a pout. Of course Allah did. What was he thinking, anyway?

Four pairs of eyes with dark rings underneath turned to look at Carl as he entered team leader Bak's office. No one could have any doubt that the team was under extreme pressure. On the wall hung a big map of Valby Park showing crucial aspects of the current case: the crime scene; where the murder weapon, an old-fashioned cut-throat razor, had been found; the place where the witness saw the victim and the suspected perpetrator together; and finally, the route the witness took through the park. Everything had been measured and thoroughly analysed, and none of it made any sense.

'Our talk is going to have to wait until later, Carl,' said Bak, tugging at the sleeve of the black leather jacket that he'd inherited from the former homicide chief. That jacket was Bak's most treasured possession, proof that he was particularly fantastic, and he rarely took it off. The rumbling radiators were pumping out at least forty degrees of heat into the room, but it didn't matter. Besides, he was probably counting on heading out the door at any moment.

Carl looked at the photos pinned up on the bulletin board behind the team members, and it was not an encouraging sight. Evidently the body of the victim had been mutilated after death. Deep gashes in the chest, half of one ear cut off. On his white shirt a cross had been drawn with the victim's own blood. Carl assumed that the cut-off ear had served as the pen. The frost-covered grass around the bicycle had been trampled flat, and the bike had also been smashed, so the spokes in the front wheel were completely crushed. The victim's satchel lay open on the ground, and textbooks from the business school were scattered all over.

'Our talk has to wait until later, you say? OK. But before then could you just ignore your brain-death for a moment and tell me what your key witness says about the individual she saw talking to the victim right before the murder?'

The four men looked at him as if he'd desecrated a grave.

Bak's eyes had a dead expression. 'It's not your case, Carl. We'll talk later. Believe it or not, we're really busy up here.'

He nodded. 'Oh sure, I can see that in your well-fed faces. Of course you're busy. I imagine that you've already sent people out to search the witness's place of residence after she was hospitalized, right?'

The others exchanged glances. Annoyed, but also with a questioning look.

So they hadn't. Excellent.

Marcus Jacobsen had just sat down in his office when Carl came in. As usual, the homicide chief was well groomed. The parting in his hair was sharp as a knife, his eyes attentive and alert.

'Marcus, did you search the witness's residence after

her suicide attempt?' asked Carl, pointing at the case folder that was lying in the middle of Jacobsen's desk.

'What do you mean?'

'You haven't found the piece missing from the victim's ear, have you?'

'No, not yet. Are you saying that it might be in the witness's home?'

'If I were you, I'd go and look for it, boss.'

'If it really was sent to her, I'm sure she got rid of it.'

'So look through the rubbish bins down in the yard. And take a good look in the toilet.'

'It would have been flushed away by now, Carl.'

'Haven't you heard the story about the shit that kept reappearing no matter how many times the toilet was flushed?'

'OK, Carl. I'll take it under advisement.'

'The pride of the department, Mr Yes-man Bak, didn't want to talk to me.'

'Well, then you'll just have to wait, Carl. Your cases aren't about to run off anywhere.'

'I just wanted you to know. It's going to set me back in my schedule.'

'Then I suggest you take a look at one of the other cases in the meantime.' He picked up his pen and tapped it on the edge of the desk. 'So, about that strange guy you have working for you downstairs . . . You're not involving him in any of the investigative work, are you?'

'Well, you know, considering the huge department I'm in charge of, there's not much chance that he'll hear about what goes on.'

Jacobsen tossed his pen on to one of the piles of

documents. 'Carl, you've taken an oath of confidentiality, and the man isn't a police officer. Just keep that in mind.'

Carl nodded. He'd be the one to decide what was discussed and where. 'How on earth did you find Assad? Through the employment office?'

'I have no idea. Ask Lars Bjørn. Or ask the man himself.'

Carl raised a finger. 'By the way, I'd like to have a floor plan of the basement, to scale, and showing the points of the compass.'

Jacobsen was looking a bit tired again. There weren't many people who dared make such strange requests of him. 'You can print out a floor plan from the departmental intranet, Carl. It's easy!'

'Here,' said Carl, pointing at the floor plan spread out in front of Assad. 'Here you can see that wall over there, and here's where you've put your prayer rug. And here's the arrow pointing north. So now you can position the rug in exactly the right place.'

The eyes that turned to look up at him were full of respect. They were going to make a good team.

'Two people called with the telephone for you. I told both of them that you would be pleased to call them back sometime.'

'Who were they?'

'That man who is the director in Frederikssund, and a lady who talked like a machine that cuts through metal.'

Carl sighed heavily. 'Vigga. That's my wife.' So she'd found out what his new phone number was. Any chance of peace and quiet was now gone.

'Wife? You have a wife?'

'Oh, Assad, it's too complicated to get into right now. Let's get to know each other better first.'

Assad pursed his lips and nodded. A trace of sympathy passed over his solemn face.

'Assad, how exactly did you get this job, anyway?'

'I know Lars Bjørn.'

'You know him?'

Assad smiled. 'Yes, I do. I was in his office every single day for a whole month to get job.'

'You pestered Lars Bjørn about getting a job?'

'Yes, I love police.'

Carl didn't call Vigga back until he was in his living room in Rønneholt Park, breathing in the aroma of the hash that Morten was cooking while listening to emotional operatic arias. He'd thrown together the concoction from what had once been a genuine Parma ham from Super-Best.

Vigga was OK in small doses, as long as Carl was allowed to decide how much of her to take. It had been difficult over the years, but now that she'd left him, certain rules of the game applied.

'Damn it, Vigga,' he said. 'I don't like you calling me at work. You know how busy we are.'

'Carl, sweetheart. Didn't Morten tell you that I'm freezing out here?'

'I'm not surprised. It's a garden cottage, Vigga. It was cobbled together out of shitty building materials. Old boards and crates that were already surplus and worthless in 1945. You can just move somewhere else.'

'I'm not moving back in with you, Carl.'

He took a deep breath. 'I certainly hope not. It would be hard to squeeze you and your assembly line of confirmation-aged lovers into the sauna downstairs with Morten. But there are plenty of other houses and flats that do have central heating.'

'I've got a really good solution for the whole thing.'

No matter what she had in mind, it already sounded expensive. 'A really good solution would be a divorce, Vigga,' said Carl. Sooner or later it had to happen. Then she would demand half the value of the house, and during the past few years it had increased considerably, brought on by the insane rise in the housing market in spite of fluctuations. He should have simply demanded a divorce while houses still cost half of what they did today. It was as simple as that. But it was too late now, and he'd be damned if he was going to move.

He turned his eyes to the vibrating ceiling under Jesper's room. Even if I took out a loan when we divorced, my expenses couldn't possibly be more than they are now, he thought. In that case, he imagined she'd have to take back responsibility for her son. They had the biggest electricity bill on this side of town; there was no doubt about that. Jesper had to be the energy company's elite customer number one.

'Divorce? No, I don't want a divorce, Carl. I've tried that before, and it wasn't a good thing. You know that.'

He shook his head. Then what the hell did she call the situation they'd been living in for the past couple of years?

'I want to have a gallery, Carl. My very own gallery.'

OK, here it came. In his mind he saw Vigga's paintings, which were nothing more than metre-high, deranged blotches of pink and bronze gilding. A gallery? Good idea, if she wanted to make more space in her garden cottage.

'A gallery, you say? And I imagine that it will have a gigantic furnace. So then you can sit there all day, warming yourself on all the millions of kroner that are going to come pouring in.' Sure. He could see the whole scam.

'You've always been the sarcastic type,' said Vigga. And then she laughed. It was the laugh that got to him every time. That damn seductive laugh. 'But it's really a fantastic idea, Carl. There would be so many possibilities if I had my own gallery. Can't you just picture it? And maybe one day Jesper will have a famous mother. Wouldn't that be fun?'

Infamous, Vigga. That's the proper word, he thought. But what he said was: 'So you've already found a place, is that right?'

'Oh, Carl, it's so charming. And Hugin has already talked to the owner.'

'Hugin?'

'Yes, Hugin. He's a very talented painter.'

'Better between the bed sheets than on the canvases, I'd guess.'

'Come on, Carl.' She laughed again. 'Be nice.'

14

2002

Merete had been waiting on the restaurant deck. She'd told Uffe to hurry up just before the door to the men's room slammed behind him. Only waiters were still in the cafeteria at the other end of the ferry; all the passengers had gone down to their cars. Uffe needs to hurry up, she thought, even though the Audi was at the back of the line.

And that was the last full thought she managed to formulate in her former life.

The attack came from behind and it was so surprising that she didn't even have time to scream. But she did notice the hand pressing the rag hard against her mouth and nose, and then, more vaguely, she was aware of someone pushing the black button that opened the door to the stairwell down to the car deck. Finally, she was conscious only of a couple of distant noises and the sight of all the metal walls in the stairwell whirling around, and then everything went black.

The cement floor underneath her when she woke up was cold, very cold. She lifted her head, feeling an intense pounding inside. Her legs felt heavy, and she could hardly raise her shoulders off the floor. She forced herself into a sitting position and tried to orient herself in the pitch dark. She considered shouting but didn't dare; instead she took a deep breath, without making a sound. Then she cautiously stretched out her hands to test if there was anything close by. But there was nothing.

For a long time she just sat there before venturing to stand up, slowly, every nerve on alert. She was determined to lash out at even the slightest sound. She would hit as hard as she could. Hit and kick. She sensed that she was alone, but she might be wrong.

After a while she felt more clear-headed, and then the fear came creeping in, like an infection. Her skin grew hot, her heart beat harder and faster. Her eyes, blinded by the dark, flickered nervously. She'd read and seen so many terrible things.

About women who disappeared.

Then she took a hesitant step forwards, holding out her hands. There might be a hole in the floor, an abyss just waiting to swallow her up. There might be sharp implements and glass. But her foot found the floor, and there was still nothing in front of her. All of a sudden she stopped and stood motionless.

Uffe, she thought, feeling her jaw start to quiver. He was on board the ship when it happened.

It took a couple of hours for her to sketch a floor plan of the room in her mind. The space seemed to be rectangular. Maybe twenty to twenty-five feet in length and at least fifteen feet wide. She had run her fingers over the cold walls; on one of them, at eye level, she'd found a couple of glass panes that felt like two enormous portholes. She'd hammered on them with her shoe, jumping back at each blow. But the glass didn't break. Then she'd touched the edges of something that felt like an arched doorway set into the wall, although maybe not, because there was no door handle. She'd slid her hands over the wall, in the hope of finding a handle or maybe a light switch somewhere. But the surface was smooth and cold.

After that she systematically explored the whole room. She cautiously paced from one end to the other, turned around, took a step to the side, and then made her way back. Upon reaching the far wall, she repeated the whole exercise. When she was done, she concluded that she and the dry air were all alone in the room.

I need to wait over there, next to what feels like a door, she thought. She would sit down at the base of it so she wouldn't be visible through the glass panes. When someone came in, she'd grab their legs and give them a yank. She'd try to kick the person hard in the head over and over.

Her muscles tensed and her skin felt clammy. She might have only the one chance.

After she'd sat there so long that her body had grown stiff and her senses were dulled, she got to her feet and went over to the opposite corner to squat down and pee. She needed to remember which corner she had used. One corner as a toilet. One where she sat and waited by the door, and one where she would sleep. The smell of urine was strong in the desolate cage. She hadn't had anything to drink since sitting in the ship's cafeteria, and that could easily have been hours ago. Of course it was possible that she'd been unconscious for only an hour or two, but it could also have been a whole day or more. She had no idea. All she knew was that she wasn't hungry, just thirsty.

She stood up, pulled up her trousers, and tried to remember.

She and Uffe had been the last passengers near the toilets. They were probably also the last ones on the sun deck. At any rate, the two men over by the big picture windows were gone when she and Uffe passed by. She had nodded to the waitress who came out of the cafeteria, and she'd seen a couple of kids punch the door opener before disappearing below deck. Nothing else. She hadn't noticed anyone coming that close to her. Her only thought had been that Uffe needed to hurry up and come out of the toilet.

Oh God, Uffe! What had happened to him? He was so unhappy after he'd hit her. And he'd been so dismayed that his baseball cap was gone. There were still red patches on his cheeks when he went into the toilet. So what kind of shape could he be in by now?

She heard a click from above that made her cringe. Then she quickly fumbled her way over to the corner with the arched door. She had to be ready if someone came in. Then there was another click, and her heart felt as if it might hammer apart. Only when the fan overhead started up did she realize she could relax a little. The clicking sound must have come from some sort of relay switch.

She stretched towards the warm air; it was life-giving. What else did she have to cling to?

And she remained standing there like that until the fan stopped, leaving her with the feeling that the warm air might be her only contact with the outside world. She closed her eyes tight and made herself concentrate so that the sobs trying to force their way out would be kept at bay.

It was a terrible thought. But maybe it was true. Maybe she'd be left here for all eternity. Hidden away to die. And nobody knew where she was; even she didn't know. It could be anywhere. Several hours' drive from the ferry-boat landing. In Denmark or Germany, anywhere at all. Maybe even further away than that.

And with death slowly emerging as the likely end to this whole scenario, she imagined the weapon that thirst and hunger would aim at her. The lingering death, in which her body would short-circuit bit by bit, the relay switches of self-preservation shutting down one after the other. And at last the apathetic, ultimate slumber that would set her free.

There aren't many people who will miss me, she thought. Uffe, of course. He would miss her. Poor, poor Uffe. But she'd never let anyone but her brother get close to her. She'd locked out everyone else and caged herself in.

She tried very hard to hold back the tears, but without success. Was this really what life had held for her? Was it going to end like this? Without children, without happiness, without having a chance to realize all that she'd dreamed of doing during the years she was alone with Uffe? Without being able to fulfil the obligation that she'd taken on ever since her parents died?

It was a bitter, depressing feeling, and infinitely lonely. That was why she now heard herself sobbing quietly.

She was overwhelmed by the awareness that Uffe would be all alone in the world, and she imagined that this was the most terrible thing that could happen to her. For a long time it filled her consciousness completely. She was going to die alone, like an animal, silently and unaccounted for, while Uffe and everyone else would have to live on without knowing. And when she had exhausted all her tears, it occurred to her that maybe this wasn't over yet. And things might get worse. She could be in for a cruel death. She might have been relegated to a fate so horrible that death would come as a relief. But first she might have to endure pain and bestiality. She'd heard all about such things. Exploitation, rape and torture. Maybe eyes were watching her right now. Cameras with infrared sensors observing her through the glass. Eyes that meant to harm her. Ears that were listening.

She looked towards the glass panes and tried to appear calm.

'Please, have mercy on me,' she whispered softly into the darkness.

15

2007

A Peugeot 607 is considered to be a relatively quiet vehicle, but that was hardly the case during Assad's frantic parking manoeuvres on the road directly outside Carl's bedroom window.

'Awesome,' muttered Jesper as he stared out the window. Carl couldn't recall the last time his stepson had said even one word so early in the morning. But it sure as hell was appropriate.

'I left you a note from Vigga,' Morten called out after Carl as he headed out the door. But he wasn't about to read any note from Vigga. The prospect of receiving an invitation to look at galleries in the company of an undoubtedly narrow-hipped artist named Hugin who painted big blotches on canvas wasn't exactly at the top of Carl's list right now.

'Hello,' greeted Assad as he stood leaning against the driver's door. On his head he wore a camel-hair cap of unknown origin. He looked like anything but a private chauffeur assigned to the criminal police department, if such a title even existed. Carl glanced up at the sky. It was pale blue and clear, the temperature was tolerable.

'I know just exactly the location of Egely,' said Assad, pointing at the GPS as Carl got into the passenger seat. Carl cast a weary glance at the image on the screen. He saw an X on a road that was a comfortable distance from the waters of Roskilde Fjord, so that the residents of the nursing home wouldn't be likely to fall in, but close enough so the director would have a good view of most of the delights of northern Zealand, if he ever bothered to look out of the window. That was where institutions for mentally disturbed patients were often placed. God only knew for whose sake the location had actually been chosen.

Assad started the engine, put the car in reverse, and sped backwards along Magnolievangen, stopping only when the rear of the vehicle was halfway up on the grass embankment on the other side of Rønneholt Parkvei. Before Carl's body could even react, Assad had slammed through the gears and was now cruising along at ninety kilometres an hour, where the speed limit was only fifty.

'Stop, damn it!' yelled Carl just before they entered the roundabout at the end of the road. But Assad merely gave him a sly look, like a cab driver in Beirut, and yanked the steering wheel hard to the right. The next second they were headed for the motorway.

'Fast car!' shouted Assad, flooring the accelerator as they entered the slip road.

Maybe it would put a damper on him if Carl pulled that cap down over his rapturous face.

Egely was a whitewashed building that splendidly proclaimed its purpose. No one ever entered voluntarily, and it was far from easy for anyone to get out. It was obvious that this was not a place for finger-painting or guitar lessons. This was where people with money and status placed the weak members of their families.

Private care, in the spirit of the government itself.

The director's office matched the overall impression, and

the director himself, an unsmiling, bony and pallid-looking man, suited the interior as if specifically designed for it.

'Uffe Lynggaard's expenses here are paid by the proceeds from funds deposited in the Lynggaard trust,' replied the director to Carl's question.

Carl glanced at the bookshelf, which held numerous case files, many of them labelled with the word 'trust'.

'I see. And how exactly was the trust created?'

'An inheritance from his parents, who were both killed in a car accident which also injured Uffe. And an inheritance from his sister, of course.'

'She was a member of parliament, so I don't imagine we're talking about large sums of money.'

'No, but the sale of their house brought in two million kroner, when a presumption of death was handed down by court order not too long ago. Thank God for that. At the moment the trust is worth about twenty-two million kroner, but I'm sure you already know that.'

Carl whistled softly. He hadn't known that. 'Twenty-two million, at five per cent interest. I suppose that would pay for Uffe's expenses, wouldn't it?'

'Well yes, it just about covers things, after taxes.'

Carl gave him a wry look. 'And since he's been here, Uffe hasn't said anything about his sister's disappearance?'

'No, he hasn't spoken a word since the car accident, as far as I've been told.'

'Have you done anything to help get him going?'

At that the director took off his glasses and peered at Carl from under his bushy eyebrows. He was the epitome of seriousness. 'Uffe Lynggaard has been thoroughly examined. He has scar tissue from bleeding in the speech centre of his brain, which is explanation enough for his muteness. But he also suffered severe trauma from the accident. The death of his parents, his own injuries. As you may know, he was seriously hurt.'

'Yes, I read the report.' He hadn't actually, but Assad had, and the man hadn't stopped jabbering about it as they cruised along the motorways of northern Zealand. 'He spent five months in the hospital with severe internal bleeding in his liver, spleen and lung tissue. His vision was also impaired.'

The director gave a brief nod. 'That's correct. It says in his medical file that Uffe Lynggaard was unable to see for several weeks. He had massive retinal bleeding.'

'What about now? Is his body functioning as it should, from a physiological perspective?'

'By all indications, yes. He's a strong young man.'

'He's nearly thirty-four years old. So he's been in this condition for twenty-one years.'

The pale man again nodded. 'So you can understand why you're not going to get anywhere with him.'

'And you won't let me talk to him?'

'I don't think it would serve any purpose.'

'He was the last one to see Merete Lynggaard alive. I'd like to see him.'

The director straightened up. Now he looked out at the fjord, as Carl had predicted he would. 'I don't think I'm going to allow it.'

Pompous idiots like him deserved to be stabbed with a blunt knife. 'You don't trust me to behave myself, but I think you should.'

'Why is that?'

'Are you familiar with the police?'

The director turned to look at Carl. His face was an ashen grey, his brow furrowed. Years spent behind a desk had worn him out, but there was nothing wrong with his mind. He had no idea what Carl meant by that question, only that silence would not be to his benefit.

'What exactly are you getting at?'

'We police officers are an inquisitive lot. Sometimes we've got a question burning in our minds and we just have to find an answer. This time it's obvious.'

'And the question is?'

'Where do your patients get their money? Five per cent of twenty-two million, minus taxes of course, is just a drop in the bucket. Do your patients receive full value for their money, or is the price too high when the state funding is added in? And is the price the same for everybody?' Carl nodded to himself, drinking in the light coming off the fjord. 'New questions always keep popping up when we can't get an answer to the one we're initially interested in. That's just how policemen are. We can't help ourselves. Maybe it's a disease, but who the hell could we consult to find a cure?'

Maybe now there was a hint of colour in the director's face. 'I don't think we're going to reach any kind of middle ground here.'

'So why don't you let me see Uffe Lynggaard? To be perfectly honest, what harm could it do? You haven't locked him up in a damned cage or anything, have you?'

The pictures in Merete Lynggaard's case file didn't do full justice to her brother, Uffe. The police photographs, the sketches from the preliminary examination, and a couple of press photos had all shown a young man with a bowed figure. A pale fellow who looked like what he apparently was: an emotionally retarded, passive, slow-witted person. But reality revealed something different.

Uffe was sitting in a pleasant room with pictures on the wall and a view that was at least as good as the one from the director's office. His bed had been newly made up, and his shoes were freshly polished. His clothes were clean and had nothing institutional about them. He had strong arms and long blond hair. He was broad-shouldered and presumably quite tall. Many would call him handsome. There was nothing drivelling or pathetic about Uffe Lynggaard.

The director and supervisory nurse watched from the doorway as Carl moved about the room, but he wasn't going to give them any reason to criticize his behaviour. He would come back again soon, even though he didn't really have the energy for it. He'd be better prepared next time, and then he would talk to Uffe. But that could wait for now. In the meantime there was plenty for him to study in Uffe's room. The picture of his sister, smiling at them. His parents, with their arms around each other as they laughed at the camera. The drawings on the wall, which bore no resemblance to the childish drawings usually found on walls in this type of place. Happy drawings. Not ones that might reveal something about the horrible event that had robbed Uffe of speech.

'Are there more drawings? Are there any in there?' Carl asked, pointing at the wardrobe and dresser.

'No,' replied the nurse. 'No, Uffe hasn't drawn anything since he came here. These drawings are all from his home.'

'So what does Uffe do to keep himself occupied during the day?'

She smiled. 'Lots of things. He takes walks with the staff, he goes for a run out in the park. Watches TV. He loves that.' The nurse seemed like a kind person. She was the one Carl would consult next time.

'What does he watch?'

'Whatever's on.'

'Does he react to the programmes?'

'Sometimes. He likes to laugh.' She shook her head with pleasure, smiling even more broadly.

'He laughs?'

'Yes, he laughs like a baby. Not self-conscious at all.'

Carl glanced at the director, standing there like a block of ice, and then at Uffe. Merete's brother hadn't taken his eyes off Carl since he entered the room. Carl had noticed that. Uffe was observant, but if you looked at him more closely, you could see that his gaze was not fully conscious. His eyes weren't dead, but whatever Uffe saw, it apparently didn't sink in very deep. Carl had an urge to startle him, just to see what would happen, but that too could wait.

He took up position next to the window and tried to catch Uffe's eye. Uffe clearly took things in but failed to comprehend fully what he saw. There was something there, and yet there wasn't.

'Move over to the other seat, Assad,' Carl told his assistant, who'd been waiting behind the wheel of the car.

'The other seat? You do not then want me to drive?' he asked.

'I'd like to keep this car a while longer, Assad. It has anti-lock brakes and power steering, and I'd like it to stay that way.'

'And what does that mean then, that you are saying?'

'That you should sit next to me and pay attention to how I'd like you to drive. If I ever let you drive again, that is.'

Carl keyed in their next destination on the GPS, ignoring the flood of Arabic words issuing from Assad's mouth as he slunk around the car to the passenger's side.

'Have you ever driven a car in Denmark?' Carl asked as they were well on their way towards Stevns.

Assad's silence was answer enough.

They found the house in Magleby on a side road all the way out by the fields. Not a smallholder's residence or a restored farmhouse, like most in the area, but a genuine brick house from the period when the facade mirrored the soul of a building. There was a dense grove of yew trees, but still the house loomed over them. If the property had been sold for two million kroner, then somebody had got themselves a real bargain. And somebody else had been cheated.

The name on the brass doorplate said: 'Antique Dealers' and 'Peter & Erling Møller-Hansen'. But the person who opened the door looked more like an aristocrat. Delicate complexion, deep blue eyes, and fragrant lotion generously applied all over.

The man was cooperative and accommodating. He politely took Assad's cap from him and invited both men into a front hall filled with Empire furniture and other bric-a-brac.

No, they hadn't known Merete Lynggaard or her brother. Not personally, that is, although most of the Lynggaards' possessions had come with the house, but they were not of any value.

The man offered Carl and Assad green tea served in paper-thin porcelain cups. He sat on the edge of the sofa with his knees together and his feet splayed out, ready to act the role of the responsible citizen to the best of his abilities.

'It was terrible that she drowned like that. It must be an awful way to die. My husband almost died in a waterfall in Yugoslavia once, and that was a horrible experience, let me tell you.'

Carl noticed Assad's confused expression when the man said 'my husband', but a quick glance was enough to wipe the look off his face. Assad obviously still had a lot to learn about the diversity of Danish living arrangements.

'The police collected all the documents belonging to the Lynggaards,' said Carl. 'But since then have you found any diaries, letters or faxes, or maybe just some phone messages that might shed new light on the case?'

The man shook his head. 'Everything was gone.' He made a sweeping gesture with his arm, taking in the whole living room. 'The furniture was still here, but it was nothing special, and there wasn't much left in the drawers other than office supplies and a few souvenirs. Scrapbooks with stickers, a few photos, and things like that. I think they must have been quite ordinary people.'

'What about the neighbours? Did they know the Lynggaards?'

'Oh, well, we don't socialize much with the neighbours, and they haven't lived here very long, anyway. They said something about having come back to Denmark from abroad. But no, I don't think the Lynggaards spent much time with anyone else in town. A lot of people didn't even know that she had a brother.'

'So you haven't run into anyone around here who knew them?'

'Oh, sure. Helle Andersen. She took care of the brother.'

'She is the home help,' said Assad. 'The police interviewed her, but she knew nothing. Except that there came a letter. For Merete Lynggaard, that is. It came the day before she drowned. The home help was the one who received it.'

Carl raised his eyebrows. He really needed to read through the damn case documents himself.

'Did the police find the letter, Assad?'

He shook his head.

Carl turned back to their host. 'Does this Helle Andersen live near by?'

'No, in Holtug on the other side of Gjorslev. But she'll actually be here in ten minutes.'

'Here?'

'Yes, my husband is ill.' He looked down at the floor. 'Very ill. So she comes over to help out.'

Fortune smiles on the clueless, thought Carl, and then asked if they might have a tour of the house.

It turned out to be an odyssey in quirky furniture and huge gilded frames. The obligatory amassing of things from a life spent working in an auction house. But the kitchen had been completely remodelled; all the walls painted and the floors refinished. If there was anything left from when Merete Lynggaard lived in the house, it could only be the silverfish skittering about on the dark floor of the bathroom.

'That Uffe, he was so sweet.' A stocky face with dark circles under her eyes and ruddy, plump cheeks were Helle Andersen's trademarks. The rest of her was covered by a light blue smock in a size that was unlikely to be found in the local clothes shop. 'It was crazy to think that he would do anything to hurt his sister, and that's what I told the police. That they couldn't have been more wrong.'

'But witnesses saw him hit his sister,' said Carl.

'He could get a bit wild at times. But he didn't mean anything by it.'

'But he's a big, strong man. Maybe he happened to push her into the water by accident.'

Helle Andersen rolled her eyes. 'Impossible. Uffe was the epitome of gentleness. Sometimes he'd get so upset about something that it would make me upset too, but not very often.'

'You cooked for him?'

'I took care of all sorts of things. So that everything would be nice and neat when Merete came home.'

'And you didn't see her very often?'

'Once in a while.'

'But not on any of the days right before she died?'

'Oh yes. There was one evening when I took care of Uffe. But then he got so upset, like I said before, that I called Merete to say she had to come home. And she did. He was really in a bad way that time.'

'Did anything out of the ordinary happen that evening?'

'Only the fact that Merete didn't come home at six o'clock like she usually did. Uffe didn't like that. He couldn't understand it was something we'd already talked about and arranged.'

'But she was a member of parliament. Surely this must have been a frequent occurrence?'

'No, not really. Only once in a while, if she had to take a trip. And then it was only for a night or two.'

'So she'd been out travelling on that evening?'

At that point Assad shook his head. It was damned annoying, how much he knew.

'No, she'd gone out to eat,' said Helle.

'I see. Who did she eat with? Do you know?'

'No, nobody knows.'

'Is that also in the report, Assad?'

He nodded. 'Søs Norup, the new secretary, saw Merete write down the name of the restaurant in her diary. And someone inside the restaurant remembered that he saw her there. Just not with who.'

There was clearly a lot that Carl needed to study in that report.

'What was the name of the restaurant, Assad?'

'I think it was called Café Bankeråt. Could that be right?'

Carl turned back to the home help. 'Do you know if Merete was on a date? Was she out with a boyfriend?'

A dimple an inch deep appeared in the woman's cheek. 'She might have been. But she didn't say anything about it to me.'

'And she didn't mention anything when she came home? After you called her, I mean?'

'No, I left. Uffe was so upset.'

They heard a clattering sound, and the present owner of the house came into the room wearing an expression of pathos, as if the tea tray he was carrying contained all the secrets of gastronomy. 'Homemade,' was his only remark as he placed several small pudding-like cakes on silver plates in front of them.

They stirred memories from a lost childhood. Not good memories, but memories all the same.

Their host handed out the cakes, and Assad demonstrated immediately that he appreciated the offering.

'Helle, it says in the report that someone gave you a letter the day before Merete Lynggaard disappeared. Can you describe it in more detail?' Her statement was undoubtedly included in the report, but she was just going to have to repeat what she'd already said.

'It was a yellow envelope, and the paper was almost like parchment.'

'How big was it?'

She showed them with her hands. Apparently an A5.

'Was anything on the envelope? A stamp or a name?'

'No, nothing.'

'So who brought it over? Did you know the person?'

'No, I didn't. The doorbell rang, and a man was standing outside. He handed me the envelope.'

'That's a bit strange, don't you think? Normally letters come with the post.'

She gave him a little, confidential nudge. 'We do have a postman. But this was later in the day. It was actually right in the middle of the news on the radio.'

'At noon?'

She nodded. 'He just handed me the envelope, and then he left.'

'Didn't he say anything?'

'Yes, he said that it was for Merete Lynggaard. That was all.'

'Why didn't he put it in the letter box?'

'I think it was urgent. Maybe he was afraid that she wouldn't see it as soon as she came home.'

'But Merete must have known who brought the letter. What did she say about it?'

'I don't know. I had left by the time she came home.'

Assad nodded again. So that too was in the report.

Carl gave his assistant a professional look, which meant: It's standard procedure to ask these types of questions multiple times. Let him chew on that for a while.

'I thought that Uffe couldn't be left at home alone,' he then interjected.

'Oh yes, he could,' she replied, her eyes shining. 'Just not late at night.'

At that point Carl wished he was back at his desk in the basement. He'd spent years having to drag information out of people, and by now his arms were feeling very tired. A couple more questions and then they had to be on their way. The Lynggaard case was obviously hopeless. She'd fallen overboard. Things like that happened.

'And it might have been too late if I hadn't put the envelope where she'd find it,' said the woman.

He saw how her eyes shifted away for a moment. Not towards the little pudding cakes. Away. 'What do you mean?'

'Well, she died the next day, didn't she?'

'That wasn't what you were just thinking about, was it?'

'Of course.'

Seated next to Carl, Assad put his cake down on the table. Strangely enough, he'd also noticed her evasive manoeuvre.

'You were thinking about something else. I can tell. What did you mean, that it might have been too late?'

'Just what I said. That she died the next day.'

He looked up at the cake-happy host. 'Would you mind if I spoke to Helle Andersen in private?'

The man didn't look pleased, and Helle Andersen didn't either. She smoothed out her smock, but the damage was done.

'Tell me, Helle,' Carl said, leaning towards her after the antique dealer had left the room. 'If you know anything at all that you've been keeping to yourself, now is the time to tell me. Do you understand?'

'There wasn't anything else.'

'Do you have children?'

The corners of her mouth drooped. What did that have to do with the case?

'OK. You opened the envelope, didn't you?'

She jerked her head back in alarm. 'Of course I didn't.'

'This is perjury, Helle Andersen. Your children are going to have to do without you for a while.'

For a stout country girl, she reacted with extraordinary speed. Her hands flew up to her mouth, her feet shot under the sofa, her entire abdomen was sucked in as she tried to create a safe distance between herself and the dangerous police animal. 'I didn't open it.' The words flew out of her mouth. 'I just held it up to the light.'

'What did the letter say?'

Her eyebrows practically overlapped. 'All it said was: "Have a nice trip to Berlin." '

'Do you know what she was going to do in Berlin?'

'It was just a fun trip with Uffe. They'd done it a couple of times before.'

'Why was it so important to wish her a nice trip?'

'I don't know.'

'Who would have known about the trip, Helle? Merete lived a very private life with Uffe, as I understand it.'

She shrugged. 'Maybe somebody at the Folketing. I don't know.'

'Wouldn't they just send her an email?'

'I really don't know.' She was obviously feeling pinned down. Maybe she was lying. Maybe she was just sensitive to pressure. 'It might have been something from the council,' she ventured. It was another blind alley.

'So the letter said: "Have a nice trip to Berlin." Anything else?'

'Nothing else. Just that. Really.'

'No signature?'

'No. That was all.'

'And the messenger, what did he look like?'

She hid her face in her hands for a moment. 'All I noticed was that he was wearing a really nice overcoat,' she said in a subdued voice.

'You didn't see anything else? That can't be right.'

'It's true. He was taller than me, even though he was standing down on the step. And he was wearing a scarf. It was green. And it covered the lower half of his face. It was raining, so that was probably why. He also had a slight cold, or at least that's how he sounded.'

'Did he sneeze?'

'No, he just sounded like he had a cold. Sniffled a bit, you know.'

'What about his eyes? Blue or brown?'

'I'm pretty sure they were blue. At least I think so. Maybe they were grey. But I'd recognize them, if I saw them again.'

'How old was he?'

'About my age, I think.'

As if that piece of information would help.

'And how old are you?'

She gave Carl a slightly indignant look. 'Not quite thirty-five,' she replied, looking down at the floor.

'What kind of car was he driving?'

'He didn't come by car, as far as I could tell. At least there wasn't any car parked outside.'

'You don't think he *walked* the whole way out here, do you?'

'No, probably not.'

'But you didn't watch him leave?'

'No. I needed to give Uffe something to eat. He always had lunch while I listened to the news programme on the radio.'

They talked about the letter as they drove. Assad didn't know anything more about it. The police investigation had come to a dead end as far as it was concerned.

'But why the hell was it so important to deliver such an unimportant message? What did it really mean? I could understand it if the message were from a woman friend and the letter was perfumed and came in a little envelope with flowers on it. But not in such an anonymous envelope and with no signature.'

'I think that Helle, she does not know very much,' Assad replied as they turned on to Bjælkerupvej, which was where Social Services for Stevns municipality was located.

Carl looked over at the buildings. It would have been nice to have a court order in his back pocket before going inside.

'Stay here,' he said to Assad, whose face virtually glowed with satisfaction.

Carl located the director's office after making a few inquiries.

'Yes, that's right. Uffe Lynggaard received care from the Home Nursing Group,' she said as Carl put his police badge back in his pocket. 'But we're a bit disorganized at the moment when it comes to archiving former cases. Municipal reforms, you know.'

So the woman seated opposite him knew nothing about the case. He'd have to talk to somebody else. Surely someone in the place had to remember Uffe Lynggaard and his sister. Just a tiny scrap of information could turn out to be valuable. Maybe someone had been to their house numerous times and had noticed something that might give him a lead.

'Could I speak to the person who was responsible for his care back then?'

'I'm afraid she's retired now.'

'Could you give me her name?'

'No, I'm sorry. Only those of us who work here at City Hall can discuss former cases.'

'But none of the employees know anything about Uffe Lynggaard, is that correct?'

'Oh, I'm sure someone does. But, like I said, we're not at liberty to discuss the case.'

'I realize that it's a matter of confidentiality, and I know that Uffe Lynggaard is not under state guardianship. But I didn't drive all the way out here to go back home empty-handed. Could you let me see his case file?'

'You know very well that I can't let you do that. If you'd like to speak with our attorney, you're welcome to do so. The files aren't accessible right now, anyway. And Uffe Lynggaard no longer lives in this district.'

'So the documents have been transferred to Frederiks-sund?'

'I'm not at liberty to say.'

What a patronizing bitch.

Carl left her office and paused outside in the hallway for a moment, looking around. 'Excuse me,' he said to a woman who came walking towards him, seemingly too tired to put up much of a fight. He pulled out his police badge and introduced himself. 'Could you possibly help me find out the name of the person who handled cases in Magleby ten years ago?'

'Ask in there,' said the woman, pointing to the office he had just exited.

So it was going to take a court order, paperwork, phone calls, waiting time, and more phone calls. He just didn't have the energy for all that.

'I'll remember this the next time you need my help,' he said to the woman, giving her a slight bow.

*

The last stop on their expedition was the Clinic for Spinal Cord Injuries in Hornbæk. 'I'll drive myself up there, Assad. Can you take the train home? I'll drop you off in Køge. There's an express train to the Central Station.' Assad nodded, not looking terribly enthusiastic. Carl had no idea where the man lived. He'd have to ask him sometime.

He glanced at his odd companion. 'We'll start working on a different case tomorrow, Assad. This one is going nowhere.' Not even that promise set off any fireworks in Assad's face.

At the clinic Hardy had been moved to another ward, and he wasn't looking good. His skin was OK, but darkness lurked in his blue eyes.

Carl put his hand on Hardy's shoulder. 'I've been thinking about what you said last time, Hardy. But it's not going to work. I'm really sorry. I just can't do it. Do you understand?'

Hardy didn't say a word. Of course he understood; at the same time, of course, he didn't.

'How about if you help me out instead, Hardy? I'll give you all the facts, and you can take your time thinking them over. I could use some extra input, you know? I don't give a flying fuck about any of it, but if you help me out, then at least we'll have something to laugh about together.'

'You want me to laugh, Carl?' said Hardy, turning his head away.

All in all, it had been a really shitty day.

16

2002

All sense of time vanished in the darkness, and with it the rhythms of her body. Day and night merged like Siamese twins. There was only one fixed point in the day for Merete, and that was the click from the retractable hatch in the arched door.

The first time she heard the distorted voice on the loudspeaker, the shock was so explosive that she was still trembling when she lay down to sleep.

But if she hadn't heard the voice, she would have been dead of thirst and hunger; she knew that. The question was whether that might have been a better alternative.

She had noticed the thirst and dryness in her mouth disappearing. She'd noticed the fatigue dulling her hunger, the fear being replaced by sorrow, and the sorrow by an almost comforting acknowledgement that death was approaching. And that was why she lay there calmly, waiting for her body to give up, when a grating voice revealed that she was not alone and that she ultimately was going to have to surrender to someone else's will.

'Merete,' said the woman's voice without warning. 'We're sending in a plastic container. In a moment you'll hear a clicking sound and a hatch will open over in the corner. We've seen that you've already found it.'

Maybe she'd imagined that a light was turned on,

because she pressed her eyes closed and tried to gain control over the shock waves that were flashing along her nerve endings. But there was no light in the room.

'Can you hear me?' shouted the voice.

She nodded, breathing hard. Now Merete noticed how cold she was. How the lack of sustenance had sucked all the fat out of her body. How vulnerable she was.

'Answer me!'

'Yes. Yes, I hear you. Who are you?' She stared into the darkness.

'When you hear the click, go over to the hatch at once. Don't try to crawl inside. You won't be able to do it. After you take out the first container, there will be another. One of them is a bucket that you can use as a toilet to relieve yourself. The other bucket holds water and food. Each day we'll open the hatch, and then we'll exchange the old containers with new ones. Do you understand?'

'What is this all about?' She listened to the echo of her own voice. 'Have I been kidnapped? Is it money you want?'

'Here comes the first one.'

There was a scraping in the corner, and a slight whistling sound. Merete moved towards that sound and noticed that the bottom of the arched door set into the wall opened to deliver a hard container the size of a wastebasket. When she pulled it out and set it on the floor, the hatch closed for ten seconds and then reopened, this time revealing a slightly taller bucket that was presumably supposed to serve as a dry toilet.

Her heart was pounding. If the containers could be exchanged so swiftly, that meant someone had to be standing

118

on the other side of the door. Another human being very close.

'Won't you please tell me where I am?' She crawled forwards on her knees until she was sitting right under the place where she thought the loudspeaker was located. 'How long have I been here?' She raised her voice a bit. 'What do you want from me?'

'There's a roll of toilet paper in the food box. You'll get another one each week. When you need to wash, use water from the container that's inside the toilet bucket. Remember to take it out before using the toilet. There's no drain in the room, so be sure to lean over the bucket to wash.'

The sinews in her neck were stretched taut. A shadow of anger fought with the tears, and her lips quivered. Snot ran from her nose. 'Am I supposed to sit here in the dark . . . the whole time?' she sobbed. 'Can't you turn on a light? Just for a moment? Please!'

Again the clicking sound and a little whistle, and the hatch shut.

After that came many, many days when she heard only the fan, turned on weekly for ventilation, and the daily clattering and whistling of the hatch door. At times the intervals in between seemed interminable; at other times it felt as if she'd just lain down after a meal when the next buckets arrived. The food was the only physical bright spot for her, even though it was a monotonous diet without any real flavour. A few potatoes and overcooked vegetables along with a scrap of meat. The same every day. As if there were a bottomless pot of stew, always simmering out there in the light, in the world on the other side of the impenetrable wall.

She had thought that at some point she would get so used to the dark that the details of the room would emerge, but that didn't happen. The darkness was irrevocable, as if she were blind. Only her thoughts could send any light into her existence, and that wasn't easy.

For a long time she was truly afraid of going mad. Afraid of the day when all control slipped out of her hands. She made up images of the world and the light and the life outside. She took refuge in all the nooks and crannies of her brain – those areas that usually become silted up with the ambitions and trivialities of life. And memories of the past slowly surfaced. Tiny moments with hands that held her. Words that caressed and comforted. But also memories of loneliness and yearning and tireless striving.

Then she fell into a rhythm in which day and night consisted of long periods of sleep, eating, meditation and running on the spot. She would run until the slamming of her feet on the floor began to hurt her ears, or until she fell over with fatigue.

Every fifth day she received new underwear and tossed the used ones into the dry toilet. It was disgusting to think that strangers were handling the garments. But they never replaced the other clothing she wore, so she took good care of it. Took care when she sat down on the bucket or lay down carefully on the floor to sleep. Cautiously smoothed out her clothes when she changed her underwear, and rinsed with water any pieces of the fabric that she could feel were getting dirty. She was glad that she'd had such good-quality clothes on the day they took her. A down jacket, scarf, blouse, underwear, trousers and thick socks. But as the days passed, her trousers hung looser and looser, and the soles of her shoes began to feel thin. I need to run in my bare feet, she thought, and she yelled into the darkness: 'Couldn't you turn up the heat a little? Please?' But the ventilator in the ceiling hadn't produced a sound for a long time now.

The light in the room was switched on after the buckets had been changed one hundred and nineteen times. An explosion of white suns blasted down on her, making her topple over backwards with her eyes closed tight and tears trickling out of their corners. It felt as if the light were bombarding her retinas, sending waves of pain up into her brain. All she could do was sink down into a squatting position and hold her hands over her eyes.

As the hours passed, she slowly moved her hands from her face and opened her eyes ever so slightly. The light was still overwhelming. She was held back by the fear that she'd already lost her sight, or that she would now lose it if she moved too quickly. And that was how she was sitting when the loudspeaker with the woman's voice hammered shock waves through her body for the second time. She reacted to the sound like a gauge that jumps too quickly. Each word sent a stab right through her. And the words were terrifying.

'Happy birthday, Merete Lynggaard. Congratulations on reaching the age of thirty-two. Yes, today is the 6th of July. You've been sitting here for one hundred and twenty-six days, and our birthday present to you is that we won't be turning off the light for a year.'

'Oh God, no. You can't do this to me,' she moaned. 'Why are you doing this?' She stood up, holding her hands over her eyes. 'If you want to torture me to death, then just do it!' she screamed.

The woman's voice was ice-cold, a bit deeper than the last time. 'Take it easy, Merete. We don't want to torture you. On the contrary, we're going to give you a chance to avoid what could be even worse for you. All you have to do is answer your own very relevant question: Why are you having to endure all this? Why have we put you in a cage like an animal? Answer your own question, Merete.'

She leaned her head back. This was terrible. Maybe she should just keep quiet. Sit down in a corner and let them say whatever they wanted.

'Answer the question, Merete, or you're going to make things even worse for yourself.'

'I don't know what you want me to say! Is this something political? Or are you blackmailing somebody for money? I don't know. Tell me!'

The voice behind the grating sound grew colder. 'That's not the correct answer, Merete. So now you'll have to take your punishment. It's not too bad. You can easily handle it.'

'Oh God, this can't be happening,' sobbed Merete, sinking to her knees.

Then she heard the familiar whistling from the door hatch become a hissing sound. She instantly noticed the warm air from outside streaming down on her. It smelled of grain and ploughed fields and green grass. Was this supposed to be a punishment?

'We're pumping the air pressure in your chamber up to

two atmospheres. Then we'll see if you can answer the question next year. We don't know how much pressure the human organism can stand, but we're going to find out as time goes by.'

'Dear God,' whispered Merete as she felt the pressure in her ears. 'Please don't do this. Please don't do this.'

17

2007

The sound of boisterous voices and clinking bottles could clearly be heard from the car park, giving Carl plenty of warning. Things were jumping at his house.

The barbecue gang was a little group of fanatics who all lived close by and who thought that beefsteak was so much better if it first languished for a while on a charcoal grill until it tasted neither of beef nor steak. They got together year round whenever the opportunity presented itself, and preferably on Carl's patio. He enjoyed their company. They were lively, but in moderation, and they always took their empty bottles back home with them.

He got a hug from Kenn, who liked to supervise the grill, and was handed an ice-cold can of beer. He put one of the scorched-meat briquettes on a plate and went into the living room, feeling everyone watching him indulgently. They never asked him questions if he didn't volunteer any comments; it was one of the things that he really appreciated about his neighbours. Whenever a case was rummaging around in his brain, it would be easier to track down a competent local politician than to make contact with Carl, and they all knew it. This time it wasn't a case knocking around in his brain; the only thing preoccupying his thoughts was Hardy.

Because Carl felt genuinely torn.

Maybe he should reconsider the situation. He could certainly find a way to kill Hardy without anyone raising the alarm afterwards. An air bubble in his IV, a firm hand placed over his mouth. It would be over quickly, because Hardy would offer no resistance.

But could he do it? Did he want to? It was a hell of a dilemma. To help or not to help? And what was the right kind of help? Maybe it would help Hardy more if Carl pulled himself together and went up to see Marcus and demanded to have his old cases back. When it came right down to it, he didn't give a damn who he was assigned to work with, and he didn't give a shit what *they* said about it. If it would help Hardy to nail the bastards who had shot them out in Amager, then he was the man to do it. Personally, he was sick of the case. If he did find those arseholes, he'd just shoot them down, and who would benefit from that? Not him, at any rate.

'Carl, could you lend me a C-note?' It was his stepson, Jesper, forcing his way into Carl's thought processes. The boy evidently had one foot out the door already. His pals in Lyngby knew that if they invited Jesper, there was a good chance he would arrive with some beers in tow. Jesper had friends in the neighbourhood who sold beer by the case to kids under sixteen. They cost a few kroner more, but what did that matter if he could get his stepfather to pay for the party?

'Isn't this the third time in a week, Jesper?' said Carl, pulling a hundred-kroner bill out of his wallet. 'No matter what, you're going to school tomorrow, got it?'

'OK,' he said.

'Have you done your homework?'

'Yeah, yeah.'

So he hadn't.

Carl frowned.

'Relax, Carl. I don't feel like doing my tenth year at Engholm. I'll just transfer to Allerød.'

That was little consolation. Then Carl would have to keep an eye on Jesper to make sure he did well in school.

'Keep smilin',' intoned the boy on his way to the bicycle shed.

That was easier said than done.

'Is it the Lynggaard case that's worrying you, Carl?' Morten asked as he gathered up the last of the empty bottles. He never went back downstairs until the whole kitchen sparkled. He knew his limits. The next morning his head was going to be as big and sensitive as the prime minister's ego. If anything needed cleaning, it had to be done now.

'I'm thinking mostly about Hardy, not so much about the Lynggaard case. The leads have gone cold, and nobody gives a shit about it, anyway. Including me.'

'But wasn't the Lynggaard case solved?' said Morten, sniffling. 'She drowned, didn't she? What more is there to say about it?'

'Hmm, is that what you think? But why did she drown? That's the question I keep asking myself. There was no storm, no rough seas, and she was apparently quite healthy. Her finances were good, she was attractive, she was on her way to building a big career for herself. Maybe she was a bit lonely, but at some point she would have solved that problem too.'

He shook his head. Who was he kidding? Of course the case interested him. Just like all cases in which the questions piled up, one after the other.

He lit a cigarette and grabbed a can of beer that one of the guests had opened but never drunk. It was lukewarm and tasted slightly flat.

'What annoys me the most is that she was so intelligent. It's always difficult when victims are as smart as she was. As I see it, she had no real reason to commit suicide. No obvious enemies. Her brother loved her. So why did she disappear? If that was your background, Morten, would you jump into the deep?'

He looked at Carl, his eyes red-rimmed. 'It was an accident, Carl. Haven't you ever felt dizzy when you leaned over a boat railing and looked down at the sea? But if it really was murder, then either her brother did it, or there was some political motivation, if you ask me. Why wouldn't a prospective leader of the Democrats have enemies, especially one who looked so stunning?' He nodded ponderously and had trouble raising his head again. 'Everyone hated her. Can't you see that? All the people she'd outstripped in her own party. And the ruling parties. Do you think the prime minister and his cronies were happy to see that luscious babe getting all that airtime on TV? You said yourself that she was brilliant.' Morten wrung out the dishcloth and draped it over the tap. 'Everybody knew that she'd be the one to form the opposition coalition at the next election. She knew how to pull in the votes, damn it.' He spat into the sink. 'Next time I'm not drinking any of Sysser's retsina. Where the hell does she buy that rotgut? It makes my throat as dry as a desert.'

Outside in the circular courtyard, Carl ran into several colleagues who were on their way home. Over by the far wall behind the colonnade, Bak was having an intense conversation with one of his men. They gave Carl a look as if he'd spat on them and offended their honour.

'Buffoon briefing?' he fired off, his words echoing among the pillars as he turned his back on them.

An explanation came from Bente Hansen, who had been a member of his former team. He met her in the vestibule. 'You were right, Carl. They found the piece of the victim's ear in the witness's flat. Congratulations, old boy!'

Fine. At least something was happening in the murdered cyclist case.

'Bak and his men have just been out to the National Hospital to make the witness cough up the whole story,' she went on. 'But they didn't get anywhere. She's terrified.'

'Then maybe she's not the one they should be talking to.'

'Probably not. But then who?'

'When would you be most likely to commit suicide? If you were under an insane amount of pressure, or if it was the only way to save your kids? I'd say it has something to do with her children.'

'The children don't know anything.'

'No, I'm sure they don't. But the witness's mother might.'

He looked at the bronze lamps on the ceiling. Maybe he

should ask for permission to trade cases with Bak. That would undoubtedly shake things up in this colossal building.

'So, Carl. The whole time I have gone around, thinking thoughts. I think we should go on with the case then.' Assad had already set a steaming cup of coffee in front of Carl. Next to the case files sat a couple of sweet pastries on top of the paper they'd been wrapped in. Apparently he was launching a charm offensive. At any rate, Assad had cleaned up in Carl's office, and several documents from the case were lined up on his desk, almost as if he was supposed to read them in a specific order. Assad must have been on the job since six in the morning.

'What have you found for me?' Carl pointed to the papers.

'Well, here is a bank account statement that tells just what Merete Lynggaard took out during her last weeks. But there is nothing at all with food at any restaurant.'

'Somebody else paid for her, Assad. It's not unusual for beautiful women to get off cheaply in such situations.'

'Yes, exactly, Carl. Very smart. So she got somebody else to pay. I think maybe a politician or some guy.'

'No doubt. But it wouldn't be easy to find out who it was.'

'Yes, I know that, Carl. It was five years ago.' He tapped another piece of paper. 'Here is a summary of the things that the police took from her house. I do not see any appointment diary like the woman, her new secretary, talked about. No. But maybe there is diary at Christiansborg. Maybe it will show who she was going to meet at the restaurant then.'

'She probably had her diary in her purse, Assad. And the purse disappeared along with her, didn't it?'

He nodded, looking a bit chagrined. 'Yes, but, Carl. Maybe we could ask her secretary then. There is a transcribing of her statement. She did not say anything then about the person who ate with Merete. So I think we should ask her again.'

'It's called a transcript, Assad! But that's still five years ago. If she couldn't remember anything important at the time she was asked, I'll guarantee she won't remember anything now.'

'OK! But it says she could remember that Merete Lynggaard got a telegram for Valentine's Day, but it was some time after, so. I think one could find out about something like that, couldn't one?'

'The telegram doesn't exist any more, and we don't have the exact date. So it would be hard to track down since we don't even know the name of the company that delivered it.'

'It was TelegramsOnline.'

Carl looked at him. Was it possible this guy was a diamond in the rough? It was difficult to tell as long as he was wearing those green rubber gloves. 'How do you know that, Assad?'

'Look there.' He pointed at the transcript of the statement. 'The secretary remembered that it said "Love & Kisses to Merete" on the telegram, and there were also two lips. Two red lips.'

'And?'

'Well, it had to be a telegram from TelegramsOnline. They print the name on the outside of the telegram. And they always have those two red lips.'

'Show me.'

Assad pressed the space bar on Carl's computer, and the TelegramsOnline home page appeared on the screen. And there it was, the telegram just as Assad had described it.

'OK. And are you positive that this is the only company that makes these types of telegrams?'

'Really positive, yes.'

'But you still don't have the date, Assad. Was it before or after Valentine's Day? And who was it from?'

'We can ask the company. Maybe they have a list of when telegrams were sent to Christiansborg Castle.'

'That was all done during the first police investigation, wasn't it?'

'There is nothing about this in the case file, no. But you have maybe read about something else?' He gave an acidic smile that stopped just short of insubordination.

'OK, Assad. Fair enough. You can check with the company. That's a perfect job for you. I'm a little busy right now, so why don't you use the phone in your own office.'

Carl gave him a pat on the back and ushered him out. Then he shut the door, lit a cigarette, picked up the Lynggaard file, and sat down in his chair, propping his feet on the desk.

He might as well dive in.

It was a stupid case, full of inconsistencies. They'd been searching high and low without any real prioritizing. In short, they had no plausible theories. No clear motive. If her death was suicide, what was the reason for it? The only thing that could be verified was that her car had been parked at the back of the line on the car deck. And that Merete Lynggaard had disappeared.

Then it occurred to the investigators that she had not been alone. A couple of witnesses had stated that she had argued with a young man on the sun deck. This was documented in a chance photo taken by an elderly couple on a privately arranged shopping trip to Heiligenhafen. And when the photo was made public, word came from City Hall in Store Heddinge that the man in the picture was Merete Lynggaard's brother.

Carl actually remembered it all quite well. Reprimands were handed out to the police officers who had overlooked the existence of this brother.

And new questions arose: If the brother killed her, why did he do it? And where was the brother now?

At first they thought that Uffe had fallen overboard, but then they found him a few days later, exhausted and confused, a good distance out on the flatlands of Fehmarn. It was an alert German police officer from Oldenburg who identified Uffe. They never found out how Merete's brother had managed to get so far. And Uffe himself had nothing to add to the case.

If he knew anything, he wasn't letting on.

The subsequent harsh handling of Uffe Lynggaard revealed just how far up shit creek Carl's colleagues had been.

He listened to a couple of cassette tapes from the police interviews and concluded that Uffe had remained as silent as the grave. At first they'd tried the 'good cop, bad cop' ploy, but nothing worked. Two psychiatrists had been called in; then later a psychologist from Farum who specialized in that sort of thing. Even Karen Mortensen, a social worker from Stevns municipality, had been brought in to try to pump information out of Uffe.

To no use.

Both the German and the Danish authorities had trawled the waters. Police divers had searched the area. A body that washed ashore was put on ice and later autopsied. Fishermen were told to pay particular attention to any objects they found floating in the water – items of clothing, purses, anything at all. But nothing was found that could be traced back to Merete Lynggaard, and the media went even more berserk. Merete was front-page news for almost a month. Old photographs from a secondary-school excursion when she posed in a snug swimsuit came out of hiding. Her high marks at the university were made public and became the subject of analysis by so-called lifestyle experts. New speculation about her sexual preferences made otherwise decent journalists follow in the wake of the tabloid press. And more than anything else the discovery that she had a brother provided plenty of fodder for the sleazy reporters.

Many of Merete's closest colleagues jabbered nonsense about how they had imagined something of the kind. That there was something in her private life she'd wanted to hide. Of course they couldn't have known that it would be a handicapped brother, but it had to be something like that.

Old photos of the car accident that had killed Merete's parents and handicapped Uffe appeared on the front page of the morning tabloids when interest in the case began to ebb. Nothing was off-limits. She'd been good material when alive, and she was just as good when she was dead. The hosts on the morning TV programmes had a hard time concealing their glee. The war in Bosnia, a prince consort who lost his temper, a suburban mayor's excessive consumption of red wine, a drowned member of parliament – all the same shit. So long as there were some good photographs to be had.

They printed big pictures of the double bed in Merete Lynggaard's house. It was impossible to know where they'd come from, but the headlines were cruel. Did the brother and sister have a sexual relationship? Was that the reason for her death? Why was there only one big bed in that huge house? Everybody in the whole country was supposed to think it was odd.

When they couldn't make any more hay out of that topic, the reporters threw themselves into speculations about why Uffe had been released. Was it because heavy-handed police methods had been used? Was it a miscarriage of justice? Or had the brother got off easy? Was it more a matter of the naivety of the judicial system and inadequate handling of the case? There were a few more peeps in the media about Uffe being committed to Egely. After that, news about the case finally petered out. The slow-news season in the summer of 2002 turned its focus on the weather and the birth of a Danish prince and the World Cup.

Oh yes, the Danish press knew all about what the average reader was interested in. Merete Lynggaard was old news.

And after six months the police investigation, to all

intents and purposes, was shut down. There were plenty of other cases.

Carl took out two pieces of paper and with a ballpoint pen he wrote on one of them:

SUSPECTS:

1) Uffe
2) Unknown postman – the letter about Berlin
3) The man/woman from Café Bankeråt
4) 'Colleagues' at Christiansborg
5) Murder resulting from a robbery – how much money in her purse?
6) Sexual assault

On the second piece of paper he wrote:

CHECK:

The caseworker in Stevns
The telegram
The secretaries at Christiansborg
Witnesses on the ferry *Schleswig-Holstein*

After staring at what he'd written for a moment, he added to the bottom of the second page:

The foster family after the accident – old classmates at the university. Did she have a tendency to get depressed? Was she pregnant? In love?

As Carl was closing up the case file, he got a call from

upstairs saying that Marcus Jacobsen wanted to see him in the conference room.

He nodded to Assad as he went past his assistant's little office. The guy was glued to his phone, looking serious and as if he were concentrating hard. Not the way he usually appeared when he stood in the doorway wearing his green rubber gloves. He was almost like a different person.

They were all there, everyone who was involved in the investigation of the murdered cyclist. Marcus Jacobsen pointed to the seat that Carl was supposed to take at the conference table, and then Bak began.

'Our witness, Annelise Kvist, has at long last asked for witness protection. We now know that she received threats that her children would be flayed alive if she didn't keep quiet about what she saw. She has been withholding information the whole time, and yet in her own way she has been cooperative. All along she has given us hints so that we could move forward with the case, but she has also withheld crucial information. Then came the serious threats, and after that she shut down completely.

'Let me summarize: The victim's throat was cut in Valby Park at approximately ten o'clock in the evening. It was dark and cold, and the park was deserted. Even so, Annelise Kvist saw the perpetrator talking to the victim only a few minutes before the murder occurred. That gives us reason to believe it was not premeditated. If it had been, the arrival of Annelise Kvist would presumably have thwarted the whole course of events.'

'Why was Annelise Kvist walking through the park? Why wasn't she riding her bicycle? Where was she coming from?' asked one of the new team members. He didn't know that he was supposed to wait until afterwards to ask questions if Bak was running the meeting.

Bak replied with an annoyed look. 'She'd been visiting a woman friend, and her bicycle had a flat tyre. That's why she was pushing it through the park. We know that it must have been the perpetrator she saw because there were only two sets of footprints around the crime scene. We put great effort into investigating Annelise Kvist to find any weak points in her background. Anything that might explain her behaviour when we began questioning her. We now know that she was once part of a biker gang, but we're also relatively sure that we're not going to find the killer in that environment.

'The victim was the brother of Carlo Brandt, one of the most active bikers in the Valby area, and was absolutely in "good standing", even though he did sell drugs once in a while on his own. We now also know from this Carlo Brandt that the victim was a friend of Annelise Kvist, and at some point they were apparently on intimate terms. We're looking into that now. At any rate, we've reached the conclusion that there is every indication she knew both the murderer and the victim.

'As for what frightened the witness, her mother admitted to us that Annelise has previously been subjected to physical violence. Granted it was on a milder scale, involving being punched and threatened and the like, but it had a profound effect on Annelise. The mother thinks that her daughter has only herself to blame for all of this because she spends a lot of time in bars and isn't very particular about who she brings home. But as far as we can tell,

Annelise's sexual and social habits aren't much different from those of most other young women.

'The discovery of the ear in Annelise's toilet tells us that the killer knows who she is and where she lives, but as I've mentioned, we haven't yet been able to convince her to tell us the name of the murderer.

'The children have now been sent to stay with family members south of Copenhagen, and that has softened up Annelise a bit. There is no longer any doubt that she was under the influence of drugs at the time when she ostensibly tried to commit suicide. According to the tests, a stew of various euphoriants in pill form were found in her stomach.'

Carl had kept his eyes closed during most of the session. The mere sight of Bak standing there and thrashing through things in that roundabout and tedious manner of his was enough to make his blood boil. He simply didn't feel like looking at the man. And why should he? None of this had anything to do with him. His place was downstairs in the basement; that was what he needed to keep in mind. The homicide chief had summoned him up here to give him a pat on the back because he'd pushed the investigation a step further. That was all. He would spare them any opinions he might have in the future.

'We haven't found the pill bottle, so it's possible the pills were provided in loose weight, presumably by the same perpetrator, and forced down her throat,' said Bak.

So he'd figured that much out, at least.

'All indications are that we're talking about a failed murder attempt. The threats to kill her children made the witness stop talking,' Bak went on.

At this point Marcus Jacobsen broke in. He could see that the new team members were itching to ask questions. Better to anticipate them.

'Annelise Kvist and her mother and children will be given the witness protection that the case demands,' he said. 'To start with, we're going to move them to another location, and then I'm sure we'll get her to talk. In the meantime we need to bring in the narcotics squad. I understand that a considerable amount of synthetic THC was found in her body, most likely Marinol, which is the most common kind of hash in pill form. We see it quite often in pusher circles, so let's find out where it can be bought locally. I also understand that traces of crystal meth and ethylphenidate were found. An extremely unlikely cocktail.'

Carl shook his head. The killer was certainly versatile. Slashing the throat of one victim in a park and then gently slipping pills down the throat of the other. Why couldn't his colleagues just wait until the woman started spilling the beans on her own? He opened his eyes and found the homicide chief staring right at him.

'You're shaking your head, Carl. Do you have a better suggestion? Have you got some other creative ideas that might give us a lead?' He smiled. But he was the only one in the room who did.

'All I know is that ingesting THC will make you throw up if too many other weird things are stuffed down your throat. So the guy who forced her to swallow the pills must have been really good at it, don't you think? Why don't you just wait until Annelise Kvist herself tells you what she saw? A couple of days, more or less, aren't going to make any difference. And we've got other things to keep us busy.' He glanced around at his colleagues. 'Well, at least I do.'

The secretaries were busy, as usual. Lis sat at her computer wearing a headset and pounding on the keyboard like a drummer in a rock band. Carl looked for a new, dark-haired secretary, but no one fitted Assad's description. Only Lis's colleague, the department's infamous version of 'Ilse, the She-Wolf' – called Mrs Sørensen by her co-workers – might reasonably be said to be a brunette. Carl squinted his eyes. Maybe Assad saw something in that surly face of hers that was invisible to everyone else.

'We need a decent photocopier in the basement office, Lis,' said Carl, when she stopped drumming on the keyboard and gave him a big smile. 'Could you make sure that happens by this afternoon? I know they have an extra one over in the National Investigative Centre. It hasn't even been taken out of the box.'

'I'll see what I can do, Carl,' she said. And he knew it would get done.

'I need to speak to Marcus Jacobsen,' said a crisp voice next to him. Carl turned and found himself face to face with a woman he'd never seen before. She had brown eyes. The most insanely delicious brown eyes he'd ever seen. Carl felt the bottom drop out of his stomach. Then the woman turned to the secretaries.

'Are you Mona Ibsen?' asked Mrs Sørensen.

'Yes,' the woman said.

'We've been expecting you.'

The two women smiled at each other, and Mona Ibsen

stepped aside as Mrs Sørensen got up to show her the way. Carl pressed his lips tight as he watched her disappear down the hall. She was wearing a short fur jacket, short enough so he could see the lower curves of her arse. Promising, but not a young woman, judging by her curves. Why the hell hadn't he noticed anything about her face other than the eyes?

'Mona Ibsen? Who's that?' he asked Lis, trying to sound casual. 'Something to do with the murder of the cyclist?'

'No, she's our new crisis counsellor. A psychologist. As of today she's assigned to work with all the departments here at headquarters.'

'Is that right?' He could hear for himself how foolish he sounded.

He suppressed the butterflies in his stomach and went over to Jacobsen's office, opening the door without bothering to knock. If the boss was going to bawl him out, it damn well better be for a good cause.

'Sorry, Marcus,' he said. 'I didn't know you had company.'

She was sitting so that he saw her in profile, with soft skin and lines at the corners of her mouth, more the result of smiling than boredom.

'I can come back later. Sorry for interrupting,' said Carl.

She turned to face him as he uttered these words of cringing servility. She had a distinctive mouth. Full, Cupid's-bow lips. She was clearly over fifty, and she gave him a faint smile. Damned if his kneecaps didn't turn to jelly.

'What do you want, Carl?' asked Marcus.

'I just wanted to say that I think you should ask

Annelise Kvist whether she also has a relationship with the killer.'

'We did that, Carl. She doesn't.'

'No? Well, then I think you should ask her what the killer does. Not who he is, but what he does.'

'We've already done that too, of course, but she refuses to tell us anything. Do you think they worked together?'

'Maybe, maybe not. At any rate, she's somehow dependent on this man because of the work he does.'

Jacobsen nodded. Nothing more was going to happen until they moved the witness and her family to a safe place. But at least Carl had got a look at this Mona Ibsen.

She was damned gorgeous for a crisis counsellor.

'That's all,' Carl said, with a smile that was bigger and more relaxed and virile than ever before, but it wasn't returned.

He put his hand to his chest for a moment where he felt a sudden pain near his sternum. A hell of an unpleasant sensation. Almost as if he'd swallowed air.

'Are you OK, Carl?' asked his boss.

'Oh, it's nothing. Just some after-effects, you know. I'm OK.' But that wasn't quite true. The feeling in his chest was not good at all.

'Oh, excuse me, Mona. Let me introduce you to Carl Mørck. A couple of months ago he was involved in a nasty shooting incident in which we lost one of our colleagues.'

She nodded at Carl as he tried to pull himself together. Squinted her eyes a bit. Professional interest, of course, but at least that was better than nothing.

'This is Mona Ibsen, Carl. She's our new crisis

counsellor. Maybe you'll get to know each other. We'd like to have one of our best colleagues completely back on his feet.'

Carl took a step forward and shook her hand. Get to know each other. Damn right they would.

He was still under a spell when he ran into Assad on his way down to the basement.

'I got finally through, Carl,' he said.

Carl tried to push the vision of Mona Ibsen into the back of his mind. It wasn't easy.

'Got through to what?' he asked.

'I called TelegramsOnline at least the ten times, and got only through fifteen minutes ago,' said Assad while Carl tried to collect his thoughts. 'Maybe they can then tell us who sent the telegram to Merete Lynggaard. They are working on it, at least.'

18

2003

It didn't take long at all for Merete to get used to the pressure. A slight rushing in her ears for a few days, and then it was gone. But the worst thing was not the pressure.

It was the light shining overhead.

Eternal light was hundreds of times worse than eternal darkness. The light revealed the pitiful state of her life. A freezing room. Greyish walls, sharp corners. The grey buckets, the colourless food. The light provided ugliness and coldness. It brought with it the realization that she couldn't break through this armoured box of a room. That the lifeline through the retractable door couldn't be used as a means of escape. That this cement hell was her coffin and her grave. Now she couldn't simply close her eyes and slip away whenever it suited her. The light forced its way in, even through her closed eyelids. Only when fatigue completely overwhelmed her could she fall asleep and evade it.

And time became interminable.

Every day when she finished eating and sat there licking her fingers clean, she stared into space and memorized the day. 'Today is the 27th of July 2002. I am thirty-two years and twenty-one days old. I've been here for one hundred and forty-seven days. My name is Merete Lynggaard, and I'm OK. My brother's name is Uffe, and he was born on the 10th of May 1973.' That was how she always started off. Sometimes she also named her parents, sometimes other people. Every single day she made herself remember their names. Along with lots of other things. She thought about the blue sky, the smell of other people, the sound of a dog barking. Thoughts that could lead to other thoughts that would allow her to slip out of the cold room.

She knew that one day she was going to go mad. This would be the way to escape the gloomy thoughts that kept whirling around in her head. But she fought hard against it. She was by no means ready for that.

And this was the reason why she kept away from the two metre-high portholes that she'd first located in the dark by running her hands over the walls. They were at eye level, and nothing from the other side was visible through the mirrored glass. After a few days when her eyes had adjusted to the light, she stood up very cautiously, afraid of being startled by her own reflection. And then, as she slowly raised her eyes, she finally came face to face with herself. The sight had pierced deep into her very soul, sending shivers through her body. What she saw made such a violent impression on her that she had to shut her eyes for a moment. It wasn't because she looked terrible, as she'd feared. No, that wasn't it. Her hair was matted and greasy and her skin was pale, but that wasn't it, either.

It was the fact that she was looking at a person who was lost. A person who had been condemned to death. A stranger – completely alone in the world.

'You are Merete,' she'd said out loud, watching herself enunciate the words. 'That's me standing there,' she'd said then, wishing it weren't true. She'd felt separated from her body, and yet that was her standing there. It was enough to make a person crazy.

Then she'd retreated from the portholes and squatted down. Tried to sing a bit, but the voice she heard seemed to be coming from a different person. So she curled up in a foetal position and prayed to God. And when she was done, she'd started praying again. Praying until her soul was lifted out of the insane trance and into another. And she'd sought refuge in dreams and memories, promising herself that she would never stand in front of that mirror to look at herself again.

As time passed, she learned to pay attention to the signals coming from her body. Her stomach told her when the food was late in being delivered, when the pressure was vacillating a bit, and when she slept best.

The intervals between the replacing of the buckets were quite regular. She had tried counting the seconds from the moment her stomach told her it was time, until the buckets arrived. There was at most a difference of half an hour in feeding times, so she had a schedule to hold on to, assuming that she continued to receive food once a day.

Knowing this was both a comfort and a curse. A comfort because it gave her a connection to the schedules and rhythms of the outside world. And a curse for the very same reason. Outside it was summer, then autumn, then winter; here inside it was nothing. She imagined the summer rain drenching her body, washing away the degradation and smell. She saw the glow of the midsummer-night bonfires and the Christmas tree in all its glory. Not a single day without its rhythms. She knew the dates and what they meant. Out there in the world.

So she sat alone on the bare floor, focusing her thoughts on life outside. It wasn't easy. Often it almost eluded her, but she was determined. Each day had its significance.

The day when Uffe turned twenty-nine and a half, she leaned against the cold wall and imagined herself stroking his hair as she congratulated him. In her mind she decided to bake him a cake and send it to him. First she had to buy all the ingredients. She would put on her coat and defy the autumn storms. And she would do her shopping wherever she pleased. In the culinary section on the lower floor of the Magasin department store. She would buy whatever she liked. Nothing was too good for Uffe on that special day.

And Merete counted the days as she speculated on the intentions of her kidnappers and who they might be. Sometimes a faint shadow seemed to slide across one of the mirrored panes, making her shudder. She covered her body when she washed herself. Stood with her back turned when she was naked. Pulled the toilet bucket over to the space between the panes so they wouldn't be able to see her sitting on it.

Because she knew they were there. It would be pointless if they weren't. For a while she talked to them, but she didn't do that very often any more. They never answered anyway.

She had asked them for sanitary napkins but never got any. When she was menstruating heavily, there was never enough toilet paper, and she simply had to make do with what she had.

She had also asked for a toothbrush, but didn't get that

either, and this worried her. So instead, she massaged her gums with her index finger and tried to clean between her teeth by forcing air through the spaces, but it didn't do much good. When she blew on the palm of her hand, she could smell how her breath was getting worse and worse.

One day she pulled a plastic stiffener out of the hood on her down jacket. It was a nylon stick that was suitably rigid, but too thick to use as a toothpick. So she decided to break off a piece and then started filing down the shortest section, using her front teeth. 'Be careful not to get any plastic stuck in your teeth. You'll never get it out,' she warned herself, taking her time.

When she was able to clean the spaces between her teeth for the first time in a year, she was filled with a huge sense of relief. The little stick was suddenly her dearest possession. She needed to take good care of it, along with the rest of the stiffener.

The voice spoke to her a while before she thought it would. She had awoken on her thirty-third birthday with a feeling in her stomach that told her it might still be night. She sat and stared at the mirrored panes for what seemed like hours as she tried to figure out what was going to happen next. She'd thought countless times about the question and how to answer it. Names and events and motives had passed through her mind again and again, but she still knew no more than she did a year earlier. It might have something to do with money. Maybe it was related to the Internet. Or an experiment. An insane person's attempt to show what the human organism and psyche were capable of enduring.

But she had no intention of succumbing to such an experiment. No way.

When the voice started speaking, she wasn't prepared. Her stomach hadn't yet signalled that it was hungry. The voice frightened her, but this time it was more from the tension that was released than from the shock when the silence was suddenly broken.

'Happy birthday, Merete,' said the woman's voice. 'Congratulations on your thirty-third birthday. We can see that you're doing well. You've been a good girl this year. The sun is shining.'

The sun! Oh God, she didn't want to know about that.

'Have you thought about the question? Why we're keeping you in a cage like an animal? Why you have to be put through all of this? Have you come up with a solution, Merete, or do we need to punish you again? What's it going to be? A birthday present or a punishment?'

'Give me some clue that I can use!' she shouted.

'You haven't understood the game, Merete. You have to work it out for yourself. We're going to send in the buckets, and in the meantime you can think about why you're here. There's not much time left for you to answer the question.'

For the first time she clearly heard a human being in the voice. It was not a young woman, definitely not. There was an accent in the voice that attested to a good education obtained a long time ago. A couple of 'a's pronounced deeper than usual.

'This isn't a game,' Merete protested. 'You've kidnapped me and locked me up. What do you want? Is it money? I don't know how I can help you to get the money out of the trust fund if I'm sitting here. Can't you understand that?'

'You know what, my dear?' said the woman. 'If this was about money, it would have been handled very differently. Don't you think?'

Then there was a whistling sound from the hatch door, and the first bucket appeared. Merete pulled it out as she racked her brain about what to say that might win her some time.

'I've never done anything bad in my life. I don't deserve this. Don't you understand?'

Another whistling sound, and the second bucket appeared in the hatch.

'You're getting close to the heart of the matter now, you stupid girl. Oh yes, you certainly do deserve this.'

She wanted to object, but the woman stopped her. 'Don't say another word, Merete. You haven't helped yourself the least bit, as it is. Try looking inside the bucket instead. I wonder if you'll be happy to get your present.'

Merete slowly took off the lid, as if the container might be holding a cobra with its hood distended, its poison glands tensed to the bursting point, ready to strike. But what she saw was worse.

It was a pocket torch.

'Good night, Merete. Sleep well. Now we're going to give you another atmosphere of pressure. Let's see if that helps your memory.'

First came the whistling sound from the hatch and the fragrance from outdoors. The scent of flowers and traces of sunshine.

And then the darkness was back.

19

2007

The photocopier they got from the NIC (the National Investigative Centre, as the Rapid Response Team of the National Police was now called) was brand new, and only intended to be on loan. A clear sign that they didn't know Carl, because he never gave back anything once it was transported down to the basement.

'Make a copy of all the case documents, Assad,' he said, pointing at the machine. 'I don't care if it takes all day. And when you're done, drive over to the Clinic for Spinal Cord Injuries and give my old partner, Hardy Henningsen, a summary of the case. He'll probably treat you like you're not even there, but don't let that worry you. He has a memory like an elephant and ears like a bat. So just forge ahead.'

Assad studied the symbols and buttons on the monster machine in the basement corridor. 'How does one do with it then?' he asked.

'Haven't you ever made photocopies before?'

'Not on one like this with all these drawings, no.'

Hard to believe. Was this the same man who had put up the TV screen in less than ten minutes?

'Good Lord, Assad, look. You put the original here, and then you press this button.' That much he seemed able to understand.

*

Bak's voicemail message on his mobile spouted the expected bullshit about the detective inspector not being available to take the call due to a homicide case.

Lis, the lovely secretary with the overlapping teeth, supplied the information that Bak and a colleague had gone out to Valby to make an arrest.

'Give me a heads-up when the idiot gets back, OK, Lis?' he said, and an hour and a half later she did.

Bak and his partner had already made a good start in the interrogation room when Carl barged in. The man in handcuffs was a completely ordinary-looking guy. Young and tired, with a terrible cold. 'Blow your nose,' said Carl, pointing at the thick streams of snot pouring down over the man's lips. If he were this guy, wild horses wouldn't be able to force him to open his mouth.

'Don't you understand Danish, Carl?' This time Bak's face had turned bright red. It took a lot to make that happen. 'You'll have to wait. And don't ever interrupt a colleague in the middle of an interrogation again. Understand?'

'Five minutes and I'll leave you in peace. I promise.'

It was Bak's problem if he wanted to spend an hour and a half telling Carl that he'd been brought into the Lynggaard case very late in the game, so he didn't know shit. Why the hell all this absurd beating about the bush?

But at least Carl got a phone number for Karen Mortensen, who was once Uffe's caseworker in Stevns, now retired. Also the phone number for Police Chief Claes Damsgaard, who was one of the officers in charge of the Rapid Response Team at the time. He was now on the police force for central and western Jutland, according to Bak. Why not just say that the man worked in Roskilde?

The other officer in charge of the team leading the investigation was dead. He'd lasted only two years after retiring. That was the reality when it came to the survival rate of police officers after retiring in Denmark.

A statistic that might even be something for the *Guinness Book of Records*.

Police Chief Claes Damsgaard was nothing at all like Bak. Friendly, accommodating and interested. Oh yes, he'd heard about Department Q, and yes, he certainly did know who Carl Mørck was. Wasn't he the officer who solved the case of the drowned girl at Femøren, and that fucking murder out in the Nordvest neighbourhood where an old woman was thrown out of a window? Oh yes, he certainly did know Carl, at least by reputation. The merits of good police officers weren't something to be overlooked. Carl would be welcome to come out to Roskilde for a briefing. The Lynggaard case was a sad business, so if he could help in any way, Carl should just ask.

Nice guy, Carl managed to think before the man told him that he'd have to wait three weeks because he and his wife were just heading off on a trip to the Seychelles with their daughter and son-in-law. And then he added with a burst of laughter that they wanted to get there before the islands were inundated by water from melting icebergs.

'How's it going?' Carl asked Assad, taking in the expanse of photocopies neatly stacked up along the hall, stretching all the way out to the stairs. Were there really that many documents in the case?

'I am sorry it is taking such long hours, Carl, but these magazines, they are the worst.'

Carl looked at the stacks of papers again. 'Are you copying the whole magazine?'

Assad tilted his head to one side like a puppy thinking about making a run for it. Good God.

'Look here. You just need to copy the pages that are relevant to the case, Assad. I don't think Hardy will give a damn which prince shot which pheasant during a hunting party in Smørumbavelse, do you?'

'Shot who?'

'Forget it, Assad. Just stick to the case and throw out the other pages that aren't relevant. You're doing a good job.'

He left Assad and the rumbling machine and then sat down to phone the retired social worker in Stevns municipality who had handled Uffe's case. Maybe she'd observed something that might give them a lead.

Karen Mortensen sounded nice. He could practically see her sitting in a rocking chair and crocheting tea cosies. The sound of her voice would fit in perfectly with the ticking of a grandfather clock. It was almost like phoning home to his family in Brønderslev.

But with the next sentence Carl changed his mind. In spirit she was still a civil servant. A wolf in sheep's clothing.

'I can't say anything about the Uffe Lynggaard case, or any other case, for that matter. You'll have to contact Social Services in Store Heddinge.'

'I've already tried that. Now listen here, Karen Mortensen, I'm just trying to find out what happened to Uffe's sister.'

'Uffe was acquitted of all charges,' she snapped.

'Yes, yes, I know, and that's fine. But maybe Uffe knows something that hasn't come out.'

'His sister is dead, so what good would it do? Uffe hasn't spoken a single word since his accident, so he can't help you.'

'What if I came out to visit you? Do you think I could ask you a few questions?'

'Not if it has anything to do with Uffe.'

'I simply don't understand this. When I've talked to people who knew Merete Lynggaard, I've heard that she always spoke so highly of you. She said she and her brother would have been totally lost without your attentive case-work.' She tried to say something, but Carl refused to let her interrupt. 'So why won't you at least do your best to protect Merete's reputation, now that she's not here to do it for herself? I'm sure you know that the general opinion is that she committed suicide. But what if that wasn't what happened?'

The only sound now audible on the other end of the line was a muted radio. She was still weighing the words 'spoke so highly of you'. Quite a mouthful to digest.

It took her ten seconds to swallow completely. 'As far as I know, Merete never said anything to anybody about Uffe. Only those of us at Social Services even knew of his existence.' That was what she said, but she sounded wonderfully unsure of herself.

'You're right, of course, that was true for the most part. But there were other family members. OK, they lived in

Jutland, but she did have relatives, you know.' He paused a moment for effect, giving himself time to consider what sort of family members he could invent for the situation if she insisted on pursuing the topic. But Karen Mortensen had already taken the bait. He could tell.

'Was it you personally, who visited Uffe in the past?' he asked.

'Only at the request of the police. But I was in charge of the case during all those years.'

'Was it your impression that Uffe's condition was getting worse as time passed?'

She hesitated. She was about to slip away again, so it was just a matter of holding on tight.

'I'm asking you this because I think it might be possible to get through to him today, but I could be wrong,' he continued.

'You've met Uffe?' She sounded surprised.

'Yes, of course. A very charming young man. And what a dazzling smile he has. It's hard to comprehend that there's anything wrong with him.'

'Plenty of people have thought the same thing in the past. But that's often how it is with victims of brain injuries. Merete deserved a lot of credit for keeping him from completely withdrawing into himself.'

'And you think there's a danger of that happening?'

'Absolutely. But it's true that he can seem very lively if you look at his face. And no, I don't think he got any worse over the years.'

'Do you think he understood at all what happened to his sister?'

'No, I don't think so.'

'Doesn't that seem strange? I mean, he would get upset if she didn't come home on time. Start crying, I mean.'

'If you ask me, he couldn't have seen her fall into the water. I don't think so. He would have become hysterical, and in my opinion he would have jumped in after her. As for his personal reaction, he wandered around for days down on Fehmarn. He had all the time in the world to cry and feel confused and try searching for her. When they found him, only his basal functions were left. I mean, he'd lost almost ten pounds and apparently hadn't had anything to eat or drink since he was on board the ship.'

'But maybe he pushed his sister overboard by accident and realized that he'd done something wrong.'

'Now look here, Mr Mørck! I thought that might be where you were headed.' Carl felt the wolf in her baring its teeth, so he needed to be careful. 'But instead of slamming down the phone, which is what I feel like doing, I'm going to tell you a little story to give you something to chew on.'

He tightened his grip on the receiver.

'You're aware that Uffe saw his father and mother die, right?' she asked.

'Yes.'

'It's my opinion that since that day, Uffe has been simply floating around. Nothing could replace his ties to his parents. Merete tried, but she was not his father and mother. She was his big sister, and they used to play together, and that was all. When he cried because she wasn't there, it wasn't because of a feeling of insecurity; instead, it was because he was disappointed that his playmate had forgotten him. Deep inside there is still a little boy waiting

157

for his father and mother to come back. As for Merete, sooner or later all children get over the loss of a playmate. So here's the story.'

'I'm listening.'

'I went to visit them one day. I dropped by unannounced, which didn't usually happen, but I was in the neighbourhood and just wanted to say hello. So I walked up the garden path, noticing along the way that Merete's car wasn't there. She arrived a few minutes later. She'd just gone down to do some shopping at the grocer's by the intersection. That was back when it still existed.'

'The grocery store in Magleby?'

'Yes. And when I was standing on the path, I heard a quiet babbling coming from over near their garden hot-house. It sounded like a child, but it wasn't. I didn't discover that it was Uffe until I was standing right in front of him. He was sitting on a pile of gravel on the terrace, talking to himself. I couldn't understand the words, if they really were words. But I understood what he was doing.'

'Did he see you?'

'Yes, he saw me at once, but he didn't have time to cover up what he'd been constructing.'

'And that was . . .?'

'It was a little furrow he'd dug into the gravel on the flagstones. On either side of the furrow he'd placed small twigs, and in between them he'd put a little wooden block, standing on end.'

'And?'

'You don't realize what he was doing?'

'I'm trying.'

'The gravel and the twigs were the road and the trees.

The block was the car that belonged to his father and mother. Uffe was reconstructing the accident.'

Jesus Christ. 'OK. And he didn't want you to see it?'

'He wiped out the whole thing with a single sweep of his hand. That was what convinced me.'

'About what?'

'That Uffe remembers.'

There was a moment's pause. The radio in the background suddenly became audible again, as if somebody had turned up the volume.

'Did you tell Merete about this when she came home?' he asked.

'Yes, but she thought I was reading too much into it. She said he often sat and played with whatever happened to be in front of him. That I probably startled him, and that was why he reacted the way he did.'

'Did you tell her you had the feeling he acted as if he'd been caught at something?'

'Yes, but she just thought he'd been startled.'

'And you don't agree?'

'I agree that he was startled, but that wasn't the whole explanation.'

'So Uffe understands more than we think?'

'I don't know. All I know is that he remembers the accident. Maybe it's the only thing he actually remembers. It's not at all certain he remembers anything from when his sister disappeared. It's not even certain that he remembers his sister any more.'

'Didn't they try to interview him in connection with Merete's disappearance?'

'It's difficult with Uffe. I tried to help the police get him to open up when he was under arrest. I wanted him to remember what happened on board the ferry. We put pictures of the ship's deck up on the wall and placed tiny little human figures and a model of the boat on the table next to a basin of water. We thought maybe he would play with them. I sat and watched him in secret along with one of the psychologists, but he never played with the toy ship.'

'He didn't remember anything even though it was only a few days later?'

'I don't know.'

'It would be good if we could find a tunnel into Uffe's memory. Even the slightest thing that might help me to understand what happened on the ferry, so I'd have something to go on.'

'Yes, I understand.'

'Did you tell the police about the episode with the wooden block?'

'Yes, I told the story to one of the officers with the Rapid Response Team. A Børge Bak.'

Was Børge really Bak's first name? That explained a lot.

'I know him well. But I don't recall seeing anything about this in his report. Can you say why he didn't include this information?'

'No, I don't know why. But later on it didn't come up again. Maybe it's in the report that the psychologists and psychiatrists wrote up. I didn't read it.'

'I imagine the report is kept at Egely, where Uffe was placed. Wouldn't you think so?'

'That's probably right, but I don't think it will add much to the picture of Uffe. Most of the psychologists agreed with me that whatever prompted the incident with the wooden block could have been something momentary. That Uffe really didn't remember, and that we wouldn't make any progress in the Merete Lynggaard case by browbeating him.'

'And so they dropped all the charges.'

'Yes, they did.'

20

2007

'Yes, well, I don't know what the hell we're going to do now, Marcus.' Lars Bjørn looked at him as if he'd just heard that his house had burned down.

'And you're positive that the journalists wouldn't rather talk to me or the public information officer?' asked the homicide chief.

'They expressly asked permission to interview Carl. They'd talked to Piv Vestergård, and she referred them to him.'

'Why didn't you just say that he was sick or on assignment or didn't want to talk to them? Anything at all. We can't just send him out into a trap. Those reporters from Danish Broadcasting will sink their teeth into him.'

'I know.'

'We need to make him say no, Lars.'

'I think you'd be better at that than me.'

Ten minutes later Carl Mørck was standing in the doorway, scowling.

'So, Carl,' said the homicide chief. 'Are you making any progress?'

He shrugged. 'If you ask me, Bak doesn't know shit about the Lynggaard case.'

'I see. That sounds strange. But you do?'

Carl came into the room and dropped on to a chair. 'Don't expect miracles.'

'So I take it there isn't much to report about the case?'

'Not yet.'

'Does that mean I can tell the TV news people that it's too early to interview you?'

'I'll be damned if I'm going to do any TV interviews.'

Marcus felt a welcome sense of relief rush through him, making him produce a smile that was possibly a bit exaggerated. 'I understand, Carl. When you're in the middle of an investigation, it's not something you want to do. The rest of us who are dealing with current cases have to do it, out of consideration for the public, but with old cases like yours, you need peace and quiet to do your work. I'll let them know, Carl. It's OK by me.'

'Could you make sure that I get a copy of Assad's personnel file?'

What was he, all of a sudden, a secretary for his own subordinates? 'Of course, Carl,' Marcus said. 'I'll ask Lars to see to it. Are you satisfied with the man?'

'We'll see. But for the time being, yes.'

'And dare I surmise that you're getting him involved in the investigation?'

'Yeah, you dare.' Carl gave his boss a rare smile.

'So you're using him in the investigative work?'

'Well, you know what? At the moment Assad is up in Hornbæk delivering some papers he photocopied for Hardy. You don't have anything against that, do you? You know how Hardy can sometimes think circles around the rest of us. And it will give him something to keep his mind busy.'

'Well, that seems all right.' At least he hoped so. 'How is Hardy?'

Carl shrugged.

That was what Marcus had expected. Very sad.

They nodded to each other. The session was over.

'Oh, by the way,' said Carl as he stood in the doorway. 'When you do the TV interview in my place, please don't mention that the department has only one and a half employees. Assad would be upset if he heard that. Not to mention the people who allocated the funding, I would imagine.'

He was right. It was a hell of a situation they'd got themselves into.

'Yes, and one more thing, Marcus.'

The homicide chief raised an eyebrow as he studied Carl's wily expression. Now what?

'When you see the crisis counsellor again, tell her that Carl Mørck could use her help.'

Marcus looked at his perennial troublemaker. Carl didn't seem like someone on the verge of a breakdown. The smile on his face wasn't really appropriate, considering the seriousness of the subject.

'I'm haunted by thoughts of Anker's death. Maybe it's because I see Hardy so often. Maybe she can tell me what to do about it.'

21

2007

The next day everybody was jabbering to Carl about homicide chief Marcus Jacobsen's TV performance. His fellow passengers on the S-train, people from the emergency services department, and everyone working on the third floor who would bother to condescend speaking to him. They'd all seen it. The only one who hadn't was Carl.

'Congratulations!' cried one of the secretaries across the courtyard at police headquarters, while other people seemed to be avoiding him. It was very strange.

When he poked his head into Assad's shoebox of an office, he was immediately met with a smile that nearly cracked the man's face in half. Which meant that Assad was also well informed.

'So are you very happy now?' asked Assad, already nodding on Carl's behalf.

'About what?'

'Oi! Marcus Jacobsen talked so good about our department and about you. The nicest words right from start and to finish, I want to tell you. We can be very proud, both of us, that is what my wife said too.' He gave Carl a wink. It was a bad habit. 'And so you are going to be police superintendent.'

'What?'

'Just ask Mrs Sørensen. She has papers for you I should just remember to have said.'

Assad could have saved himself the trouble because

the clacking of the Fury's heels could already be heard in the corridor.

'Congratulations,' Mrs Sørensen forced herself to say to Carl, as she gave Assad a sweet smile. 'Here's the paperwork you need to fill out. The course starts on Monday.'

'A lovely woman,' said Assad after she had once again removed her purposeful body from their office. 'What course was she talking about, Carl?'

He sighed. 'You can't become a superintendent until you go to school, Assad.'

Assad stuck out his lower lip. 'So you are going away from here?'

Carl shook his head. 'I'll be damned if I'm going away from anything at all.'

'Then that I do not understand.'

'You will. But right now, tell me what happened when you went to see Hardy yesterday.'

Assad opened his eyes wide. 'I did not like it. That big man under the covers, lying so still. Only his face showing so I could see it.'

'Did you talk to him?'

He nodded. 'It was not easy, because he said I should leave. And then a nurse came and she wanted to throw me out the door. But it was OK. She was actually very much pretty in a way.' He smiled. 'I think she noticed I thought so, then she went away.'

Carl gave him a blank look. Sometimes dreams of fleeing to Timbuktu could overwhelm him.

'What about Hardy? I asked you about Hardy, Assad! What did he say? Did you read any of the photocopies to him?'

'Yes. For two and a half hours. But then he fell completely asleep.'

'And?'

'Well, then he was sleeping.'

Carl sent a message from his brain to his hands that it was still illegal to strangle people.

Assad smiled. 'But I will go over there again. The nurse said a very nice goodbye to me when I left.'

Carl swallowed hard. 'Since you're so good at handling all the harpies, I'm going to ask you to go upstairs and flatter the secretaries one more time.'

Assad's face brightened. It was obvious he was thinking that would be better than going around wearing green rubber gloves.

Carl sat motionless at his desk for a moment, staring into space. His phone conversation with Karen Mortensen kept popping up in the back of his brain. Was there a tunnel into Uffe's mind? Was it possible to open it? Were there explanations for Merete Lynggaard's disappearance lurking somewhere inside there, and all that was needed was to press the right button? Could he use the car accident to find that button? It was becoming more and more crucial to find out.

He stopped his assistant as he was on his way out the door. 'Assad, one more thing. I need you to bring me all the information you can find about the car accident that killed Merete and Uffe's parents. Everything. Lock, stock and barrel. Pictures, the police report, newspaper clippings. Get the secretaries to help you. I want the information asap.'

'Asap?'

'That means in a hurry, Assad. There's a certain person

by the name of Uffe, and I'd like to have a little talk with him about the accident.'

'Talk with him?' murmured Assad, looking pensive.

Carl had an appointment in his lunch hour that he wished he could cancel. Last night Vigga had kept bugging him about coming to see her marvellous new gallery. It was on Nansensgade, which was not the worst place on the planet, but rent, on the other hand, cost an arm and a leg. Nothing in the world was going to force even a hint of enthusiasm from Carl at the prospect of turning his pockets inside out just so a lousy painter by the name of Hugin could display his work next to Vigga's cave paintings.

As Carl was leaving headquarters he ran into Marcus in the lobby. The chief came walking briskly towards him, keeping his eyes fixed on the terrazzo floor and its swastika patterns. He knew full well that Carl had spotted him. Nobody at police headquarters was as keen an observer as Marcus Jacobsen. You wouldn't know that by looking at him, but it was true. It was no accident that he was the boss.

'I hear you've been singing my praises, Marcus. Exactly how many cases did you tell those journalists we'd already tackled in Department Q? And according to you, we're even on the verge of a breakthrough with one of them. You have no idea how happy I am to hear that. That's really great news!'

The homicide chief looked him in the eye. It was the kind of look that demanded respect. Sure, Marcus knew he'd laid it on too thick, but he had reasons for doing so. And right now he conveyed that knowledge with a single glance. The police force always came first. The money was merely a means to an end. The goal was something the homicide chief himself would decide.

'Well,' said Carl. 'I guess I'd better be heading out if I'm going to solve a couple of cases before lunch.'

When he reached the front entrance, he turned around. 'Marcus, exactly how many salary levels am I going to go up?' he shouted, as the homicide chief disappeared past the bronze-painted chairs lining the walls. 'And by the way, Marcus. Did you have a chance to talk to that crisis counsellor yet?'

Carl stepped out into the light and stood there for a moment, blinking at the sun. Nobody was going to tell him how much gold braid would be plastered on to his dress uniform. Knowing Vigga, she probably already knew that he'd been promoted, which meant his pay raise had been spent. Who the hell felt like taking a course for that?

The premises she'd set her sights on had once been an old knitwear shop, which had since housed a publishing company, a type-setter, an art-import business and a CD shop. By now the opal glass ceiling was the only thing left of the original furnishings. The space was no more than three hundred and seventy-five square feet, but it did have charm – that much he could see. Huge windows faced the passageway down to the lakes, there was a view of a pizzeria, and at the back a view with traces of greenery. And it was almost next door to the Café Bankeråt, where Merete Lynggaard had met someone for dinner a few days before her death. There was nothing boring about Nansensgade with all of its cafés and hang-outs. It was a real Parisian-style paradise.

Carl turned around and immediately caught sight of Vigga and her boyfriend passing by the baker's window. She occupied the street with all the confidence and flair of a matador in a bullring. Her artist's outfit spoke with all the colours of the palette. She'd always been a festive one, that Vigga. The same, however, could not be said of her sickly-looking male companion, with his tight-fitting black clothes, his chalk-white skin, and dark circles under his eyes. His type could best be found inside the lead-lined coffins in a Dracula film.

'Sweeeetheart,' Vigga called, as she crossed Ahlefeldts-gade.

This was going to be expensive.

By the time the emaciated phantom had taken measurements of the whole place, Vigga had softened Carl up. He would only have to pay two-thirds of the rent; she would pay the rest herself.

She threw out her arms. 'The dough's gonna be pouring in, Carl.'

Yeah, right. Or pouring out, he thought, calculating that his share was going to come to two thousand six hundred kroner per month. Maybe he should take that fucking superintendent's course, after all.

They went over to Café Bankeråt to read through the rental agreement, and Carl took a look around. Merete Lynggaard had been here. And less than two weeks later, she had vanished from the face of the earth.

'Who owns this place?' he asked one of the girls at the bar.

'Jean-Yves. He's sitting over there.' She pointed to a

man who looked solid enough. There was nothing preten-
tiously delicate or French about him.

Carl got up. 'May I ask you how long you've owned this
fine establishment?' he asked, taking out his police badge
to show it to the man. That wasn't really necessary, judging by the man's amiable smile, but once in a while he
needed to take the thing out of mothballs.

'I took over the business in 2002.'

'Do you remember exactly when that was?'

'What's this about?'

'About a member of parliament named Merete Lynggaard. You may remember that she disappeared.'

He nodded.

'And she was here not long before she died. Were you
the owner back then?'

He shook his head. 'I took over the business from one
of my friends on March 1, 2002. But I do remember that
the police asked him if anyone here recalled who she'd
had dinner with. But nobody did.' He smiled. 'Maybe I
would have remembered if I'd been here.'

Carl smiled back. Yes, maybe. The owner seemed on
the ball. 'You came on the scene a month too late. That's
how it goes sometimes,' said Carl, shaking the man's hand.

In the meantime Vigga had signed all the papers. She'd
always been generous with her signature.

'Let me just have a look at everything,' Carl said, taking
the papers away from Hugin.

He made a show of placing them on the table in front
of him. The standard contract was filled with words too
small to read, and his eyes instantly glazed over. All those
people out there who are totally oblivious to what could

happen to them, he thought. Merete Lynggaard had sat here in this restaurant, enjoying herself as she looked out of the window on a cold February evening in 2002.

Had she expected something else out of life? Or was it really possible that even then she suspected that in a few days' time she'd be slipping away in the raw, cold waters of the Baltic?

When he got back to the office, his assistant was still fully occupied with the secretaries upstairs, and that suited Carl just fine. The emotional upset of meeting Vigga and her wandering ghost had sapped him of all energy. Only a quick little nap with his feet propped up on the desk and his thoughts buried in dreamland could put him back in the game.

He'd probably been sitting like that for only ten minutes when his meditative state was interrupted by the sensation that all police detectives know only too well – what women call intuition. It was the turmoil of experience bubbling up in his subconscious. The feeling that a number of concrete events would inevitably lead to a specific result.

He opened his eyes and looked at the notes that he'd put up on the whiteboard.

Then he got up and crossed out 'The caseworker in Stevns' on the piece of paper. Under the word 'Check' it now said: 'The telegram – The secretaries at Christiansborg – Witnesses on the ferry *Schleswig-Holstein*.'

Perhaps Merete Lynggaard's secretary had something to do with that telegram. Who had actually accepted delivery of the valentine telegram at Christiansborg? Why had he immediately assumed that it had to be Merete

Lynggaard herself? At that time there was hardly any other MP who was as busy as she was. So it was only logical that at some point the telegram had to have passed through the hands of her secretary. Not that he suspected the secretary of the vice-chair of a group to be sticking her nose in her boss's personal affairs. But wasn't it possible?

It was this possibility that was bothering him.

'So now we have the answer from TelegramsOnline, Carl,' said Assad from the doorway.

Carl looked up.

'They could not tell me what the telegram said, but they had a record of who sent it. It was some funny name.' He looked at his notes. 'Tage Baggesen. I got the phone number that he used to order the telegram. They said it came from inside the Folketing. That was all I wanted to say then.' He handed the note to Carl and had already turned to leave. 'We are investigating the car accident now. They are waiting for me upstairs.'

Carl nodded. Then he picked up the phone and punched in the number to the parliament.

The voice that answered belonged to a secretary in the office of the Radical Centre Party.

She was friendly enough, but was sorry to inform Carl that Tage Baggesen was in the Faroe Islands for the weekend. Would he like to leave a message?

'No, that's OK,' said Carl. 'I'll contact him on Monday.'

'I have to tell you that Mr Baggesen will be very busy on Monday. Just so you know.'

Then Carl asked to be transferred to the office of the Democrats.

*

This time the secretary who answered the phone sounded worn out, and she didn't know the answer to his question offhand. But wasn't there a Søs Norup who used to be Merete Lynggaard's secretary?

Carl confirmed that she was right.

No one really remembered much about Søs, because she'd been there for only a very short time. But one of the other secretaries in the office said that she thought Søs Norup had come from DJØF, the Federation of Jurists and Economists, and had gone back there instead of staying on to work for Merete Lynggaard's successor. 'She was a bitch,' Carl suddenly heard somebody say in the background, and that apparently refreshed everyone's memory.

Yes, thought Carl with satisfaction. It's the good, stable arseholes like us who are remembered best.

Then he phoned DJØF, and found out that yes, they all knew Søs Norup. But no, she hadn't come back to work for them. She had apparently vanished into thin air.

He put down the phone and shook his head. All of a sudden his job had developed into *Without a Trace* in every direction. He wasn't particularly excited at the thought of running around after a secretary who might or might not remember something about a telegram that might point to a specific person who might have gone to a restaurant with Merete Lynggaard and might know something about what her state of mind might have been five years ago. Instead, he decided to go upstairs to see how far Assad had got with their own secretaries and that damned car accident.

*

Carl found them in one of the smaller offices with faxes and photocopies and all sorts of scraps of paper spread out on the table in front of them. It looked as if Assad had set up a campaign office in a presidential election. Three secretaries sat there chattering with each other as Assad served tea and nodded diligently every time the conversation moved a small step forward. An impressive effort.

Carl knocked discreetly on the doorframe.

'So, it looks like you've found a whole lot of lovely documentation for us.' He pointed at the papers, feeling like The Invisible Man. Only Mrs Sørensen even bothered to glance at him, and that was something he could have done without.

He retreated to the hallway, and for the first time since his schooldays was filled with jealousy.

'Carl Mørck?' said a voice behind him, tearing him free of the tight grip of defeat and bringing him back on track to victory. 'Marcus Jacobsen says that you want to talk to me. Should we set up an appointment?'

He turned around and found himself looking right into the eyes of Mona Ibsen. Set up an appointment?

Hell yes.

22

2003—2005

When they turned off the light and raised the air pressure on her thirty-third birthday, Merete slept for a whole day and night. The recognition that everything was beyond her control and that she was apparently on the brink of despair knocked her out completely. Only the next day, when the food bucket once again appeared with a clatter in the hatch, did she open her eyes and try to reorient herself.

She looked up at the portholes, noticing that the hint of a glow was visible. That meant a light was on in the room next door. It produced as much light as a match, but it was there. She got on to her knees and tried to locate the source, but couldn't make out anything behind the panes. Then she turned around and surveyed the space. There was no doubt that there was now enough light in the room that in a matter of days she'd be able to distinguish all its details.

For a moment this made her happy, but then she reminded herself that no matter how weak the light was, it could also be turned off.

She was not the one who had control of the switch.

When she made a move to stand up, her hand bumped against the little metal tube lying on the floor next to her. It was the pocket torch that they'd given her. She curled her fingers tightly around it as her mind tried to work out what it all meant. The torch must mean that at some point they were going to turn off the glimmer of light entering the room. Why else would they give her a torch?

For a moment she considered switching it on, just because she could. She had long ago given up any notion of being able to control anything, so it was tempting. But she decided not to.

'You still have your eyes, Merete. Make them work,' she admonished herself as she set the torch down next to the toilet bucket under the glass panes. If she turned on the torch, she would just find herself in interminable darkness when she switched it off.

It would be like drinking salt water to assuage her thirst.

But the faint light remained on in spite of her prediction. She could make out the contours of the room and see how her limbs were wasting away. It was in this state, reminiscent of the dark twilight of winter, that almost fifteen months passed until everything was radically changed once again.

That was the day when she saw shadows behind the mirrored glass for the first time.

She'd been lying on the floor thinking about books. That was something she often did in order not to think about the life she might have had, if only she'd made different choices. When she thought about books, she could move into a whole different world. Just remembering the feeling of the dry surface and inexplicable roughness of the paper could ignite a blaze of yearning inside of her. The scent of evaporated cellulose and printer's ink. Thousands of times now she'd sent her thoughts into her imaginary library and selected the only book in the world that she knew she could recall without embellishing it. It was not the one she wanted to remember, not even the one that had made the greatest impression on her. But it was the only book that had remained completely intact in her tortured memory because of the liberating bursts of laughter she associated with it.

Her mother had read it aloud to her, and Merete had read it to Uffe. And now she sat here in the dark, trying hard to read it to herself. A philosophical little bear named Winnie the Pooh was her salvation, her only defence against madness. Pooh and all the animals in Hundred Acre Wood. And she was far away in the land of honey when a dark patch suddenly stationed itself in front of the faint light coming from the mirrored glass.

She opened her eyes wide and inhaled air deep into her lungs. The flickering was not something she was imagining. For the first time in ages she felt her skin get clammy. The way it had in the schoolyard, in the narrow and silent alleys of distant cities in the evening, and on her first days in parliament. Those were all the places where she'd been aware of this kind of clammy feeling that could only be caused by the presence of a stranger who meant her harm and was secretly watching her.

That shadow wants to hurt me, she thought, wrapping her arms around herself as she stared at the spot that slowly got bigger on one of the panes and then finally stopped moving. The shadow reached to just above the edge of the glass, as if it belonged to someone sitting on a tall stool.

Can they see me? she wondered, staring at the far wall

behind her. Yes, the white surface of the wall was very visible, so clearly it could also be seen from behind the glass, even by people who were used to moving around in the light. That meant they could see her too.

It was only a couple of hours since the food bucket had been delivered. She could tell from the rhythms of her body. Everything took place on a regular schedule, day after day. It would be many, many hours before the next bucket arrived. So why were they out there? What did they want?

She stood up very slowly and moved towards the mirrored glass, but the shadow didn't stir in the least.

Then she placed her hand against the pane on top of the dark shadow and stood there waiting, as she studied her blurry reflection. She stayed like that until she became convinced that she could no longer trust her sense of judgement. Was it a shadow or not? It could be anything at all. Why would somebody stand on the other side of the glass when they'd never done that before?

'To hell with all of you!' she shouted, feeling an electric shock pass through her body from the force of the echo.

But then it happened. Behind the glass the shadow clearly moved. A bit to one side and then back. The further away from the pane it moved, the smaller and less distinct it became.

'I know you're there!' she yelled, feeling her damp skin cool down instantly. Her lips and face trembled. 'Get away from here!' she snarled at the pane.

But the shadow stayed where it was.

Then she sat down on the floor and buried her face in

her arms. Her clothes stank, reeking of mould. She'd been wearing the same blouse for three years.

The grey light was there all the time, day and night, but it was better than total darkness or interminable light. Here, in this grey nothingness, she had a choice. She could ignore the light or she could ignore the dark. She no longer closed her eyes in order to concentrate; she allowed her brain to decide for itself what state of mind to assume.

And this grey light contained all possible nuances. Almost like the world outside, where the day could be winter-light, February-dim, October-grey, rain-saturated, crystal-clear, and thousands of other shades of the palette. Here inside, her palette consisted of only black and white, and she mixed them as her mood dictated. As long as this grey light was her canvas, she was not forsaken.

And Uffe, Winnie the Pooh, Don Quixote, the Lady of the Camellias, and Smilla all stormed through her head, filling up the hourglass and the shadowy images behind the panes. That made it so much easier to wait for her captors to make another move. She knew it would eventually come. No matter what.

And the shadow behind the mirrored glass became a daily event. Quite a while after she'd eaten, the dark patch would always appear on one of the panes. It never failed to materialize. For the first couple of weeks it was small and indistinct, but it soon grew bigger and sharper. And it came closer.

She knew that she could be seen quite clearly from the other side. One of these days they would aim spotlights on her and demand that she perform. She could only imagine what the animals behind the panes would get out of it, but she couldn't care less.

Shortly before her thirty-fifth birthday, a second shadow suddenly appeared behind the glass. It was a little bigger and not as sharp-edged, and it loomed quite a bit higher than the other one.

Another person is standing behind the first one, she thought, noticing her fear grow with the certainty that she was outnumbered; the superior force out there had now manifested itself.

It took her a couple of days to get used to this new situation, but then she decided to challenge her captors.

She began lying down under the panes to wait for the shadows. In this position she was out of their line of vision when they arrived to observe her. She refused to accommodate them, not knowing how long they would wait for her to come out of hiding. That was the whole point of the manoeuvre.

The second day, when the urge to pee came over her for the second time, she got up and looked directly into the mirrored glass. As always there was a slight glow from the subdued light on the other side, but the shadows were gone.

She repeated this routine for three days in a row. If they want to see me, they can just say so, she thought.

On the fourth day, she got ready. She lay down under the panes, patiently memorizing her books as she gripped the pocket torch tightly in her hand. She'd tested it the night before, and the light had come pouring into the room, making her dizzy and giving her an instant headache. The force of the light was overwhelming.

When it was time for the shadows to appear, she leaned her head back a bit so she could look up at the panes. Suddenly, like mushroom clouds, they were standing there in one of the portholes, closer together than ever. They must have noticed her at once, because they both moved back slightly. But after a minute or two they stepped forwards again.

At that instant she jumped up, switched on the torch, and pressed it against the pane.

The reflection of the light ricocheted off the long wall behind her, but a tiny sliver penetrated the mirrored glass and settled revealingly like faint moonlight upon the silhouettes on the other side. The pupils of their eyes, looking straight at her, contracted and then expanded again. She'd prepared herself for the shock if her plan succeeded, but she had never imagined how deeply the sight of those two indistinct faces would be burned into her consciousness.

23

2007

Carl had made appointments for two meetings at Christiansborg. He was received by a lanky woman who seemed to have frequented the place since childhood. She was able to lead him through the labyrinthine halls and up to the office belonging to the vice-chair of the Democrats with such familiarity that a snail in its shell would have envied her.

Birger Larsen was an experienced politician who had succeeded Merete Lynggaard as vice-chair of the party three days after she disappeared. Since then he'd distinguished himself by acting as the glue that was needed to hold the two vying wings of the party in reasonably close contact. Merete's disappearance had left a gaping void. The veteran leader had almost blindly selected his new heir, a female airhead with a big smile, who initially became the political spokesperson. No one, except the designated successor, was happy with his choice. It didn't take two seconds for Carl to sense that Birger Larsen would have preferred making a career for himself in some tiny business out in the sticks to working at some point under this self-satisfied potential prime minister.

The time would no doubt arrive when he wouldn't be allowed to make that decision on his own.

'Even today I still can't make any sense of the idea that Merete supposedly committed suicide,' he said, pouring

Carl a cup of lukewarm coffee. It was so tepid that he could have stuck his thumb in it with no ill effects.

'I don't think I've ever met anyone here who seemed more vital and glad to be alive.' He shrugged. 'But when it comes right down to it, what do we really know about our fellow human beings? Haven't we all had some sort of tragedy happen in our lives that we couldn't foresee?'

Carl nodded. 'Did she have any enemies here at Christiansborg?'

Larsen displayed a row of exceedingly crooked teeth when he smiled. 'Who the hell doesn't? Merete was the most dangerous woman here in terms of the future of the government, the influence of Piv Vestergård, and the likelihood of the Radical Centre Party grabbing the prime minister position. She was actually dangerous to anyone who pictured themselves in that position, and Merete would undoubtedly have achieved it for herself if only she'd been here a couple more years.'

'Do you think she'd received threats from anyone here?'

'Oh, Mørck. We MPs are too smart for anything like that.'

'Maybe she had personal relationships that could have led to jealousy or hatred. Do you know anything about that?'

'As far as I know, Merete wasn't interested in personal relationships. For her it was all work, work, work and more work. I knew her since she was a political science student, but even I was never permitted to get closer to her than she would allow.'

'And she didn't allow it?'

The man's teeth appeared again. 'You mean, was anyone

interested in her romantically? Of course, I can think of at least half a dozen men here who would gladly have given up their wives for ten minutes alone with Merete Lynggaard.'

'Did that include yourself?' Carl permitted himself a smile.

'Hmm, well, who wouldn't?' The teeth disappeared. 'But Merete and I were friends. I knew what my limits were.'

'But maybe there were others who didn't?'

'You'll have to ask Marianne Koch about that.'

'Merete's former secretary? Do you know why she was replaced?'

'Well, not really. They'd worked together for a couple of years, but it could be that Marianne got a little too personal for Merete's taste.'

'Where can I find this Marianne Koch today?'

A slyness appeared in Larsen's eyes. 'Where you just said hello to her ten minutes ago, I would imagine.'

'She's your secretary now?' Carl put down his coffee cup and pointed towards the door. 'The woman sitting out there?'

Marianne Koch was the complete opposite of the woman who had escorted Carl up to the office. She was petite, with thick, curly black hair that seemed fragrant with temptation even from the other side of the desk.

'Why weren't you still working as Merete Lynggaard's secretary during the period just before she disappeared?' he asked, after the requisite introductory remarks had been exchanged.

She knitted her brow in thought. 'I couldn't understand

it either. Not at the time, at any rate. I was actually quite ticked off at her. But then it came out that she had a disabled brother she was taking care of.'

'And?'

'Well, I thought she had a boyfriend since she was always acting so secretive and was in such a hurry to go home every day.'

He smiled. 'Was that what you told her?'

'Yes, it was dumb. I can see that now. But I thought we were closer friends than we really were. You live and learn.' She gave Carl a wry smile, revealing a whole set of dimples. If Assad ever met her, he'd never be able to get on with his life.

'Did anyone ever try to make a pass at her, here at Christiansborg?'

'Oh, yes. Men were always leaving her messages, but there was only one who made a serious attempt.'

'Would you care to reveal who that might be?'

She smiled. She was willing to reveal anything if it pleased her.

'Of course. It was Tage Baggesen.'

'OK, I've heard that name before.'

'That would really make him happy to know. I think he's held chairman positions for the Radical Centre Party for at least a thousand years.'

'Have you ever mentioned this to anyone else?'

'Yes, to the police, but they didn't seem to think it was relevant.'

'Do you?'

She shrugged.

'Were there others?'

'Lots of others, but nobody serious. She took what she needed whenever she was travelling.'

'Are you saying she was an easy lay?'

'Good Lord, is that how you interpret it?' She turned away, trying to suppress her laughter. 'No, she definitely was not. But she was no nun, either. I just don't happen to know who she went into the convent with. She never told me.'

'But her preference was for men?'

'Well, put it this way, she always laughed when the gossipmongers hinted otherwise.'

'Could you think of any reason why Merete might want to put her past behind her and create a whole new life?'

'You mean whether she might be sitting out there in Mumbai, soaking up the sun?' Marianne looked indignant.

'Some place where life might be less problematic, yes. Could you picture her doing anything like that?'

'That's totally absurd. She was extremely conscientious. I know that some people collapse like a house of cards and one fine day they just disappear, but not Merete.' She paused for a moment, looking pensive. 'But it's a lovely thought.' She smiled. 'I mean, that Merete might still be alive.'

Carl nodded. Plenty of psychological profiles had been done of Merete Lynggaard just after she disappeared, and all of them had come to the same conclusion. Merete had not simply run away from her old life. Even the tabloids dismissed that possibility.

'Did you ever hear anything about a telegram that she

received during her last week here at the castle?' he asked. 'A valentine telegram?'

The question seemed to annoy Marianne. Apparently she was still upset that she hadn't been part of Merete's life at the end. 'No. The police asked me about that, but just as I told them I have to refer you to Søs Norup, who took over my job.'

He raised his eyebrows as he looked at her. 'Are you bitter about that?'

'Of course I am. Wouldn't you be? We'd worked together for two years without any problem.'

'Do you happen to know where Søs Norup is today?'

She shrugged. Nothing could have interested her less.

'What about this Tage Baggesen? Where can I get in touch with him?'

She drew Carl a little map showing the way to Baggesen's office. It didn't look easy to find.

It took Carl nearly half an hour to find his way to the domain of Tage Baggesen and the Radical Centre Party, and it was no cakewalk. It was a mystery to him how the hell anybody could work in such a hypocritical environment. At least at police headquarters you knew what you were dealing with, where friends and enemies weren't afraid to show their true colours, and yet everyone was able to work side by side towards a common goal. Here it was just the opposite. Everybody pretended to be the best of friends, but they were all thinking only of themselves when it came to settling scores. Everything was based on kroner and øre and power, not so much on results. A big man in this place was someone who made the others seem small. Maybe it hadn't always been this way, but that's how it was now.

Tage Baggesen was obviously no exception. His role was to safeguard the interests of his distant constituency and handle the traffic policies of his party, but after one look at him, you knew better. He'd already secured himself a nice fat pension, and whatever he took in before he retired was spent on expensive clothes and lucrative investments. Carl looked up at the walls that were covered with certificates from golf tournaments and detailed aerial photographs of Baggesen's country homes all over Denmark.

He considered asking whether the man might have misunderstood which party he belonged to, but Tage Baggesen disarmed him with a friendly slap on the back and a cordial welcome.

'I suggest that you close the door,' said Carl, pointing to the corridor.

That prompted a jovial squint from Baggesen. A little trick that he used successfully in negotiating new motorways in Holstebro but it had no effect on a detective inspector whose speciality was bullshit.

'I don't think we need to do that. I've got nothing to hide from my fellow party members,' said Baggesen.

'We've heard that you took a great interest in Merete Lynggaard. You sent her a telegram among other things. And it was a valentine telegram at that.'

The man's complexion turned a bit paler, but his self-confident smile was back.

'A valentine telegram?' he said. 'I don't remember that.'

Carl nodded. The lie shone out of the man's face. Of

course Baggesen remembered. Now Carl had an opportunity to really go to work on the MP.

'When I suggested that you close the door, it was because I wanted to ask you bluntly if you were the one who murdered Merete. You were in love with her. She rejected you, and you lost control. Was that what happened?'

For a split second every cell in Tage Baggesen's brain, otherwise so self-confident, considered whether he should stand up and slam the door or whether he should work himself up into an apoplectic fit. His complexion was suddenly almost the same shade of red as his hair. He was deeply shocked, completely exposed. Sweat trickled from every pore of his body. Carl knew all the tricks in the book, but this reaction was something entirely different. If the man had anything to do with the case, and judging by his response he did, then he might as well write his own confession. If he didn't, then there was still something pushing him to the wall. His mouth gaped. If Carl wasn't careful, the man would clam up for good. Never before in his finely tuned life had Tage Baggesen heard anything like this; that much was certain.

Carl tried to smile at the man. Somehow his dramatic reaction also seemed conciliatory. As if somewhere inside that body, nourished on high-class reception delicacies, there still might be a human being.

'Now listen here, Baggesen. You left notes for Merete. Lots of notes. I can tell you that her previous secretary, Marianne Koch, kept a close eye on your advances.'

'Everyone writes notes to each other in this place.' Baggesen tried to lean back nonchalantly, but the distance to the back of his chair was too great for it to look casual.

'So you're saying the notes contained nothing of a personal nature?'

At this point the MP hauled his bulk out of his chair and went over to quietly close the door. 'It's true that I harboured strong feelings for Merete Lynggaard,' he said, looking so sincerely mournful that Carl almost felt sorry for him. 'It's been very difficult for me to get over her death.'

'I understand. I'll try to make this brief.' Carl's words were met with a grateful smile. Now the man was getting realistic.

'We know that you sent Merete Lynggaard a valentine telegram in February 2002. We received confirmation of this from the telegram company today.'

Now Baggesen looked dejected. The past was truly gnawing at him.

He sighed. 'Of course I knew that she wasn't interested in me in that way. Unfortunately. I'd known that for a long time, even back then.'

'But you still kept trying?'

He nodded without saying a word.

'What did the telegram say? Try to stick to the truth this time.'

He tilted his head a bit to the side. 'Just the usual. That I'd like to see her. I don't remember the exact words. And that's the truth.'

'And so you killed her because she wasn't interested in you?'

Now Baggesen's eyes narrowed to thin slits. His lips were closed tight. A second before the tears began running down the side of the politician's nose, Carl was inclined to arrest him. Then Baggesen raised his head and looked at him. Not as if Carl were the executioner who had placed a noose around his neck, but as if he were a father confessor to whom he could finally open his heart.

'Who would kill the one person who made life worth living?' he asked.

They sat there for a moment, looking at each other. Then Carl looked away.

'Do you know whether Merete had any enemies here? Not political adversaries. I mean real enemies.'

Baggesen wiped his eyes. 'All of us have enemies, but not what you'd call real enemies,' he replied.

'Nobody who might have had designs on her life?'

Baggesen shook his head. 'That would really surprise me. She was well liked, even by her political opponents.'

'I have a different impression. So you don't think she was working with key issues that might have proved so problematic for someone that they'd do anything to stop her? Special-interest groups that felt pressured or threatened?'

Baggesen gave Carl an indulgent look. 'Ask her own party members. She and I were not what you'd call political confidants. Far from it, I must say. Have you found out anything in particular?'

'Politicians the world over are always held accountable for their opinions, right? Opponents of abortion, animal-rights fanatics, people with anti-Muslim attitudes, or the opposite – anything at all can elicit a violent reaction. Just look at Sweden or Holland or the United States.' Carl made a motion to stand up and noticed the look of relief already appearing on the face of the MP sitting across from him. But maybe he shouldn't read too much into that. Who wouldn't want this sort of conversation to come to an end?

'Baggesen,' Carl went on. 'Maybe you'd be kind enough to get in touch with me if you happen to stumble on anything at all that I should know.' He handed the man his card. 'If not for my sake, then for your own. Not many people in this place felt as positive about Merete Lynggaard as you did, I'm afraid.'

That hit home. The tears would undoubtedly begin flowing again, even before Carl was out the door.

According to the Civil Register, Søs Norup's last place of residence was the same as that of her parents, right in the middle of Copenhagen's snooty Frederiksberg district. On the brass plate next to the front door it said: 'Wholesaler Vilhelm Norup and actress Kaja Brandt Norup.'

Carl rang the bell and heard the sound reverberating behind the massive oak door. A moment later it was supplemented by a quiet 'Yes, yes, I'm coming.'

The man who opened the door must have retired at least a quarter of a century earlier. Judging by the waistcoat he was wearing and the silk cravat around his neck, his fortune hadn't dried up yet. He stared uneasily at Carl with eyes ravaged by illness, as if this stranger on his doorstep might be the Grim Reaper. 'Who are you?' he asked bluntly, ready to slam the door.

Carl introduced himself, and again took his badge out of his pocket. He asked if he might come inside.

'Has something happened to Søs?' the man demanded to know.

'I don't know. Why do you ask? Isn't she at home?'

'She doesn't live here any more, if she's the one you're looking for.'

'Who is it, Vilhelm?' called a faint voice from behind the double doors to the living room.

'Just somebody who wants to talk to Søs, dear.'

'Then he'll have to go elsewhere,' she replied.

The wholesaler grabbed Carl's sleeve. 'She lives in Valby. Tell her we want her to come and get her things if she's planning to go on living like that.'

'Like what?'

The man didn't answer. He gave Carl the address on Valhøjvej, then slammed the door shut.

In the small co-op building there were only three names next to the intercom. In the past the place had undoubtedly been home to six families, each with four or five children. What had previously been a slum was now gentrified. It was here in this attic flat that Søs Norup had found her true love, a woman in her mid-forties whose scepticism regarding Carl's police badge manifested itself in pale lips that were pressed tight.

Søs's lips were not much friendlier. Even at first glance, Carl understood why DJØF and the Democrats' office at Christiansborg hadn't fallen apart when she left. One would have to search far and wide to find someone who presented a less sympathetic aura.

'Merete Lynggaard was a frivolous boss,' she remarked.

'You mean, she didn't take her job seriously? That's not what I heard.'

'She left everything up to me.'

'I'd think that would be a plus.' He looked at her. She

194

seemed like a woman who'd always been kept on a short leash and hated it. Wholesaler Norup and his wife, no doubt once very prominent, had probably taught Søs the meaning of blind obedience. That must have been hard to take for an only child who saw her parents as gifts from God. Carl was convinced it must have reached the point where she both detested and loved them. Detested what they stood for, and loved them for the very same thing. In Carl's humble opinion, that was why she'd moved back and forth from home all her adult life.

He glanced over at her girlfriend. Dressed in loose-fitting garb and with a smouldering cigarette hanging from her lips, she sat there making sure he wouldn't try to molest anyone. She was determined to provide Søs with a permanent anchor here from now on. That much was obvious.

'I heard that Merete Lynggaard was very satisfied with your work.'

'Oh, really.'

'I'd like to ask you about Merete's personal life. Was there any reason to think that she might have been pregnant when she disappeared?'

Søs frowned and drew back.

'Pregnant?' She said the word as if it were in the same category as contagion, leprosy and the bubonic plague. 'No, I'm positive that she wasn't.' She glanced over at her lover and rolled her eyes.

'How can you be so sure?'

'How do you think? If she was as together as everybody thought, she wouldn't have had to borrow tampons from me every time she got her period.'

'You're saying that she had her period just before she disappeared?'

'Yes, the week before. We always got our periods at the same time when I was working for her.'

He nodded. That was something she would know. 'Do you know if she had a lover?'

'I've already been asked that a hundred times before.'

'Refresh my memory.'

Søs took out a cigarette and tapped it firmly on the table. 'All the men stared at her as if they wanted to throw her down on the table. How would I know if one of them had something going on with her?'

'In the report it says that she received a valentine telegram. Did you know it was from Tage Baggesen?'

She lit her cigarette and disappeared behind a blue haze. 'No, I didn't.'

'So you don't know whether there was something going on between them?'

'Something going on? This was five years ago, as I'm sure you'll recall.' She blew a cloud of smoke right at Carl's face, eliciting a wry smile from her lover.

Carl moved back a bit. 'Now listen here. I'm going to take off in four minutes. But before I do, let's pretend that we want to help each other out, OK?' He looked Søs right in the eye; she was still trying to hide her self-loathing behind a hostile expression. 'I'll call you Søs, OK? I'm usually on first-name terms when I share a smoke with someone.'

She moved the hand with the cigarette to her lap.

'So now I'm going to ask you this, Søs. Do you know about any incidents that happened just before Merete disappeared? Anything we ought to investigate further? I'm going to rattle off a list of possibilities, so just stop me if I come to anything relevant.' The nod he gave her wasn't returned. 'Phone conversations of a personal nature? Little yellow notes that were left on her desk? People who behaved towards her in an unprofessional manner? Boxes of chocolates, flowers, new rings on her fingers? Did she ever blush while staring into space? Was she having a hard time concentrating during those last few days?' He looked at the zombie sitting across from him. Her colourless lips hadn't moved a millimetre. Another dead end. 'Did her behaviour change in any way? Did she go home earlier? Did she leave the parliament chamber to make calls on her mobile out in the corridor? Did she arrive later than usual in the morning?'

Again he looked up at Søs, giving her an emphatic nod, as if that might wake her from the dead.

She took another puff of her cigarette and then ground the butt out in the ashtray. 'Are you done?' she asked.

He sighed. Stonewalled! What else did he expect from this cow? 'Yeah, I'm done.'

'Good.' She raised her head. For a moment he saw a woman who possessed a certain gravitas. 'I told the police about the telegram and about her meeting someone at Café Bankeråt. I saw her write that down in her appointment diary. I don't know who she was going to meet, but it did make her cheeks flush.'

'Who could it have been?'

She shrugged.

'Tage Baggesen?' he asked.

'It could have been anybody. She met so many people

at Christiansborg. There was also a man who was part of a delegation who seemed interested. But there were lots of men who were interested.'

'A delegation? When was that?'

'Not long before she disappeared.'

'Do you remember his name?'

'After five years? God, no.'

'What sort of delegation?'

She gave him a surly look. 'Something to do with research on the immune system. But you interrupted me,' she said. 'Merete also received a bouquet of flowers. There was no doubt she had some sort of relationship that was quite personal. I have no idea what was connected with what, but I've told the police all this before.'

Carl scratched his neck. Where had this information been recorded?

'Who did you talk to about this, if I might ask?'

'I don't remember.'

'It wasn't Børge Bak from the Rapid Response Team, was it?'

She pointed her index finger at Carl, as if to say 'Bingo'.

That damned Bak. Did he always leave out so many details when he wrote up his reports?

Carl looked over at Søs's chosen cellmate. She wasn't exactly lavish with the smiles. Right now she was just waiting for him to disappear.

Carl nodded to Søs and stood up. Between the bay windows hung various tiny studio photographs in colour, as well as a couple of large black-and-white pictures of Søs's parents, taken in better days. They must have been quite attractive at one time, but it was hard to tell, given the way

Søs had scratched and scored all the faces in the photos. He leaned down to look at the small framed pictures. From the clothes and posture, he recognized one of the many PR photos of Merete Lynggaard. She too had lost most of her face in a network of scratches. So Søs collected pictures of people she hated. Maybe he could have won a place for himself if he'd made an effort.

For once Børge Bak was alone in his office. His leather jacket was more creased than usual. Indisputable proof that he was working hard, day and night.

'Didn't I tell you not to come barging in here, Carl?' He slammed his notepad on the desk and glared at him.

'You fucked up, Børge,' said Carl.

Whether it was the use of his first name or the accusation, Bak's reaction was instantaneous. All the furrows on his forehead went vertical, reaching right up to his comb-over.

'Merete Lynggaard got a bouquet of flowers a few days before her death. And from what I've heard, she never used to receive flowers.'

'So what?' Bak's expression couldn't have been more condescending.

'We're looking for someone who might have committed a murder. Has that slipped your mind? A lover could be a likely candidate.'

'We looked into all that.'

'But it wasn't included in your report.'

Bak shrugged. 'Take it easy, Carl. You, of all people, should talk about other people's work. The rest of us are working our arses off while you're just sitting on your backside. Don't you think I know that? I put what's important into the report, and that's that,' he said, smacking his pad on the desktop.

'You neglected to include the fact that a social worker named Karin Mortensen observed Uffe Lynggaard playing a game that indicated he remembered the car accident. Maybe he also remembers something from the day when Merete disappeared. But apparently you didn't pursue that angle very far.'

'Karen Mortensen. Karen spelled with an *e*, not an *i*, Carl. Try listening to yourself. And don't come here trying to teach me anything about being thorough.'

'Does that mean you realize how significant this piece of information from Karen Mortensen could be?'

'Shut the fuck up. We checked it out, okay? Uffe didn't remember shit about anything. That kid's got nothing upstairs.'

'Merete Lynggaard met a man a few days before she died. He was part of a delegation on research into the workings of the immune system. You didn't put anything about that in your report either.'

'No, but we looked into it.'

'So then you must know that a man got in touch with her, and there was clearly strong chemistry between them. That's what her secretary, Søs Norup, says she told you, at any rate.'

'Yes, damn it. Of course I know that.'

'Then why isn't it in your report?'

'I don't know. Probably because it turned out that the man was dead.'

'Dead?'

'Yes, burned to death in a car accident the day after Merete disappeared. His name was Daniel Hale.' He enunciated the name carefully, so that Carl would take note of what a good memory he had.

'Daniel Hale?' Apparently Søs had forgotten his name over the years.

'Yes, he was working on the placenta research that the delegation was trying to get funded. He had a laboratory in Slangerup.' Bak presented these facts with supreme self-confidence. He had a good handle on this part of the case.

'If he didn't die until the following day, he still could have had something to do with Merete's disappearance.'

'I don't think so. He came home from London on the afternoon she drowned.'

'Was he in love with her? Søs hinted that might be the case.'

'If so, I feel sorry for the man. She wasn't having any of it.'

'Are you sure, Børge?' His colleague clearly wasn't comfortable hearing Carl use his first name. So that settled things – he was going to hear it non-stop. 'Maybe it was this Daniel Hale she had dinner with at Bankeråt. What do you think, Børge?'

'Listen, Carl. There's a woman in the cyclist murder case who's talked to us, and now we're hot on the trail. I'm busy as fuck right now. Can't this wait until some other time? Daniel Hale is dead. He wasn't even in the country when Merete Lynggaard died. She drowned, and Hale didn't have shit to do with it, OK?'

'Did you try to find out whether Hale was the person

she had dinner with at Bankeråt a week earlier? There's nothing about it in the report.'

'Listen to me! The investigation finally pointed to the likelihood that her death was an accident. Besides, there were twenty of us on the case. Go ask somebody else. Now get out of here, Carl.'

24

2007

If he relied exclusively on his sense of smell and hearing, it was hard to distinguish the basement in police headquarters from Cairo's teeming alleyways on Monday morning when Carl arrived at work. Never before had that venerable building ever reeked so much of cooking smells and exotic spices, and never before had those walls heard the likes of such twisted tones.

A secretary from Admin who had just been down to the archives glared at Carl as she passed him, her arms filled with case files. Her expression said that in ten minutes the whole building was going to know that everything had run amok down in the basement.

The explanation was to be found in Assad's pygmy office, where a sea of baked goods and pieces of foil holding chopped garlic, little green bits, and yellow rice adorned the plates on his desk. No wonder it was causing raised eyebrows.

'What's going on here, Assad?' shouted Carl, turning off the half tones issuing from the cassette player. Assad merely smiled. Evidently he wasn't aware of the cultural gap that was presently in the process of gnawing its way deep under the solid foundations of police headquarters.

Carl dropped heavily on to the chair across from his assistant. 'It smells wonderful, Assad, but this is the police department. Not a Lebanese takeaway in Vanløse.'

'Here, Carl. And congratulations, Mr Superintendent, one might say,' replied Assad, handing him a buttery dough triangle. 'This is from my wife. My daughters cut out the paper.'

Carl followed Assad's hand as he gestured around the room. Now he noticed the brilliantly coloured tissue paper draped over the bookshelves and ceiling lights.

This was not going to be easy.

'I also took some to Hardy yesterday. I have read most of the case files to him out loud now, Carl.'

'Is that right?' He could just picture the nurses as Assad fed Egyptian rolls to Hardy. 'You mean you went to see him on your day off?'

'He is thinking about the case, Carl. A fine man. He is a fine man.'

Carl nodded and took a bite. He planned to go and see Hardy tomorrow.

'I have put together all the papers about the car accident on your desk, Carl. If you like I can also talk a little about what I have been reading.'

Carl nodded again. Before he knew it, his assistant would be writing the report before they were even done with the case.

In other parts of Denmark on Christmas Eve in 1986, the temperature was up to six degrees Celsius, but on Sjælland they weren't as lucky, and it had cost ten people their lives. Five of them died on a narrow country road that ran through a wooded area in the Tibirke Hills; two of them were the parents of Merete and Uffe Lynggaard.

They had tried to pass a Ford Sierra on a stretch of road where the wind had created a carpet of ice crystals, and that's where things went terribly wrong. No one was assigned blame, and no lawsuits were filed for damages. It was a simple accident, except that the outcome was anything but simple.

The car they tried to pass ended up in a tree and was still burning when the fire department arrived, while the car belonging to Merete's parents lay upside down fifty yards further away. Merete's mother was thrown through the windscreen and landed in the thickets, her neck broken. Her father was not as lucky. It took him ten minutes to die. Half of the engine block had punctured his abdomen and a tree branch had pierced his ribcage. It was assumed that Uffe remained conscious the whole time, because when the firemen cut him out of the car, he watched their efforts with wide-open, frightened eyes. He refused to let go of his sister's hand, even when they pulled her out on to the road to give her first aid. He never let go, even for a second.

The police report was simple and brief, but the newspaper reports were not. It was too good a story.

In the other car, a little girl and her father died instantly. The circumstances were especially tragic because only the older boy escaped relatively unharmed. The mother was in the last stages of pregnancy, and the family had been on its way to the hospital. While the firemen tried to put out the blaze under the bonnet of the car, the mother gave birth to twins with her head resting on the body of her dead husband and one leg pinned beneath the car seat. In spite of heroic efforts to cut all of them out of the car in time, one of the babies died, and the newspapers had a guaranteed front-page story for Christmas Day.

Assad showed Carl both the local rags and the national papers, and all of them had picked up on the newsworthiness of the story. The photographs were heart-rending. The car in the tree and the torn-up road; the new mother on her way in the ambulance with a sobbing boy at her side; Merete Lynggaard lying on a stretcher in the middle of the road with an oxygen mask over her face; and Uffe, who was sitting on the thin layer of snow with frightened eyes, firmly gripping the hand of his unconscious sister.

'Here,' said Assad, taking two pages from the *Gossip* tabloid out of the case file, which he'd taken from Carl's desk. 'Lis found out that some of these pictures were also used in the newspapers when Merete Lynggaard was elected to the Folketing,' Assad added.

All in all, the photographer who just happened to be in the Tibirke Woods on that particular afternoon had certainly got his money's-worth out of the few hundredths of a second it took to snap those pictures. He was also the one who had photographed the funeral of Merete's parents – this time in colour. Sharp, well-composed press shots of a teenage Merete Lynggaard holding her stunned brother by the hand as the urns were interred in Vestre Cemetery. There were no photographs from the other funeral. It took place in the utmost privacy.

'What the hell is going on down here?' a voice broke in. 'Is it your fault that it stinks like Christmas Eve upstairs in our office?'

Sigurd Harms, one of the police sergeants from the second floor, was standing in the doorway. He stared with astonishment at the orgy of colours hanging from the lights.

'Here, Sigurd Fart-Nose,' said Carl, handing him one

of the spicy, buttery rolls. 'Just wait until Easter. That's when we burn incense, too.'

A message was delivered from upstairs saying that the homicide chief wanted to see Carl in his office before lunch. Jacobsen wore a gloomy and preoccupied expression as he looked up from reading the documents in front of him and invited Carl to have a seat.

Carl was about to apologize for Assad and explain that all that deep-frying wouldn't happen again in the basement; he had the situation under control. But he never got that far before a pair of new detectives came in and sat down against the wall.

Carl gave them a crooked smile. He didn't think they were there to arrest him because of a few samosas, or whatever those spicy, doughy things were called.

When Lars Bjørn and Detective Inspector Terje Ploug, who'd taken over the nail-gun case, entered the room, the homicide chief flipped the case file closed and turned to Carl. 'I want you to know that I've called you in because two more murders were discovered this morning. The bodies of two young men were found in a car-repair shop outside Sorø.'

Sorø, thought Carl. What the devil did that have to do with them?

'They were both found with ninety-millimetre nails from a Paslode nail gun in their skulls. I'm sure that reminds you of something, right?'

Carl turned his head to look out of the window, staring at a flock of birds flying over the buildings across the road. He could feel his boss's eyes fixed on him, but that wasn't going to do him much good. What had happened in Sorø yesterday didn't necessarily have anything to do with the case out in Amager. Even on TV shows they used nail guns as weapons these days.

'Will you take it from here, Terje?' he heard Marcus Jacobsen say, as if from far off.

'Sure. We're convinced that it's the same perpetrators who killed Georg Madsen in the barracks out in Amager.'

Carl turned to face him. 'And why is that?'

'Because Georg Madsen was the uncle of one of the victims in Sorø.'

Carl turned back to watch the birds again.

'We've got a description of one of the individuals who apparently was at the scene when the murders were committed. Police Detective Stoltz and his team in Sorø want you to drive down there today to compare your description with theirs.'

'I didn't see shit. I was unconscious.'

Terje Ploug gave Carl a look that he didn't care for. He of all people must have studied the report in detail, so why was he playing dumb? Hadn't Carl insisted that he was unconscious from the moment he was shot in the temple until they put the IV drip in his arm in the hospital? Didn't they believe him? What possible reason could they have for wanting to speak with him?

'In the report it says that you saw a red-checked shirt before the shots were fired.'

The shirt. Was that all this was about? 'So they want me to identify a shirt?' he replied. 'Because if that's what they need, I think they should just email me a photo of it.'

'They've got their own reasons, Carl,' Marcus interjected. 'It's in everyone's interest that you drive down to Sorø. Not least your own.'

'I don't really feel like it.' He glanced at his watch. 'Besides, it's already getting late.'

'You don't really feel like it? Tell me, Carl, when is it that you have an appointment to see the crisis counsellor?'

Carl pursed his lips. Did Marcus really have to announce that to the whole department?

'Tomorrow.'

'Then I think you should drive to Sorø today, and you'll have your reaction to the experience fresh in your mind when you see Mona Ibsen tomorrow.' He flashed Carl a phoney smile and picked a file off the top of the tallest stack on his desk. 'Oh, and by the way, here are copies of the documents we received from Immigration regarding Hafez el-Assad. You can take them with you.'

Assad ended up doing the driving. He'd brought along some of the spicy rolls and triangles in a lunch box and shovelled them in his mouth as they shot along the E20. Sitting there behind the wheel, he was a happy and contented man, as evidenced by his smiling face. He moved his head from side to side in time to whatever music was playing on the radio.

'I got your papers from the Immigration Service, Assad, but I haven't read them yet,' said Carl. 'Why don't you tell me what they say?'

For a second his driver gave him an alert look as they roared past a procession of lorries. 'My birth date, where I come from, and then what I did there. Is that what you mean, Carl?'

'Why were you granted permanent residency, Assad? Does it say that too?'

He nodded. 'Carl, I would be killed if I went back. That is how it is. The government in Syria was not really very happy with me, you understand.'

'Why not?'

'We did not just think the same. And that is enough.'

'Enough for what?'

'Syria is a big country. People just disappear.'

'OK, so you're sure that you'll be killed if you go back?'

'That is how it is, Carl.'

'Were you working for the Americans?'

Assad turned his head sharply to look at Carl. 'Why do you say that?'

Carl looked away. 'No reason, Assad. Just asking.'

The last time Carl visited the old Sorø police station on Storgade, it was part of District 16, under the Ringsted police force. Now it belonged to southern Jutland and Lolland-Falster's police district, but the bricks were still red, the mugs behind the counter were the same, and the workload hadn't got any lighter. What benefits were achieved by moving people from one box into another was a question worthy of *Who Wants To Be A Millionaire?*.

Carl was expecting one of the detectives at the station to ask him for yet another description of a checked shirt. But they weren't that amateurish. A welcome party, four men strong, was waiting for him in an office the size of Assad's, looking as if each of them had lost a family member in connection with the violent events of the night before.

'Jørgensen,' announced one of them, holding out his hand. It was ice-cold. A few hours earlier this same Jørgensen had undoubtedly been staring into the eyes of a couple of men who'd had their lives blown away with a pneumatic nail gun. And in that case, he probably hadn't slept a wink all night.

'Do you want to see the crime scene?' asked one of the officers.

'Is that necessary?'

'It's not completely identical to the scene in Amager. They were killed in a car-repair shop. One in the garage and one in the office. The nails were fired at close range, since they went all the way in. We had to look closely even to see them.'

One of the other officers handed a couple of A4-size photos to Carl. They were right. The heads of the nails were just barely visible in the skull. There wasn't even any significant bleeding.

'As you can see, they were both working. There was dirt on their hands and they were wearing boiler suits.'

'Was anything missing?'

'Zilch!'

Carl hadn't heard that expression in a while.

'What were they working on? Wasn't it late at night? Were they moonlighting, or what?'

The detectives exchanged glances. This was clearly a question they were still working on.

'There were footprints from hundreds of shoes. Looks like they never cleaned the place,' Jørgensen added. This wasn't going to be an easy case for him. 'We want you to have a close look at this, Carl,' he went on as he picked up a corner of a cloth that was covering the table. 'And don't say anything until you're sure.'

He took off the cloth to reveal four shirts with big red checks, lying side by side like lumberjacks taking a nap on the forest floor.

'Do any of these look like the one you saw at the crime scene in Amager?'

It was the strangest line-up Carl had ever taken part in. Which of these shirts did it? That was the question. It was almost a joke. Shirts had never been his speciality. He wouldn't even be able to recognize his own.

'I realize it's difficult after such a long time, Carl,' said Jørgensen wearily. 'But it would be a big help if you could try.'

'Why the hell do you think the perp would be wearing the same shirt months later? Even you lot must change your gear once in a while out here in the sticks.'

Jørgensen ignored the remark. 'We just want to try everything.'

'And how can you be sure that the witness who saw the alleged killer from a distance and, to cap it all, at night, would be able to remember how a red-checked shirt looked with such accuracy that you could use it as a lead in the investigation? These shirts look like four peas in a pod, damn it! OK, they're not identical, but there must be thousands of other shirts that look just like them.'

'The guy who saw the shirt works in a clothing shop. We believe him. He was very precise when he drew a picture of it.'

'Did he also draw a picture of the man inside it? Wouldn't that have been better?'

'As a matter of fact, he did. Not a bad drawing, but not

great either. It's not as easy to draw a person as it is to draw a shirt.'

Carl looked at the sketch they now placed on top of the shirts. An ordinary-looking guy. If he didn't know better, the man could be a photocopier salesman in Slagelse. Round glasses, clean-shaven, innocent-looking eyes, with a boyish set to his mouth.

'I don't recognize him. How tall did the witness say he was?'

'At least six feet, maybe more.'

Then the detective took the drawing away and pointed at the shirts. Carl studied each of them. Offhand, they all looked pretty much the same.

Then he closed his eyes and tried to picture the shirt in his mind.

'What happened then?' asked Assad on the way back to Copenhagen.

'Nothing. They all looked the same to me. I can't really remember that damn shirt any more.'

'So maybe then you got a picture of them to take home?'

Carl didn't answer. He was far away in his thoughts. At the moment he was seeing Anker lying dead on the floor next to him, and Hardy gasping on top of him. Why the fuck hadn't he shot those men? All he'd had to do was turn around when he heard them on their way into the barracks, and then none of this would have happened. Anker would be sitting next to him behind the wheel of the car instead of this strange being named Assad. And Hardy! Hardy wouldn't be chained to a bed for the rest of his life, for fuck's sake.

'Could they not just send you the pictures right away first, Carl?'

He looked at his driver. Sometimes those eyes of his had such a devilishly innocent expression under the inch-thick eyebrows.

'Yes, Assad. Of course they could have.'

He checked out the signs posted above the motorway. Only a couple of kilometres to Tåstrup.

'Turn off here,' he said.

'Why?' asked Assad as the car crossed the solid lines and took the exit ramp on two wheels.

'Because I want to take a look at the place where Daniel Hale died.'

'Who?'

'The guy who was interested in Merete Lynggaard.'

'How do you know about that, Carl?'

'Bak told me. Hale was killed in a car crash. I have the police report with me.'

Assad gave a low whistle, as if car wrecks were a cause of death reserved only for people who were very, very unlucky.

Carl glanced at the speedometer. Maybe Assad should let up a little on the speed, before they ended up in the statistics as well.

Even though it was five years since Daniel Hale lost his life on the Kappelev highway, it wasn't hard to see traces left by the accident. His car had crashed into a building, which afterwards had undergone rudimentary repairs, and most of the soot had been washed off, but as far as Carl could tell, the majority of the insurance money must have gone to other uses.

He looked down the long expanse of open road. What bad luck for the man to drive right into that ugly building. Only thirty feet to either side and his car would have sailed into the fields.

'Very unlucky. What do you say, Carl?'

'Damned unlucky.'

Assad kicked at the tree stump still standing in front of the scarred wall. 'He drove into the tree, and the tree snapped like a stick, and then he rammed into the wall and the car started to burn, right?'

Carl nodded and turned around. He knew that further along was a side road. It was apparently from that road that the other vehicle had pulled out, as far as he could remember from the police report.

He pointed north. 'Daniel Hale came from that direction, driving his Citroën from Tåstrup. According to the other driver and the police measurements, they crashed at that spot there.' He pointed at the line in the middle of the road. 'Maybe Hale fell asleep. In any case, he drove over the centre line and ran right into the oncoming vehicle. Then Hale's car was flung back, right into the tree and the building. The whole thing didn't take more than a split second.'

'What happened to him, the man in the other car?'

'Well, he landed out there,' said Carl, pointing to a flat piece of land that the EU had allowed to go fallow years ago.

Assad gave another low whistle. 'And him nothing happened to?'

'No. He was driving some sort of gigantic 4x4. You're out in the country now, Assad.'

His partner looked as if he knew exactly what Carl was talking about. 'There are also many 4x4's in Syria,' he said.

Carl nodded, but he wasn't really listening. 'It's strange, isn't it, Assad?' he then said.

'What? That he drove into the building?'

'No, that he happened to die the day after Merete Lynggaard disappeared. The man that Merete had just met and who might have been in love with her. Very strange.'

'You think maybe it was suicide? That he was so sad because she disappeared down into the sea?' Assad's expression changed a bit as he looked at Carl. 'He killed himself maybe because he was the one who murdered Merete. It has happened before, Carl.'

'Suicide? No. Then he would have rammed the building on purpose. No, it definitely wasn't suicide. And besides, he couldn't have killed her. He was on a plane when Merete disappeared.'

'OK.' Assad touched the scarred surface of the wall. 'So maybe it could not be him either who brought the letter that said, "Have a nice trip to Berlin."'

Carl nodded and looked at the sun, which was about to settle in the west. 'You could be right.'

'What are we doing then here, Carl?'

'What we're doing?' He stared out over the fields, where the first weeds of spring were already taking hold. 'I'll tell you, Assad. We're investigating. That's what we're doing.'

25

2007

'Thank you for arranging this meeting for me, and for agreeing to see me again so soon.' He shook hands with Birger Larsen, adding, 'This won't take long.' He looked around at the familiar faces gathered in the Democrats' vice-chairman's office.

'All right, Mørck. I've invited all of the people who worked with Merete Lynggaard just before she disappeared. You might recognize a few of them.'

Carl nodded to everyone. Yes, he did recognize some of them. A number of the politicians sitting here might be able to knock the present government out of power during the next election. One could always hope so, at least. Here sat the party spokesperson in a knee-length skirt; a couple of the more prominent members of parliament; and a few people from the party office, including the secretary Marianne Koch, who sent Carl a flirtatious look, reminding him that in only three hours he was due to be cross-examined by Mona Ibsen.

'As Birger Larsen has no doubt told you, we're investigating Merete Lynggaard's disappearance one more time, before we close the case. And in that connection, I need to find out anything that might help me to understand Merete's behaviour during those last few days, as well as her state of mind. It's my impression that back then, at quite an early stage in the investigation, the police came to the conclusion that she fell overboard by accident, and they were probably right. If that was the case, we'll never know for certain what happened. After five years in the sea, her body would have decomposed long ago.'

Everyone nodded, looking both solemn and sad. These were the people that Merete would have counted among her colleagues. Perhaps with the exception of the party's new 'crown princess'.

'Many things have turned up that point to an accident,' Carl continued, 'so you'd have to be a bit of a conspiracy nerd to think otherwise. At the same time, we in Department Q are a bunch of sceptical devils, and that's probably why we were given this assignment.' Everyone smiled a bit. At least they were listening. 'So I'm going to ask all of you a number of questions, and don't hesitate to speak up if you have anything to say.'

Most of them nodded again.

'Do any of you remember whether Merete had a meeting with a group lobbying for placenta research shortly before she disappeared?'

'Yes, I do,' said someone from the party office. 'It was a delegation put together for the occasion by Bille Antvorskov from BasicGen.'

'Bille Antvorskov? You mean *the* Bille Antvorskov? The billionaire?'

'Yes, that's right. He put together the group and arranged a meeting with Merete. They were making the rounds.'

'Making the rounds? With Merete Lynggaard?'

'No.' The woman smiled. 'That's what we call it when a special-interest lobby meets with all the parties, one after the other. The group was trying to put together a majority of votes in the Folketing.'

'Would there be a record of the meeting anywhere?'

'Yes, there should be. I don't know whether it was printed out, but we might be able to find it on the computer belonging to Merete's secretary.'

'Does that computer still exist?' asked Carl. He could hardly believe what he was hearing.

The woman from the party office smiled. 'We always save the hard drives when we change operating systems. When we switched to Windows XP, at least ten hard drives had to be replaced.'

'Aren't all of you on a network?'

'Yes, we are, but back then Merete's secretary and a few others weren't hooked up to it.'

'Paranoid, perhaps?' He smiled at the woman.

'Maybe.'

'Would you be willing to try to find the minutes of that meeting for me?'

She nodded again.

He turned to the rest of the group. 'One of the participants at that meeting was a man named Daniel Hale. From what I've heard, he and Merete were interested in each other. Is there anyone here who can confirm or expand on this?'

Several people exchanged glances. Apparently he'd hit home again. Now it was just a matter of who wanted to answer.

'I don't know his name, but I saw her talking to a man down in Snapstinget, the MPs' restaurant.' It was the party spokesperson who decided to take the floor. She was an irritating but tough young lady who looked good on TV and would obviously hold major ministry posts in the future, when the right time came. 'She looked very pleased to see him, and she seemed rather distracted while she was talking with the chairpersons from the Socialist's and Radical Centre's health committees.' She smiled. 'I think plenty of people noticed.'

'Because Merete didn't usually act that way? Is that what you mean?'

'I think it was the first time anyone here had ever seen Merete's attention waver. Yes, it was highly unusual.'

'Could he have been this Daniel Hale that I mentioned?'

'I don't know.'

'Is there anyone else who knows about this?'

They all shook their heads.

'How would you describe the man?' was Carl's next question for the party spokesperson.

'He was slightly hidden by the pillar he was sitting behind, but he was slim and well dressed and suntanned, as far as I remember.'

'How old was he?'

She shrugged. 'A little older than Merete, I think.'

Slim, well dressed, a little older than Merete. If she hadn't said that he was suntanned, the description would have applied to all the men in the room, including himself, if one didn't mind adding five or ten years at the wrong end.

'I imagine there must have been a lot of documents from Merete's time that couldn't simply be dumped on her successor.' He nodded at Birger Larsen. 'I'm thinking about appointment diaries, notebooks, handwritten notes and things like that. Were those sorts of things just thrown out or shredded? No one could really know whether she would be coming back, could they?'

Again it was the woman from the party office who responded. 'The police took some of it, and some of it was discarded. I don't think much was left.'

'What about her appointment diary? Where did that end up?'

She shrugged. 'Not here, anyway.'

Marianne Koch broke in. 'Merete always took her diary home with her.' Her tone of voice did not invite contradiction. 'Always,' she emphasized.

'What did it look like?'

'It was a very ordinary time system calendar, in a worn, reddish-brown leather cover. A daily planner, appointment book, notebook and phone list all in one.'

'And it hasn't turned up,' Carl added. 'That much I know. So we have to assume that it disappeared into the sea with her.'

'I don't believe that,' the secretary replied at once.

'Why not?'

'Because Merete always carried a small purse, and the diary simply wouldn't fit inside. She almost always put it in her briefcase, instead, and I can guarantee that she wouldn't take her briefcase along to stand on the sun deck of a ship. She was on holiday, after all, so why would she take it with her? It wasn't in her car, either, was it?'

Carl shook his head. Not as far as he could recall.

Carl had been waiting a long time for the crisis counsellor with the lovely arse, and now he was starting to feel uneasy. If she'd arrived on time, he would have let his natural charm guide him forward, but now, after having repeated his lines in his mind and practised his smiles for more than twenty minutes, he was feeling deflated.

She didn't look particularly guilt-stricken when she finally made her arrival on the third floor, but she did apologize. It was the sort of self-confidence that drove Carl wild. It was also what he'd fallen for when he first met Vigga. That and her infectious laugh.

Mona Ibsen sat down across from him. The light from outside on Otto Mønsteds Gade shone on the back of her neck, creating a halo around her head. The soft light revealed delicate lines on her face; her lips were sensual and a deep red. Everything about her signalled high class. Carl locked eyes with her so as not to dwell on her voluptuous breasts. Nothing in the world could make him want to break out of the state he was in.

She asked him about the case out in Amager. Wanted to know about the specific timeline, actions and consequences. She asked him about everything that was of no significance, and Carl laid it on thick. A little more blood than in reality. Shots that were a little more powerful, sighs a little deeper. And she stared at him intently, making note of the key points in his story. When he got to the moment when he had to talk about the impression it had made on him to see his dead and wounded friends and how badly he'd been sleeping ever since, she pushed her chair back from the table, placed her business card in front of him, and began to pack up her things.

'What's going on?' he asked as her notebook disappeared into her leather briefcase.

'It seems to me that you should be asking yourself that

question. When you're ready to tell the truth, make another appointment to see me.'

He gave her a frown. 'What does that mean? Everything I just told you is exactly how it happened.'

She pulled the briefcase close to the slight curve of her stomach under the tight skirt. 'First of all, I can tell by looking at you that you have no trouble sleeping. Second, you've really been exaggerating the details of your whole account. Or did you think I hadn't read the report in advance?' He was about to protest when she held up her hand. 'Third, I can see it in your eyes when you mention Hardy Henningsen and Anker Høyer. I don't know why, but you've got some unfinished business with that incident. And when you mention your two colleagues who weren't as lucky to escape with their lives and limbs intact, it reminds you of something, and you practically come unglued. When you're ready to tell me the truth, I'll be happy to see you again. Until then, I can't help you.'

He uttered a small sound that was meant as a protest, but it died out of its own accord. Instead, he looked at her with an expression of desire that women no doubt could read but could never know for sure was there.

'Wait a minute,' he forced himself to say before she went out the door. 'You're probably right. I just didn't realize it.'

He frantically considered what he could say to her before she turned around and made a move to leave.

'Maybe we could talk about it over dinner?' The words just flew out of his mouth.

He saw that he'd misfired badly. It was such a stupid thing to say that she didn't even bother to deride him.

Instead, she gave him a look that expressed concern more than anything else.

Bille Antvorskov had just turned seventy and was a regular guest on TV 2's *Good Morning Denmark* and other talk shows. He was a so-called expert, and was therefore presumed to know something about everything between heaven and earth. That's how it was when Danes took someone seriously; they went all out. But the man also looked good on camera. Authoritative and mature, with striking brown eyes, a distinctive jaw, and an aura that paired the wits of a street kid with the discreet charm of the bourgeoisie. And then there was the undeniable fact that he'd amassed a fortune in record time, one that would soon be reckoned among the largest in all of Denmark. On top of which, it was a fortune that had been built on high-risk medical projects carried out in the public interest, which led Danish viewers to prostrate themselves with admiration and respect.

Personally, Carl couldn't stand the man.

Even in the receptionist's office, Carl was made aware that time was short and Bille Antvorskov was a busy man. Seated along the wall were four gentlemen, and it was obvious that none of them wanted anything to do with the others. They had placed their briefcases on the floor between their feet and their laptops on their knees. They were all busy as hell, and they all dreaded what they would encounter behind the closed door.

The secretary smiled at Carl, but she didn't really mean it. He had summarily forced his way into her appointment book; she just hoped he wouldn't do it again.

Her boss received Carl with a characteristically wry

smile and asked politely if he'd ever been in this part of the office complex on the edge of Copenhagen's harbour. Then he gestured towards the huge picture windows that stretched from one wall to the other, sketching a glass mosaic of the multifarious state of the entire world: the ships, harbour, cranes, water and sky, fighting for attention in all their grandiosity.

The view from Carl's office wasn't quite as good.

'You wanted to talk to me about the meeting at Christiansborg on the 20th of February 2002. I have it here,' said Antvorskov, typing on the computer keyboard. 'Well, look at that: it's a palindrome. How funny.'

'Say what?'

'The date: 20.02.2002. It's the same whether you read it backwards or forwards. I can also see that I was visiting my ex-wife at precisely 20:02. We celebrated with a glass of champagne.' And then he added in English, 'Once in a lifetime!' After which he smiled, and that part of the entertainment was over.

'I take it you wanted to know what the meeting with Merete Lynggaard was about?' he went on.

'Yes, that's right. But first I'd like to hear something about Daniel Hale. What was his role at the meeting?'

'Hmm. It's funny that you should mention it, but he didn't actually have a role there. Daniel Hale was one of our most important developers of laboratory techniques. Without his lab and his excellent co-workers, a great number of our projects would have just hobbled along.'

'So he didn't participate in project development?'

'Not the political or financial side of development, no. Only the technical side.'

'Then why was he at the meeting?'

Antvorskov bit his cheek for a moment, a conciliatory habit. 'As far as I remember, he phoned and asked to attend. I no longer recall the reason, but apparently he was planning to invest a lot of money in new equipment, and he needed to keep up to date with political developments. He was a very diligent man; that may have been why we worked so well together.'

Carl caught the man's self-admiration. Some businessmen made it a virtue to hide their light under a bushel. Bille Antvorskov was of a different breed.

'What was Hale like as a person, in your opinion?'

'As a person?' Antvorskov shook his head. 'I have no idea. Reliable and conscientious as a subcontractor. But as a person? I have no idea.'

'So you didn't have anything to do with him privately?'

This provoked the famous Bille Antvorskov growl that was supposed to pass for laughter. 'Privately? I never set eyes on him until the meeting at Christiansborg. Neither he nor I had time for that. And besides, Daniel Hale was never at home. He would fly from Herod to Pilate in an instant. One day in Connecticut, the next day in Aalborg. Back and forth, constantly. I've probably scraped together a few free miles myself, but Daniel Hale must have left behind enough to fly a class of school kids around the world at least a dozen times.'

'So you'd never met him before that meeting?'

'No, never.'

'But there must have been meetings, discussions, price negotiations. Things like that?'

'You know what? I have staff to handle those things.

226

I knew Daniel Hale by reputation, we had a few phone conversations, and then we were in business. The rest of the collaborative work was handled by Hale's people and mine.'

'OK. I'd like to talk to someone here at the company who worked with Hale. Is that possible?'

Bille Antvorskov sighed so heavily that the tightly upholstered leather chair he was sitting on creaked. 'I don't know who's still here. That was five years ago, after all. There's a lot of turnover in our business. Everyone's always looking for new challenges.'

'I see.' Was the idiot really admitting that he couldn't hold on to employees? He couldn't be. 'Could you possibly give me the address of his company?'

Antvorskov frowned. He had staff to handle that.

Even though the buildings were six years old, they looked as if they'd been constructed only a week ago. 'InterLab A/S' it said in three-foot-tall letters on the sign in the middle of the landscape of fountains in front of the car park. Apparently the business was doing just fine without its helmsman.

In the reception area Carl's police badge was scrutinized as if it were something he'd bought in a practical joke shop, but after a ten-minute wait a secretary arrived to speak with him. He told her that he had questions of a private nature, and with that he was immediately escorted out of the lobby and into a room with leather chairs, birchwood tables and several glass cabinets full of beverages. Presumably it was here that foreign guests first encountered InterLab's efficiency. Proof of the laboratory's high status was everywhere. Awards and certificates from all over the world covered one whole wall, while another two displayed diagrams and photographs of various projects. Only the wall facing the Japanese-inspired driveway leading up to the building had any windows, and the sun was blazing in.

Apparently it was Daniel Hale's father who founded the firm, but this was long ago, judging by the photos on the wall. Daniel had successfully followed in his father's footsteps in the short time that he'd been boss, and clearly he'd done so with pleasure. There was also no doubt that he'd been loved and given plenty of incentives in the right direction. A single photo showed father and son standing close together, smiling happily. The father wore a jacket and waistcoat, symbolizing the old days that were on their way out. The son had not yet come of age, which was obvious from his smooth cheeks and big smile. But he was ready to make his mark.

Carl heard footsteps approaching.

'What was it you wanted to know, sir?' said a plump woman wearing flats.

The woman introduced herself as the public relations manager. The name on her ID badge, which was clipped to her lapel, was 'Aino Huurinainen'. Finns had such funny-sounding names.

'I'd like to talk to someone who worked closely with Daniel Hale in the time before he died. Someone who knew him well privately. Someone who knew what his thoughts and dreams were.'

She looked at him as if he'd assaulted her.

'Could you put me in touch with someone like that?'

'I don't think anyone knew him better than our sales director, Niels Bach Nielsen. But I'm afraid he doesn't wish to speak with you about Mr Hale's personal life.'

'And why not? Does he have something to hide?'

She gave him another look as if he were making a serious attempt to provoke her. 'Neither Niels nor Daniel had anything to hide. But Niels has never recovered from Daniel's death.'

He caught the undertone. 'You mean they were a couple?'

'Yes. Niels and Daniel were together through thick and thin, both in private and at work.'

For a moment Carl stared into her pale blue eyes. He wouldn't have been surprised if she suddenly doubled over with laughter. But that didn't happen. What she had just said was no joke.

'I didn't know that,' he said.

'I see,' she replied.

'You wouldn't happen to have a photograph of Daniel Hale, would you? One that you could spare?'

She stretched out her arm a few inches to the right and grabbed a brochure lying on the glass counter next to half a dozen bottles of Ramlösa mineral water.

'Here,' she said. 'There ought to be at least ten of them.'

He didn't get through to Bille Antvorskov on the phone until he'd had a lengthy discussion with the billionaire's grumpy secretary.

'I've scanned a picture that I'd like to email to you. Have you got a couple of minutes to take a look at it?' he said, after identifying himself.

Antvorskov acquiesced and gave Carl his email address. Carl clicked the mouse and looked at the computer screen as he transferred the file.

It was an excellent picture of Daniel Hale that he'd scanned from the brochure the public relations woman had given him. A slender blond man, quite tall, suntanned and well dressed, as everyone had noticed over in the MPs' restaurant. There was nothing about his appearance to indicate he was gay. Apparently he had other sexual inclinations. About to come out of the closet as a heterosexual, thought Carl, as he pictured the man, crushed and burned to death on the Kappelev highway.

'OK, the email has arrived,' said Bille Antvorskov on the other end of the line. 'I'm opening the attachment now.' There was a pause that seemed to go on for a very long time. 'What am I supposed to do with this?'

'Can you confirm that it's a photo of Daniel Hale? Was this the man who took part in the meeting at Christiansborg?'

'This man? I've never seen him before in my life.'

26

2005

When she turned thirty-five, the sea of light from the fluorescent tubes on the ceiling returned, thus causing the faces behind the mirrored panes to vanish.

This time not all of the tubes in the reinforced-glass fixtures went on. One day they're going to have to come in and change them or the room will end up in eternal darkness, she thought. They're still standing there, spying on me, and they don't want to have to stop. One day they'll come inside and change the tubes. They'll bleed off the pressure ever so slowly, and then I'll be waiting for them.

They'd increased the pressure again on her last birthday, but that no longer worried her. If she could handle four atmospheres, she could also handle five. She didn't know what the limit was, but they hadn't come anywhere near it yet. Just like the previous year, she had hallucinations for a couple of days. It felt as if the background of the room was spinning around while the rest remained in sharp focus. She had sung and felt light-hearted, reality had become meaningless. This time everything returned to normal after only a couple of days. Then she began noticing a howling sound in her ears. At first it was very faint, so she yawned and tried to equalize the pressure as best she could, but after two weeks the sound became permanent. An utterly clear tone, like the one accompanying

231

the test pattern on TV. Higher in register, purer, and a hundred times more enervating. It'll go away, Merete, you'll get used to the pressure. Just wait, one morning it'll be gone when you wake up. It'll be gone, it'll be gone, she promised herself. But promises based on ignorance always prove disappointing. When the high-pitched tone had lasted for three months and she was about to go crazy from lack of sleep and the constant reminder that she was living in a death chamber at the mercy of her executioner, she began working out in her mind how she would take her own life.

She knew now that it would all end with her dying anyway. The woman's face had not displayed the slightest grounds for hope. Those piercing eyes were a clear indication they would not allow her to escape. Not ever. So it would be better to die by her own hand. To decide for herself how it would happen.

The room was completely empty aside from the toilet bucket and the food bucket, the pocket torch, the two plastic stiffeners from her down jacket – one of which she'd made into a toothpick – a couple of rolls of toilet paper, and the clothes she was wearing. The walls were smooth. There was nothing to which she could tie the sleeves of her jacket, nothing from which her body could dangle until it was delivered from this life. The only possibility left to her was to starve herself to death. Refuse to eat the monotonous diet, refuse to drink the small amount of water they allowed her. Maybe that was what they were waiting for. Maybe she was part of some sick wager. Since time immemorial, human beings had always transformed the suffering of fellow humans into entertainment. Each stratum of human history had revealed an infinitely thick layer of callousness. And the sediment forming new layers was constantly piling up; she was finding that out for herself now. That was why she made the decision.

She pushed the food bucket aside, stood herself in front of one of the portholes and declared that she would no longer eat any of the food. She'd had enough. Then she lay down on the floor and wrapped herself in her ragged clothes and her dreams. According to her calculations, it had to be 6 October. She figured she'd last a week. At that time she would have lived for thirty-five years, three months and one week. To be more precise: twelve thousand, eight hundred and sixty-four days, although she wasn't entirely sure. She would have no headstone. There would be no birth date or death date to see anywhere. Not a thing left after her death that might link her to the time she'd spent in this cage, where she'd spent this last long period of her life. Other than her killers, she was the only one who would know the date of her death. And she alone would know it beforehand, with more or less accuracy. On approximately the 13th of October 2005, she intended to die.

On the second day of her refusal to eat, they shouted to her to trade out the buckets, but she refused. What could they do? Either leave the bucket in the hatch of the airlock door or take it back. It was all the same to her.

So they left the bucket in the hatch and repeated the same ritual over the next couple of days. The old bucket out and a new one in. They yelled at her. Threatened to increase the pressure and then let all the air out. But how could they use death as a threat when it was death she desired? Maybe they would come in, maybe they wouldn't, she didn't care. She let her mind run amok with thoughts and images and memories that could push the nowling in her ears away, and on the fifth day, everything merged into one. Dreams of happiness, her political work, Uffe standing alone on the ship, love that had been shoved aside, the children she'd never had, *Mr Bean* and quiet days in front of the television. And she noticed how her body slowly loosened its grip on its unfulfilled needs. Gradually she lay lighter on the floor; a strange stagnation took over, and time passed as the food in the bucket next to her began to rot.

Everything was as it should be, and then all of sudden she felt a throbbing in her jaw.

In her listless condition, it felt at first like a vibration from outside. Just enough to make her open her eyes slightly, but nothing more. Are they coming in? What's happening? she thought briefly, and then fell back into a silent torpor until a couple of hours later when she awoke with a pain as sharp as a knife stabbing into her face.

She had no idea what time it was; she had no idea if they were out there; and she screamed as she'd never screamed before in that barren room. Her whole face felt as if it had split in two. The pain in her tooth felt like a jackhammer pounding in her mouth, and there was nothing she could do to fight it. Oh God, was this the punishment for taking her life into her own hands? She'd neglected looking after herself for only five days, and now this torment. Cautiously she stuck her finger inside her mouth and felt the abscess around the back molar. That tooth had always been a weak point, providing a steady income for her dentist. A bad spot, which her homemade toothpick had tried to keep clean every day. She carefully pressed on the abscess and felt the pain explode through bone and marrow. She doubled over, opened her mouth wide, and gasped frantically for air. A short time ago her body had succumbed to lethargy, but now it had awakened to this torturous agony. She felt like an animal that would have to chew off its own paw to slip out of a trap. If pain was a defence against death, then she was more alive now than ever before.

'Ohhh!' she sobbed. It hurt so much. She reached for her toothpick and slowly held it up to her mouth. Cautiously she tried to find out whether something stuck in her gums had caused the infection, but as soon as the tip touched the abscess, her tooth once more exploded in agony.

You have to puncture it, Merete. Come on, she told herself, weeping, and jabbed at it again. The little that was left in her stomach threatened to come up. She had to puncture the abscess, but she couldn't. She simply couldn't do it.

Instead she crawled over to the airlock door to see what they'd put in the bucket that day. Maybe there was something that might offer some relief. Or perhaps a little drop of water on the abscess would make it stop throbbing so badly.

She looked down at the bucket and saw temptations she'd never dared dream of before. Two bananas, an apple, a piece of chocolate. It was totally absurd. They were trying to bait her hunger. Force her to eat, and now she couldn't. Couldn't and wouldn't.

She grimaced at the next stabs of pain that nearly knocked her over. Then she took out all the pieces of fruit and placed them on the floor, thrust her hand in the bucket and grabbed the water bottle. She stuck her finger in the water and held it up to the abscess, but the icy-cold water didn't have the expected effect. There was the pain and there was the water, and they had absolutely nothing to do with each other. The water couldn't even assuage her thirst.

So she moved away, curled up in a foetal position underneath the mirrored panes, and prayed a silent prayer for God's forgiveness. At some point her body would give up; she knew that. She would have to live her last days in pain.

Eventually it, too, would give up.

The voices came to her as if she was in a trance. They were calling her name. Entreating her to answer them. She opened her eyes and noticed at once that the abscess had stopped throbbing, and that her limp body was still lying next to the toilet bucket beneath the mirrored panes. She stared up at the ceiling, noticing that one of the fluorescent tubes had started to flicker faintly in the fixture high above her. She'd heard voices, hadn't she? Were they real?

Then a clear voice that she'd never heard before spoke: 'That's right, she took out the fruit.'

It's real, she thought, but she was too weak to be startled.

It was a man's voice. Not a young man, but not an old man either.

She immediately raised her head, but not so much that they'd be able to see her from outside.

'I can see the fruit from where I'm standing,' said a woman's voice. 'It's over there on the floor.' It was the same woman who had spoken to Merete once a year; the voice was unmistakable. Apparently the people outside had been calling to her and had then forgotten to shut off the intercom.

'She's crawled over between the windows. I'm sure of it,' the woman went on.

'Do you think she's dead? It's been a week, you know,' said the man's voice. It sounded so natural, but it wasn't. This was her they were talking about.

'It would be just like her to do something like that, the little slut.'

'Should we equalize the pressure and go in and have a look?'

'What were you planning to do with her then? All of the cells in her body have acclimated to five atmospheres of pressure. It would take weeks to decompress her body. If we open the door now, she'll not only get the bends, she'll explode on the spot. You've seen her faeces and how it expands. And her urine, how it bubbles and boils. Keep in mind that she's been living in a pressure chamber for three and a half years now.'

'Can't we just pump up the pressure again after we find out whether she's still alive?'

The woman outside didn't answer, but it was clear that under no circumstances was that going to happen.

Merete's breathing became more and more laboured. The voices belonged to devils. They'd flay her and sew her back together for an eternity, if they could. She was in the inner circle of hell. The place where the torments never ceased.

Come on in, you bastards, she thought, cautiously pulling the pocket torch closer as the whining in her ears got louder. She was going to plant it in the eye of the first person who came near her. Blind the vile creature who dared to set foot in her holy chamber. It was the one thing she'd manage to do before she died.

'We're not doing anything until Lasse gets back. Do you hear me?' said the woman in a tone of voice that demanded obedience.

'But that'll take forever. She'll be dead long before then,' replied the man. 'What the hell should we do? Lasse is going to be furious.'

Then came a silence that was nauseating and oppressive, as if the walls of the room were about to contract and leave her there, like a louse squeezed between two fingernails.

She clutched the pocket torch even tighter in her hand and waited. All of a sudden the pain was back with a wallop. She opened her eyes wide and drew air deep into her lungs to release the pain in a reflexive scream, but no sound came out. Then she got herself under control. The feeling of nausea remained, and the sensation that she was about to throw up made her regurgitate, but she didn't say a word. She merely tilted her head back and let the tears flow down her face and over her parched lips.

I can hear them, but they mustn't hear me, she chanted soundlessly over and over. She clutched her throat, fanned her hand over the bulge in her cheek, and rocked back and forth, clenching and unclenching her free hand ceaselessly. Every nerve fibre in her body was aware of the excruciating pain.

And then the scream came. It had a life of its own. Her body demanded it. A deep, hollow scream that went on and on and on.

'She's there. Do you hear that? I knew it.' There was a clicking sound from a switch. 'Come out so we can see you,' said the revolting female voice. Only then did they discover that something was wrong.

'Wait a minute,' she said. 'The switch is stuck.'

Then the woman started tapping on the intercom switch, but it did no good.

'Have you been lying there eavesdropping on what we were saying, you little bitch?' She sounded like an animal. Her voice was raw, honed with years of cruelty and callousness.

'Lasse will fix it when he gets here,' said the man outside. 'He'll fix it. It really doesn't matter.'

Now it felt as if her jaw would split in two. Merete didn't want to react, but she had no choice. She had to stand up. Anything to distract the hammering sense of panic in her body. She propped herself up on her knees, noticing how weak she was, then pushed off and managed to sit back on her heels, feeling the fire ignite again inside her mouth. She set one knee on the floor and managed to stand halfway up.

'Good Lord, look at you, girl,' said the ghastly voice outside, and then it began to laugh. The laughter struck Merete like a hailstorm of scalpels. 'You have a toothache,' said the laughing voice. 'Ye gods, the filthy slut has a tooth-ache. Look at her.'

Merete turned abruptly to face the mirrored panes. The mere act of moving her lips felt worse than death. 'I'll get my revenge one day,' she whispered, pressing her face close to the pane. 'I'll get my revenge. Just wait.'

'If you don't eat, you're going to end up burning in hell without ever having that satisfaction,' snarled the woman, but there was something more in her voice. Like a cat playing with a mouse, and the cat wasn't done playing yet. They wanted their prisoner to live. Live for as long as they had decided, and no longer.

'I *can't* eat,' Merete groaned.

'Is it an abscess?' asked the man's voice.

She nodded.

'You'll have to deal with it yourself,' he said coldly.

Merete stared at her reflection in one of the portholes. The poor woman before her had hollow cheeks and her eyes looked as if they might fall out of her head. The upper part of her face was distorted from the abscess, and the dark circles under her eyes told their own story. She looked deathly ill, and she was.

She set her back against the glass and slowly slid down to the floor. There she sat, with tears of anger in her eyes and a new awareness that her body wanted to live and was capable of doing so. She would take whatever was in the bucket and force herself to swallow it. The pain would either kill her or it wouldn't; time would tell. In any case, she would not give up without a fight, because she had just made a promise to that awful bitch out there. A promise she was determined to keep. At some point that disgusting woman would get a taste of her own medicine.

For a moment Merete's body felt calm, like a shattered landscape in the eye of a hurricane, and then the pain was back. This time she screamed as uninhibitedly as she could. She felt the pus from her gum flow on to her tongue and how the throbbing of the toothache spread all the way to her temple.

Then she heard the whistling of the airlock door, and a new bucket came into view.

'Here! We've put some first aid in the bucket for you. Go ahead and take it,' laughed the woman's voice outside.

Merete quickly crawled over to the hatch on all fours and pulled out the bucket. She looked inside.

Way down at the bottom, lying on a piece of fabric just like a surgical instrument, was a pair of tongs.

A big pair of tongs. Big and rusty.

27

2007

Carl's morning had been an oppressive one. First bad dreams and then Jesper's griping at breakfast had drained him of energy even before he sank into the driver's seat of his car, only to discover the petrol gauge pointing to empty. The forty-five minutes that he then spent sitting in the exhaust fumes of the small stretch of motorway between Nymøllevej and Værløse didn't do much to encourage the side of his personality that might manifest charm, amiability and patience.

When he was finally sitting at his desk in the basement of police headquarters, he found himself staring at the sparks of energy apparent in Assad's morning-fresh face. That was when he considered going upstairs to Marcus Jacobsen's office and smashing a few chairs so he'd be sent off someplace where they'd take good care of him. Where he would only need to pay attention to all the world's misfortunes when the evening news appeared on TV.

Carl nodded wearily to his assistant. If he could only get the man to contain his high spirits for a moment, then perhaps his own inner batteries might have a chance to recharge. He glanced at the coffeemaker, saw that it was empty, and then accepted the tiny cup that Assad handed him.

'I do not entirely understand it, Carl,' said Assad. 'You say that Daniel Hale is dead, but he was not the one who came to the meeting at Christiansborg. So who was that man then?'

'I have no idea, Assad, but Hale had nothing to do with Merete Lynggaard. Whoever came in Hale's place did, however.' He took a sip of Assad's mint tea. Without the four or five spoonfuls of sugar, it might actually be drinkable.

'But how could this other guy know that the billionaire who was boss of the meeting up at Christiansborg had never seen Daniel Hale in reality then?'

'That's a good question. Maybe this man and Hale knew each other somehow.' Carl set his cup on the desk and looked up at the bulletin board, where he had pinned up the brochure from InterLab A/S with Daniel Hale's well-groomed likeness.

'So it was not Hale who delivered the letter, was it? And he was not the man who had dinner with Merete Lynggaard at the Bankeråt, right?'

'According to Hale's colleagues, he wasn't even in the country at the time.' Carl turned to look at his assistant. 'What did the police report say about Daniel Hale's car after the accident? Do you remember? Was everything a hundred per cent in order? Did they find any defects that might have caused the accident?'

'You mean, were the brakes fine?'

'The brakes. Steering mechanism. Everything. Was there any sign of sabotage?'

Assad shrugged. 'It was difficult to see anything, because the car burned up, Carl. But it was then probably believed to be an ordinary accident, as I can understand that report.'

That was how Carl remembered it too. Nothing suspicious.

'And there were no witnesses who can say otherwise?'

They exchanged glances.

'I know, Assad. I know.'

'Only him, the man who drove into him.'

'Exactly.' Without thinking, Carl took a gulp of the mint tea, which made him shudder. He certainly wasn't going to get addicted to this swill.

Carl considered taking a cigarette or a throat lozenge out of the desk drawer, but he didn't have enough energy even for that. It was a hell of a development. Here he was, just about to close up the damn case and now this turn of events had to happen, pointing to unexplored aspects. An endless workload suddenly loomed before him, and this was just one case. There were forty or fifty more stacked on the desk in front of him.

'What about him, the witness in the other car, Carl? Shouldn't we talk to that man who Daniel Hale crashed into?'

'I've got Lis trying to track him down.'

For a moment Assad looked thoroughly disappointed.

'But I've got a different assignment for you.'

An oddly blissful change in mood brought a smile to his lips.

'I want you to drive down to Holtug in Stevns and talk to the home help, Helle Andersen, one more time. Ask her if she recognizes Daniel Hale as the man who personally delivered the letter. Take his picture with you.' He pointed at the bulletin board.

'But he was not the one, it was him, the other one who –'

Carl stopped Assad with a wave of his hand. 'You know that, and I know that. But if she says no, as we expect her to do, then ask her whether Daniel Hale looked anything like the guy with the letter. We need to get a better description of the man, OK? And one more thing: Ask her whether Uffe was there and might have caught a glimpse of the man who brought the letter. And finally, ask her whether she remembers where Merete used to put her briefcase when she came home. Tell her it's black and has a big rip on one side. It was her father's, and he had it in the car when the accident happened, so it must have meant a lot to her.' Carl raised his hand again as Assad was about to say something. 'And afterwards, drive over to see the antique dealers who bought Merete's house in Magleby and ask them if they've seen a briefcase like that anywhere. We'll talk about everything tomorrow, OK? You can take the car home with you. I'll take cabs today, and later I can catch the train home.'

By now Assad was flailing his arms about.

'Yes, Assad?'

'Just a minute, right? I have to find a writing book. Will you please just say everything one more time?'

Hardy had looked worse. Previously his head resembled something that had melted into the pillow, but now it was lifted enough so that the fine blood vessels were visible, pulsing in his temples. He lay there with eyes closed, and he seemed more peaceful than he had in a long time. For a moment Carl thought maybe he should leave. Some of the equipment had been removed from the room, even though the respirator was of course still pumping. All in all, it seemed a good sign.

He turned carefully on his heel and was just taking a step towards the door when Hardy's voice stopped him.

'Where are you going? Can't you stand to see a man flat on his back?'

Carl turned around and saw Hardy lying exactly as when he'd entered the room.

'If you want people to stay, you ought to make some sort of sign that you're awake, Hardy. You could open your eyes, for example.'

'No. Not today. I don't feel like opening my eyes today.'

Carl needed to hear that one again.

'If there's going to be any difference in my days, then I should be allowed to decide whether or not to open my eyes, OK?'

'Yeah. OK.'

'Tomorrow I'm planning on looking only to the right.'

'OK,' said Carl, even though Hardy's words hurt deep in his soul. 'You've talked to Assad a couple of times now, Hardy. Was it all right with you that I sent him over here?'

'It sure as hell wasn't,' he said, hardly moving his lips.

'Yeah, well, I did. And I've been thinking of sending him over here as often as I need to. Do you have any objections?'

'Only if he brings those spicy, grilled things again.'

'I'll let him know.'

Something that might be interpreted as laughter slipped out of Hardy's body. 'They made me shit like I've never shit before. The nurses were really upset.'

Carl tried not to picture the scene. It didn't sound pleasant.

'I'll tell Assad, Hardy. No spicy, grilled things next time.'

'Is there anything new in the Lynggaard case?' asked Hardy. This was the first time since he was paralysed that he'd expressed curiosity about anything. Carl could feel the heat rising to his cheeks. In a moment he'd probably have a lump in his throat, too.

'Yeah, you bet.' And then he told Hardy about the latest development with Daniel Hale.

'You know what I think, Carl?' Hardy said afterwards.

'You think the case has got a new lease of life.'

'Exactly. The whole thing stinks to high heaven.' He opened his eyes for a moment and looked up at the ceiling before he closed them again. 'Do you have any political leads to investigate?'

'Not in the slightest.'

'Have you talked to the press?'

'What do you mean?'

'One of the political commentators at Christiansborg. They've always got their noses in everything. Or what about the tabloids? Pelle Hyttested at *Gossip*, for instance. That little weasel has been gleefully digging dirt out of the woodwork at Christiansborg ever since he was fired from *Aktuelt*, so he's an old hand there by now. Ask him, and you'll know more than you do now.' A smile appeared on Hardy's face, and then it was gone.

I'll tell him now, thought Carl, and then he spoke very slowly so that it would sink in properly, right from the start. 'There's been a murder down in Sorø, Hardy. I think it's the same guys who were out in Amager.'

Hardy's expression didn't change. 'And?' he said.

'Yeah, well, the same circumstances, the same weapon, the same red-checked shirt presumably, the same group of people, the same –'

'I said, "And?"'

247

'Well, that's why I'm telling you all this.'

'I said, "And?" Meaning, "And what the hell do I care?"'

Gossip's editorial office was in that in-between phase when the weekly deadline had been met and the next issue was just starting to take shape. A couple of journalists glanced at Carl without interest as he walked through the open office landscape. Apparently they didn't recognize him, which was just as well.

He found Pelle Hyttested preening his well-trimmed but skimpy red beard over in a corner where an eternal lethargy had descended upon the senior journalists. Carl was well acquainted with Hyttested's reputation as a scumbag and an arsehole that only money could stop. It was incomprehensible why so many Danes loved to read the overwrought trash that he wrote, but his victims didn't share their enthusiasm. There was a long queue of lawsuits waiting outside Hyttested's door, but the editor-in-chief held a protective hand over his favourite little demon. To hell with it if the editor-in-chief had to pay a few fines along the way.

The man cast a brief glance at Carl's police badge and turned back to his colleagues.

Carl placed a hand on his shoulder. 'I've got a couple of questions for you, I said.'

Hyttested looked right through him when he turned to face Carl again. 'Can't you see I'm working? Or maybe you'd like to take me down to the station . . .'

It was at this point that Carl pulled from his wallet the thousand-kroner note that he'd been saving for months and stuck it in front of the journalist's nose.

'What was it you wanted to see me about?' asked the man, trying to suck up the bill with his eyes. Maybe he was working out in his mind how many late-night hours the money could keep him going at Andy's Bar.

'I'm investigating the disappearance of Merete Lynggaard. My colleague Hardy Henningsen thinks you might be able to tell me whether Merete had any reason to fear somebody in political circles.'

'Fear somebody? That's an odd way to put it,' he said, stroking the almost invisible tufts of hair on his face. 'Why are you asking me about this? Has something new turned up in that case?'

Now the cross-examination was moving in the wrong direction.

'Something new? No, nothing like that. But the case has reached the point where certain questions need to be resolved once and for all.'

Hyttested nodded, obviously unimpressed. 'Five years after she disappeared? Come on, you've got to be kidding. Why don't you tell me what you know instead, and then I'll tell you what I know.'

Carl waved the banknote again so the man's attention would be drawn to what was essential.

'So you have no knowledge of anyone who might have been especially angry with Merete Lynggaard at the time? Is that what you're telling me?'

'Everybody hated the bitch. If it hadn't been for her fucking beautiful tits, she would have been tossed out long ago.'

Not a supporter of the Democrats, Carl gathered. It could hardly come as a surprise. 'OK, so you don't know anything.' He turned to the others in the room. 'Do any of you know anything? Anything at all. It doesn't have to be related to Christiansborg. Maybe some wild rumours. Or people who were seen around her while your paparazzi were on the prowl. Vague impressions. Ring any bells?' He looked at Hyttested's colleagues. It would be easy to diagnose at least half of them as brain-dead. They looked at him with blank eyes that said they didn't give a shit.

He turned around to look at the rest of the office. Maybe one of the younger journalists who still had some life in his skull would have something to say. If not from first-hand experience, then maybe third- or fourth-hand. This was gossip central, after all.

'Did you say that Hardy Henningsen sent you here?' asked Hyttested as he crept closer to the thousand-kroner note. 'Maybe it was you who fucked things up for him. I remember very clearly reading something about a Carl Mørck. Isn't that your name? You're the one who took cover under one of your colleagues. The guy who lay underneath Hardy Henningsen and played dead. That's you, right?'

Carl felt the Greenland ice cap creeping up his spine. How in the world had the guy come to that conclusion? All of the internal hearings had been closed to the public. No one had ever even hinted at what this shithead was now insinuating.

'Are you saying that because you want me to grab you by the collar, crush you flat and then shove you under the carpet, so you'll have something to write about next week?' Carl moved in so close that Hyttested chose to fix his eyes on the banknote again. 'Hardy Henningsen was the best colleague anyone could ever have. I would have died for him, if I could. Do you get me?'

Hyttested looked over his shoulder to give his co-workers a triumphant look. Shit. Now the headline for the next issue was in the bag, and Carl was the casualty. Now all they needed was a photographer to immortalize the situation. He'd better get out while he could.

'Do I get the thousand kroner if I tell you which photographer specialized in taking pictures of Merete Lynggaard?'

'What good would that do me?'

'I don't know. Maybe it would help. You're a cop, aren't you? Can you really afford to ignore a tip?'

'Who is it?'

'You should try talking to Jonas.'

'Jonas who?' Now there were only a few inches between the thousand kroner and Hyttested's greedy fingers.

'Jonas Hess.'

'Jonas Hess? Yeah, OK. Where do I find him? Is he here in the office right now?'

'We don't hire guys like Jonas Hess. You'll have to look him up in the phone book.'

Carl made a mental note of the name and then in a flash stuffed the thousand kroner back in his pocket. The jerk was going to write about him in the next issue, no matter what. Besides, he'd never in his life paid for information, and it would take somebody of an entirely different calibre than Hyttested before that ever changed.

'You would have died for him?' Hyttested yelled after

Carl, as he strode between the rows of cubicles. 'Then why didn't you, Carl Mørck?'

He got Jonas Hess's address from the receptionist, and a taxi dropped him in front of a tiny stucco house on Vejlands Allé, which had become silted up over the years with the detritus of society: old bicycles, shattered aquariums, and glass flagons from ancient home-brewing projects, mouldy tarpaulins that could no longer hide the rotting boards underneath, a plethora of bottles, and all sorts of other junk. The owner of the house would be an ideal candidate for any one of those home make-over programmes on TV. Even the most inept of landscape architects would be welcome here.

A bicycle lying in front of the door and the quiet growling from a radio behind the filthy windows indicated that somebody was home. Carl leaned on the doorbell until his finger started to ache.

Finally he heard from inside: 'Cut that out, damn it.'

A ruddy-faced man displaying the unmistakable signs of a massive hangover opened the door and tried to focus on Carl in the blinding sunlight.

'What the hell's the time?' he asked, as he let go of the doorknob and retreated inside. There was no need for a court order to follow him in.

The living room was of the type shown in disaster movies after the comet has split the earth in two. The homeowner threw himself on to a sagging sofa with a satisfied sigh. Then he took a huge gulp from a whisky bottle as he tried to localize Carl out of the corner of his eye.

Carl's experience told him this man would not exactly be an ideal witness.

He said hello from Pelle Hyttested, hoping that would break the ice a bit.

'He owes me money,' replied Hess.

Carl was about to show the photographer his badge, but changed his mind and stuck it back in his pocket. 'I'm from a special police unit that's trying to solve mysteries about some unfortunate people,' he said. A statement like that couldn't possibly scare anyone off.

Hess lowered the bottle for a moment. Maybe that was too many words for him to process, considering his condition.

'I'm here to talk to you about Merete Lynggaard,' Carl ventured. 'I know that you sort of specialized in her.'

Hess tried to smile, but acid indigestion prevented it. 'There aren't many who know that,' he said. 'And what about her?'

'Do you have any pictures of her that you haven't published?'

Hess doubled over, trying to suppress a laugh. 'Jesus, how can you ask such a stupid question? I've got at least ten thousand of them.'

'Ten thousand! That sounds like a lot.'

'Listen here.' He held up his hand with the fingers splayed out. 'Two or three rolls of film every other day for two to three years – how many photos would that make?'

'A lot more than ten thousand, I would think.'

After an hour, and helped along by the calories contained in neat whisky, Jonas Hess was finally alert enough that he could lead the way, without staggering, to his darkroom, which was in a little building made of breeze blocks behind the house.

Here things were quite different from inside his house. Carl had been in plenty of darkrooms before, but none as sterile and neat as this one. The difference between the man in the house and the man in the darkroom was unsettling.

Hess pulled out a metal drawer and dived in. 'Here,' he said, handing Carl a folder labelled: 'Merete Lynggaard: 13 November 2001 to 1 March 2002.' 'Those are the negatives from the last period.'

Carl opened the folder, starting at the back. Each plastic sleeve contained the negatives from a whole roll of film, but in the last sleeve there were only five shots. The date had been meticulously printed on it: 1 March 2002 ML.

'You took pictures of her the day before she disappeared?'

'Yes. Nothing special. Just a couple of shots in the parliament courtyard. I often stood in the gate, waiting.'

'Waiting for her?'

'Not just for her. For all the Folketing politicians. If you only knew what surprising groupings I've seen appear on that stairway. All it takes is waiting, and one day it happens.'

'But there were apparently no surprises that day, as far as I can see.' Carl took the plastic sleeve out of the folder and placed it on the light table. So these pictures were taken on Friday, when Merete Lynggaard was on her way home. The day before she disappeared.

He leaned down to get a closer look at the negatives.

There it was: she had her briefcase under her arm.

Carl shook his head. Incredible. The very first picture he looked at, and he already had something. Here was the proof in black and white. Merete had taken the briefcase home with her. An old, worn-out case with a rip on one side and everything.

'Could I borrow this negative?'

The photographer took another gulp of whisky and wiped his mouth. 'I never lend out my negatives. I don't even sell them. But we can make a copy; I'll just scan it. I assume the quality doesn't have to be fit for a queen.' He took in a big breath, then hawked a bit as he laughed.

'Thanks, I'd really appreciate a copy. You can send the bill to my department.' Carl handed the man his card.

Hess looked at the negatives. 'Yeah, well, that day there wasn't anything special. But there hardly ever was when it came to Merete Lynggaard. The biggest deal was in the summertime if it got cold and you could see her nipples through her blouse. I got good money for those shots.'

Again there was that hawking laughter as he went over to a small red refrigerator propped up on a couple of containers that had once held darkroom chemicals. He took out a beer, and seemed to offer it to his visitor, but the contents vanished before Carl even had time to react.

'Of course the scoop would be to catch her with a lover, right?' Hess said, looking for something else to toss down his throat. 'And I think that's what I caught on film a few days earlier.'

He slammed the fridge shut and picked up the folder to leaf through it. 'Oh yeah, then there are the ones of Merete talking to a couple of members of the Denmark

Party outside the Folketing chambers. I've even made contact prints of these negatives.' He chuckled. 'I didn't take the pictures because of who she was talking to but because of the woman standing over there, behind them.' He pointed to a person standing close to Merete. 'I guess you can't see it very well when the image is this size, but just take a look when it's blown up. That's the new secretary, and she's totally gaga about Merete Lynggaard.'

Carl leaned closer. It was definitely Søs Norup. But with an entirely different air about her than there had been in her dragon's lair in Valby.

'I have no idea whether there was anything going on between them, or whether it was just all in the secretary's imagination. But what the hell! Don't you think that photo would have brought in a nice sum one day?' Hess mused as he turned the page to the next set of negatives.

'Here it is,' he said, placing a moist finger in the middle of the plastic sleeve. 'I remembered it was on the 25th of February, because that's my sister's birthday. I thought I could buy her a nice present if that picture turned out to be a goldmine. Here it is.'

He took out the plastic sleeve and placed it on the light table. 'See, that was the shot I was thinking about. She's talking to some man out on the steps of the parliament building.' Then he pointed at the photo just above it. 'Take a look at that picture. I think she looks upset. There's something in her eyes that shows she's uncomfortable.' He handed Carl a magnifying glass.

How the hell could anyone see something like that in a negative? Her eyes were nothing but two white dots.

'She noticed me taking pictures, so I split. I don't think

she got a good look at me. Afterwards I tried to photograph the man, but the only shot I got was from behind because he left the courtyard in the other direction, towards the bridge. But it was probably just some random guy who tried to accost her as he went by. There'd be plenty of others if they thought they could get away with it.'

'Do you have contact prints of this series too?'

Hess swallowed a couple more acid eruptions, looking as if his throat was on fire. 'Prints? I can make you some if you run down to the off-licence and buy me some beer in the meantime.'

Carl nodded. 'But first I have a question for you. If you were so obsessed about getting a picture of Merete Lynggaard with a lover, you must have taken photos of her at her house in Stevns. Am I right?'

Hess didn't look up as he studied the pictures they'd been looking at.

'Of course. I was down there lots of times.'

'So there's something I don't understand. You must have seen her with her handicapped brother, Uffe. Yes?'

'Oh sure, plenty of times.' Hess put an 'X' on the plastic sleeve next to one of the negatives. 'Here's a really good shot of her and that guy. I can give you a copy. Maybe you'll know who he is. Then you can tell me, OK?'

Carl nodded again. 'But why didn't you take any good pictures of Merete and Uffe together, so the whole world would know why she was always in such a hurry to get home from Christiansborg?'

'I didn't do it because a member of my own family is handicapped. My sister.'

'But you take photographs for a living.'

Hess gave him an apathetic look. If Carl didn't go and get those beers soon, he wasn't going to get any copies.

'Hey, you know what?' replied the photographer, looking Carl right in the eye. 'Just because somebody is a shit, it doesn't mean he has no integrity. Like yourself, for example.'

Carl walked along the pedestrian street from Allerød Station, noting with annoyance that the street scene was looking more and more miserable. Concrete boxes camouflaged as luxury flats were already towering over the Kvickly supermarket, and soon even the snug old, one-storey houses on the other side of the road would be gone. What had previously been a picturesque feast for the eyes had now turned into a tunnel of dolled-up concrete. A few years ago he wouldn't have thought it possible, but now it had reached his own town. Thanks to politicians like Erhard Jakobsen in Bagsværd, Urban Hansen in Copenhagen, and God only knew who in Charlottenlund. Homey, precious townscapes shattered. An abundance of mayors and town councils with no taste. These hideous new buildings were clear proof of that.

The barbecue gang at Carl's house in Rønneholt Park was in full swing, thanks to the continuing good weather. It was 6:24 p.m. on 22 March 2007 – and spring had officially arrived.

In honour of the day, Morten had donned flowing robes that he'd bartered for during a trip to Morocco. Dressed in that outfit, he could have easily started up a new sect in ten seconds flat. 'Just in time, Carl,' he said, dumping some spare-ribs on to his plate.

His neighbour Sysser Petersen already seemed a bit tipsy, but bore it with dignity. 'I just don't feel like doing this any more,' she said. 'I'm going to sell my dump and move.' She took a big gulp of red wine. 'Down at Social Services we spend more time filling out stupid forms than helping citizens. Did you know that, Carl? Let those smug government ministers give it a try. If they had to fill out forms to get their free dinners and free chauffeurs and free rent and their enormous salaries and free junkets and free secretaries and all that other shit, they wouldn't have any time left for eating or sleeping or driving or anything else. Can't you just picture it? If the prime minister had to sit down and tick off a list of what he wanted to discuss with his ministers before the meeting even got started? In triplicate, printed out from a computer that only worked every other day. And first he'd have to get it approved by some government official before he was even allowed to speak. It would wear the man out.' And with that, she threw back her head and howled with laughter.

Carl nodded. Soon the discussion would turn to the cultural minister's right to muzzle the media, or whether there was anyone who remembered the arguments for breaking up the counties of Denmark, or the hospitals or the tax system, for that matter. And the talk wouldn't end until the last drop had been drunk and the last spare-rib sucked clean.

He gave Sysser a little hug, patted Kenn on the shoulder, and took his plate up to his room. They were all more or less in total agreement. More than half of the country wished the prime minister would go to hell, and they would keep wishing the same thing tomorrow and the day after, until finally all the misfortune that he'd brought flooding in over Denmark and its citizens had been rectified. It would take decades.

But Carl had other things on his mind at the moment.

28

2007

At three o'clock in the morning Carl opened his eyes to pitch darkness. In the back of his mind he had a vague memory of red-checked shirts and nail guns and a clear sense that one of the shirts in Sorø did have the right pattern. His pulse was racing and his mood was glum; he was definitely not feeling good. He simply didn't have the energy to think about the case, but who could stop the nightmares or keep his sheets from getting clammy?

And now he had to deal with that slimy journalist Pelle Hyttested. Was he going to start digging around? Was one of the headlines in the next issue of *Gossip* really going to be about a police detective who had fucked up?

What a mess. Just the thought of it made his abdominal muscles contract so they felt like armour plate for the rest of the night.

'You look tired,' said the homicide chief.

Carl dismissed the comment with a wave of his hand. 'Have you told Bak that he needs to be here?'

'He'll be here in five minutes,' said Marcus, leaning forward. 'I noticed that you haven't signed up for the management course yet. The deadline is coming up soon, you know.'

'I guess I'll just have to wait until next time, won't I?'

'You know we have a plan here, don't you, Carl? When

your department starts showing results, it would be only natural that you got help from your former colleagues. But it won't do any good if you don't have the authority that the title of police superintendent would give you. You don't really have a choice, Carl. You *have* to take that course.'

'It won't make me a better investigator, sitting in a classroom sharpening pencils.'

'You're the head of a new department here, and the title goes along with the baggage. You're taking the course – or you'll have to find somewhere else to do your investigating.'

Carl stared out of the window at the Golden Tower in Tivoli Gardens, which a couple of workmen were making ready for the new season. Four or five times up and down on that monstrous ride and Marcus Jacobsen would be begging him mercy.

'I'll take that into consideration, Mr Superintendent.'

The mood was a bit chilly when Børge Bak came in with his black leather jacket draped neatly over his shoulders.

Carl didn't wait for the homicide chief to initiate the conversation. 'So, Bak! That was a hell of a job you lot did on the Lynggaard case. You were up to your necks in signs that everything wasn't as it should be. Had the whole team caught sleeping sickness, or what?'

Bak's eyes were like steel when their eyes met, but Carl was damned if he was going to look away.

'So now I want to know if there's anything else in the case that you're keeping to yourself,' Carl went on. 'Was there someone or something that put the brakes on your excellent investigation, Børge?'

262

At this point the homicide chief was clearly considering putting on his reading glasses so he could hide behind them, but the scowl on Bak's face demanded some sort of intervention.

'If we just ignore the last couple of remarks that Carl delivered in his inimitable style' – Marcus raised his eyebrows as he glanced at Carl for a moment – 'then it's easy to understand his point of view, since he's just discovered that the deceased Daniel Hale was not the man that Merete Lynggaard met at Christiansborg. Which is something that should have been uncovered during the previous investigation. We have to give him that.'

Bak's hunched shoulders produced a couple of folds in his leather jacket, the only sign of how tense this information was making him feel.

Carl went for the jugular. 'That's not all, Børge. Did you happen to know, for example, that Daniel Hale was gay? Or that he was out of the country during the period when he presumably was in contact with Merete Lynggaard? You should have taken the trouble to show Hale's photo to Merete's secretary, Søs Norup, or to the head of the delegation, Bille Antvorskov. Then you would have known at once that something wasn't right.'

Bak slowly sat down. Thoughts were clearly swirling around in his head. Of course he'd been involved in tons of cases since then, and the workload in the department had always been onerous, but damned if Bak wasn't feeling an urge to squirm.

'Do you think we can still rule out the possibility that some sort of crime was committed?' Carl turned to look at his boss. 'What do you think, Marcus?'

'We assume that you're going to investigate the circumstances surrounding Daniel Hale's death. Am I right, Carl?'

'We're already working on that.' Again he turned to Bak. 'I've got a former colleague up in Hornbæk in the Clinic for Spinal Cord Injuries who's really on the ball and knows how to think.' He tossed the photos on the desk in front of Marcus. 'If it hadn't been for Hardy, I wouldn't have come in contact with a photographer by the name of Jonas Hess and acquired a couple of photos. They prove that Merete Lynggaard brought her briefcase home with her from Christiansborg on her last day there; they catch her lesbian secretary showing a great interest in her boss; there are ones of Merete having a conversation with someone on the stairs of Christiansborg a few days before she disappeared. A meeting that apparently upset her.' He pointed to the photo of her face and the uneasy look in her eyes. 'It's true that we only have a picture of the guy from the back, but if you compare his hair and posture and height, he actually looks a lot like Daniel Hale, even though that's not who he is.' Carl then placed one of the photos of Hale from the InterLab brochure next to the others.

'Now I ask you, Børge Bak: Don't you think it's rather odd for her briefcase to disappear somewhere between Christiansborg and Stevns? Because you never did find it, did you? And don't you think it's also odd that Daniel Hale should die the day after Merete's disappearance?'

Bak shrugged. Of course he thought so; the idiot just didn't want to admit it.

'Briefcases go missing,' he said. 'She could have left it at a petrol station or somewhere else on her way home. We searched her house and her car, which was still on the ferry. We did what we could.'

'Oh, right. OK, you say she might have forgotten it at a petrol station, but are you sure about that? As far as I can tell from her bank statement, she didn't take care of any errands on her way home that day. You didn't do your homework very well, did you, Bak?'

By now Bak looked ready to explode. 'I'm telling you that we put a lot of effort into searching for that briefcase.'

'I think both Bak and I realize that there's more work for us to do here,' the boss tried to mediate.

More work for 'us', he'd said. Was everybody suddenly going to start meddling in the case?

Carl looked away from his boss. No, of course Marcus Jacobsen didn't mean anything by it. Because no help was ever going to be forthcoming from upstairs. Carl knew all too well how things were run in this place.

'I'm going to ask you again, Bak. Do you think we've covered everything now? You didn't include Hale in your report, and there was nothing about Karen Mortensen's observations regarding Uffe Lynggaard. Is there anything else missing, Børge? Can you tell me that? I could use some support right now. Do you get it?'

Bak stared down at the floor as he rubbed his nose. In a second he'd raise his other hand to stroke his comb-over. He could have jumped up and made a hell of a ruckus, considering all the insinuations and accusations being levelled at him. That would have been perfectly understandable, but when it came right down to it, Bak was a detective with a capital *D*. And right now his mind was far away.

Jacobsen gave Carl a look that said 'take it easy', and so Carl kept his mouth shut. He agreed with Marcus. Bak should be given a little time to think.

They sat like that for a whole minute before Bak raised his hand to touch his comb-over. 'The skid marks,' he said. 'The skid marks from the Daniel Hale accident, I mean.'

'What about them?'

Bak looked up. 'As it says in the report, there were none on the road from either of the vehicles. I mean not even a shadow of a mark. It seemed as if Hale wasn't paying attention and simply veered over the line into the other lane. Then: Kapowwww!' He clapped his hands together. 'No one managed to react before the collision occurred. That was the assumption.'

'Yeah, that's what it says in the police report. Why are you mentioning this now?'

'I was driving past the accident site a few weeks later and remembered where it happened, so I stopped to take a look.'

'And?'

'As the report said, there were no skid marks, but it was easy to see where the accident occurred. They hadn't yet removed the shattered, scorched tree or repaired the wall, and tracks from the other vehicle were still visible in the field.'

'But? You're leading up to something here, right?'

Bak nodded. 'But then I discovered that there actually were some marks seventy-five feet further along the road towards Tåstrup. They were already rather blurry, but I could see they were quite short, only about a foot and a half long. And I thought to myself: What if these marks were from the same accident?'

Carl was having trouble following Bak and was annoyed when his boss beat him to it. 'So they were marks left by someone trying to avoid a collision?' Marcus asked.

'They could have been, yes.' Bak nodded.

'So you mean Hale was about to collide with something – and we don't know what that was – but then he put on the brakes and swerved around it?' Marcus went on.

'Yes.'

'And then there was a vehicle in the oncoming lane?' Jacobsen nodded. It sounded plausible.

Carl raised his hand. 'The report says that the collision occurred in the oncoming lane. But it sounds like you're saying that wasn't necessarily the case. You think it happened in the middle of the road, and at precisely that spot the oncoming vehicle had nothing to do with it. Am I right?'

Bak took a deep breath. 'That's what I thought for a moment, but then I decided otherwise. But now I can see it might have been a possibility, yes. Something or someone could have come into his lane, so Hale had to swerve, and then an oncoming vehicle rammed into his car at full speed right near the central line. Maybe even deliberately. Maybe we could have found signs of acceleration further along in the oncoming lane if we'd gone another hundred yards down the road. Perhaps the other vehicle sped up in order to be in the perfect position to ram Hale's car as he swerved into the centre of the road to avoid colliding with someone or something.'

'And if that something was a person who stepped into the lane, and if that person and the individual who ran into Hale were in cahoots, then it's no longer an accident. It's homicide. And if that's true, there's also reason to believe that Merete Lynggaard's disappearance was part of the same crime,' concluded Jacobsen, jotting down a few notes.

'It's possible.' Bak was frowning. He wasn't feeling very good about things at the moment.

Carl stood up. 'There were no witnesses, so we're not going to find out anything more. Right now we're looking for the driver of the other vehicle.' He turned to face Bak, who seemed to have shrunk inside his black leather jacket.

'I had a suspicion things might have happened the way you just described, Bak. So I just want you to know that you've been a big help, in spite of everything. Be sure to come and see me if you remember anything else, OK?'

Bak nodded. He was looking solemn. This had nothing to do with his personal reputation; it had to do with a professional assignment and resolving it properly. The man deserved some respect for that.

Carl almost felt like giving him a pat on the back.

'I have the good and the bad news after my drive to Stevns, Carl,' said Assad.

Carl sighed. 'I don't care which I hear first, Assad. Just go ahead and fire away.'

Assad perched himself on the edge of Carl's desk. Before long he'd be sitting on Carl's lap.

'OK, the bad first.' If it was normal for him to accompany bad news with that kind of smile, then he was really going to split his sides laughing when he delivered the good news.

'The man who drove into Daniel Hale's car is dead too,' Assad said, clearly eager to see Carl's reaction. 'Lis phoned and said it. I have written it just down here.' He pointed to a number of Arabic symbols that could just as well have meant it was going to snow in the Lofoten Islands in the morning.

Carl didn't have the energy to react. It was so annoying and so typical. Of course the man was dead. Had he really expected anything else? That he was alive and kicking and would immediately confess that he'd impersonated Hale, murdered Lynggaard, and then killed Hale afterwards? Nonsense!

'Lis said that he was a thug from out in the sticks, Carl. She said that he was in prison several times for dumb driving. Do you know what she means by "thug" and "sticks"?'

Carl nodded wearily.

'Good,' said Assad, and continued reading aloud from his hieroglyphics. At some point Carl was going to have to suggest that his assistant write his notes in Danish.

'He lived in Skævinge in northern Zealand,' he went on. 'They found him dead then in his bed with quite a lot of vomit in his windpipe and with an alcohol of at least a thousand. He had also taken pills.'

'I see. When did this happen?'

'Not long after the accident. In the report it says that the whole shit with him came from that.'

'You mean he drank himself to death because of the accident?'

'Yes. Because of post-dramatic stress.'

'It's called post-*traumatic* stress, Assad.' Carl drummed his fingers on the desk and closed his eyes. There may have been three people out on the road when the collision took place; if so, it was most likely murder. And if it was murder, then the thug from Skævinge really did have something to drink himself to death over. But where was the third person, the man or woman who had waded out in front of Daniel Hale's car, if that was what actually happened? Had he or she also killed themselves with booze?

'What was the man's name?'

'Dennis. Dennis Knudsen. He was twenty-seven when he died.'

'Do you have the address where he lived? Are there any relatives? Family members?'

'Yes. He lived with his father and his mother.' Assad smiled. 'A lot of twenty-seven-year-olds in Damascus do that too.'

Carl raised his eyebrows. That was as far as Assad's Middle Eastern experiences came into the discussion at the moment. 'You said you also had some good news.'

As predicted, Assad's smile was so big that it practically split his face open. With pride, one would expect.

'Here,' he said, passing Carl a black plastic bag that he'd set down on the floor.

'OK. And what's this, Assad? Forty pounds of sesame seeds?'

Carl got up, stuck his hand inside, and instantly touched the handle. Suspecting what it was, shivers ran down his spine as he pulled the object out of the plastic bag.

It was exactly as he thought: a worn briefcase. Just like in Jonas Hess's photograph, with a big rip not only on the side but also on the top.

'What the hell, Assad!' said Carl, slowly sitting down. 'Is her diary inside?' He felt a tingling in his arm when Assad nodded. It felt as if he were holding the Holy Grail.

He stared at the briefcase. Take it easy, Carl told himself, and then opened the locks and flipped up the lid. There they all were. Her time system calendar in brown leather. Her Siemens mobile phone and charger, handwritten notes on lined paper, a couple of ballpoint pens, and a packet of Kleenex. It *was* the Holy Grail.

'How . . . ?' was all he could muster. And then he wondered whether he ought to give it to forensics first, for a closer examination.

Assad's voice sounded far away. 'First I went to see Helle Andersen. She was not home, but then her husband called her on the phone. He was in bed with a hurt back and said sounds. When she came, I showed her the picture of Daniel Hale, but him she could not remember having seen before.'

Carl stared at the briefcase and its contents. Patience, he thought. Assad would get to the briefcase eventually.

'Was Uffe there when the man brought the letter? Did you remember to ask her that?' He was trying to keep Assad on track.

Assad nodded. 'Yes. She says that he was standing right next to her the whole time. He was very interested. He was always that when the doorbell rang.'

'Did she think the man with the letter looked like Hale?'

Assad wrinkled his nose. A good imitation of Helle Andersen. 'Not very much. But a little bit. The man with the letter was maybe not as old as him. His hair was a little darker and a little more masculine. Something about his eyes and so on, but that was all she had to say about it.'

'So then you asked her about the briefcase, right?'

Assad's smile returned. 'Yes. She did not know where it was. She remembered it, but she did not know if Merete Lynggaard brought it home with her on the last night then. Because she was not there – remember?'

'Assad, get to the point. Where did you find it?'

'Next to the furnace in their utility room.'

'You went to the house in Magleby to see the antique dealer?'

He nodded. 'Helle Andersen said that Merete Lynggaard did everything every day the same way. She noticed this herself over the years. Always the same way. She threw off her shoes in the utility room, but first she looked always in the window. At Uffe. She took every day right away her clothes off and laid it by the washing machine. Not because it was dirty, but because that was where it just lay. She also always put on a bathrobe. And she and her brother watched the same video films then.'

'And what about the briefcase?'

'Well, the home help did not really know about that, Carl. She never saw where Merete put it, but she thought then that it was either in the front hall or the utility room.'

'How the hell were you able to find it near the furnace in the utility room when the whole Rapid Response Team couldn't. Wasn't it visible? And why was it still there? I have a pretty good feeling that those antique dealers are very meticulous when it comes to cleaning. How'd you find it?'

'The antique dealer gave me complete permission to look around the house on my own, so I just played it all through in my head.' He tapped his knuckles on his skull. 'I kicked off my shoes and hung my coat on the hook in the utility room. I just pretended, because the hook was not there any more. But then I pictured in my head that she maybe was holding something in both hands. Papers in one hand and the briefcase in the other. And then I thought that she could not take off her coat without first putting the other things down that she had in her hands first.'

'And the furnace was the closest thing?'

'Yes, Carl. Just right next to me.'

'But afterwards, why didn't she take the briefcase with her into the living room or her home office?'

'I will get to that, Carl, just in a minute. I looked up at the furnace, but the briefcase was not there so. I did not think it would be, either. But do you know what I saw, Carl?'

Carl just stared at him. Obviously Assad would answer his own question.

'I saw that just between the furnace and the ceiling there was at least a whole three feet of air.'

'Fantastic,' replied Carl feebly.

'And then I thought that she would not lay the briefcase down on the dirty furnace because it once belonged to her father, so she took care of it.'

'I don't quite follow you.'

'She did not *lay* it, Carl. She *set* it up on the furnace then. The way you set a briefcase on the floor. There was plenty of room.'

'So that's what she did, and then it toppled over behind the furnace.'

Assad's smile was confirmation enough. 'The rip on the other side is new. See for yourself.'

Carl closed the briefcase and turned it around. It didn't look very new, in his opinion.

'I wiped off the briefcase because it was covered with dust, so maybe the rip looks a little dark now. But it looked very fresh when I found it. This is true, Carl.'

'Confound it, Assad – you wiped off the briefcase? And I suppose you've also touched everything inside?'

He was still nodding, but with less enthusiasm.

'Assad.' Carl took a deep breath so he wouldn't sound too harsh. 'Next time you find something important in a case, you keep your mitts off it, OK?'

'Mitts?'

'Your hands, damn it, Assad. You can destroy valuable evidence when you do something like that. Do you understand?'

He nodded. No longer enthusiastic. 'I pulled my sleeve down over my hand, Carl.'

'OK. Good thinking, Assad. So you think the other rip happened in the same way?' He turned the briefcase around again. The two rips were undeniably similar. So the old rip hadn't come from the car accident back in 1986.

'Yes. I think it was not the first time that the briefcase fell behind the furnace. I found it completely squeezed tight in between the pipes behind the oil furnace. I had to tug and pull to get it out. Merete tried the same thing, I am just sure of that.'

'And why didn't it ever fall down more than twice?'

'It probably did, because there was a big draught from

the wind in the utility room when you opened the door, but maybe it did not fall all the way down.'

'Let's go back to my other question. Why didn't she take it with her into the house?'

'She wanted to have her peace when she was home. She did not want to hear her mobile telephone, Carl.' Assad raised his eyebrows, and his eyes grew big. 'This is what I think.'

Carl looked inside the briefcase. Merete brought it home; that much seemed logical. Inside were her appointment diary and maybe also notes that in certain situations might prove useful. But she usually brought home lots of documents to review; there was always plenty of work she could be doing. She had a landline, but very few people had that number. Her mobile was for a wider circle; that was the number on her business card.

'And you don't think she could hear her mobile inside the house if she left it in her briefcase in the utility room?'

'No way,' said Assad in English.

Carl hadn't realized he knew any English.

'So, here you are. Two grown men having a cosy little chat?' said a bright voice behind them.

Neither of them had heard Lis from the homicide department come down the hallway.

'I have a couple more things for you. They came in from the south-east Jutland district.' Her perfume filled the room, almost a match for Assad's incense, but with an entirely different effect. 'They apologize for the delay, but some of the staff have been off sick.'

She handed the folders to Assad, who was profuse in

his eagerness to accommodate, then gave Carl a look that could stir any man deep in the groin.

He stared at Lis's moist lips and tried to recall when he'd last had any intimate contact with the opposite sex. The image of a pink two-room flat belonging to a divorcée clearly appeared all too clearly in his mind. She'd had lavender blossoms in a bowl of water and tea-light candles and a blood-red cloth draped over the bedside lamp. But he couldn't remember the woman's face.

'What did you say to Bak, Carl?' asked Lis.

He emerged from his erotic reverie and looked into her light blue eyes, which had turned a bit darker now.

'Bak? Is he wandering around upstairs whining?'

'Not at all. He went home. But his colleagues said that he was as pale as a ghost after talking to you in the boss's office.'

Carl connected Merete Lynggaard's mobile to the charger, hoping the battery wasn't dead. Assad's eager fingers – shirtsleeves notwithstanding – had touched everything inside the briefcase, so a forensic examination would be hopeless. The damage had already been done.

Only three pages in the notebook had any writing on them; the rest were blank. The notes were mostly about the municipal home-help arrangement and schedule planning, respectively. Very disappointing and no doubt indicative of the daily life that Merete had left behind.

Then he stuck his hand into a side pocket and pulled out three or four crumpled pieces of paper. The first was a receipt from the 3rd of April 2001 for a Jack & Jones jacket. The rest were some of those folded sheets of white A4 paper that could be found in the bottom of any healthy boy's schoolbag. Handwritten in pencil, more or less illegible, and of course undated.

Carl aimed the desk lamp at the top one, smoothing it out a bit. Only ten words. 'Can we talk after my presentation regarding the tax reform?' Signed with the initials TB. Countless possibilities, but 'Tage Baggesen' would be a good guess. At least that was what Carl chose to believe.

He smiled. Yeah, that was a good one. Baggesen had wanted to talk to Merete Lynggaard, had he? Well, it probably hadn't done him much good.

Carl smoothed out the next piece of paper and quickly scanned the message; it gave him an entirely different feeling in his bones. This time the tone was very personal. Baggesen was backed into a corner. It said:

'I don't know what will happen if you go public with it, Merete. I beg you not to. TB.'

Then Carl picked up the last sheet of paper. The writing had been almost completely rubbed off, as if it had been taken out of the briefcase over and over. He turned it this way and that, deciphering the sentences one word at a time.

'I thought we understood each other, Merete. The whole situation pains me deeply. I implore you again: Please don't let it go any further. I'm in the process of divesting myself of the whole thing.'

This time there were no initials serving as a signature, but there was no doubt that the handwriting was the same.

Carl grabbed the phone and punched in the number for Kurt Hansen.

A secretary in the office of the Conservative Party answered. She was polite but told him that unfortunately Kurt Hansen was unavailable at the moment. Would he care to wait on the line? As far as she could tell, the meeting would be finishing in a couple of minutes.

Carl looked at the pieces of paper lying in front of him as he waited with the receiver to his ear. They had been in the briefcase since March 2002, and most likely for a whole year prior to that. Maybe it was something trivial, but maybe it wasn't. Maybe Merete Lynggaard had kept them because they might be important at some point, but maybe not.

After listening to a few minutes of chit-chat in the background, Carl heard a click and then Kurt Hansen's distinctive voice.

'What can I do for you, Carl?' asked the MP, not bothering with any introductory remarks.

'How can I find out when Tage Baggesen proposed legislation for a tax reform?'

'Why the hell would you want to know that, Carl?' He laughed. 'Nothing could be less interesting than what the Radical Centre thinks about taxes.'

'I need to establish a specific time.'

'Well, that's going to be difficult. Baggesen presents legislative proposals every other second.' He laughed again. 'OK, joking aside. Baggesen has been the traffic policy chairman for at least five years. I don't know why he withdrew from the tax chairmanship. Wait just a minute.' Hansen placed his hand over the phone as he mumbled something to someone in his office.

'We think it was in early 2001 under the old government.

Back then he had more opportunity for that sort of she-nanigan. Our guess is March or April 2001.'

Carl nodded with satisfaction. 'OK, Kurt. That fits in with what I thought. Thanks. You couldn't transfer me to Tage Baggesen, could you?'

He heard a few beeps on the line before he was connected with a secretary who told him that Baggesen was out of the country on a fact-finding trip to Hungary, Switzerland and Germany to take a look at tram networks. He'd be back on Monday.

Fact-finding trip? Tram networks? They had to be kidding. A holiday was what Carl would call it. Pure and simple.

'I need his mobile number. Would you be so kind as to tell me what it is?'

'I don't think I'm allowed to do that.'

'Now listen here, you're not talking to some farmer from Funen. I can find out that number in a matter of minutes, if I have to. But don't you think Tage Baggesen would be sorry to hear that your office refused to assist me?'

There was a lot of crackling on the line, but it was still possible to hear that Baggesen's voice sounded anything but enthusiastic.

'I've got some old messages here, and I just need to have an explanation from you,' said Carl, his tone mild. He'd already seen how the guy could react. 'It's nothing special; just a formality.'

'Go ahead.' The sharp tone of voice was clearly trying to distance itself from their conversation three days ago.

Carl read the messages, one after the other. By the time

he got to the last one, Baggesen seemed to have stopped breathing on the other end of the line.

'Baggesen?' said Carl. 'Are you still there?'

And then he heard only a beeping on the phone.

I hope he doesn't throw himself into the river now, thought Carl, trying to remember which one ran through Budapest. He took down the piece of paper with the list of suspects and added Tage Baggesen's initials to item number four: '"Colleagues" at Christiansborg.'

He had just put down the phone when it began to ring.

'Beate Lunderskov,' said a woman's voice. Carl had no idea who she was.

'We've examined Merete Lynggaard's old hard drive, and I'm sorry to say that it has been very efficiently wiped clean.'

Now it dawned on Carl who she was. One of the women from the Democrats' office.

'But I thought you kept hard drives because you wanted to save the information on them.'

'That's true, but apparently nobody informed Merete's secretary, Søs Norup.'

'What do you mean?'

'Well, she's the one who erased it, according to the note printed very neatly on the back. It says: "Formatted on 20 March 2002, Søs Norup." I'm holding it in my hand.'

'But that was almost three weeks after Merete disappeared.'

'Yes, so it would appear.'

Damn Børge Bak and his gang. Had they done anything in this investigation by the book?

'Couldn't we send it in for closer analysis? There must be people who can retrieve erased data that's been buried deep,' said Carl.

'I think that's already been done. Just a minute.' He could hear her rummaging around, and then she was back, a note of satisfaction in her voice. 'Yes, here's the report. They tried to reconstitute the data at the Down Under shop on Store Kongensgade in early April 2002. There's a detailed explanation as to why they weren't successful. Do you want me to read it to you?'

'That's not necessary,' he replied. 'Søs Norup apparently knew how to make a proper job of it.'

'Apparently. She was a very meticulous sort of person.' Carl thanked her and hung up.

He sat there staring for a moment before he lit a cigarette. Then he picked up Merete Lynggaard's worn diary from the desk and opened it with a feeling that bordered on reverence. That was the way he always felt when he had the chance to examine a lifeline to the last days of a murder victim.

Like the notes he'd already seen, the handwriting in the diary was almost illegible and showed signs of great haste. Capital letters written down in a hurry. *N*s and *G*s that weren't closed up; words that ran into each other. He started with the meeting with the placenta special-interest group on Wednesday, 20 February 2002. Further down on the page it said: 'Café Bankeråt 6:30 p.m.' That was all.

On the following days there was hardly a line that wasn't filled in; quite a hectic schedule, he could see, but no remarks of a personal nature.

As he approached Merete's last day at work, a feeling of

desperation began settling over him. There was absolutely nothing that might give him any leads. Then he turned to the last page. Friday, 1 March 2002. Two committee meetings and another with lobbyists. That was all. Everything else had been lost to the past.

He pushed the book away and looked down at the empty briefcase. Had it really spent five years behind the furnace for no good reason? Then he picked up the diary again and leafed through the rest of the pages. Like most people, Merete Lynggaard had used only the calendar and the phone list in the back.

He began running through the phone numbers from the beginning. He could have skipped to *D* or *H*, but he wanted to keep his disappointment at bay. Under *A*, *B* and *C* he recognized ninety per cent of the names. There was little similarity with his own phone book, which was dominated by names like Jesper and Vigga and a sea of people who lived in Rønneholt Park. It was easy to conclude that Merete hadn't had many personal friends. In fact, none at all. A beautiful woman with a brain-damaged brother and a hell of a lot of work – and that was it. He reached the letter *D*, knowing that he wouldn't find Daniel Hale's phone number there. Merete didn't list her contacts by their first names, the way Vigga did; different strokes for different folks. Who the hell would look up Sweden's prime minister under *G* for Göran? Besides Vigga, that is.

And then he saw it. The moment he turned the page to *H*, he knew that the whole case had reached a turning point. They'd talked about an accident, they'd talked about suicide, and finally they'd ended up high and dry. Along the way there had been indications that something was odd about the Lynggaard case, but this page in the phone book practically screamed it out loud. The whole appointment diary was filled with hastily jotted notes. Letters and numbers that even his stepson could have written neater, and that told him nothing. There was nothing pretty about her handwriting; it wasn't at all what might be expected of a rising star like Merete. But nowhere had she changed her mind about what she'd written. Nothing had been corrected or edited. She knew what she wanted to write every time. Carefully considered, unerring. Except here in her phone book under the letter *H*. Here something was different. Carl couldn't be certain that it had anything to do with Daniel Hale's name, but deep inside, where a cop plumbs his last reserves, he knew that he'd hit the bull's-eye. Merete had crossed out a name with a thick line of ink. It was no longer possible to read, but underneath it had once said 'Daniel Hale' and a phone number. He was sure of it.

Carl smiled. So he was going to need the help of the forensic team after all. They'd better do a good job of it, and quickly.

'Assad,' he called. 'Come in here.'

For a moment he heard some clattering out in the corridor, and then Assad was standing in the doorway holding a bucket and wearing green rubber gloves.

'I've got a job for you. The tech guys need to find a way to read this number.' He pointed to the crossed-out line. 'Lis can tell you what the procedure is. Tell them we need it asap.'

*

Carl knocked cautiously on the door to Jesper's room, but of course got no response. Not home, as usual, he thought, noting the absence of the hundred and twelve decibels that normally bombarded the door from inside. But it turned out that Carl was mistaken, which became apparent when he opened the door.

The girl whose breasts Jesper was groping under her blouse let out a shriek that pierced right to the bone, and Jesper's furious expression underscored the gravity of the situation.

'Sorry,' said Carl reluctantly as Jesper got his hands untangled, and the girl's cheeks turned as red as the background colour of the Che Guevara poster hanging on the wall behind them. Carl knew her. She was no more than fourteen, but looked twenty. She lived on Cedervangen. Her mother had probably looked just like her at one time, but over the years had come to the bitter realization that it wasn't always an advantage to look older than one was.

'What the hell are you doing here, Carl?' shouted Jesper as he jumped up from the sofa bed.

Carl apologized again and mentioned that he had, in fact, knocked on the door, as the generation gap echoed through the house.

'Just go on with . . . what you were doing. I just have a quick question for you, Jesper. Do you know where you put your old Playmobil toys?'

Jesper looked as if he was ready to hurl a hand grenade at his stepfather. Even Carl could see that the question was rather ill-timed.

He nodded apologetically to the girl. 'I know it sounds strange, but I need them for my investigation.' He turned to look at Jesper, who was glaring at him. 'Do you still have those plastic figures, Jesper? I'd be happy to pay you for them.'

'Get the hell out of here, Carl. Go downstairs and see Morten. Maybe you can buy some from him. But you'll need a fat chequebook for that.'

Carl frowned. What did a fat chequebook have to do with it?

It might have been a year and a half since Carl had last knocked on the door to Morten's flat. Even though his lodger moved about upstairs like one of the family, his life in the basement had always been sacrosanct. After all, he was paying his part of the rent, which made all the difference, so Carl didn't really want to know anything about Morten or his habits that might damage the man's standing. And that was why he stayed away.

But his worries turned out to be groundless, because Morten's place was unusually boring. If you disregarded a couple of very broad-shouldered guys and some girls with big tits on posters that were at least three feet high, his basement flat could have been any senior citizen's home on Prins Valdemars Allé.

When Carl asked him about Jesper's Playmobil toys, Morten led the way to the sauna. All the houses in Rønneholt Park were originally equipped with a sauna, but in ninety-nine per cent of the cases they had either been torn down or now functioned as a storage room for all sorts of junk and debris.

'Go ahead and have a look,' said Morten, proudly throwing open the sauna door to reveal a room filled from floor to ceiling with shelves bulging with the type of toys that flea markets couldn't even give away a few years back. Kinder Egg figures, *Star Wars* characters, Ninja Turtles and Playmobil toys. Half of the house's plastic content was on those shelves.

'See, here are two original figures from the series at the toy trade show in Nürnberg in 1974,' said Morten. He proudly picked up two small figurines wearing helmets.

'Number 3219 with the pickaxe and number 3220 with the traffic cop's signs intact,' he went on. 'Isn't it insane?'

Carl nodded. He couldn't have thought of a better word.

'I'm only missing number 3218, and then I'll have the complete set of workmen. I got box 3201 and 3203 from Jesper. Look, aren't they fantastic? It's hard to believe that Jesper ever played with them.'

Carl shook his head. He had definitely thrown away his money on Muscleman Max, or whatever the hell the figure was called; that much was very clear.

'And he only charged me a couple of thousand. That was so nice of him.'

Carl stared at the shelves. If it were up to him, he would have hurled a few well-chosen remarks at both Morten and Jesper, about how he used to get two kroner an hour for spreading manure, back when the price of a hot dog with two pieces of bread rose to one krone and eighty øre.

'Could I borrow a few of them until tomorrow? Preferably those over there,' he said, pointing to a little family with a dog and lots of other stuff.

Morten Holland looked at him as if he'd lost his mind. 'Are you crazy, Carl? That's box 3965 from the year 2000.

I've got the whole set with the house and balcony and everything.' He pointed at the top shelf.

He was right about that. There stood the house in all its plastic glory.

'Do you have any others I could borrow? Just until tomorrow night?'

Morten had a strangely stunned look on his face.

Carl probably would have got the same reaction if he'd asked permission to kick him hard in the nuts.

It was going to be a busy Friday. Assad had a morning appointment at the offices of the Immigration Service, which was the new name the government had assigned to its old system of sorting out aliens, the Immigration Administration, in order to put a nice face on the situation. In the meantime, Carl would be running all over town taking care of business.

The previous evening he had slipped the little Playmobil family out of Morten's treasure chamber while his lodger was on duty at the video shop. Right now, the toys were lying on the seat next to him, giving him cold and reproachful looks as he headed into the wilds of northern Zealand.

The house in Skævinge, where the driver Dennis Knudsen had been found after suffocating on his own vomit, was like all the other houses on the road. None of them had even a trace of beauty, yet in their slovenly, workmanlike way, they seemed oddly harmonious with their worn terraces and breeze-block construction. In terms of durable material, the Eternit roofing appeared to match the ready-to-discard, lustreless windows.

Carl had expected a solid-looking construction-worker to open the door, or at least the female equivalent. Instead, he found himself facing a woman in her late thirties with such an indeterminate and delicate appearance that it was impossible to determine whether she frequented the corridors of management or worked for an escort service in expensive hotel bars.

Yes, he was welcome to come in; and no, unfortunately both of her parents were dead.

She introduced herself as Camilla and led the way to a living room where traditional Christmas plates, skinny, triangular Amager shelves and knotted rya rugs made up a significant part of the scenery.

'How old were your parents when they died?' asked Carl, trying to ignore the rest of the hideous decor.

She sensed what he was thinking. Everything in the house was from a past era.

'My mother inherited the place from my grandmother, so it's mostly her things in the house,' she said. It was obvious that this was not how her own residence would look. 'I inherited everything and just got divorced, so I'm going to fix the place up, if I can find the right builder to do the job. So you're lucky to find me here.'

Carl picked up a framed photograph from the best piece of furniture in the room, a bureau in walnut veneer. It was a picture of the whole family: Camilla, Dennis and their parents. It had to be at least ten years old, and the parents were beaming like suns in front of a silver wedding anniversary banner. It said: 'Congratulations on 25 Years, Grete and Henning.' Camilla was wearing tight jeans that left nothing to the imagination, and Dennis had on a black leather vest and a baseball cap with the logo for Castrol Oil. So all in all it was banners and smiles and happy days in Skævinge.

On the mantelpiece stood a few more photographs.

Carl asked who everyone was, and from what she said, he got the feeling that the family hadn't had a large circle of friends.

'Dennis was crazy about anything that drove fast,' said Camilla, taking him to the room that had once belonged to Dennis Knudsen.

A couple of lava lamps and a pair of massive speakers were to be expected, but otherwise the room was very different from the rest of the house. The furniture was made of light wood and it all matched. The wardrobe was new and filled with nice clothes on hangers. The walls were covered with a sea of certificates, all neatly framed, and above them, on birchwood shelves up near the ceiling, stood all the trophies that Dennis had won over the years. By Carl's rough estimate there were at least a hundred, maybe more. It was pretty overwhelming.

'As you can see,' she said, 'Dennis won every competition he entered. Motorcycle speedways, stock-car races, tractor pulls, rallies, and all classes of motor racing. He was a natural talent. Good at almost everything that interested him, even writing and maths, and all sorts of other things. It was very sad that he died.' She nodded, her eyes welling up. 'His death took the life out my father and mother. He was such a good son and little brother. He really was.'

Carl gave her a sympathetic look, but he was puzzled. Could this really be the same Dennis Knudsen that Lis had described to Assad?

'I'm glad you're going to look into the circumstances of his death,' Camilla said. 'I just wish you'd done it while my parents were still alive.'

Carl looked at her, trying to figure out what was behind her words. 'What do you mean by "the circumstances"? Are you thinking about the car accident?'

She nodded. 'Yes, the accident and then Dennis's death a short time afterwards. Dennis would sometimes go on a drinking binge, but he'd never taken drugs before. And that's what we told the police. It was unthinkable, as a matter of fact. He'd worked with teenagers and warned them against taking drugs, but the police wouldn't listen. All they saw was his criminal record and how many speeding tickets he'd had. So they'd already convicted him in their minds before they even found those disgusting ecstasy pills in his sports bag.' Her eyes narrowed. 'But it didn't make sense, because Dennis never touched anything like that. It would have slowed down his reactions when he drove. He hated that kind of shit.'

'Maybe he was tempted by the idea of making some quick cash and planned to sell the drugs. Maybe he was just going to try them out. You wouldn't believe the sort of things we see at police headquarters.'

Now the lines around her mouth hardened. 'Somebody got him to take those drugs, and I know who it was. That's what I told the police back then.'

Carl pulled out his notebook. 'Is that right?' His inner bloodhound raised its head and sniffed at the wind, catching the scent of something unexpected. He was fully alert now. 'And who might that be?'

She went over to one end of the room and took down a photograph hanging from a nail sticking out of the wallpaper that obviously hadn't been changed since the house had been built in the early sixties. Carl's father had taken a

291

similar photo when Carl won a swimming trophy in Brønderslev. It was a dad's proud documentation of how great and talented his son had become. Carl guessed that Dennis was ten or twelve in the photo, looking handsome in his go-kart gear, and proud as punch about the little silver shield he was holding in his hand.

'That kid there,' said Camilla, pointing to a blond boy standing behind Dennis, with one hand on his friend's shoulder. 'They called him Atomos, but I don't know why. They met at a motocross track. Dennis was crazy about him, but Atomos was a little shit.'

'So the two of them kept in touch after they grew up?'

'I'm not really sure. I think they lost contact when Dennis was sixteen or seventeen, but during his last years I know they were seeing each other again, because Mum was always complaining about it.'

'And why do you think Atomos might have had something to do with your brother's death?'

She looked at the photograph with a sorrowful expression. 'He was just a real prick, and ugly deep down in his soul.'

'That's a strange way of putting it. What exactly do you mean?'

'He was fucked up inside his head. Dennis said I was talking nonsense, but it was true.'

'So why was your brother friends with him?'

'Because Atomos was always the one who encouraged Dennis to drive. Plus he was a couple of years older. Dennis looked up to him.'

'Your brother suffocated on his own vomit. He'd taken five pills and had a blood-alcohol level of four point one.

I don't know how much he weighed, but no matter what, he made a good job of it. Do you know whether he had any reason to drink? Was this new behaviour for him? Was he particularly depressed after the accident?'

She looked at him with sad eyes. 'Yes, my parents said that the accident had a terrible effect on him. Dennis was a fantastic driver. It was the first accident he'd ever been involved in, and a man died, besides.'

'According to my information, Dennis was in jail twice for reckless driving, so he couldn't have been all that fantastic.'

'Ha!' She gave him a scornful look. 'He never drove recklessly. When he was speeding on a motorway, he always knew how far ahead the lane was free. The last thing he wanted was to endanger the life of anyone else.'

How many sociopaths would never have been hatched if their families had only been paying attention? How many idiots were allowed to cling to the bonds of blood? Carl had heard the same story a thousand times before. My brother, my son, my husband is innocent.

'You seem to have a high regard for your brother. Don't you think you're being a little naive?'

She grabbed Carl's wrist and leaned so close that he could feel her fringe brushing the bridge of his nose.

'If your investigative work is as limp as your dick, you might as well leave right now,' she snarled.

Her reaction was surprisingly fierce and provocative. So it probably wasn't the corridors of management that she frequented, Carl thought, drawing his face away.

'My brother was all right. Do you hear me?' she went on. 'And if you want to make any progress in what you're farting around with, I advise you to remember what I just said.' Then she patted him on the crotch and stepped back. It was a shocking metamorphosis. Suddenly she seemed gentle and open and credible again. It was a hell of a profession he'd got himself involved in.

He frowned and took a step towards her. 'The next time you touch my equipment, I'm going to puncture your silicon boobs and then claim it happened because you resisted arrest after threatening to slug me with one of your brother's ugly trophies. When I slap the cuffs on you, and you're waiting for the doctor as you stare at the blank white wall of a prison cell in Hillerød, you'll dream about taking back that pat you gave me. Shall we proceed, or do you have anything to add regarding my nobler parts?'

She kept her cool. Didn't even smile. 'I'm just saying that my brother was OK, and you'll just have to believe me.'

Carl gave up. It was no use trying to make her change her mind.

'Right,' he said. 'So how do I find this Atomos?' he asked, taking a step back from the chameleon. 'Don't you remember anything else about him?'

'You know what? He was five years younger than me. I couldn't have cared less about him back then.'

Carl smiled wryly. Interests could certainly change over the years.

'Any distinguishing marks? Scars? What about his hair? His teeth? Is there anyone else in town who knew him?'

'I don't think so. He came from a children's home up in Tisvildeleje.'

She paused for a moment, thinking with her eyes

averted. 'Wait a minute. I think the place was called God-havn.' She handed the framed photograph to Carl. 'If you promise to bring it back, you can try showing the picture to the staff at the home. Maybe they can answer your questions.'

Carl had come to a stop at an intersection sparkling with sunlight. He was sitting in the car, thinking. He could drive north to Tisvildeleje to talk to the staff at the children's home, in the hopes that somebody still remembered a boy named Atomos who lived there twenty years ago. Or he could drive south to Egely and play a game about the past with Uffe. Or he could park his vehicle on the side of the road and set his brain on cruise control while he took a nap for a few hours. The last option was especially tempting.

On the other hand, if he didn't put the Playmobil figures back on Morten's shelf in time, there was a real risk that he might lose his lodger, along with a big chunk of rent money.

So he released the handbrake and turned left to drive south.

It was lunchtime at Egely, and the aroma of thyme and tomato sauce had settled over the landscape as Carl parked his car. He found the director sitting alone at a long teak table on the terrace outside his office. As on the previous occasion, he was impeccably dressed, with a sun hat on his head and a napkin tucked into his collar. He was tentatively nibbling at a small serving of lasagne that took up only a corner of his plate. He was clearly not the sort who lived for worldly pleasures. The same could not be said of his administrative co-workers and a couple of nurses who sat thirty feet away, chattering vociferously as they attacked the food piled on their plates.

They saw Carl come round the corner and suddenly fell silent, which made other sounds suddenly seem very loud: the nest-builders, giddy with spring, noisily fluttering about in the bushes; the clattering of dishes from inside the dining hall.

'Bon appétit,' said Carl as he sat down at the director's table without waiting for an invitation. 'I'm here to ask you something about Uffe. Did you know he played a game where he was supposedly reliving the accident that left him handicapped? Karen Mortensen, a caseworker in Stevns, observed him playing that game shortly before Merete Lynggaard died. Did you know about it?'

The director nodded slowly and took another bite of his food. Carl looked at the plate. Evidently the last bites would have to disappear before the undisputed king of Egely deigned to carry on a conversation with a mere commoner.

'Is there anything about it in Uffe's case file?' asked Carl.

Again the director nodded, as he continued to chew very slowly.

'Has it ever happened since?'

The man shrugged.

'Did it happen again or didn't it?'

The director shook his head.

'I'd like to see Uffe alone today. Just for ten or fifteen minutes. Is that possible?'

The director didn't reply.

So Carl waited until the man finished his lunch, wiped his mouth on a cloth napkin, and licked his teeth with his tongue. A single gulp of ice water and then he looked up.

'No, you can't be alone with Uffe,' was his answer.

'Dare I ask why not?'

The director gave him a condescending look. 'Your profession is a pretty far cry from what we do here, isn't it?' He didn't wait for Carl to respond. 'We can't risk having you cause a setback in Uffe Lynggaard's development. That's the way it is.'

'Is he in a period of development? I didn't know that.'

Carl noticed a shadow fall across the table and turned around to face the supervisory nurse, who gave him a friendly nod, immediately stirring up memories of better treatment than the director was willing to offer.

She gave her boss an authoritative look. 'I'll take care of this. Uffe and I are going out for a walk now, anyway. I can accompany Mr Mørck.'

It was the first time Carl had stood next to Uffe Lynggaard, and he now saw how tall he was. Long, lanky limbs and a posture that indicated he spent his time sitting down, hunched over a table.

The nurse had taken Uffe's hand, but apparently he didn't care much for that. When they reached the thickets near the fjord, he let go of her hand and sat down in the grass.

'He likes to watch the cormorants. Don't you, Uffe?' she said, pointing at a colony of prehistoric-looking birds perched in clusters of semi-dead trees covered with bird shit.

'I've brought something that I'd like to show Uffe,' said Carl.

She looked with alert interest at the Playmobil figures and car that he pulled out of a plastic bag. She was quick on the uptake – he'd noticed that the first time – but maybe not quite as accommodating as he'd hoped.

She placed her hand on her nurse's badge, presumably to give her words added weight. 'I know about the episode that Karen Mortensen described. I don't think it would be a good idea to repeat it.'

'Why not?'

'You want to try to replay the accident while he watches, right? You're hoping it will open something up in him.'

'Yes.'

She nodded. 'I thought so. But to be honest, I don't know if I should let you.' She made a motion to get up, but then hesitated.

Carl cautiously placed his hand on Uffe's shoulder and squatted down next to him. Uffe's eyes shone happily in the reflection from the waves, and Carl understood him. Who wouldn't want to disappear into this beautiful clear and blue March day?

Then Carl set the Playmobil car on the grass in front of Uffe and one by one put the figures in the car seats. The father and mother in front, the daughter and son in back.

The nurse watched closely every move Carl made. He might have to come back another day and repeat the experiment. But right now he wanted to convince her that at least he knew enough not to abuse her trust. That he regarded her as an ally.

'Vroooom,' he said warily, driving the car back and

forth in front of Uffe on the grass, to the great distress of a couple of bumblebees flitting among the flowers.

Carl smiled at Uffe and smoothed out the tracks left by the car. That was clearly what interested Uffe most. The flat-pressed grass that sprang back up.

'Now we're going out driving with Merete and Mum and Dad, Uffe. Oh, look at this, we're all together. Look, we're driving through the woods! Look how lovely it is.'

Carl glanced at the woman in the white uniform. She looked nervous, the lines around her mouth showing traces of doubt. He had to be careful not to go too far. If he shouted, she would flinch. She was much more into the game than Uffe, who was just sitting there with the sun glinting in his eyes, letting everything around him mind its own business.

'Look out, Dad,' warned Carl, imitating a woman's voice. 'It's slippery, you might skid.' He gave the car a little jolt. 'Watch out for the other car – it's skidding too. Help, we're going to crash into it.'

He made the sound of a car braking and metal scraping the undercarriage of the car. Now Uffe was watching. Then Carl tipped the car over, and the figures tumbled out on to the ground. 'Look out, Merete! Look out, Uffe!' he shouted in a high voice. The nurse leaned towards Carl and put her hand on his shoulder.

'I don't think . . .' she said, shaking her head. In a second she would take Uffe by the arm and pull him to his feet.

'Bam!' said Carl and made the car roll along the grass, but Uffe didn't react.

'I don't think he's really here,' said Carl, assuring the

nurse with a wave of his hand that the performance was over. 'I have a photograph that I'd like to show to Uffe,' he went on. 'Is that OK? Then I promise to leave you in peace.'

'A photograph?' she asked, as Carl pulled all the pictures out of his plastic bag. Then he took the photos of Dennis Knudsen that he'd borrowed from his sister and lay them on the grass while he held up the brochure from Daniel Hale's company in front of Uffe.

It was clear that Uffe was curious. He was like a monkey in a cage, who, after looking at thousands of humans making faces, finally sees something new.

'Do you know this man, Uffe?' asked Carl, studying his face attentively. The slightest twitch might be the only signal he'd get. If there was any possible response from Uffe's sluggish mind, Carl had to make sure he saw it.

'Did he come to your house in Magleby, Uffe? Was this the man who brought the letter to you and Helle? Do you remember him?' Carl pointed to Daniel Hale's bright eyes and blond hair. 'Was this the man?'

Uffe stared at the picture with a blank expression. Then his eyes shifted downward until he was looking at the photos on the grass in front of him.

Carl followed his gaze and noted how Uffe's pupils suddenly contracted as his lips parted. The reaction was very clear. Just as real and visible as if someone had dropped a carjack on his toes.

'What about this man? Have you seen him before, Uffe?' asked Carl, quickly moving the silver anniversary photo of Dennis Knudsen's family close to Uffe's face. 'Have you?' Carl noticed that the nurse was standing behind him now, but he didn't care. He wanted to see Uffe's pupils contract again. It was like having a key in his hand and knowing that it was the right one, but not which lock it would open.

But now Uffe was looking straight ahead, quite calm, and his eyes had glazed over.

'I think we should stop now,' said the nurse as she tentatively touched Uffe's shoulder. Maybe all Carl needed was twenty seconds more. Maybe he would have been able to reach him if only they'd been alone.

'Didn't you see his reaction?' asked Carl.

She shook her head.

Damn it.

Then he put the framed photo back on the ground next to the other one he'd borrowed in Skævinge.

At that instant a jolt passed through Uffe's body. First in his torso, where his chest sucked in, then his right arm, which jerked up at an angle in front of his stomach.

The nurse tried to calm Uffe, but he paid no attention to her. He started taking short, shallow breaths. Both the nurse and Carl heard it, and she began to protest loudly. But Carl and Uffe were alone together at that moment. Uffe in his own world, on his way into Carl's. Carl saw his eyes slowly grow bigger. Like a shutter in an old-style camera, they widened, pulling in everything around them.

Uffe looked down again, and this time Carl followed his gaze towards the grass. Uffe was very much present now.

'So you *do* recognize him?' asked Carl, picking up the picture of Dennis Knudsen on his parents' silver wedding anniversary again and holding it up. But Uffe swept it aside like a sulky child and began uttering noises that didn't sound like a normal kid's whimpering; it was more like an asthmatic who couldn't get enough air. His breathing was almost a wheezing, and the nurse shouted for Carl to leave.

He followed Uffe's eyes again, and this time there was no doubt. They were fixed on the other photograph Carl had brought. The picture of Dennis Knudsen with his friend Atomos, standing behind, leaning against Dennis's shoulder.

'Is this how he should look instead?' asked Carl, pointing at the young Dennis in his go-kart outfit.

But Uffe was looking at the boy behind Dennis. Never before had Carl seen a person's eyes so riveted on something. It was as if the boy in the picture had taken possession of Uffe's innermost soul, as if these eyes in an old photograph were burning Uffe like fire, even as they also gave him life.

And then Uffe screamed. He screamed so loud that the nurse shoved Carl down on the grass and took Uffe in her arms. He screamed so that Egely's tenants began howling as well.

He screamed so masses of cormorants lifted off from the trees, leaving everything deserted.

30

2005-2006

It had taken Merete three days to wiggle the tooth loose, three nightmarish days and nights in hell. Every time she placed the jaws of the tongs around the throbbing beast and the blast waves of infection sucked all strength out of her, she had to muster her courage again. A slight nudge to one side and her entire organism shut down. Then a few seconds of heart-pounding fear before the next twist of the tongs, and thus the process continued without end. Several times she tried to yank hard, but her strength and courage failed her the moment the rusty metal clinked against the tooth.

When she finally reached the moment when pus began steadily streaming out of the gum and the pressure eased for a moment, she collapsed in tears of gratitude.

She knew they were watching her out there. The one they called Lasse hadn't yet arrived, and the button on the intercom was still stuck. They didn't say anything to each other, but she could hear them moving around and breathing. The more she suffered, the harder they breathed, almost as if it excited them sexually, and her hatred towards them grew. Once she got the tooth out, she'd be able to look to the future. Yes, she would exact her revenge, but first she had to be able to think.

So once again she placed the foul-tasting metal jaws

around the tooth and wiggled it, never doubting that she had to get the job done. That tooth had caused her enough damage; now the pain had to end.

She eventually pulled it out one night when she was alone. It was hours since she'd last heard any sign of life from outside, so the relieved laughter that slipped out in the echoing space was hers and hers alone. The taste of the infection was refreshing. The throbbing that caused the blood to flow freely in her mouth was like a caress.

She spat on her hand every few seconds and smeared the bloody mass on the mirrored panes, first one, then the other. And when the blood no longer flowed, her work was done. A small square, eight by eight inches, on one of the portholes was all that remained unbloodied. Now she'd robbed them of their pleasure in watching her whenever they felt like it. Finally she was in control of when she would appear in their field of vision.

When they put the food in the hatch the next morning, the woman's curses woke her up.

'The little slut has covered the windows with filth. Look at that! She's smeared shit over the whole thing, that pig.'

She heard the man say that it looked more like blood, and the woman snarled, 'So that's the gratitude we get for giving you the tongs? So you could smear your filthy blood all over everything? If that's your way of saying thank you, then you're going to have to pay for it. We're turning off the lights. Let's see what you say to that, bitch. Maybe then you'll wipe off that mess. And until you do, you're not getting any more food.'

She heard them make a move to take back the food bucket in the airlock, but she ran over and stuck the tongs into the carousel. They weren't going to cheat her out of this last portion. So she pulled out the food bucket at the last second, right before the hydraulic mechanism let go of the tongs. The mechanism spun around with a whistling sound, and then the hatch door closed.

'That trick may have worked today, but it won't work tomorrow!' yelled the woman outside. The fury in her voice was consoling. 'I'll give you spoiled food until you wipe off the windowpanes. Do you hear me?' And then the fluorescent lights in the ceiling went out.

Merete sat still for a while, staring at the faint brown stains on the mirrored panes and the small clear patch that was slightly brighter. She noticed that the woman tried to reach it so she could look in, but Merete had deliberately placed it too high. She couldn't even remember the last time she'd felt such joyous triumph stream through her body. It wouldn't last long – that much she knew – but under the circumstances, such moments were the only things she had to live for.

That, plus visions of revenge, dreams of freedom, and to stand face to face with Uffe again one day.

That night she switched on the pocket torch for the last time. She went over to the little blank space on the pane and shone the light inside her mouth. The hole in her gum was enormous, but it looked all right, at least as far as she could tell. The tip of her tongue agreed. The healing process had already begun.

After a few minutes the light of the torch grew fainter, so she got down on her knees to examine the closing mechanism around the airlock door. She'd seen it thousands of times before, but now she might have to memorize exactly how it looked. Who knew whether the ceiling lights would ever be turned on again?

The airlock door was convex and presumably conical, so it could make a tight seal to close off the space. The lower section, which was the hatch in the door, was about thirty inches high, and here too it was almost impossible to feel where the sections joined. A metal peg had been welded on the front, at the bottom, so the hatch door would stop in a fully open position. She examined it thoroughly until the light from the torch died out.

Afterwards she sat in the dark, considering what she could do.

There were three things she wanted to control. First, what other people could see of her; that was something she'd already dealt with. A long, long time ago, right after she'd been kidnapped, she'd meticulously searched all the surfaces and walls for the tiniest suggestion of a camera, but there was nothing. The monsters who were holding her prisoner had put their faith in the mirrored panes. They shouldn't have done that. It was the reason that she could now move about unobserved.

Second, she was determined to make sure she didn't lose her mind. There had been days and nights when she'd disappeared inside herself, and there had been weeks when her thoughts had run in circles, but she had never allowed her brain to stop. When she'd realized where that might lead, she forced herself to think about others who had endured similar situations. People who had been condemned to solitary confinement for decades without being convicted of any crime. There were plenty of examples in world history and in literature. Papillon, the Count of Monte Cristo, and so many others. If they could do it, so could she. She had forcibly directed her thoughts to books and films and the best memories of her life, and she'd snapped out of it again.

Because she would continue to be herself, Merete Lynggaard, until the day she left this place. That was a promise, and she was determined to keep it.

And when that day finally arrived, she would be in control of how she would die. That was the third thing. The woman outside had said before that it was Lasse who made the decisions, but if the situation arose, the she-wolf could easily take matters into her own hands. Hatred had seized control of the woman before, and it could happen again. Only a second of insanity was necessary in order for her to open the airlock and equalize the pressure. That moment was very likely to come.

For almost four years Merete had sat in this cage, but the woman had also been marked by the passing of time. Maybe her eyes had sunk deeper, maybe there was something in her voice. In these circumstances it was hard to tell how old the woman was, but she was old enough to fear what life might have in store. And that made her dangerous.

In the meantime, it didn't seem as if the two people out there knew much about technical matters. They couldn't even fix a button that was stuck, so they probably couldn't equalize the pressure by any other method than opening the airlock; at least that was what Merete hoped. So if she made sure that they couldn't open the hatch door unless she allowed them to, she would have enough time to commit suicide. The tongs would serve as her instrument. She could grip her arteries with the tongs and tear them apart if those two people outside suddenly decided to release the pressure inside the room. She didn't really know what would happen then, but the woman's comment that Merete would explode from inside was terrifying. No death could be worse. Which was why she wanted to decide when and how it would happen.

If this Lasse happened to return and had other plans for her, she would not have any naive illusions. Of course the room must have means of equalizing pressure other than through the hatch door. Maybe the ventilation system could also be used. She had no idea why this room had originally been built, but it must have been expensive. So she assumed that whatever it was originally intended to house must have had a certain value or importance. Which meant there had to be some kind of device in case of emergency. She'd caught a glimpse of small metal nozzles up under the light fixture on the ceiling. Not much bigger than her little finger, but surely that would be enough. Maybe that was how fresh air was pumped into the space, or maybe the nozzles could be used to equalize the pressure. But one thing was certain: If this Lasse wanted to harm her, he undoubtedly knew which buttons to push.

Until then, she would just try to concentrate on countering the threats that seemed most imminent. So she unscrewed the cap on the bottom of the pocket torch, took out the batteries, and noted with satisfaction how hard and strong and sharp the metal of the torch was.

The distance from the edge of the hatch door to the floor was only about an inch, so if she dug a hole right below the peg that had been welded on to stop the hatch door when it opened, she'd be able to position the torch in the hole to prevent the door from opening.

She hugged the torch to her chest. Here was a tool that gave her the feeling she could control something in her life, and that was an indescribably welcome sensation. Like the first time she took birth-control pills. Like the time she defied their foster family and took off, hauling Uffe along with her.

Digging into the concrete floor was much, much harder than she had imagined. The first couple of days passed quickly, since she still had food and water, but when the bucket with the good food was empty, the strength in her fingers swiftly gave out. She knew that she had very few energy reserves, but the food that had been delivered over the past few days had been completely inedible. They were really taking their revenge. The stench alone kept her from eating anything in the buckets. The food reeked like the rotting carcasses of diseased animals. Every night she spent five or six hours using the edges of the pocket torch to scrape at the floor under the door, and that took its toll on her too. At the same time, it would be no use if she made a sloppy job of it; that was the problem. The hole had to be just the right size to hold the torch tightly, and since the torch itself was her digging tool, she had to keep twisting it into the hole to make sure it had the proper diameter and then carefully scrape off the concrete in paper-thin layers.

By the fifth day she'd dug out less than an inch, and gastric juices were starting to burn her insides.

The witch had repeated her demands every day at exactly the same time. If Merete didn't wipe off the glass panes, the old woman refused to turn the lights back on, and she would deliver only spoiled food. The man had tried to mediate, but without success. There they were now, making their demands. Merete didn't give a damn about the light, but her intestines were screaming. If she didn't eat, she'd get sick, and she didn't want to be sick.

She looked up at the reddish film on the panes; there was a faint light showing through the clear patch.

'If it's so important to you, give me something I can use to wipe the panes clean!' she finally yelled.

'Use your sleeve and your piss, then we'll turn the light on and give you some food!' the woman shouted back.

'All right, but you'll have to send in a new jacket.'

At that the woman started in with her disgusting stabbing laughter that went straight to the marrow. She didn't answer, just laughed until her lungs were empty. Then it was silent again.

'I won't do it,' said Merete. But she did.

It didn't take long, but it felt like years of defeat.

Even though they still stood out there once in a while, they couldn't see what she was doing. When she sat over by the door she was in a blind spot, just like when she sat on the floor between the two mirrored panes. If they decided to come unannounced by night, they would immediately hear the scraping sound of the pocket torch, but they never came. That was the advantage of the system they had put in place. She knew that she had the night to herself.

When she had scraped out almost an inch and a half of concrete, her existence, which had always been so predictable, changed. She had been sitting under the flickering fluorescent lights waiting for food as she figured out that it would soon be Uffe's birthday. It was already the month of May, at any rate. May for the fifth time since she'd been imprisoned. May 2006. She had been sitting next to the toilet bucket, cleaning her teeth and thinking about Uffe, clearly picturing the sun dancing in a blue sky. 'Happy birthday to you,' she sang in a hoarse voice, picturing Uffe's happy face. Somewhere out there he was doing fine – she was sure of it. Of course he was doing fine. That was what she'd told herself so often.

'It's that button, Lasse,' said the woman's voice suddenly. 'We can't get it to come back out again, so she's been able to hear everything we say.'

The image of sun and blue sky disappeared instantly, and her heart began to hammer. It was the first time she had heard the woman address the man they called Lasse.

'For how long?' replied a muted voice that made Merete hold her breath.

'Since the last time you were here. Five or six months.'

'Have you said anything she shouldn't hear?'

'Of course not.'

For a moment there was silence. 'Soon it won't matter anyway. Go ahead and let her hear what we say. At least until I decide something else.'

That remark felt like the blow of an axe to Merete.

'Soon it won't matter anyway.' What wouldn't matter? What did he mean? What was going to happen?

'She's been a real bitch while you were gone. She tried to starve herself to death, and once she blocked the hatch door. Then she smeared her own blood on the panes so we couldn't see through them.'

'Our chum told me she had a toothache for a while. I wish I could have seen that,' said Lasse.

The woman outside laughed dryly. They knew that Merete was sitting inside, listening to everything they said. What made them act like that? What had she ever done to them?

'You monsters – what did I ever do to you?' she shouted at the top of her lungs as she stood up. 'Turn off the light in here so I can see you! Turn off the light so I can look into your eyes while you talk!'

Again she heard the woman laugh. 'Dream on, girl!' she shouted back.

'You want us to turn off the lights?' Lasse chuckled. 'Sure, why not?' he said. 'This could be the moment when the whole thing really starts. Then we'll have some interesting days ahead of us until it's over.'

Those were terrible words. The woman tried to object, but the man silenced her with a few harsh remarks. Then the lights above her in the ceiling suddenly went out.

Merete stood still for a moment, her pulse racing as she tried to get used to the faint light streaming into the room from outside. At first she saw the beasts out there merely as shadows, but slowly they became more distinct. The woman reached only to the bottom edge of one of the portholes; the man was much taller. Merete assumed he was Lasse.

Slowly he stepped closer. His blurry figure took form. Broad shoulders, well-proportioned figure. Not like the other tall, thin man.

She felt simultaneously an urge to curse them and to beg them to take pity on her. Anything that might make them tell her why they had done this to her. Here he was, the man who made the decisions. This was the first time she was seeing him, and there was something disturbingly exciting about the moment. She sensed that he alone would decide whether she should be allowed to know more, and now she was going to demand her rights. But when he took a step closer and she saw his face, the words refused to come out.

She looked with shock at his mouth. Saw the crooked smile freeze. Saw his white teeth slowly appear. Saw everything gather itself into a whole and shoot electrical charges through her body.

Now she knew who Lasse was.

31

2007

Out on the lawn at Egely, Carl apologized to the nurse for the episode with Uffe. Then he threw the photographs and Playmobil figures into the plastic bag and strode towards the car park, while Uffe kept on screaming in the background. It was only when Carl started up the engine that he noticed the chaotic scene as staff members tore down the slope. That was the end of his investigative efforts on the grounds of Egely. Fair enough.

Uffe's reaction had been very strong. So now Carl knew that in some way or another Uffe was present in the same world as everyone else. Uffe had looked into the eyes of the boy named Atomos in the photo, and it had shaken him badly. There was no doubt about that. This signified an unusually big step forwards.

Carl pulled over next to a field and tapped in the name of the Godhavn children's home on the car's Internet system. The phone number appeared at once.

He didn't have to offer much in the way of explanation. Apparently the staff were used to having the police call them, so there was no need to beat about the bush.

'Don't worry,' he said. 'None of your residents has done anything wrong. I'm calling about a boy who lived at the home in the late eighties. I don't know his real name, but he was called Atomos. Does that name ring a bell?'

'In the late eighties?' said the staff member on duty. 'No, I haven't been here that long. We have case files on all the children, but they're probably not listed under nicknames like that. Are you sure you don't have some other name we could look up?'

'No, sorry.' Carl glanced over at the fields that reeked of manure. 'Do you know of any staff member who worked there back then?'

'Hmm. Not among the full-time employees. I'm pretty sure of that,' she said. 'But, let me see . . . oh, that's right, we do have a retired colleague, John, who comes in a couple of times a week. He just can't bear to stay away, and the boys would miss him if he didn't come in. I'm sure he worked here back then.'

'He wouldn't happen to be there today, would he?'

'John? No, he's on holiday. The Canary Islands for one thousand two hundred and ninety-five kroner. How could he resist? as he likes to say. But he'll be back on Monday, so I'll see if we can get him to come in. It's mostly for the boys' sake. They like him. Give us a call on Monday, and we'll see what we can do.'

'Could you give me his home number?'

'No, I'm sorry. It's against our policy to give out personal phone numbers for staff members. You never know who might be asking for it.'

'My name is Carl Mørck. I think I already told you that. I'm a police detective, you may recall.'

She laughed. 'I'm sure you can track down his number if you're so clever, but I suggest that you wait until Monday and call us back. OK?'

Carl leaned back in his car seat and looked at his watch.

It was almost one o'clock. He could still make it back to the office in time to check out Merete Lynggaard's mobile, if the battery was still working after five years, which was doubtful. If it was dead, they'd have to get a new one.

Out in the fields, screeching clusters of seagulls rose to the sky behind the hills. A vehicle came rumbling underneath them, whipping up dust and dirt. Then the top of the driver's cab appeared. It was a tractor, a huge Landini with a blue cab, lumbering steadily along the ploughed field. That was the sort of thing a person knew if he'd grown up with shit on his wooden clogs. So it's time to spread the manure here too, he thought as he turned on the engine, about to drive off before the stench blew over towards him and settled in the car's air conditioning system.

At that very moment he caught sight of the farmer inside the Plexiglass windows. He was wearing a baseball cap, and all of his attention was focused on his work and the prospect of having a record harvest this summer. He had a ruddy face, and his shirt was red-and-black-checked. A real lumberjack-patterned shirt. Easily recognizable.

Fuck, he thought. He'd forgotten to call his colleagues in Sorø and tell them which type of shirt pattern he thought he could remember the shooter wearing out in Amager. He sighed at the thought. If only they hadn't involved him in all that. Soon they'd probably be asking him to come back and point out the shirt for a second time.

He punched in the number and got hold of the officer on duty. He was immediately transferred to the head of the investigation, the one they called Jørgensen.

'This is Carl Mørck in Copenhagen. I think I can confirm that one of the shirts you showed me matched the one worn by the perp out in Amager.'

Jørgensen didn't respond. Why the hell didn't he at least clear his throat so Carl would know he hadn't croaked in the meantime on the other end of the line?

'Ahem,' said Carl, thinking it might prompt a reaction, but the man didn't say a word. Maybe he'd put his hand over the mouthpiece.

'I've been having dreams the past few nights, you see,' Carl went on. 'More scenes from the shooting incident have come back to me. Including a picture of the shirt. I can see it really clearly now.'

'Is that so?' said Jørgensen at last after yet another resounding silence on the line. He might at least have mustered a few cheers.

'Don't you want to know which shirt on the table I'm thinking of ?'

'And you think you can remember?'

'If I can remember the shirt after getting a bullet in my head and three hundred and thirty pounds of paralysed deadweight on top of me while I was being sprayed with a gallon of my best colleagues' blood, don't you think I can remember how those damned shirts were laid out after four days?'

'It doesn't really seem normal.'

Carl counted to ten. It was very possible it wasn't normal on Storgade in Sorø. That was probably also why he'd ended up in a police department with twenty times as many homicide cases as Jørgensen.

But what he said was: 'I'm also good at playing the Memory Game.'

A pause to let the words sink in. 'Oh, really! Well, then I'd certainly like to hear what you can tell me.'

Damn, what a country bumpkin the man was.

'The shirt was the one on the far left,' said Carl. 'The one closest to the window.'

'OK,' replied Jørgensen. 'That matches what the witness told us.'

'Good. I'm glad. Well, that was all. I'll send you an email so you have it in writing.' By now the tractor in the field had come precariously close. The spray of piss and manure that pounded out of the hoses and on to the ground was truly a joy to behold.

Carl rolled up the window on the passenger side and was just about to end the conversation.

'Just a moment, before you go,' said Jørgensen. 'We've taken in a suspect. Well, just between the two of us, I can say that we're convinced we've caught one of the perpetrators. When do you think you can come down here for the line-up? Some time tomorrow?'

'A line-up? No, I can't do that.'

'What do you mean?'

'Tomorrow is Saturday, and it's my day off. When I'm done sleeping, I'm going to get up and make myself a cup of coffee and then go back to bed. I may do that all day long, you never know. Besides, I never saw the perps out in Amager, which I've actually said many times, in case you take a look at the reports. And since the man's face wasn't revealed to me in my dreams, you can conclude that I haven't seen him since. So I'm not coming in. Is that OK with you, Jørgensen?'

Another pause, for Christ's sake. This was more enervating than politicians who constantly inserted an 'er' or 'um' between every other word in their nauseating, long-winded sentences.

'Only you can decide whether it's OK or not,' said Jørgensen. 'It was your friends was suffered at the hands of this man. We've searched the suspect's place of residence, and several of the things we found indicate a connection between the events in Amager and Sorø.'

'That's good, Jørgensen. Good luck, then. I'll follow the story in the newspapers.'

'You do know that you'll be asked to testify in court, don't you? It's your identification of the shirt that helps to link the two crimes.'

'Yeah, yeah. I'll be there. Happy hunting.'

Carl cut off the connection and noted an unpleasant feeling in his chest. A much stronger sensation than before. Maybe it was due to the unbelievably offensive odour that had seeped into the car, but it could also be a sign of something more serious.

For a minute he just sat and waited until the pressure in his rib cage eased up a bit. Then he returned the wave the farmer had sent him, and started the motor. After Carl had driven about five hundred yards along the road, he slowed down, opened the window, and began gasping for air, arching his back as much as he could to release the tension. Then he pulled over and began sucking the air deeper and deeper into his lungs. He'd seen other people suffering from this type of panic attack, but experiencing it inside his own body was totally surreal. He opened the car door, cupped his hands around his mouth to decrease the effect of hyperventilation, and flung the door all the way open.

'Damn it!' he shouted, doubling over as he staggered along the ditch with a piston pounding in his bronchial tubes. Overhead the clouds were spinning, the sky closing in around him. He dropped to the ground with his legs off to the side and fumbled after the mobile in his jacket pocket. He was damned if he'd die of a heart attack without having anything to say about it.

A car slowed down on the road. The people inside couldn't see him in the ditch, but he could hear them. 'That looks odd,' said a voice, and then the car drove on. If I had their licence number, I'd show them, all right. That was the last thought Carl had before everything went black.

When he came to, he was holding his mobile pressed to his ear, with an awful lot of dirt around his mouth. He licked his lips, spat out some grime, and looked around in confusion. He put his hand to his chest; the pressure was still there but not as bad, and he concluded that things may not be as dire as he'd thought. Then he hauled himself to his feet, staggered back to the car, and tumbled into the driver's seat. It wasn't even one thirty, so he hadn't been out for long.

'What's going on, Carl?' he asked himself. His mouth was dry and his tongue felt twice as thick as normal. His legs were like ice, while his torso was drenched in sweat. Something had gone very wrong with his body.

'You're about to lose control,' he heard a voice bellow inside of him. And then his mobile rang.

Assad didn't ask him how he was feeling. Why should he? 'We have now a problem, Carl,' was all he said as Carl swore to himself.

'The technicians do not dare remove the crossed-out line in Merete Lynggaard's phone book,' Assad continued, undaunted. 'They say that the number and the crossed-out line were made with the same ballpoint pen, so even though they have dried up different, there is much too big a risk that both layers disappear.'

Carl put his hand on his chest again. Now it felt as if he'd swallowed air. It hurt like hell. Was he really having a heart attack? Or did it just feel like he was?

'They say we have to send it all to England. Something about combining some kind of digitalizing process with a chemical emersion, or whatever they said.' He was probably waiting for Carl to correct the terms that he'd used, but Carl wasn't correcting anything at the moment. He had enough to deal with as he squeezed his eyes shut and summoned all his willpower to get rid of the awful spasms that were pumping through his torso.

'I think it takes too long, the whole thing. They say that we will not have the results until three or four weeks. Don't you agree?'

He tried to concentrate, but Assad didn't have the patience to wait.

'Maybe I should not tell you this, Carl, but I think I can count really good on you, so I will tell you anyway. I know a guy who can do this for us.' Assad paused for some sort of acknowledgement, but he waited in vain. 'Are you there now still, Carl?'

'Yes, damn it,' he snapped. Then he inhaled deeply,

expanding his lungs to the limit. It hurt like hell for a moment before the pressure eased. 'Who is he?' Carl asked, trying to relax.

'You do not want to know that, Carl. But he is very good. He is from the Middle East. I know him real well enough, and he is good. Should I set him on the job?'

'Just a minute, Assad. I need to think.'

Carl stumbled out of the car and stood there for a moment, doubled over, his head hanging and his hands on his knees. That sent the blood flowing back to his brain. His face was ablaze but the pressure in his chest faded. Oh, that felt good. In spite of the stench from the farmer's field that wafted past him like a disease, the air out there felt almost refreshing.

When he straightened up, he felt fine.

He picked up his mobile. 'OK, Assad, I'm back. We can't have a passport counterfeiter doing work for us. Do you hear me?'

'Who says he is a passport counterfeiter? I did not say that.'

'So what then?'

'He was just good at doing this kind of thing, where he came from. He can remove stamp marks so you cannot see them. It should be simple for him to remove a little ink. You do not need to know more then. And I will not tell him what he is doing this for. He is fast, Carl. And it will cost nothing. He owes me favours.'

'How fast?'

'We have it on Monday if we want.'

'Then go ahead and give him the shit, Assad. Go ahead.'

Assad muttered something on the other end of the line. Presumably 'OK' in Arabic.

'Just one more thing, Carl. Mrs Sørensen from upstairs in the homicide department wants me to tell you that the witness, that woman in the cyclist case, has started to talk a little bit. And she –'

'Stop right there, Assad. That's not our case.' Carl got back in the car. 'We have enough to do as it is.'

'Mrs Sørensen did not say it exactly to me, but I think upstairs they want your opinion, I mean without asking you, like directly.'

'Go up there and pump her for information, Assad. And then go and visit Hardy on Monday morning and tell him about it. I'm sure it would amuse him more than me. Take a cab out there, and then I'll see you back at headquarters later. OK? In the meantime, keep your chin up, Assad. Say hello to Hardy for me and tell him I'll be out to visit him sometime next week.'

Carl ended the conversation and peered out the windscreen, which looked as though it had been through a shower. But it wasn't rain; he could smell what it was from inside the car. It was pig's piss, à la carte. The springtime country menu.

Sitting on Carl's desk was a sumptuously decorated monster of a tea apparatus, sputtering away. If Assad had thought that the oil flame would keep the mint tea good and hot until his boss returned, he was mistaken, because by now all the water in the kettle had boiled off and the bottom was making creaking noises. Carl blew out the flame and dropped heavily on to his chair, noticing the pressure in his chest again. He'd heard it all before. A warning, then relief. Then maybe another brief warning and after that: you're dead. Bright prospects for a man who had buckets full of years that had to be poured out before he could retire.

He took out Mona Ibsen's business card and weighed it in his hand. Twenty minutes next to her soft, warm body and he'd probably feel much better. The question was whether he'd feel just as good if he had to make do with the company of her soft, warm eyes.

He picked up the phone and punched in her number; as it rang, the pressure in his chest returned. Was it a life-affirming heartbeat or a warning of the opposite? How could he tell?

He was gasping for air as she answered the phone.

'Carl Mørck here,' he said awkwardly. 'I'm ready to make a full confession.'

'Then you'd better go over to St Peter's Church,' she said drily.

'No, honestly. I had a panic attack today; at least I think that's what it was. I'm not feeling well.'

'All right then. Monday at eleven o'clock. Should I phone in a prescription for a sedative, or can you make it through the weekend?'

'I can make it,' he said, although he wasn't too sure about that as he put down the phone.

Time kept ticking away mercilessly. In less than two hours Morten would be home from his afternoon shift at the video shop.

Carl took Merete Lynggaard's phone out of the charger

and switched it on. It said: 'Enter PIN code.' At least the battery was still working. Good old reliable Siemens.

He punched in 1-2-3-4 and got an error message. Then he tried 4-3-2-1, and got the same message. After that he had only one shot left before he'd have to send the phone off to the experts. He opened the case file and found Merete's birth date. Of course, she might just as well have used Uffe's birth date. He leafed through the documents until he found it. Then again, it might also be a combination of the two, or something else altogether. He decided to combine the first two digits of their birth dates, starting with Uffe's. He punched in the numbers.

When the display showed a smiling Uffe, with his arm around Merete's neck, the pressure in Carl's chest vanished for a moment. Someone else might have uttered a triumphant cheer, but Carl didn't have the energy for that. Instead, he leaned back and hauled his feet up on the desk.

As the constriction in his chest returned, he opened the list of incoming and outgoing calls and went through all the numbers from 15 February 2002 until the day Merete Lynggaard disappeared. It was a long list. Some of them he'd have to look up in the companies' archives. Numbers that had been changed and then changed again. It sounded tedious, but after an hour, a clear pattern emerged: during the entire period, Merete had communicated only with colleagues and spokespersons for various special-interest groups. Thirty calls alone were from her own secretariat, including the very last call, made on 1 March.

That meant that any calls from the fake Daniel Hale must have gone through the landline at Christiansborg. If there had been any calls, that is.

Carl sighed and used his foot to push a stack of papers to the middle of his desk. His right leg was itching to give Børge Bak a good kick up the backside. If the original investigative team had ever had a call list for Merete's office phone, it must have been lost, because there was nothing like that in the case file.

Well, he'd just have to leave that issue for Assad to take care of on Monday morning, while he went to see Mona Ibsen for a therapy session.

The selection of Playmobil toys in the toy shop in Allerød wasn't bad; on the contrary. But the prices sure were steep. He couldn't fathom how the local citizenry could afford to bring kids into the world. He chose the absolute cheapest set he could find with more than two figures – a police car with two officers for two hundred and sixty-nine kroner and seventy-five øre, and asked for the receipt. He was pretty certain that Morten would want to come in and exchange the set, anyway.

As soon as Morten arrived home, Carl confessed what he'd done. He took the pieces that he'd borrowed out of the plastic bag and handed his lodger the newly purchased set as well. He told Morten he was more than sorry, and he would never do it again. In fact, he would never set foot in Morten's domain when he wasn't home. Morten reacted as Carl had expected, but it was still a surprise to see how this big, flabby example of how destructive a fatty diet and the lack of exercise could be, was able to tense up his body with such physical rage. How the human body could quiver so much with indigation or that disappointment could be expressed with so many different words. Not only had he stepped on Morten's mega-long toes, he had apparently flattened them totally on the laminated parquet floor.

Carl was looking with dismay at the little plastic family standing on the edge of the kitchen table, wishing that this had never happened, when the pressure in his chest returned in a whole new form.

Morten was so busy declaring that Carl would have to find himself a new lodger, that he didn't notice Carl's distress. Not until he collapsed on the floor with cramps from his neck to his navel. This time the pains were not confined to Carl's chest. His skin felt too tight, his muscles were surging with blood circulation, and he had stomach-muscle spasms that forced his internal organs up against his spine. It didn't really hurt, but he almost couldn't breathe.

In a matter of seconds Morten was bending over him, his eyes wide, asking Carl if he needed a glass of water. A glass of water? What good would that do? Carl thought as his pulse danced to its own irregular beat. Was Morten planning to pour the water over him so his body would have a nice little reminder of a sudden summer shower? Or was he thinking of forcing the water down his throat between his clenched teeth, which at the moment were whistling from the low pressure in his pinioned lungs?

'Yeah, thanks, Morten,' Carl forced himself to say. Anything so they could at least meet halfway, there in the middle of the kitchen floor.

By the time Morten had recovered enough to settle into the most squashed corner of the sofa, his sense of alarm had been replaced by a more pragmatic attitude.

If an otherwise level-headed guy like Carl could accompany his apology with such a dramatic breakdown, then he must have really meant it.

'OK. So we agree to forget all about this little episode, right, Carl?' said Morten, looking solemn.

Carl nodded. He'd agree to anything that would give him some peace and quiet and a few hours to recover before Mona Ibsen started digging around inside him.

32

2007

Carl had hidden a couple of half-empty bottles of whisky and gin behind some books on the living-room bookshelf – booze that Jesper hadn't yet sniffed out and magnanimously contributed to one of his improvised parties.

Carl drank most of both bottles before a sense of calm finally descended over him, and the weekend's endless hours were spent in a deep, deep sleep. Only three times in two days did he get up to grab from the fridge whatever it had to offer. Jesper wasn't home, and Morten had left to visit his parents in Næstved, so who cared if the food was past its expiry date and the menu was an awkward mish-mash of ingredients?

When Monday arrived, it was Jesper's turn to try to rouse Carl out of bed for a change. 'Get up, Carl. What's with you? I need money for food. There's nothing left in the fucking fridge.'

Carl looked at his stepson with eyes that refused to comprehend, let alone accept, the daylight. 'What time is it?' he mumbled. For a moment he couldn't even remember what day it was.

'Come on, Carl. I'm going to be late as hell.'

He glanced at the alarm clock that Vigga had so generously left for him. This was a women who had no respect for the extent of the night-time hours.

He stared at the clock, suddenly wide awake. It was ten minutes past ten. In less than fifty minutes he needed to be sitting on a chair, looking into the exquisite eyes of psychologist Mona Ibsen.

'So you're having a hard time getting out of bed these days?' she ascertained, casting a quick glance at her watch. 'I can see that you're still sleeping badly,' she went on, as if she'd been corresponding with his pillow.

He was annoyed. Maybe it would have helped if he'd had time for a shower before he rushed out the door. I hope I don't stink, he thought, turning his face slightly towards his armpit.

She looked at him calmly as she sat across from him, hands resting in her lap, legs crossed, and clad in black velvet trousers. Her hair was cut in wisps, shorter than before, her eyebrows a thundering black. All in all quite terrifying.

He told her about his collapse out in Farmer Shite's fields, perhaps expecting some show of sympathy.

Instead, she went straight for the jugular. 'Do you feel that you failed your colleagues during the shooting episode?'

Carl swallowed hard a few times, and rambled on about how he could have taken out his gun faster and about instincts that might have become blunted by years spent dealing with criminal elements.

'You feel that you failed your friends. That's my opinion. And in that case, you're going to continue to suffer unless you acknowledge that things couldn't have happened any other way.'

'Things could always have happened differently,' he said.

She ignored his remark. 'You should know that I'm also treating Hardy Henningsen. Which means I'm seeing the case from two sides, and I should have recused myself. But there are no regulations requiring me to, so I need to ask if you wish to continue talking to me, now that you know this. You have to realize that I can't say anything about what Hardy has told me, just as whatever you tell me will naturally also remain confidential.'

'That's OK,' said Carl, but he didn't really mean it. If it weren't for her downy-fine cheeks and lips that simply cried out to be kissed, he would have stood up and told her to go to hell. 'But I'm going to ask Hardy about it,' he said. 'Hardy and I can't have secrets from each other; that just won't work.'

She nodded and straightened her back. 'Have you ever found yourself in other situations you felt you couldn't handle?'

'Yes,' he said.

'When?'

'Right now.' He sent her a penetrating look.

She ignored it. Cold broad.

'What would you give to still have Anker and Hardy around?' she asked, and then quickly fired off four more questions that stirred up a strange feeling of grief inside Carl. With every question she looked him in the eye and then wrote down his answers on her notepad. It felt as if she wanted to push him to the edge. As if he would have to fall dramatically before she was prepared to reach out and catch him.

She noticed that his nose was running before he did. She lifted her gaze to look at him, and then took note of the moisture that had started collecting in his eyes.

Don't blink, dammit, or the tears will fall, he told himself, not understanding what was going on inside him. He wasn't afraid to cry, and he had nothing against her seeing his tears; he just didn't know why it was happening at this particular moment.

'Go ahead and cry,' she said in the same worldly-wise manner that someone might use to encourage a gluttonous infant to burp.

When they ended the session twenty minutes later, Carl had had enough of spilling his guts. Mona Ibsen, on the other hand, seemed satisfied as she shook his hand and gave him another appointment. She assured him again that the outcome of the shooting incident couldn't have been prevented, and that he would undoubtedly regain his sense of equilibrium after a few more sessions.

He nodded. In a certain sense he did feel better. Maybe because her scent overshadowed his own, and because her handshake felt so light and soft and warm.

'Call me if there's anything you want to talk about, Carl. It doesn't matter whether it's something big or small. It might be important for the work we'll be doing together. You never know.'

'Well, then, I've already got a question for you,' he said, trying to draw her attention to his sinewy and purportedly sexy hands. Hands that had often won high praise from the ladies.

She noticed his posturing, and smiled for the first time.

Behind her soft lips were teeth even whiter than Lis's up on the second floor. A rare sight in an age where red wine and caffeinated beverages made most people's teeth look like smoked glass.

'So what's the question?' she asked.

He pulled himself together. It was now or never. 'Are you currently involved with someone?' He was startled how clumsy that sounded, but it was too late to take back his words. 'Sorry,' he said, shaking his head. He was having a hard time figuring out how to go on. 'I just wanted to ask if you might be receptive to a dinner invitation some day.'

Her smile stiffened. Gone were the white teeth and the silky skin.

'I think you need to get back on your feet before you engage in that sort of offensive, Carl. And you'd be wise to choose your victims with greater care.'

He felt disappointment settling throughout his entire endocrine system as she turned her back and opened the door to the hallway. Damn it all, anyway. 'If you don't think you're a good choice,' he grumbled, 'then you have no idea what an amazing effect you have on the opposite sex.'

She turned around and held out her hand to show him the ring on her finger.

'Oh yes, I'm aware of it,' she said, retreating from the field of battle.

He was left standing there, shoulders drooping. In his own eyes he was one of the best detectives the kingdom of Denmark had ever produced, so he wondered how in the world he'd managed to overlook something so elementary.

*

Someone from the Godhavn children's home called to tell Carl they'd got hold of the retired teacher, John Rasmussen, and that on the following day he'd be in Copenhagen to visit his sister. He wanted to pass on the message that he'd always been interested in seeing police headquarters, so he'd be happy to pay Carl a visit between ten and ten thirty, if that was OK. Carl couldn't call him back, because it was the home's policy not to give out private phone numbers, but he could leave a message if he wouldn't be able to meet with Rasmussen.

It wasn't until after Carl put down the phone that he returned to reality. His failed efforts with Mona Ibsen had disconnected certain parts of his brain, and the job of reconnecting them had only just started. So the teacher from Godhavn, who'd been on holiday in the Canary Islands, was going to come and see him. It might have been reassuring to hear that the man actually remembered the boy known as Atomos before Carl agreed to play tour guide at police headquarters. But what the hell.

He took a deep breath and tried to chuck Mona Ibsen and her catlike eyes out of his system. There were plenty of threads in the Lynggaard case that needed to be tied up, so he'd better get started before self-pity sank its claws into him.

One of the first tasks was to ask Helle Andersen, the home help from Stevns to take a look at the photos he'd borrowed from Dennis Knudsen's house. Maybe she too could be persuaded to come down to headquarters for a tour guided by a detective inspector. Anything so he wouldn't have to drive across the Tryggevælde River again.

He called her number and got hold of her husband who claimed to still be on sick leave with unbelievably bad pain in his back, but who otherwise sounded surprisingly fit. He said 'Hi, Carl' as if they'd gone to Scout camp together and eaten out of the same pail.

Listening to him was like sitting next to an old aunt who'd never snagged a husband. Of course he'd be happy to get Helle to come to the phone if she were at home. No, she was always busy with her clients until at least . . . But wait a minute, he thought he heard her car in the driveway. She'd bought herself a new one, by the way, and he could always hear the difference between a 1.3- and a 1.6-litre engine. And it was true what the man on TV said; damned if those Suzukis didn't deliver what they promised. At any rate it was great to get rid of their old Opel for a good price. The husband's voice churned on and on while his wife could be heard announcing her arrival in the background with a shrill: 'Hi, O-o-o-le! Are you home? Did you stack up the firewood?'

Lucky for Ole that Social Services didn't hear that question.

Helle Andersen was cordial and obliging when she finally caught her breath. Carl thanked her for talking to Assad the other day and then asked if she would be able to receive by email some photos he'd scanned.

'Right now?' she asked, and in the next breath was probably going to explain why this wasn't the most favourable moment. 'I've brought home a couple of pizzas.' Here it came. 'Ole likes them with lettuce on top, and it's not much fun when the lettuce has a chance to sink into the cheese.'

Carl had to wait twenty minutes before she called him back, and it sounded as if she hadn't quite swallowed the last mouthful.

'Did you get the email I sent?'

'Yes,' she told him. She was sitting there looking at the three files.

'Click on the first one and tell me what you see.'

'That's Daniel Hale. Your assistant already showed me a picture of him. But I've never seen him before.'

'Then click on the second file. What about that one?'

'Who's that?'

'That's what I'm asking you. His name is Dennis Knudsen. Have you ever seen him before? Maybe a few years older than in the picture?'

She laughed. 'Not wearing a silly cap like that, at any rate. No, I've never seen him before. I'm sure of it. He reminds me of my cousin Gorm, but Gorm is at least twice as fat.'

It seemed to be a family trait.

'What about the third picture? It shows a person talking to Merete at Christiansborg shortly before she disappeared. I know you can only see him from the back, but is there anything about him that seems familiar? His clothes, hair, posture, height, body type, anything at all?'

She paused for a moment, which was a good sign.

'I'm not sure, since the picture only shows him from the back, as you said. But I may have seen him before. Where did you think I would have seen him?'

'That's what I was hoping you'd tell me.'

Come on, Helle, thought Carl. How many possibilities could there be?

'I know you're thinking about the man who delivered

336

the letter. I did see him from behind, but he had on very different clothes, so it's not easy to tell. He looks familiar, but I can't say for sure.'

'Then you shouldn't say anything, dear,' said the allegedly back-damaged pizza eater in the background.

Carl had to make an effort not to sigh. 'OK,' he said. 'I have one last photo that I'd like to send you.' He clicked on his email.

'It's here,' she said ten seconds later.

'Tell me what you see.'

'I see a picture of the guy who was also in the second picture, I think. Dennis Knudsen. Wasn't that his name? Here he's only a boy, but that funny expression on his face is unmistakable. What odd cheeks he has. Yes, I'll bet he drove go-karts when he was a boy. My cousin Gorm did too, strangely enough.'

That was probably before he weighed a thousand pounds, Carl was tempted to say. 'Take a look at the other boy standing behind Dennis. Do you recognize him?'

There was silence on the phone. Not even the malingerer husband said a word. Carl waited. Patience was supposedly a virtue for detectives. So it was just a matter of living up to this maxim.

'This is really creepy,' Helle Andersen said at last. Her voice seemed to have shrunk. 'That's him. I'm positive that's him.'

'The man who brought the letter to you at Merete's house? Is that who you mean?'

'Yes.' Another pause, as if she needed to gauge the photo against the ravages of time. 'Is he the man you're looking for? Do you think he had something to do with what happened to Merete? Should I be scared of him?' She sounded genuinely worried. And maybe at one time she would have had reason to be.

'It was five years ago, so you have nothing to fear, Helle. Take it easy.' He heard her sigh. 'So you think this is the same man who brought the letter. Are you sure now?'

'It has to be. Yes, I'm sure of it. His eyes are so distinctive, you know what I mean? Oh, this is making me feel weird.'

It's probably just the pizza, thought Carl as he thanked the woman and put down the phone. Then he leaned back in his chair.

He looked at the tabloid photos of Merete Lynggaard that were lying on top of the case folder. Right now Carl felt more strongly than ever that he was the link between the victim and perpetrator in this case. For the first time he felt that he was on the right track. This Atomos had lost his grip on life during childhood and grown up to do the devil's work, to use a colourful phrase. The evil inside him had led him to Merete; the question was why and where and how? Maybe Carl would never find the answers, but he was going to try.

Mona Ibsen could sit and polish her wedding ring in the meantime.

Next he sent the pictures to Bille Antvorskov. In less than five minutes Carl had an answer in his email inbox. Yes, one of the boys in the pictures did look like the man who'd been part of the group at Christiansborg. But Antvorskov couldn't swear that it was the same person.

That was enough for Carl. He was sure that Antvorskov

was not the sort to swear to anything without first examining it from head to toe.

The phone rang. It wasn't Assad or the man from the Godhavn children's home, as he expected. Of all people on earth to be calling him at this moment, God help him, it was Vigga.

'What happened to you, Carl?' she said, her voice quavering.

He tried to decipher what was going on but didn't come up with anything before she launched into him.

'The reception started half an hour ago, and not a soul has turned up. We have ten bottles of wine and twenty bags of snacks. If you don't show up either, I simply don't know what I'm going to do.'

'At your gallery? Is that what you mean?'

A couple of sniffles told him that she was about to start sobbing.

'I didn't know anything about any reception.'

'Hugin sent out fifty invitations the day before yesterday.' She sniffled one last time and then pulled the real Vigga out of the goody bag. 'Why can't I count on your support at least? You're an investor in the gallery, after all!'

'Try asking your wandering phantom.'

'Who are you calling a phantom? Hugin?'

'Do you have other lice like him crawling all over you?'

'Hugin is just as concerned as I am that this gallery is a success.'

Carl didn't doubt it. Where else could the man exhibit his torn-off scraps of underwear ads and smashed McDonald's Happy Meal figures splattered with the cheapest paint you could find?

'I'm just saying, Vigga, that if Einstein actually remembered to post the invitations on Saturday, as you claim, then they won't show up in anyone's letter box until they get home from work sometime later today.'

'Oh my God, no! Damn it!' she groaned.

So there was probably a man in black who wasn't getting laid tonight.

Carl couldn't resist feeling gleeful.

Tage Baggesen knocked on the doorframe to his office just as Carl was lighting the cigarette that had been yelling and nagging at him for hours.

'Yeah, what is it?' said Carl, his lungs filled with smoke. Then he recognized the man clad in a nicely acquitted state of mild intoxication that sent a scent of cognac and beers wafting into the room.

'I just wanted to apologize for cutting off our phone conversation so abruptly the other day. I needed time to think, now that everything is going to be made public.'

Carl invited Baggesen to sit down and asked if he'd like something to drink, but the MP dismissed the offer with a wave of his hand as he took a seat. No, he wasn't thirsty.

'Which things did you specifically have in mind?' asked Carl, trying to make it sound as if he had more up his sleeve, which wasn't the case at all.

'Tomorrow I plan to resign from my position in parliament,' said Baggesen, looking around the room with weary eyes. 'I'm going to meet with the chairman after we're done talking here. Merete told me this would happen if I didn't listen, but I didn't want to believe her. And then I did what I never should have done.'

Carl narrowed his eyes. 'Then it's good that the two of us clear the air before you start making confessions to everyone and his uncle.'

The stout man nodded and bowed his head. 'I bought some stocks in 2000 and 2001, and made a killing on them.'

'What kind of stocks?'

'All sorts of shit. And then I hired a new stockbroker who advised me to invest in weapons factories in the United States and France.'

Not the sort of thing that the manager at Carl's local bank in Allerød would recommend to his customers as a sound investment for their savings. He took a deep drag on his cigarette and then stubbed it out in the ashtray. No, Carl could see that these weren't the kind of investments leading member of the pacifist Radical Centre Party would want to be known for.

'I also leased two of my properties to massage parlours. I didn't know about it in the beginning, but I soon found out. They were located in Strøby Egede, near where Merete lived, and people were starting to talk. I had a lot of different things going on at the time. Unfortunately, I bragged about my business deals to Merete. I was so in love with her, and she couldn't have cared less about me. Maybe I was hoping that she'd show more interest in me if I acted like a big shot, but of course it didn't make any difference.' He reached up to massage the back of his neck. 'She wasn't like that at all.'

Carl fixed his eyes on the cloud of smoke until it was swallowed up by the room. 'And she asked you to stop what you were doing?'

'No, she didn't ask me to stop.'

'What then?'

'She said that she might say something by mistake to her secretary, Marianne Koch. It was clear what she meant. If that secretary found out anything, everybody else would know about it in seconds. Merete just wanted to warn me.'

'Why was she interested in your business affairs?'

'She wasn't. That was the whole problem.' He sighed and buried his head in his hands. 'I'd been making advances for so long that she finally just wanted to get rid of me. And that was how she got her way. I'm positive that if I'd continued pressuring her, she would have leaked the information. I don't blame her. What the hell was she supposed to do?'

'So you decided to leave her alone, but you kept running your business ventures?'

'I cancelled the lease agreements for the massage parlours, but I kept the stocks that I owned. I didn't sell them until shortly after 9/11.'

Carl nodded. There were plenty of people who had made a fortune from that catastrophe.

'How much did you make?'

Baggesen looked up. 'Nearly ten million kroner.'

Carl stuck out his lower lip. 'And then you killed Merete because she was going to blow the whistle on you?'

That gave the member of parliament a start. Carl recognized the man's frightened expression from the last time they'd gone a round together.

'No, no! Why on earth would I do that? What I did wasn't illegal, you know. The only thing that would have happened is what's going to happen today.'

'You would have been asked to leave your party instead of resigning?'

Baggesen's eyes flicked around the room and didn't stop until he saw his own initials on the list of suspects on the whiteboard.

'You can cross me off your list now,' he said and stood up.

Assad didn't show up at the office until three o'clock, which was considerably later than would be expected of a man with his modest qualifications and precarious position. For a second Carl weighed how useful it would be to bawl him out, but Assad's cheerful expression and enthusiasm didn't exactly invite an ambush.

'What the hell have you been doing all this time?' he asked instead, pointing at the clock.

'Hardy sends you his greetings, Carl. You sent me yourself up there, remember?'

'You've been talking to Hardy for seven hours?' He pointed again at the clock.

Assad shook his head. 'I told him what I knew about the cyclist murder then, and do you know what he said?'

'He told you who he thinks the killer is?'

Assad looked surprised. 'You know Hardy pretty very well, Carl. Yes, that is actually what he did.'

'He didn't give you a name, though. Am I right?'

'A name? No, but he said to look for a person who was important for the witness's children then. That it probably was not a teacher or somebody in the day-care centres but somebody they were really dependent on. The ex-husband of the witness or a doctor or maybe someone the children saw up to a lot. A riding instructor or something. But it had to be a person who had something to do with both of the children. I have also just said it up on the second floor.'

'Oh really,' said Carl, pursing his lips. It was astounding how well informed Assad suddenly was. 'I can just imagine Bak must have been over the moon.'

'Over the moon?' Assad considered Carl's choice of words. 'Maybe. How would that make him look?'

Carl shrugged. Now Assad was his old self again. 'So what else have you been doing?' Judging by the way Assad's eyebrows danced, Carl guessed that he had something up his sleeve.

'Look what I have here, Carl.' He took Merete Lynggaard's worn leather diary out of a plastic shopping bag and set it on the desk. 'Take a look. Isn't the man so good?'

Carl opened the phone book to the letter *H* and immediately saw the transformation. Yes, the man had truly done a spectacular job. The thick line through the phone number was now gone; the number was a bit faded but clearly legible: 'Daniel Hale, 25772060'. It was amazing. Even more amazing than the speed with which Carl's fingers tapped on the computer keyboard to check the number.

He couldn't resist looking it up. But without any luck, of course.

'It says it's an invalid number. Call Lis and ask her to check out the number asap. Tell her it might well have been disconnected five years ago. We don't know which mobile company issued it, but I'm sure she can find out. Hurry up, Assad,' said Carl, giving his assistant a pat on his granite-like shoulder.

*

Carl lit a cigarette, leaned back, and summed up what they knew so far.

Merete Lynggaard had met the fraudulent Daniel Hale at Christiansborg and had possibly carried on a flirtation with him, but then dropped him after a few days. It was unusual for her to do something like crossing out his name in her phone book; it almost seemed ritualistic. No matter what the reason for doing so, meeting the man who called himself Daniel Hale had undoubtedly been a radical experience in Merete's life.

Carl tried to picture her in his mind. The beautiful politician with her whole life ahead of her, who happened to meet the wrong guy. An impostor, a man with evil intentions. Several people had linked him to the boy called Atomos. The home help in Magleby thought the boy was very likely identical to the man who had brought the letter with the message: 'Have a nice trip to Berlin.' And according to Bille Antvorskov, Atomos was the same person who later claimed to be Daniel Hale. The same boy that Dennis Knudsen's sister claimed had exerted great influence over her brother in childhood. And by all accounts he was also the one who many years later convinced his friend Dennis to crash into the car driven by the real Daniel Hale, thereby causing his death. Complicated, and yet not really.

By now quite a lot of evidence had piled up: there was Dennis Knudsen's peculiar death shortly after the car accident. There was Uffe's much too strong reaction when he saw the old photo of Atomos, who was most likely the person Merete later met as Daniel Hale. A meeting that must have required a great deal of planning.

345

And finally, there was the disappearance of Merete Lynggaard.

Carl felt acid indigestion etching its way up and almost wished he could have a sip of Assad's sickly sweet tea.

Carl hated waiting when it wasn't necessary. Why the hell couldn't he talk to that fucking teacher from the Godhavn children's home right this minute? The boy nicknamed Atomos must have a real name and a Civil Registry number. Something that would still be valid today. He wanted to know what it was. Now!

He stubbed out his cigarette and took down the lists from the whiteboard, scanning what he had written.

SUSPECTS:

1) Uffe
2) Unknown postman – the letter about Berlin
3) The man/woman from Café Bankeråt
4) 'Colleagues' at Christiansborg – TB+?
5) Murder resulting from a robbery – how much money in her purse?
6) Sexual assault

CHECK:

The telegram
The secretaries at Christiansborg
Witnesses on the ferry *Schleswig-Holstein*

The foster family after the accident – old classmates at the university. Did she have a tendency to get depressed? Was she pregnant? In love?

Next to 'Unknown postman' Carl now wrote in parentheses: 'Atomos as Daniel Hale.' Then he crossed out item number four with Tage Baggesen's initials and the question about her being pregnant at the bottom of the second page.

In addition to item number three, he still had items five and six left on the first list. Even a small amount of money could have tempted the sick brain of some robber. But item number six, the possible sexual-assault motive, seemed unlikely, given the circumstances and time frame on board the ferry.

With regard to the items on the second list, he still hadn't talked to the witnesses on the ferry, the foster family or university classmates. As for the witnesses, their statements had offered nothing useful, and the other points he'd written down were no longer relevant. It was obvious that Merete had not committed suicide, in any case.

No, these lists aren't going to get me any further, thought Carl. He studied them for a few more minutes and then tossed them in the wastebasket, which had to be put to good use, after all.

He picked up Merete's phone book and held it close to his eyes. Assad's contact had certainly done a hell of a job. The crossed-out line was completely gone. It was really unbelievable.

'Tell me who did this!' Carl shouted across the hall, but Assad stopped him from saying anything else with a wave of his hand. Carl saw that his assistant had the phone glued to his ear as he sat at his desk, nodding his head. He didn't look very animated; on the contrary. No doubt it hadn't been possible to find out the name of the subscriber for the old mobile number listed in the telephone registered under the name of Hale.

'Was there a prepaid calling card in the mobile?' he asked when Assad came in holding a scrap of paper and fanning away the cigarette smoke with disapproval.

'Yes,' he replied, handing Carl the note. 'The mobile belonged to a girl at Tjørnelys middle school in Greve. She reported it stolen from her coat, which she hung up outside the classroom on Monday 18th February 2002. The theft was not reported until a few days later, and no one knows who did it.'

Carl nodded. So now they knew the name of the subscriber, but not who stole the mobile and then used it. That made sense. He was now convinced that everything was connected. Merete Lynggaard's disappearance was no accident. A man had approached her with dishonest intentions, and set off a chain of events that ended with no one having seen the beautiful Folketing politician since. In the meantime, more than five years had passed. Naturally Carl feared the very worst.

'Lis is asking now if she should keep going on the case,' said Assad.

'What do you mean?'

'Should she look for a link between those conversations there from the old phone in Merete's office with this number?' Assad pointed at the little scrap of paper where he had neatly printed in block letters: '25772060, Sanne Jønsson, Tværager 90, Greve Strand.' So Assad was capable of writing something that was legible after all.

Carl shook his head at himself. Had he really forgotten to compare the lists of phone calls? Damned if he wasn't

348

going to have to start making notes for himself before Alzheimer's Lite took over.

'Of course,' he replied in an authoritative tone. In that way they might be able to establish a timeline in communication that showed a pattern in the course of the relationship between Merete and the Daniel Hale impostor.

'But you know what, Carl? It will take a couple of days, and Lis does not have time right now. She says that it will be fairly so difficult after such a long time then. Maybe it cannot even be done.' Assad looked downright mournful.

'Tell me now, Assad. Who do you know that does such nice work?' said Carl, weighing Merete's appointment diary in his hand.

But Assad refused.

Carl was just about to explain that this sort of secrecy wasn't helping his chances of keeping his job, but then the phone rang.

It was the director from Egely, and his disdain for Carl practically dripped out of the receiver. 'I want you to know that Uffe Lynggaard took off a short time after your utterly insane assault on him last Friday. We have no idea where he is right now. The police in Frederikssund have been alerted, but if anything serious happens to him, Carl Mørck, I promise I am going to torment you for the rest of your career.'

Then he slammed down the phone, leaving Carl in a thundering void.

Two minutes later the homicide chief called and asked Carl to come upstairs to his office. He didn't need to elaborate; Carl recognized the tone.

He'd been summoned. Now.

33

2007

The nightmare started as soon as he passed the newsstand outside the Allerød station, headed for work. The expanded Easter issue of *Gossip* had come out a week early, and even those who had only a passing acquaintance with Carl now knew that it was his photo, Detective Inspector Carl Mørck, that graced a corner of the front page, right under the lead story about the impending wedding of the Danish prince and his French sweetheart.

A couple of locals moved aside in embarrassment as they bought sandwiches and fruit. 'Police Detective Threatens Journalist' screamed the headline. And underneath in smaller letters it said: 'The Truth about the Fatal Shots'.

The clerk seemed truly disappointed when Carl chose not to personally invest his hard-earned money in a copy of *Gossip*. But he'd be damned if he'd contribute even one øre to Pelle Hyttested's livelihood.

Quite a few people on the train stared at Carl, and again he felt the pressure settling in his rib cage.

Things didn't get better at police headquarters. He'd finished the previous work day listening to the homicide chief reprimand him because of Uffe's disappearance. Now he was summoned upstairs again.

'What are you staring at, you morons?' he snarled as he

walked past a couple of colleagues who didn't exactly look as if they were aggrieved on his behalf.

'Well, Carl. The question is: What are we going to do with you?' said Marcus Jacobsen. 'I'm afraid that next week I'll be seeing headlines saying you've been psychologically terrorizing some poor retarded person. I'm sure you realize that the media is going to have a field day if anything happens to Uffe Lynggaard.' He pointed at the newspaper. There was a picture of a scowling Carl, taken years earlier at a crime scene. Carl recalled how he'd kicked the press out of the cordoned-off area, and how furious the journalists had been.

'So let me ask again: What are we going to do with you, Carl?'

Carl picked up the tabloid with annoyance and scanned the text in the centre of the yellow-and-red layout splotches. They really knew how to drag a man through the mud, those gossip-spewing, low-life reporters.

'I never made any sort of statement about the case to anyone at *Gossip*,' he said. 'All I said was that I would have gladly given up my own life for Hardy and Anker. That's it. Just ignore it, Marcus, or get our lawyers to go after them.'

He tossed the tabloid on the desk and stood up. Now he'd given his testimony, and it was the truth. What the hell was Marcus going to do about it? Fire him? That would certainly produce some more good headlines.

His boss gave him a resigned look. 'The crime programme on Channel 2 called. They want to talk to you. I told them to forget it.'

'OK,' replied Carl. His boss probably didn't dare do otherwise.

'They asked me if there was anything to the *Gossip* story about you and the shooting episode out in Amager.'

'Is that right? Then I'd like to hear what you told them.'

'I said that the whole thing was pure bullshit.'

'OK, that's good.' Carl nodded doggedly. 'Is that what you really think?'

'Carl, I'm going to tell you something, and I want you to listen carefully. You've been on the force for a long time now. How many times during your career have you seen a colleague being pushed into a corner? Think about the very first time you were a cop on the night beat in Randers, or wherever the hell it was, and all of a sudden you found yourself face to face with a bunch of shit-faced farmboys who didn't like your uniform. Do you remember what that felt like? Then, as the years pass, situations come up that are a hundred times worse. I've been through it. Lars Bjørn and Bak have been through it. And plenty of former colleagues who now make their living doing something else have been through it too. Life-threatening situations. With axes and hammers, metal rods, knives, broken beer bottles, shotguns, and all sorts of weapons. How many times can a person handle that sort of situation, and when does he decide he just can't take it any more? Who knows? It's impossible to predict, don't you think? We've all been up shit creek at one time or another. Anyone who hasn't is not a real cop. We just have to go out there, knowing that we might be out of our depth once in a while. That's our job.'

Carl nodded, feeling the pressure in his chest take on a

new form. 'So what's the verdict on all this, boss?' he said, pointing at the tabloid. 'What do you have to say about it? What do you think?'

The homicide chief looked at Carl with a calm expression. Without saying a word, he got up and opened the window facing Tivoli. Next he picked up the newspaper, bent over, and pretended to wipe his backside with it. Then he tossed the whole mess out into the street.

He couldn't have been more explicit about his opinion.

Carl felt a smile tugging at his lips. Some pedestrian down on the street below was going to be the lucky recipient of a free copy of the TV schedule.

He nodded to his boss. Marcus's reaction had actually been quite touching.

'I'm close to having new information in the Lynggaard case,' he said in return, and waited to be given permission to leave.

Jacobsen nodded back with a certain show of approval. It was in these sorts of situations that he demonstrated why he was so well liked, and why he'd been able to hold on to the same beautiful woman for more than thirty years. 'Just remember that you still haven't signed up for the management course, Carl,' Jacobsen interjected. 'And you need to do that in the next two days. Do you hear me?'

Carl nodded, but didn't mean anything by it. If his boss was going to insist that he take the course, Marcus would first have to deal with the union.

The four minutes that it took Carl to walk from the homicide chief's office down to the basement were a gauntlet of scornful looks and disapproving attitude. You're a disgrace to us all, said some of those eyes. But I don't give a shit, he thought. They should be giving him their support instead; then he probably wouldn't have this feeling of a big fat axe hacking into his chest.

Even Assad had seen the article, but at least he gave Carl a pat on the back. He thought the picture on the front page was nicely in focus, but the tabloid cost too much.

It was refreshing to hear a different point of view.

At ten o'clock sharp the phone rang; it was from 'the cage', the front desk at police headquarters. 'There's a man here who says he has an appointment with you, Carl,' said the duty officer coldly. 'Are you expecting somebody named John Rasmussen?'

'Yes, send him down.'

Five minutes later they heard hesitant footsteps out in the corridor and then a cautious 'Hello, is anybody here?'

Carl forced himself to get up. In the doorway he came face to face with an anachronism wearing an Icelandic sweater, corduroy trousers and the whole hippie outfit.

'I'm John Rasmussen, the one who was a teacher at the Godhavn children's home. We have an appointment,' he said, holding out his hand with a sly expression. 'Hey, wasn't that your picture on the front page of one of the tabloids today?'

It was enough to drive you mad. Dressed in that sort of get-up, the man really should have known better than to stare.

After that they quickly established that John Rasmussen did remember Atomos, and then they agreed to go over the case before they took a tour of police headquarters. That would allow Carl the chance to get off with giving him a mini-tour of the ground floor and a brief look out in the courtyards.

The man seemed pleasant enough, if a bit long-winded. Not at all the type that delinquent boys would have the patience to put up with, in Carl's opinion. But there were probably still a few things that Carl didn't know about delinquent boys.

'I'll fax you what we have about him up at the home; I've already arranged with the office staff that it would be OK. But I have to tell you that there isn't much. Atomos's case file disappeared a few years ago, and when we finally found it behind a bookshelf, at least half of the documents were missing.' He shook his head, making the loose skin under his chin wobble.

'Why did he end up in your institution?'

Rasmussen shrugged. 'Problems on the home front, you know. And he'd been placed with a foster family that probably wasn't the best choice. Which can provoke a reaction, and sometimes things go too far. He was apparently a good kid, but he wasn't given enough challenges and he was too smart. And that makes for an ugly combination. You see kids like that everywhere in the ghettos where the foreign workers live. They're practically exploding with untapped energy, those young people.'

'Was he mixed up in any sort of criminal activity?'

'I suppose he was, in a sense, but I think it was only minor stuff. I mean, OK, he had a fierce temper, but I don't remember him being at Godhavn because of anything violent. No, I don't recall anything like that, but it was twenty years ago, after all.'

Carl pulled his notepad closer. 'I'm going to ask you a few quick questions, and I'd appreciate it if you'd keep your answers brief. If you can't answer a question, we'll just move on. You can always go back to it, if you think of an answer later. OK?'

The man gave a friendly nod to Assad, who offered him one of his viscous, burning-hot substances in a dainty little cup decorated with gold flowers. Rasmussen accepted the cup with a smile. He was going to regret it.

Then he turned to look at Carl. 'OK,' he said. 'I understand.'

'What's the boy's real name?'

'I think it was Lars Erik or Lars Henrik, or something like that. He had a very common last name. I think it was Petersen, but I'll tell you in my fax.'

'Why was he called Atomos?'

'It was a nickname his father had given him. Apparently he really looked up to his father, who'd died a few years earlier. I think his father was an engineer and had something to do with the nuclear research station at Risø, or some place like that. But I'm sure you can find out more details when you have the boy's name and CR number.'

'Do you still have his CR number?'

'Yes. It disappeared with the other documents from his file, but we had a bookkeeping system that was linked to funding from the municipalities and the national government, so the number has been restored to his file.'

'How long was he in your institution?'

'I think he was there about three or four years.'

'That was a long time, considering his age, wasn't it?'

'Yes and no. That's how it goes sometimes. It wasn't

possible to find another place for him in the system. He refused to live with a new foster family, and his own family wasn't able to look after him until then.'

'Have you heard from him since? Do you know what happened to him?'

'I happened to see him, just by chance, some years later, and he seemed to be doing fine. I think it was in Helsingør. He was apparently working as a steward or a first mate, or something like that. He was wearing a uniform, at any rate.'

'You mean, he was a seaman?'

'Yes, I think so. Something along that line.'

I have to get hold of the crew list for the *Schleswig-Holstein* ferry from Scandlines, Carl said to himself, wondering if it had ever been requisitioned. Again he saw Bat's conscience-stricken face before him from last Thursday, when they were sitting in Marcus Jacobsen's office.

'Just a minute,' he said to Rasmussen, and then told Assad to go upstairs and find Bak. He needed to ask him whether they'd ever received a list of personnel on the ferry that Merete Lynggaard had taken. And if so, where was it now?

'Merete Lynggaard? Is this about her?' asked the man, his eyes sparkling like Christmas lights. He took a big gulp of the syrupy tea.

Carl gave him a smile that radiated how incredibly pleased he was to be asked that question. Then he went back to his own questions, without replying.

'Did the boy have psychotic tendencies? Do you remember if he was able to show empathy?'

The teacher looked at his empty cup as if he were still

thirsty. Apparently he was one of those people whose taste buds had been tempered back in the macrobiotic days. Then he raised his grey eyebrows. 'A lot of the boys who come to us are emotionally abnormal. Of course some of them are given a medical diagnosis, but I don't remember that happening with Atomos. I do think he was able to show empathy. At least he worried about his mother a lot.'

'Was there any reason for that? Was she a drug addict or something?'

'No, not at all. But I seem to recall that she was quite ill. That was why it took so long before his family could take him back.'

The tour of police headquarters was brief. John Rasmussen turned out to be an insatiable observer, and he commented on everything he saw. If it had been up to him, he would have examined every square foot of the buildings. No detail was too insignificant for Rasmussen, so Carl pretended he had a pager in his pocket that was beeping. 'Oh, sorry, I just received the signal that there's been another murder,' he told the man with a solemn look that the teacher immediately adopted. 'I'm afraid I'll have to say goodbye now. Thanks for your help, Mr Rasmussen. And I'll count on receiving a fax from you within an hour or two. All right?'

Silence had settled over Carl's domain. On his desk in front of him was a message from Bak saying that he knew nothing about any ferry-boat personnel list. Why the hell had Carl expected anything else?

He could hear the murmur of prayers coming from the

corner of Assad's cubbyhole where the rug was positioned, but otherwise no other sound. Carl felt tossed by the storm and swept by the wind. The phone had been ringing off the hook for over an hour because of the fucking tabloid article. Everyone had called, from the police commissioner, who wanted to give him a word of advice, to local radio stations, website editors, magazine journalists, and all sorts of other vermin that crawled about on the fringes of the media world. Apparently Mrs Sørensen upstairs was finding it amusing to transfer all the calls to Carl, so now he'd switched the phone to silent and activated the caller-ID function, which displayed the number of the incoming call. The problem was that he'd never been good at remembering numbers. But at least for now he didn't have to put up with anyone else accosting him.

The fax from the Godhavn teacher was the first thing that managed to haul Carl out of his self-imposed torpor.

As expected, Rasmussen was a polite man, and he took the opportunity to offer his thanks and praise to Carl for taking the time to show him around headquarters. The other pages were the promised documents, and in spite of their brevity, they were a gold mine.

The real name of the boy called Atomos was Lars Henrik Jensen. His CR number was 020172-0619, so he was born in 1972. Today he would be thirty-five, which meant that he and Merete Lynggaard were approximately the same age.

Lars Henrik Jensen – what an insanely ordinary name, thought Carl wearily. Why the hell hadn't Bak or one of those other clowns on the original investigative team been smart enough to print out the crew list from the

Schleswig-Holstein? Who knew if it was even possible to dig up the duty roster from so long ago?

He pursed his lips. It would be a huge step forward if it turned out that this guy had worked on the ferry back then, but hopefully that could readily be revealed by making an inquiry to Scandlines. He read over the faxes one more time and then grabbed the phone to call the main Scandlines office.

A voice started speaking even before he had punched in the number. For a moment he thought it was Lis, but then Mona Ibsen's wax-coated, velvety voice rolled into his ear, leaving him holding his breath.

'What happened?' she asked. 'The phone didn't even ring.'

Yes, that was a good question. She must have been transferred to his phone at the same instant that he picked it up.

'I saw today's issue of *Gossip*,' she said.

He swore under his breath. Not her too. If that shitty tabloid only knew how many readers he'd brought in this week, they'd probably put his likeness under their masthead permanently.

'This is a rather unusual situation, Carl. How has it made you feel?'

'Well, it's not the best thing that's ever happened to me, I have to admit,' he told her.

'You should come and see me again soon,' she said.

Somehow the offer didn't seem quite as attractive as it had before. Most likely because of the signal-disrupting wedding ring that had caused interference with his antennas.

'I have a feeling that you and Hardy won't be free, in a

psychological sense, until the killers have been caught. Do you agree, Carl?'

He felt the distance between them grow. 'No, not at all,' he said. 'It has nothing to do with those bastards. People like us have to live with danger all the time.' He tried hard to recall Marcus's lecture from earlier that day, but this erotic individual's breathing on the other end of the line wasn't helping. 'You have to consider that there are plenty of times in a cop's professional past when things didn't go wrong. Sooner or later its bound to happen.'

'I'm glad to hear you say that,' she replied. Hardy must have said something similar. 'But you know what, Carl? It's pure bullshit! I'm going to expect to meet with you on a regular basis, so we can figure this whole thing out. Next week there won't be anything more about you in the tabloids, so we should be able to work in peace and quiet.'

The man Carl talked to at Scandlines was very accommodating. As with similar cases of missing persons, the company had a case file on Merete Lynggaard at hand, and they were able to confirm that the personnel list from that sad day had indeed been printed out back then, with a copy delivered to the police Rapid Response Team. All crew members, both above and below decks, had been interviewed, but unfortunately no one had any information that might indicate what had happened to Merete during the crossing.

Carl felt like banging his head against the wall. What the hell had the police done with that list in the meantime? Used it for a coffee filter? To hell with Bak & Company, and everyone like them.

'I have a CR number,' he told the secretary. 'Could you run a search on it?'

'Not today,' he replied. 'I'm sorry, but the whole accounting department is away taking a course.'

'OK. Is the list in alphabetical order?' Carl asked. It wasn't. The captain and his closest subordinates had been listed first; that was common procedure. On board a ship, everyone knew his or her place in the hierarchy.

'Could you check for the name Lars Henrik Jensen?'

The man on the other end of the line gave a weary laugh. Apparently the list was a real whopper.

In the time that it took Assad to finish yet another prayer, splash his face with water from a little bowl in the corner, blow his nose with an expressive blast, and then put on yet another pot of candied water to boil, the clerk in the Scandlines office managed to complete his search. 'No, there's no Lars Henrik Jensen,' he said, and with that the phone call was over.

It was damned depressing.

'Why do you look so gloomy, Carl?' asked Assad with a smile. 'Do not think any more about that stupid picture in that stupid paper. Just think about if you had broken all your arms and legs – that would have been much worse then.'

Undeniably a strange consolation.

'I found out that boy Atomos's real name, Assad,' said Carl. 'I had a feeling that he worked on board the ship Merete disappeared from, but he didn't. That's why I look like this.'

Carl received a well-placed thump on the back. 'But you found out about the list of the ship's crew anyway then. Good job, Carl,' said Assad, using the same tone of voice as when a toddler has successfully used the potty.

'Well, it didn't really lead to anything, but we'll keep plugging away. His CR number was in the fax from God-havn, so I'm sure we'll find the guy. Thank God we've got access to all the official registries we have use for.'

He typed in the number on the computer, with Assad standing behind him, and felt like a child about to open a Christmas present. The best moment for every police detective was when the identity of a prime suspect was about to be revealed.

But instead came disappointment.

'What does that mean, Carl?' asked Assad, pointing at the computer screen.

Carl took his hand off the mouse and stared up at the ceiling. 'It means the number can't be found. No one in the whole kingdom of Denmark has that particular CR number. It's that simple.'

'Didn't you write it wrong then? Are you sure that is what the fax says?'

Carl checked. Yes, he'd copied the number correctly.

'Maybe it is then not the right number.'

Good guess.

'Maybe somebody changed it.' Assad took the fax from Carl, frowning as he studied the number. 'Look at this, Carl. I think someone changed one number or two. What do you think? Isn't it like scratched in there and there?' He pointed at two of the last four digits. It was hard to see, but on the fax copy there did seem to be a faint shadow surrounding two of the typed numbers.

'Even if only two numbers were changed, Assad, there would be hundreds of possible combinations.'

'Yes, and so what? Mrs Sørensen can type in the CR numbers in a half, fast hour, if we send some flowers upstairs to her.'

It was unbelievable how the guy had wormed his way into the good graces of that shrew. 'As I said, there could be hundreds of possibilities, Assad. And if somebody changed two numbers, maybe they changed all ten. We need to get the original document from Godhavn and examine it more closely before we start trying out number combinations.'

Carl called the institution immediately and asked them to send the original document to police headquarters by messenger, but they refused to comply. They didn't want the original to get lost.

Then Carl explained how important it was. 'It's likely that you've had a counterfeit document in your archives for years.'

His assertion had no effect. 'No, I don't think so,' came the self-confident reply. 'We would have discovered it when we reported the information to the authorities to renew our funding.'

'I see. But what if the counterfeiting occurred a long time after the client left the institution? Who on earth would discover it then? You have to consider the possibility that this new CR number didn't appear in your books until at least fifteen years after Atomos left.'

'I'm sorry, but we still can't let you have the original document.'

'OK, then we'll have to get a court order. I find your

attitude less than cooperative. We're investigating a possible murder here. Keep that in mind.'

Neither the fact that they were investigating a murder nor the threat of court involvement was going to do any good; Carl knew that from the start. Appealing to a person's ego was far more effective. Because who wanted to be saddled with a derogatory label? Not people in the Social Services system, at any rate. The phrase 'less than cooperative' was such an understatement that it packed a lot of punch. 'The tyranny of the quiet remark', as one of Carl's instructors at the police academy liked to call it.

'You'll need to send us an email first, with a request to see the original,' said the staff member.

Finally he'd hit home.

'So what was the real name then of that Atomos boy, Carl? Do we know how he got a nickname like that?' asked Assad afterwards, his foot resting on the open drawer of Carl's desk.

'They told me it was Lars Henrik Jensen.'

'Lars Henrik. Strange name. Not many people could be called that.'

Probably not where Assad comes from, thought Carl. He was considering making a sarcastic remark when he noticed the oddly pensive expression on Assad's face. For a moment he looked completely different than usual. More present, more focused. More of an equal, somehow.

'What are you thinking, Assad?' he asked.

It was as if a film of oil slid over his eyes, and their colour changed. He frowned and grabbed the Lynggaard file. It took only a second for him to find what he was looking for.

'Can that be a coincidence?' he asked, pointing to a line on the top document.

Carl looked at the name and then realized which report Assad was holding.

For a moment Carl tried to picture everything in his mind, and then it happened. Somewhere inside of him, where cause and effect were not weighed against each other, and where logic and explanations never challenged consciousness, in that place where thoughts could live freely and be played out against each other – right there in that spot, things fell into place, and he understood how it all fitted together.

34

2007

The biggest shock was not to look into the eyes of Daniel, the man to whom she had been so attracted. Nor was it the realization that Daniel and Lasse were one and the same person, even though that made her legs weak. No, the worst thing was knowing who he really was. It simply drained everything out of her. All that remained was the heavy weight of guilt that had rested on her shoulders her entire adult life.

It wasn't really his eyes that she recognized – it was the pain she saw in them. The pain and the despair and the hatred, which in a split second had taken over this man's life. Or rather, the boy's life. She knew that now.

Because Lasse was only fourteen on that frosty clear winter day when he looked out of the window of his parents' car and saw in another car a girl, full of life and thoughtless, teasing her brother so vigorously on the back seat that she diverted her father's attention. Diverted for a few milliseconds her father's sense of judgement and prevented him from gripping the steering wheel. Those precious fractions of a second of lapsed vigilance, which could have spared the lives of five people and prevented three others from being maimed. Only Merete and the boy named Lasse had escaped from the accident with their lives and health intact. And precisely for that reason, it was between the two of them the account now had to be settled.

She understood that. And she surrendered to her fate.

During the next months the man whom she'd once been attracted to under the name of Daniel, and now detested as Lasse, appeared in the outer room every single day to look at her through the porthole. Some days he merely stood there, observing her as if she were a civet cat in a cage, about to fight to the death with a superior force of cobra snakes; on other days he spoke to her. Only rarely did he ask her any questions. He had no need to. It was as though he knew what her answers would be.

'When you looked into my eyes from your car, at the moment when your father was passing us, I thought you were the most beautiful girl I'd ever seen in my whole life,' he said one day. 'But the next second when you grinned at me, and didn't bother to notice what a ruckus you were causing in your own car, I knew even then that I hated you. That was the instant before our car spun around, and my little sister sitting next to me broke her neck against my shoulder. I heard it snap, do you realize that?'

He stared at her intently, trying to make her look away, but she refused to avert her eyes. She did feel shame, but that was all. The hatred was mutual.

Then he told his story about the moments that had changed everything. About how his mother tried to give birth to the twins in the wreck of the car, and how his father, whom he had loved and admired so much, stared at him with a loving expression as he died with his mouth agape. About the flames that crept up along his mother's leg, which was jammed fast under the front seat. About his beloved little sister, so sweet and playful, who lay crushed beneath him; and about the second twin to be born, who lay in such an awkward position, with the umbilical cord wrapped around his neck; and the other one, who lay on the windscreen wailing as the flames approached.

His words were terrible to hear. She remembered all too clearly their desperate screams as his story savaged her with guilt.

'My mother can't walk; she's been crippled ever since the accident. My brother never went to school; he was never able to learn what other children learn. We all lost our lives because of what you did back then. How do you think it feels to have a father, a sweet kid sister, and the prospect of two little brothers, and then all of a sudden nothing is left? My mother always had a fragile psyche, but even so, she was sometimes able to laugh light-heartedly. Until you came into our lives, that is, and she lost everything. Everything!'

By that point the woman had come into the room, and she seemed clearly upset by his account. Maybe she was crying. Merete couldn't be sure.

'How do you think I felt during those first few months, all alone with a foster family that beat me? A boy like me, who had never experienced anything but love and security in his life. There wasn't a single moment when I didn't want to strike back at that shithead who insisted that I call him "Dad". And the whole time I could see you before me, Merete. You and your lovely, irresponsible eyes that annihilated everything I ever loved.' He paused for so long that the words he spoke next were shockingly clear. 'Oh, Merete, I promised myself that I would take revenge on you and all the others, no matter what the cost. And you know what? Today I feel good. I've exacted revenge on all of you fuckers who took our lives away. You should know that once I even considered killing your brother. But then one day while I was watching you, I saw what a hold he had on you. How much guilt there was in your eyes when the two of you were together. How much his presence clipped your wings. Did I really want to lighten that burden for you by killing him, too? And besides, wasn't he another one of your victims? So I let him live. But not my foster-father, and not you, Merete. Not you.'

He'd been sent to the children's home after the first time he tried to kill his foster-father. The family never told the authorities what he'd done, or that the deep gash in the foster-father's forehead had come from the blade of a shovel. They just said that the boy was sick in the head, and that they could no longer take responsibility for him. That way they could get another foster-child from the state, to make money off.

But the wild beast inside Lasse had been awakened. No one would ever take control of him or his life again.

After that episode, five years, two months and thirteen days passed before the insurance claims were paid, and his mother felt well enough to allow Lasse, now an adult, to move back home to live with her and his handicapped brother. One of the twins had been burned so badly that his life couldn't be saved, but the other had survived in spite of the cord wrapped around his neck.

Lasse's infant brother had been placed with a family while their mother was in the hospital and the rehabilitation centre, but she brought him home before he turned three. His face and chest had scars from the fire, and he had very poor motor control because of the oxygen deprivation he'd suffered. But he was his mother's solace for a couple of years while she regained her strength so that Lasse could come home. The family received a million and a half kroner in compensation for their ruined lives. A million and a half for the loss of his father and his successful business, which no one else was able to run; for the loss of a little sister and the infant twin brother, along with his mother's loss of mobility and the whole family's well-being. A paltry million and a half kroner. When Merete was no longer their daily focus of attention, Lasse was going to direct his revenge at the insurance people and the lawyers who had cheated his family out of the compensation they deserved. That was something Lasse had promised his mother.

Merete had a great deal to pay for.

Time was about to run out; she knew that. Anxiety and relief grew inside of her at the same time. The almost five years in this loathsome captivity was consuming her, but eventually it would have to come to an end. Of course it would.

By the time New Year's Eve arrived in 2006, the pressure in the room had long since been increased to six atmospheres, and since then all of the fluorescent lights but one had flickered constantly. A festively clad Lasse appeared, together with his mother and brother on the other side of the mirrored panes to wish Merete a Happy New Year, adding that this would be the last New Year of her life.

371

'We know the date of your death, if we think about it, don't we, Merete?' he'd said at the time. 'It's so logical. If you add up the years and months and days that I was forced to be away from my family until the day when I captured you like the animal you are, then you'll know when you're going to die. You must suffer in loneliness exactly as long as I did, but no more. Figure it out, Merete. When the time comes, we'll open the airlock. It will be painful, but it probably won't last long. The nitrogen has been accumulating in your fatty tissues, Merete. Of course you're very thin, but you have to remember that there are pockets of air everywhere inside your body. When your bones expand and the bone fragments start bursting inside your tissues, when the pressure under your fillings makes them explode in your mouth, when you feel the pain whistling through your shoulder and hip joints, then you'll know that the time has come. Figure it out. Five years, two months and thirteen days, starting on the 2nd of March 2002, then you'll know what it will say on your tombstone. You can always hope that the blood clots in your lungs and brain will paralyse you, or that your lungs will explode and knock you unconscious or kill you fast. But don't count on it. And who says that I'll let it happen quickly?'

So she was going to die on the 15th of May 2007. If she was right in calculating that today was February 13th, then it would be ninety-one days from now – exactly forty-four days since the start of the new year. She had lived every day since New Year's Eve in the awareness that she would put an end to things before they ever reached that date.

But until that time, she was determined to carry on, ignoring all gloomy thoughts and cherishing the best of her memories.

This was how she was mentally preparing herself to say goodbye to the world. She often held up the tongs to look at the sharp jaws, or pick up the longer plastic stiffener from her jacket and consider snapping it in half and sharpening the two pieces on the cement floor. It was going to have to be one of these tools. She would lay down in the corner under the mirrored panes and puncture the arteries in her wrists. Thank God they were easy to see, since her arms were so thin.

It was this state of mind that had kept her going until today. After the airlock delivered the food bucket, she once again heard the voices of Lasse and his mother outside. Both sounded irritable, and their argument took on a life of its own.

So the bastard and the bitch don't always see eye to eye, she thought. This cheered her up.

'What's the matter, little Lasse, can't you keep your mother under control?' she shouted. Of course she knew that an insolent remark like that would bring reprisals; she knew what the witch out there was like.

But it turned out that she didn't know her well enough. She'd thought the woman's spitefulness would mean she'd get little or no food for a couple of days. Merete had no idea it would rob her of the right to determine her own life.

'Watch out for her, Lasse,' snarled the old woman. 'She'll turn us against each other, if she can. And she'll cheat you, believe me. You'd better watch out for her.

She's got a pair of tongs in there, and she could easily try to use them on herself if need be. Do you really want her to have the last laugh? Do you, Lasse?'

There was a pause that lasted only a couple of seconds, then the sword of Damocles was hanging over her head.

'You heard what my mother said, didn't you, Merete?' His voice sounded cold coming through the loudspeakers.

What good would it do for her to reply?

'From now on, you're keeping back from the windows. I want to be able to see you at all times. Get it? Move the toilet bucket over to the far wall. Now! If you in any way try to starve yourself or hide or injure yourself, I promise you that I'll lower the pressure in the room faster than you can react. Then if you stab yourself, the blood will gush out of you like a waterfall. You'll feel everything exploding inside before you black out, I promise you. I'm going to set up cameras so we can observe you night and day from now on. We'll aim a couple of floodlights at the windows at full power. And I can change the air pressure by remote control, by the way. So you can go to the guillotine now, or you can wait until later. But who knows, Merete? Maybe we'll all drop dead tomorrow. Maybe we'll be poisoned by the lovely salmon we're going to have for dinner. You never know. So just hold on. Maybe one day a prince will arive on a white horse and give you a lift. Where there's life, there's hope – am I right? So hold out, Merete. But stick to the rules.'

She looked up at one of the panes. She could just barely make out Lasse's silhouette. A grey angel of death – that's what he was. Hovering out there in life, nursing a sick, sinister mind that she hoped would torture him for ever.

'How did you kill your foster-father? The same bestial way?' she shouted, expecting to hear him laugh. But she didn't expect to hear the other two laughing as well. So all three were out there now.

'I waited ten years, Merete. And then I went back, with forty pounds more muscle weight, and with so much contempt for the man, I thought that, alone, might be enough to kill him.'

'And you figured that would get you some respect?' she retorted and then laughed at him.

Anything that might rain on his victory parade was worth dishing out.

'I beat him to death. That made him respect me, don't you think? Not exactly a refined method, but so what? I took my time bashing him to pieces. I wanted to give him a taste of his own medicine – nothing else would satisfy me.'

Merete felt her stomach turn over. The man was completely insane. 'You're just like him, you ridiculous sick animal,' she whispered. 'It's too bad you weren't caught back then.'

'Caught? Did you say caught?' Again he laughed. 'How would that happen? It was harvest time, and his old, piece-of-shit reaping machine was standing ready, out in the field. It wasn't hard to tip him into the machinery once it was going. He'd always had lots of peculiar ideas, the prick– such as going out to work in the fields at night. So no one was surprised when he died that way. And he wasn't missed, let me tell you.'

'Oh, you're really a big man, Lasse. I'm so impressed. Who else have you killed? Do you have something more on your conscience?'

She hadn't figured he would stop there, but she was still deeply shocked when he told her how he'd exploited Daniel Hale's profession to get close to her, and how he'd impersonated the man and then murdered him. Daniel Hale had never done anything to Lasse; he just needed to be eliminated so that Lasse's real identity wouldn't be revealed by chance. And the same went for Lasse's helper, Dennis Knudsen. He too had to die. No witnesses. Lasse was cold as ice.

'My God, Merete,' she whispered to herself. 'How many people have you destroyed without even knowing it?'

'Why didn't you just kill me, you arsehole?' she shouted at the window. 'You had the chance. You said yourself that you'd been watching me and Uffe. Why didn't you just stab me with a knife when I was out in the garden? I'm sure you were there, weren't you?'

For a moment he didn't speak. When he did, he carefully enunciated each word, so she'd understand the depth of his cynicism. 'First of all, that would have been too easy. I wanted us to watch you suffer for the same amount of time as we had. Besides, dear Merete, I wanted to get close to you. I wanted to see you vulnerable. I wanted to shake up your life. You were supposed to learn to love this Daniel Hale, and then you were supposed to learn to fear him. You would take one last trip with Uffe, convinced that something remained unresolved and waiting for you when you came home. That gave me a great sense of satisfaction, I want you to know.'

'You're sick in the head!'

'Sick? Am I? I can tell you this is nothing compared to what I felt on the day I found out that my mother had applied to the Lynggaard Foundation for help so she could move back home after she was discharged from the hospital. Her application was denied on the grounds that the fund was intended exclusively for use by the descendants of Lotte and Alexander Lynggaard. My mother was asking your fucking filthy-rich foundation for a measly hundred thousand kroner, and the board said no, even though they knew who she was and what had happened to her. So she had to spend several more years in institutions. Now do you understand why she hates you so much, you spoiled bitch?' The psychopath had started to cry. 'A fucking hundred thousand kroner. What difference would that have made to you and your brother? None, whatsoever!'

She could tell him that she knew nothing about this, but it didn't matter. She'd already paid her debt to him. Long ago.

That very evening Lasse and his brother set up cameras and turned on the floodlights. Two blindingly bright objects that turned night into day and revealed the overwhelming squalor of her prison; once again she had a full view of the room in all its filthy detail. It was so terrible to be confronted with her own degradation that she chose to keep her eyes closed for the first twenty-four hours. The place of execution may have been put on display, but the condemned chose darkness.

Later they stretched wires across both mirrored panes to a pair of detonators, which could break the glass in a so-called emergency. Finally, right outside, they rolled into possition cylinders containing compressed oxygen and hydrogen, as well as 'flammable liquids', as they called it.

Lasse informed her that everything was ready. After her body had exploded, they would run her through their composter, and then they'd blow up the whole fucking place. The explosion would be audible for miles. This time the insurance company would have to pay. Unforeseen accidents such as this had to be prepared meticulously, and all evidence permanently obliterated.

'Believe me, that's not going to happen,' she said to herself, planning her revenge.

After a couple of days she sat down with her back to the windows and began digging in the concrete with the tongs. In a few more days she'd be finished, and the tongs surely would be too. Then she'd have to use the plastic toothpicks to puncture her arteries, but that didn't matter. It could be done, and that was enough.

The digging took her more than a few days. It was more like a week, but by then the grooves were deep enough to withstand almost anything. She'd covered them with dust and dirt from the corners of the room. One letter after another. Once the fire experts from the insurance company came to inspect the scene to find out what had caused the blaze, she was certain that at least a few of the words would be discovered, and then they'd probably be able to figure out the rest of the message. It said:

Lasse, the owner of this building, murdered his step-father and Daniel Hale and one of his friends, and after that he murdered me.

Take good care of my brother, Uffe, and tell him that his sister thought about him every single day for more than five years.

Merete Lynggaard, 13 February 2007, kidnapped and imprisoned in this godforsaken place since 2 March 2002.

35

2007

What Assad had come across was a name mentioned in the police report from the deadly accident on Christmas Eve 1986, when Merete Lynggaard's parents died. The report listed three individuals who were killed in the other vehicle: a newborn baby, a girl who was only eight, and the driver of the car, Henrik Jensen, who was an engineer and the founder of a company called Jensen Industries. After that the report became less specific, as indicated by a row of question marks in the margin. According to a handwritten note, the firm was supposedly 'a flourishing enterprise that produced airtight steel containment linings'. There was another brief remark underneath. It said: 'a source of pride for Danish industry', and was apparently also a statement by a witness.

Assad had remembered correctly. Henrik Jensen was the name of the driver killed in the other car. And it was true that name was exceedingly similar to Lars Henrik Jensen. No one could claim that Assad was stupid.

'Take out the tabloids again, Assad,' said Carl. 'Maybe they published the names of the survivors. It wouldn't surprise me if the boy in the other car was Lars Henrik, named after his father. Do you see his name anywhere?' Carl suddenly regretted making Assad do all the work, so he stretched out his hand. 'Give me a few of the tabloid articles. And a couple of those over there,' he said, pointing at clippings from the morning papers.

There were horrifying photos from the accident. They were displayed in a lurid context, side by side with pictures of inconsequential people, greedy for fame. The sea of flames surrounding the Ford Sierra had consumed everything, as the photo of the charred wreck documented. It was a real miracle that a couple of medics happened to be driving past and were able to pull the passengers out before the cars burned. According to the police report, the fire department hadn't been able to reach the scene as quickly as normal. The slippery road had simply been too dangerous.

'Here it says then that the mother was named Ulla Jensen, and both her legs were crushed,' said Assad. 'I can't tell you the name of the boy. It doesn't say. They just call him the "couple's eldest child". But here they write that he was fourteen years old.'

'That fits with the year Lars Henrik Jensen was born, if we can rely at all on that manipulated Civil Registry number from Godhavn,' said Carl. He was studying a couple of clippings from the noon editions of the newspapers.

There was nothing in the first one. The story was printed next to some unimportant reports about political squabbles and minor scandals. The trademark of this newspaper was to follow specific guidelines for what was guaranteed to sell, no matter what it might be. This was apparently an enduring precept because if Carl exchanged this five-year-old issue with one from yesterday, he'd be hard-pressed to know which was more recent.

He was cursing the media and leafing through the next newspaper, when he turned the page and saw the name. It practically jumped out at him. Just what he'd been hoping for.

'Here it is, Assad!' shouted Carl, his eyes nailed to the page. At that moment he felt like a hawk that had spotted its prey from the treetops and then dove in for the kill. A fabulous find. The pressure in Carl's chest vanished, and an odd feeling of relief passed through his body.

'Listen to this, Assad. "The survivors in the vehicle that was torpedoed by wholesaler Alexander Lynggaard's car were Henrik Jensen's wife, Ulla Jensen, age 40, one of her newborn twins, and their eldest child, Lars Henrik Jensen, age 14."'

Assad put down the clipping he was holding. His dark brown eyes were squeezed almost shut by a huge smile.

'Hand me the police report from the accident, Assad.' Carl wanted to see whether the CR numbers of those involved might be listed. He ran his finger down the report but found only the numbers for the two drivers, Merete's father and Lars Henrik's father.

'If you have the father's CR number, can you just also find the son's number fast, Carl? Then we can maybe compare it to the one we got on the boy from Godhavn.'

Carl nodded. That should be easy enough. 'I'll check and see what I can find out about Henrik Jensen, Assad,' he said. 'In the meantime, go and ask Lis to check up on the CR numbers. Tell her that we're looking for an address for Lars Henrik Jensen. If he doesn't have a place of residence in Denmark, ask her to find out where the mother lives. And if Lis does find his CR number, get her to print out all his addresses since the accident. Take the folder with you, Assad. And hurry.'

Carl got on the Internet and searched for 'Jensen Industries', but came up empty. Then he searched for 'airtight steel containment linings for nuclear reactors', which resulted in a list of various companies, especially in France and Germany. Then he tried the words 'lining for containments', which, as far as he knew, covered more or less the same terminology as 'airtight steel containment linings for nuclear reactors'. That didn't get him anywhere either.

He was about to give up when he found a pdf file that mentioned a company in Køge, and there he saw the sentence 'a source of pride for Danish industry' – exactly the same wording as had been included in the police accident report. So this must have been where that quote came from. He sent a silent thank-you to the traffic cop who had dug a little deeper into the material than was normally required. Carl bet the man had eventually ended up working as a detective.

That was as much as he could find out about Jensen Industries. Maybe he had the name wrong. He put in a call to the Registry of Companies and learned that no firms were listed under any Henrik Jensen with that particular CR number. Maybe the company was owned by foreigners, maybe it was registered under another name by a different group of owners, or it could be part of a holding company and registered under the holding company's name.

Carl took out his ballpoint pen and crossed off the company name on his notepad. As things now stood, Jensen Industries was nothing more than a blank spot in the high-tech landscape.

He lit a cigarette and watched the smoke rise up to the network of pipes on the ceiling. One day the smoke alarms out in the corridor were going to catch a whiff and set off an infernal racket that would send all the employees in the building out on the street in infernal disarray. He smiled and took an extra-deep drag before blowing a thick cloud towards the door. It would put a stop to his little illegal pastime, but it would almost be worth it just to see Bak and Bjørn and Jacobsen standing outside looking up with anxious annoyance at the windows of their offices, with their hundreds of yards of shelf space filled with archived atrocities.

Then he recalled what John Rasmussen from Godhavn had said – that the father of Atomos, aka Lars Henrik Jensen, might have had something to do with the nuclear research facility at Risø.

Carl looked up the phone number. It might be a dead end, but if there was anyone who knew something about airtight steel containment linings for nuclear reactors, it would be the people at Risø.

The person on duty was very helpful and transferred him to an engineer named Mathiasen, who in turn transferred him to a man named Stein who again passed him on to a Jonassen. Each engineer sounded older than the previous one. Jonassen introduced himself simply as Mikkel, and he was busy, but OK, he was willing to spend five minutes helping the police. What was it Carl wished to know?

He sounded particularly smug when he heard Carl's question. 'You want to know whether I've ever heard of a company that made linings for containments here in Denmark in the mid-eighties?' he said. 'Yes, of course. HJ Industries was probably one of the world leaders.'

'HJ Industries' the man had said. Carl could have kicked

himself. HJ for Henrik Jensen. H-J I-n-d-u-s-t-r-i-e-s. What else?! It was that simple. You'd think the staff over at the Registry of Companies could have suggested something like that when he phoned for Pete's sake.

'Henrik Jensen's company was actually called Trabeka Holding. Don't ask me why. But the name HJI is still known the world over. Their standards remain the industry's benchmark. It was a sad thing that Henrik Jensen died so suddenly, and that the company was forced to close soon afterwards. But the twenty-five employees couldn't keep going without his leadership, nor could the company continue to exist without his high demands for quality. Besides, it had just undergone big changes, moving to a different location and expanding, so it was very unfortunate that he died right then. Major assets and expertise were lost. If you ask me, the business could have been saved if Risø had intervened, but back then management lacked the political support to do that.'

'Can you tell me where HJI was located?'

'Yes, the factory was in Køge for a long time. I made several visits there myself. But right before the accident it was moved to a site just south of Copenhagen. I'm not sure exactly where. I can try to find my old phone book; it's here somewhere. Can you hold on for a minute?'

It took a good five minutes while Carl listened to the man rummaging around in the background as he used his doubtlessly vast intellect to plumb the most vulgar depths of the Danish language. He sounded as if he was really pissed off at himself. Carl had seldom heard anything like it.

'No, I'm sorry,' said Jonassen after he'd finished cursing. 'I can't find it, even though I never throw anything out. Typical. But talk to Ulla Jensen, his widow. I assume she's still alive; she can't be very old. She should be able to tell you everything you want to know. A truly fine woman. Too bad she had to suffer so much.'

Carl decided to meet him halfway. 'Yes, it's too bad,' he said, ready to ask one last question.

But the engineer was just getting started. 'It was really brilliant, what they were doing at HJI. Just consider the welding techniques. The welds were practically invisible, even if you X-rayed them using the absolutely most advanced equipment. But they also had all sorts of techniques for finding leaks. For instance, they had a pressure chamber that could go up to sixty atmospheres to test the durability of their products. Probably the biggest pressure chamber I've ever seen. With incredibly high-tech control systems. If the containment linings could withstand that much pressure, you knew the nuclear energy reactors were getting first-class equipment. That was HJI. Always top-notch.'

The man was so enthusiastic, it almost sounded as if he'd had stock in the business.

'You don't happen to know where Ulla Jensen is living today, do you?' Carl interjected.

'Nope, but I'm sure you can find out by checking the Civil Registry. I assume she still lives on the company site. They couldn't throw her out, as far as I know.'

'Somewhere south of Copenhagen, you said?'

'Yes, exactly.'

How on earth could he say 'exactly' about a location as imprecise as 'south of Copenhagen'?

'If you're particularly interested in this sort of thing, I'd be happy to invite you down here to visit,' said the man.

Carl thanked him but declined the offer, citing that he was very pressed for time. In reality, he'd always wanted to flatten Risø with a thousand-ton steamroller and sell the scraps to some one-horse town in Siberia as road paving. So when it came to an invitation to take a tour of such an enterprise, it would be a shame to waste his time, since Jonassen had already remarked that he was a busy man.

By the time Carl put down the phone, Assad had been standing in the doorway for several minutes.

'What is it, Assad?' he asked. 'Did we get what we needed? Did they check the CR numbers?'

Assad shook his head. 'I think myself that you need to go upstairs and talk to them, Carl. They're totally . . .' he twirled his finger around beside his temple '. . . up in their heads today.'

Carl approached Lis with caution, moving along the wall like a tomcat in rut. Sure enough, she was looking very frazzled. Her short hair, normally so cheerfully tousled, was now plastered down so it looked like a motorbike helmet. Standing behind her, Mrs Sørensen flashed Carl a fierce look, and he could hear people shouting at each other in the offices. It was really pitiful.

'What's going on?' he asked Lis when he finally caught her eye.

'I don't know. When we try to log on to government databases, we're denied entry. It's as if all the passwords have been changed.'

'But the Internet is working fine.'

'Yes, but try to log on to the CR files or the tax authority, and you'll see what I mean.'

'You're going to have to wait, just like everybody else,' gloated Mrs Sørensen in her flat-sounding voice.

He stood there for a moment, trying to figure out another way to get the information, but gave up when he saw Lis's screen display one error message after another.

He shrugged. What the hell. It wasn't really urgent, anyway. A man like him knew how to turn a *force majeure* to his advantage. If the electronics had decided to shut down, then it must be a sign that he should station himself in the basement and hold a profound dialogue with the coffee cups for an hour or two, his feet propped up on his desk.

'Hi, Carl,' he heard someone say behind him. It was Marcus Jacobsen, wearing a dazzling white shirt and neatly pressed tie. 'I'm glad you're up here. Could you come to the cafeteria for a second?' Carl could tell it wasn't a question. 'Bak's giving a briefing, and I think you'll have a certain interest in what he has to say.'

There must have been at least fifteen people in the cafeteria, with Carl standing at the very back, and the homicide chief off to one side. Up front, with the windows behind them, stood a couple of narcotics officers, Vice-Superintendent Lars Bjørn, and Børge Bak and his second-in-command. Bak's colleagues all looked extremely pleased.

Lars Bjørn turned over the floor to Bak, and everyone knew what he was going to say.

'This morning we made an arrest in the cyclist murder case. At this very moment the accused is consulting with his lawyer, and we're convinced that a written confession will be made available before the end of the day.'

He smiled and patted his comb-over. The morning was all his. 'The key witness, Annelise Kvist, provided us with a detailed statement after being assured that the suspect had been arrested, and her statement supports our view a hundred per cent. The individual in question is a highly respected and professionally active physician, a specialist with a practice in Valby. In addition to stabbing the drug dealer in Valby Park to death, he also played a role in Annelise Kvist's alleged suicide attempt, and issued death threats against her children.' Bak pointed to his assistant, who continued the report.

'During a search of the suspect's residence, we found more than six hundred and fifty pounds of various types of narcotics, which are now being identified by our technicians.' He paused for a moment to let the reaction die down. 'There is no doubt that the doctor has built up a large and extensive network of colleagues, and they've all made significant sums from the sale of various types of prescription drugs – from methadone to diazepam, phenobarbital and morphine – and from the importation of drugs such as amphetamines, zopiclone, THC, or acetophenazine. As well as large quantities of neuroleptics, soporifics and hallucinogens. Nothing was too big or too small for the accused. Apparently he had customers for everything.

'The man who was murdered in Valby Park was the ringleader behind the distribution of these drugs to people who went to clubs, in particular. We're guessing that the victim tried to blackmail the doctor, and the latter made short work of things, but that the murder was not premeditated. Annelise Kvist witnessed the killing, and she happened to know the doctor. Because of this, the doctor was able to track her down and force her to keep quiet.' The officer stopped, and Bak took over.

'We now know that right after the murder, the doctor went to see Annelise Kvist at her home. He specializes in bronchial diseases and Annelise's daughters were two of his asthma patients; both are very dependent on the medicine they take. On that evening at Annelise's flat, the doctor displayed a dramatically violent behaviour, and he forced her to give her children pills, or he said he would kill them. The pills caused their alveoli to constrict, which was life-threatening. He then gave them an injection, which was the antidote. It must have been extremely traumatic for a mother to watch her daughters turn blue in the face, unable to communicate with her.'

Bak looked around the room. Everyone was nodding at what he said. He went on.

'Afterwards the doctor claimed that the girls would have to make regular visits to his office to receive the antidote, or they would suffer a fatal relapse. That was how he kept the mother quiet.

'We can thank Annelise's mother for the fact that we eventually located our key witness. She knew nothing about the intervening scene that had been played out in her daughter's flat that night, but she did know that her daughter had witnessed the murder. She got Annelise to say so the next day when she saw what a state of shock her daughter was in. The only thing the mother didn't find out was who the murderer was; Annelise refused to tell her. So when we brought Annelise Kvist in for questioning at her mother's insistence, she was a woman undergoing a deep inner crisis.

'Today we also know that the doctor went to see Annelise again a couple of days later. He warned her that if she talked, he'd kill the girls. He used words like "flay them alive" and pushed her so far that he was able to force her to take a deadly cocktail of pills.

'You all know the rest of the story. The woman was hospitalized, her life was saved, and she clammed up completely. But what you don't know is that our investigation received a great deal of help from our new Department Q, which is headed by Carl Mørck.'

Bak turned to Carl. 'You didn't participate in the actual investigation, Carl, but you set in motion several trains of thought. My team and I would like to thank you for that. We'd also like to thank your assistant, whom you used as a messenger between us and Hardy Henningsen, who also provided us with valuable input. We've sent Hardy some flowers, just so you know.'

Carl was dumbfounded. A couple of his former colleagues turned towards him and attempted to wring smiles out of their stony faces, but the others didn't budge.

Lars Bjørn took over. 'A lot of people have worked on this case. We also want to thank you boys,' he added, pointing to the two narcotics cops. 'Now it's up to you to unravel the ring of drug-dealing doctors. We know it's going to be a huge job. On the other hand, those of us in homicide can now turn our attention to other matters, and we're glad about that. There's plenty to keep all of us busy up here on the third floor.'

Carl waited until almost everyone had left the room. He knew how hard it must have been for Bak to give him any sort of praise. So he went over to shake hands with him. 'I didn't deserve that, but I'd like to say thanks, Bak.'

Børge Bak looked at Carl's outstretched hand for a moment and then started packing up his papers. 'Don't thank me. I would never have done it if Marcus Jacobsen hadn't ordered me to.'

Carl nodded. So once again they knew where each of them stood.

Out in the hall, panic was spreading. All the office workers were clustered around the boss's door, and everyone had a complaint.

'OK, OK. We don't yet know what's wrong,' said homicide chief Marcus Jacobsen. 'But from what the police commissioner has told us, no official database can be accessed at the moment. Somebody has hacked into the central servers and changed all the passwords. We don't know yet who's behind it. There aren't many who'd be capable of doing something like this, so we're pulling out all the stops to find the culprits.'

'You've got to be kidding,' someone said. 'How can it be possible?'

Jacobsen shrugged. He tried to look calm and composed, but probably wasn't.

Carl told Assad that the work day was over since there was nothing more they could do. Without the information from the Civil Registration System they wouldn't be able to track Lars Henrik Jensen's movements. It would just have to wait.

As Carl drove north to the Clinic for Spinal Cord

Injuries, he heard on the radio that a letter had been sent to the media by an angry citizen who claimed to have infected all the official government databases with a virus. It was assumed the individual was a civil servant who held a key position but may have been laid off due to municipal reforms. But so far nothing could be confirmed. Computer experts tried to explain how it was possible to access such well-protected data, and the prime minister called the culprits 'the worst kind of bandits one can imagine'. Security experts specializing in data transmission were already in full swing, he claimed, and everything would soon be back in working order. Of course whoever was to blame could expect a very long prison sentence. The Prime Minister was just about to compare the situation to the attacks on the World Trade Center, but stopped short of doing so.

The first smart thing he'd done in a long time.

There was, in fact, a bouquet of flowers from Bak's team on Hardy's bedside table, but even the smallest petrol station kiosk could have come up with something nicer. Hardy didn't care. He couldn't see the flowers anyway since the nurses had moved him over to the window so he could look out.

'I'm supposed to say hello from Bak,' Carl told him.

Hardy gave him a look that might be described as surly, but in reality was indefinable. 'What does that fucking creep have to do with me?'

'Assad gave him your tip, and now they've made an arrest that's going to stick.'

'I haven't given anybody a damn tip about anything.'

'Sure you did. You said that Bak should take a look at everyone who might be giving medical treatment to the key witness, Annelise Kvist.'

'What case are we talking about?'

'The cyclist murder, Hardy.'

He frowned. 'I don't have a clue what you're talking about, Carl. You've tossed that idiotic case about Merete Lynggaard in my lap, and that psychologist bitch keeps harping on the shooting incident out in Amager. That should be plenty. I have no idea what this cyclist murder case is about.'

Now it wasn't only Hardy who was frowning. 'Are you sure Assad didn't mention the cyclist case to you? Are you having trouble with your memory, Hardy? It's OK to tell me.'

'Aww, fuck off, Carl. I don't feel like listening to this bullshit. My memory is my worst enemy. Can't you understand that?' Hardy sputtered, his eyes crystal clear.

Carl raised his hand in an apologetic gesture. 'Sorry, Hardy. I must have been misinformed by Assad. It happens.'

But deep inside he wasn't taking it nearly as casually.

That sort of thing couldn't and wouldn't happen again.

36

2007

He sat down at the breakfast table with his oesophagus burning from acid indigestion and sleep still weighing heavily on his shoulders. Neither Morten nor Jesper said a word to him, which was standard procedure for his stepson but definitely an ominous sign when it came to his lodger.

The morning paper was lying neatly on a corner of the table, and the top story was Tage Baggesen's voluntary resignation from his parliamentary position, citing health reasons. Morten kept his head bowed silently over his plate, steadily chewing, as Carl reached page six and sat gaping at a grainy photo of himself.

It was the same picture that *Gossip* had used of him the day before, but this time it was next to a slightly faded outdoor photo of Uffe Lynggaard. The caption was far from flattering:

'The head of Department Q, in charge of the investigation of "cases deserving special scrutiny", as designated by the Denmark Party, has appeared in the news in the past two days under particularly unfortunate circumstances.'

The article didn't focus on the *Gossip* story, but the reporter had conducted interviews with staff members at Egely, and they all complained of Carl's heavy-handed methods. They also blamed him for Uffe's disappearance. The supervisory nurse was portrayed as especially furious. She used phrases such as 'abuse of our willingness to help', and 'psychological rape' and 'manipulation'. The article ended with the words: 'As of press time, it has not been possible to get any comment from the police department.'

It would be hard to find a more evil villain than Carl Mørck in a spaghetti Western. An amazing piece of reporting, considering what had really happened.

'I've got a final exam today,' said Jesper, rousing Carl from his reverie.

Carl looked at him over the top of the newspaper. 'In what?'

'Maths.'

That didn't sound good. 'Have you studied for it?'

Jesper shrugged and got up. As usual, he paid no attention to the plethora of utensils he'd slathered with butter and jam or the rest of the mess he'd left on the table.

'Just a second, Jesper,' Carl said. 'What does that mean?'

His stepson turned to look at him. 'It means that if I don't do well, I might not quality for the fifth and sixth forms at Allerød. Too bad!'

Carl pictured Vigga's reproachful face and lowered the newspaper. The acid revolt in his system was really starting to hurt.

Out in the car park folks were already joking about yesterday's database breakdown. A couple of people had no idea what they were going to do at work. One's job was dealing with building permits, and the other's was medical reimbursements, and both of them usually spent their time staring at computer screens all day.

On the car radio Carl heard several mayors express criticism of the municipal government reforms, which had indirectly sparked the whole mess. Other people called in to rant about the fact that the ongoing miserable situation with overworked and overburdened municipal employees was now going to get even worse. If the culprit who had shut down the databases ever dared to show up at one of the many hard-hit city halls, the closest emergency ward would no doubt have its hands full.

At police headquarters everyone was more hopeful; the individual who had caused the problem had already been arrested. As soon as they'd received an explanation from the accused – an older woman who was a computer programmer in the Interior Ministry – to explain how to repair the damage, they would make the whole story public. It would only be a few more hours before everything would return to normal. Total control of society by government bureaucrats, which so many people were sick and tired of, had been re-established.

Poor woman.

Oddly enough, Carl managed to make it down to the basement without running into any of his colleagues, and that was a good thing. The news in the morning papers about Carl's clash with a psychologically handicapped man in an institution in northern Zealand had undoubtedly already spread to even the lowliest office in that enormous building.

He just hoped that Marcus Jacobsen's Wednesday meeting with the commissioner and the other police chiefs wouldn't focus entirely on the news story.

He found Assad in his office and wasted no time launching into him.

After a few seconds Assad started looking groggy.

Cheerful assistant that he was, he'd never seen this side of Carl before. But his boss now let him have the full brunt of his anger.

'You lied to me, Assad,' Carl barked, fixing his eyes on the man. 'You never even mentioned the cyclist murder to Hardy. You came up with all those conclusions yourself, and yes, they were good ones, but what you said to me was something else altogether. I simply won't have it. Do you hear me? This will have consequences.'

He could almost hear the wheels creaking inside Assad's head. What was going on in there? Did he have a guilty conscience or what?

Carl chose to really let him have it. 'Don't bother saying anything, Assad! You're not bullshitting me any more! Who the hell are you, really, Assad? I'd like to know. And what were you doing since you weren't visiting Hardy?' He waved off Assad's objections. 'Yeah, all right, I know you went there, but you never stayed very long. So spit it out, Assad. What's going on?'

Assad's silence couldn't hide his nervousness. Carl caught glimpses of a hunted animal in the man's calm expression. If they'd been enemies, Assad presumably would have leaped up to strangle him.

'Just a second,' said Carl. He turned to look at the computer and brought up Google onto the screen. 'I've got a couple of questions for you. You get me?'

Assad didn't answer.

'Are you listening at all?'

Assad murmured something even fainter than the hum of the computer. It was apparently meant as an affirmative reply.

'It says in your file that you and your wife and two daughters came to Denmark in 1998. You were in the Sandholm refugee camp from 1998 until 2000, and then you were granted asylum.'

Assad nodded.

'That was fast.'

'Not back then, Carl. Things are different now.'

'You're from Syria, Assad. What city? It doesn't say in your file.'

He turned around and saw that Assad's expression was darker than he'd ever seen it.

'Am I under your interrogation, Carl?'

'Yes, you could say that. Any objections?'

'There are many things I will not tell you, Carl. You will have to respect that then. I have had a bad life. It is mine, not yours.'

'I understand that. But what city are you from? Is that such a hard question to answer?'

'I come from a suburb of Sab Abar.'

Carl typed in the name. 'That's in the middle of nowhere, Assad.'

'Did I say it was not, Carl?'

'How far would you say it is from Damascus to Sab Abar?'

'A day's journey. More than two hundred kilometres.'

'A day's journey?'

'Things take time there. First you have to go through the city, and then there are the mountains.'

That matched with what Carl saw on Google Earth. It would be hard to find a more desolate place. 'Your name is Hafez el-Assad. At least that's what it says in the

Immigration Service's documents about you.' He typed in the name on Google and found it instantly. 'Isn't that a rather unfortunate name to be carrying around?'

Assad shrugged.

'The name of a dictator who ruled Syria for twenty-nine years! Were your parents members of the Baath Party?'

'Yes, they were.'

'So you were named after him?'

'Several people in my family have that name. I can tell you that.'

Carl looked into Assad's dark eyes. The man was in a different state than usual.

'Who was Hafez el-Assad's successor?' Carl asked abruptly.

Assad didn't even blink. 'His son Bashar. Should we then not stop this now, Carl? It is not good for us.'

'You might be right. So what was the name of the first son, the one who died in a car crash in 1994?'

'I do not remember right now.'

'You don't? That's odd. Here it says that he was his father's favourite and chosen successor. His name was Basil. I'd think that everyone your age in Syria would be able to tell me that without hesitation.'

'That is correct. His name was Basil.' Assad nodded. 'But there are so quite many things that I have forgotten, Carl. I do not *want* to remember. I have . . .' He searched for the word.

'Suppressed them?'

'Yes, that sounds right enough.'

OK, if that's how he's going to act I'm not going to get

any further like this, thought Carl. He was going to have to shift gears.

'You know what I think, Assad? I think you're lying. Your name isn't Hafez el-Assad at all. It was just the first name that came into your head when you applied for asylum. Am I right? I can just imagine that the guy who falsified your papers had a good laugh over it, didn't he? Maybe he's even the same man who helped us with Merete's phone book. Am I getting warm?'

'I think we should make a stop now, Carl.'

'Where are you really from, Assad? Well, I'm used to the name, so why change now, even though it's really your surname, isn't it, Hafez?'

'I am Syrian, and I come from Sab Abar.'

'You mean a suburb of Sab Abar?'

'Yes, north-east of downtown.'

It all sounded very plausible, but Carl had a hard time accepting the information at face value. Maybe ten years and hundreds of interrogations ago. But not any more. His instincts were grumbling. The way Assad reacted wasn't quite right.

'You're actually from Iraq, aren't you, Assad? And you've got skeletons in the closet that would get you deported from Denmark and sent back to where you came from. Am I right?'

Assad's expression changed again. The lines on his forehead were erased. Maybe he'd caught sight of a way out; maybe he was just telling the truth.

'Iraq? Not at all. Now you are sounding dumb, Carl,' he said, offended. 'Come home and see my things, Carl. I brought a suitcase from home. You can talk to my wife.

401

She understands a little English. Or my girls. Then you will know that what I am telling you is right then, Carl. I am a political refugee, and I have been through a lot of bad things. I do not want to talk about it, Carl, so, could you please leave me in peace? It is true that I did not spend a lot of time with Hardy, the way I said, but it is very far, up to Hornbæk. I am trying to help my brother come to Denmark, and that takes time too, Carl. I'm sorry. I will tell you things straight in the future.'

Carl leaned back. He was almost to the point where he wanted to smother his sceptical brain in the sugar water that Assad was dishing out. 'I don't understand how you could acclimate yourself so quickly to doing police work, Assad. I certainly appreciate your help. You're a spooky kind of guy, but you do have skills. Where does it come from?'

'Spooky? What is that? Something to do with ghosts and things like that?' He gave Carl a guileless look. Yes, he did have skills, all right. Maybe he had a natural talent. Maybe everything he'd said was true. Perhaps it was just Carl who was turning into a sulky grouch.

'It doesn't say anything about your education in the file, Assad. What kind of training did you have?'

He shrugged. 'There was not very much, Carl. My father owned a small company that sold tinned goods. I know everything about how long a tin of stewed tomatoes can last at fifty degrees Celsius.'

Carl tried to smile. 'And then you couldn't keep out of politics, and you ended up with the wrong name. Is that it?'

'Yes, something like that.'

'And you were tortured?'

'Yes. Carl, I do not want to talk about that. You have

not seen how I can get when I feel bad. I cannot talk about it, OK?'

'OK.' Carl nodded. 'And from now on you're going to tell me what you're doing during work hours. Do you get me?'

Assad gave his boss a thumbs-up.

The expression in Carl's eyes allowed Assad's gaze to relax. Then he held up his hand for a high-five, and Assad smacked it.

So that was that.

'OK, Assad. Let's move on. We've got other things to think about,' said Carl. 'We need to locate this Lars Henrik Jensen. I'm hoping it won't be long before we'll be able to log on to the Civil Registration System, but until then, let's try to find his mother, Ulla Jensen. A man out at Risø . . .' He saw that Assad wanted to ask him what Risø was, but that could wait. 'A man told me that she lives south of Copenhagen.'

'Is Ulla Jensen an unusual name?'

Carl shook his head. 'Now that we know the name of the father's company, we have more angles we can check. To start off, I'm going to call the Registry of Companies. We can only hope that it hasn't been shut down too. In the meantime, go through the address-finder directory and look for the name Ulla Jensen. Try Brøndbyerne and then move south. Vallensbæk, maybe Glostrup, Tåstrup, Greve-Kildebrønde. Don't search all the way to Køge, because that's where the company was located before. Try north of there.'

Assad looked relieved. He was just about to go out the door but turned around to give Carl a hug. His beard stubble

403

was like needles, and his aftershave was some cheap knock-off brand, but the sentiment was genuine.

Carl sat at his desk for a moment, letting the feeling wash over him after Assad had waltzed across the hall to his own office. It was almost like having his old team back.

The answer came from both sources at once. The Registry of Companies had been functioning without interruption throughout the computer crash, and it took only five seconds on the keyboard for them to identify HJ Industries. It was owned by Trabeka Holding, a German firm, and they'd be happy to look for more information if Carl was interested. They couldn't see who the owners were, but that could be found out if they contacted their German colleagues. After they gave Carl the address, he shouted over to Assad that he could stop his search, but Assad shouted back that he'd already found a couple of possible addresses.

They compared results. There it was. Ulla Jensen lived on the site of the bankrupt HJ Industries, on Strøhusvej in Greve.

Carl looked it up on the map. It was only a few hundred yards away from where Daniel Hale had burned to death on the Kappelev highway. He remembered standing there. It was the road he'd looked down as they'd surveyed the countryside. The road with the windmill.

He felt the adrenalin starting to pump faster. Now they had an address. And they could drive there in twenty minutes.

'Should we call down there first then, Carl?' Assad handed him the phone number.

He gave his helper a blank look. So it wasn't always pearls of wisdom that fell from the man's lips. 'That's a great idea, Assad, if we want to find an empty house.'

Originally it must have been an ordinary farm with a farmhouse, pigsty and barn arranged around a cobblestone courtyard. The house was so close to the road that they could look right into the rooms. Behind the whitewashed buildings were three or four larger ones. A couple of them had presumably never been put to use. This seemed in any case true of a building thirty to forty feet high, with gaping holes where the windows should have been set in. It was incomprehensible that the authorities had ever allowed something like that to be built. It completely ruined the view down to the fields, where yellow carpets of rapeseed gave way to meadows so green that the colour couldn't possibly be reproduced in any painting.

Carl scanned the landscape but didn't see a soul. Not near any of the buildings, either. The farmyard seemed just as neglected as everything else. The whitewash on the house was flaking off. Piled up by the road, a little further to the east, were heaps of junk and building debris. Aside from the dandelions and flowering fruit trees that towered over the corrugated Eternit roof, the whole place looked terribly bleak.

'There is no car in the courtyard, Carl,' said Assad. 'Maybe it was a long time ago when somebody lived here.'

Carl clenched his teeth, trying to fend off his disappointment. His guts told him that Lars Henrik Jensen wasn't here. Damn it. Damn it to hell.

'Let's go in and look around, Assad,' he said as he parked the car fifty yards further along the road.

They set off in silence. Through the hedge they reached the back of the house and a garden where fruit bushes and ground-elder were fighting for space. The bay windows of the house were grey with dirt and age. Everything seemed deed.

'Look at this,' whispered Assad, pressing his nose against one of the windowpanes.

Carl leaned in to look. The inside of the house seemed abandoned too. It was almost like Sleeping Beauty's castle, except there were no banners or thorn bushes. Dust covered the tables, the books and newspapers, and all sorts of papers. In one corner cardboard boxes were piled up that had never been unpacked, and there were carpets that were still rolled up.

Here was a family whose life had been interrupted during a happier time.

'I think they were in the process of moving in when the accident happened, Assad. That's what the man at Risø said too.'

'Yes, but look over there in the back then.'

Assad pointed at a doorway on the other side of the room. Light was streaming in, and the floor behind was polished and shiny.

'You're right,' said Carl. 'It looks different.'

They made their way through a herb garden where the bumblebees buzzed around flowering chives and reached the other side of the house, down in one corner of the courtyard.

Carl moved close to the windows, which were fastened

shut. Through the first panes he was able to get a glimpse of a room with bare walls and a couple of chairs. He pressed his forehead against the window and saw the room take shape. There was no doubt it was in use. A couple of shirts lay on the floor. The blankets on the box mattress had been pushed aside, and on top of them lay a pair of pyjamas, a kind that he was certain he'd seen in a department store catalogue not long ago.

He concentrated on controlling his breathing and instinctively placed his hand on his belt, where he'd worn his service weapon for years. But it was months since he'd carried a gun.

'Someone slept in that bed recently,' he said quietly to Assad, who was looking through the windows a little further away.

'Somebody was also here,' said Assad.

Carl went over and looked inside. Assad was right. The kitchen was neat and clean. Through a door in the wall directly across from them, they could see the dusty living room that they had looked into from the other side. It was like a mausoleum. A sacred place, not to be disturbed.

But the kitchen had definitely been in use quite recently.

'A deep freezer, coffee on the table, an electric kettle. There are also a couple of full bottles of cola over there in the corner,' said Carl.

He turned towards the pigsty and the other buildings behind it. They could continue their search without getting a court order, but they'd have to suffer the consequences afterwards if it proved to be fruitless since they couldn't very well claim that the opportunity would be lost if they searched the house at some other time. Actually, they could wait until morning. Yes, it might even be better to come back the next day. Maybe someone would be home by then.

He nodded. It was probably best to wait and follow proper legal procedures. He took a deep breath. In reality, he didn't feel like doing either.

As Carl stood there thinking, Assad suddenly took off. For a man with such a compact, heavy body, he was surprisingly nimble. He crossed the yard in a couple of bounds and then went out into the road to wave down a farmer who was driving his tractor.

Carl went over to join them.

'Yes,' he heard the farmer say as he approached, the tractor idling. 'The mother and son still live there. It's a bit odd, but apparently she's set up home in that building over there.' He pointed to the last of the adjacent buildings. 'I think they must be in. At least, I saw her outside this morning.'

Carl showed the man his police badge, which prompted the farmer to turn off the tractor.

'What about the son?' said Carl. 'Is his name Lars Henrik Jensen?'

The farmer squinted one eye to think. 'Nay, I don't think that's his name. He's a real strange, tall one. What the devil is his name?'

'So it's not Lars Henrik?'

'No, that's not it.'

See-saws and merry-go-rounds. Back and forth and up and down. Carl had been through this rollercoaster ride, countless times before. And he was sick and tired of it, among other things.

'You say they live in that building over there?' Carl pointed.

The farmer nodded, launching a blob of snot over the bonnet of his brand-new Ferguson tractor.

'How do they make a living?' asked Carl, gesturing at the open countryside.

'I don't know. I lease a few acres from them. Kristoffersen, over there, leases some too. They've got some fallow land that's subsidized, and she must also have a small pension. And a couple of times a week a van arrives from somewhere, bringing plastic items for them to clean, I think. It also brings them food. I think the woman and her son manage somehow.' He laughed. 'This is farm country, you know. Out here we usually have everything we need.'

'An official van from the municipality?'

'No, it sure isn't. It's from some shipping company or something like that. It's got a sign on the side that you sometimes see on ships on TV, but I don't know where it's from. All that stuff with oceans and seas has never interested me.'

After the farmer chugged off towards the windmill, Carl and Assad studied the buildings beyond the pigsty. Strange that they hadn't noticed them from the road, because they were quite large. It was probably because the hedges had been planted so close together and had already sprouted leaves, thanks to the warm weather.

In addition to the three buildings surrounding the courtyard and the unfinished structure, there were three low buildings located close together next to a level area covered with gravel. Presumably at one time the plan had been to lay asphalt over there. By now weeds had sprung up everywhere, and the only gap in the greenery was a wide path connecting all the buildings.

Assad pointed at the narrow wheel tracks on the path. Carl had already noticed them. The width of a bicycle wheel, but parallel. Most likely from a wheelchair.

Carl's mobile rang, shrill and loud just as they were approaching the building that the farmer had pointed out. He saw Assad's expression as he cursed himself for not turning off the ringtone.

It was Vigga. Nobody could match her ability to call him at the most inconvenient moments. He'd stood in the ooze of putrefying corpses as she asked him to bring home cream for their coffee. She'd called him when his mobile lay in his jacket pocket under a bag in the police car, as he was in hot pursuit of some suspects. Vigga was good at that sort of thing.

He set the ringtone to OFF.

It was then that he raised his head and looked straight into the eyes of a tall, gaunt man in his twenties. His head was strangely elongated, almost deformed, and one entire side of his face was marred by the craters and stretched skin created by burn scars.

'You can't come here,' he said in a voice that belonged neither to an adult nor a child.

Carl showed him his police badge, but the man didn't seem to understand what it meant.

'I'm a police officer,' Carl said in a friendly tone. 'We'd like to talk to your mother. We know this is where she lives. I'd appreciate it if you'd ask her if we could come in for a moment.'

The young man didn't seem impressed by either the

badge or the two men. So he probably wasn't as simple-minded as he first appeared.

'How long am I going to have to wait?' asked Carl brusquely. The man gave a start. Then he disappeared inside the house.

A few minutes passed, as Carl felt the pressure increase in his chest. He cursed the fact that he hadn't taken his service weapon out of the armoury at police headquarters even once since he'd come back from sick leave.

'Stay behind me, Assad,' he said. He could just picture the headlines in tomorrow's newspaper: 'Police detective sacrifices assistant in shooting drama. For the third day in a row, Detective Inspector Carl Mørck from Department Q creates a scandal.'

He gave Assad a shove to emphasize the seriousness of the situation and then took up position close to the door. If they came out carrying a shotgun or anything like that, at least his assistant's head wouldn't be the first thing the muzzle pointed at.

Then the young man came out and invited them in.

She was sitting in a wheelchair, smoking a cigarette. It was hard to guess her age, since she looked so grey and wrinkled and worn out, but judging by the age of her son, she couldn't be more than sixty-one or sixty-two. She sat hunched over and her legs looked strangely awkward, like branches that had been snapped in half and then had to find some way to grow back together. The car crash had really left its mark on her; it was pitiful and sad to see.

Carl looked around. It was a huge room. A good twenty-five hundred square feet or more, but in spite of the twelve-foot-high ceiling, the place reeked of tobacco. He followed the spiralling smoke from her cigarette up to the skylights. There were only ten Velux windows, so the room was quite dim.

There were no walls for separate rooms. The kitchen was closest to the front door, the toilet off to one side. The living-room area, filled with furniture from IKEA and with cheap rugs on the cement floor, extended for fifteen or twenty yards and then ended at the space where the woman presumably slept.

Aside from the nauseating air in the room, everything was meticulously neat. This was where she watched TV and read magazines and apparently spent most of her life. Her husband had died, so now she had to manage as best she could. At least she had her son to help her out.

Carl saw Assad's eyes making a slow survey of the room. There was something devilish in his eyes as they slid over everything, occasionally pausing to zoom in on some detail. He was extremely focused, his arms hanging at his sides and feet planted firmly on the floor.

The woman was reasonably friendly, although she shook hands only with Carl. He made the introductions and told her not to be nervous. They were looking for her elder son, Lars Henrik. They wanted to ask him some questions; nothing special, it was just a routine matter. Could she tell them where they might find him?

She smiled. 'Lasse is a seaman,' she said. So she called him Lasse. 'He's not home right now, but he'll be back ashore in a month. So I'll let him know. Do you have a business card I can give him?'

'No, unfortunately.' Carl attempted a boyish smile, but

the woman wasn't buying it. 'I'll send you my card when I get back to the office. I'd be happy to.' He tried the smile again. This one was better timed. It was the golden rule: first say something positive, then smile in order to seem sincere. To do it in reverse could mean anything: flattery, flirtation. Anything that was to one's advantage. The woman knew that much about life, at least.

Carl made as if to leave and grabbed hold of Assad's sleeve. 'All right, Mrs Jensen, we have a deal. By the way, what shipping line does your son happen to work for?'

She recognized the sequence of statement and smile. 'Oh, I wish I could remember. He works on so many different ships.' And then came her smile. Carl had seen yellow teeth before, but never any as yellow as hers.

'He's a first officer. Isn't that right?'

'No, he's a steward. Lasse is a good cook. He's always been good with food.'

Carl tried to picture the boy with his arm on Dennis Knudsen's shoulder. The boy they called Atomos because his deceased father had manufactured something for nuclear reactors. When had the son developed his knowledge about cooking? In the home of the foster family who beat him? In Godhavn? When he was a young boy at home with his mother? Carl had also been through a lot in life, but he couldn't fry an egg. If it weren't for Morten Holland, he didn't know what he'd do.

'It's wonderful when things go well for one's children. Are you looking forward to seeing your brother again?' Carl asked the disfigured young man who was watching them suspiciously, as if they'd come to steal something.

His gaze shifted to his mother, but her expression

didn't change. So her son wasn't about to say a word; that much was clear.

'Where is your son's ship sailing at the moment?'

She looked at Carl, her yellow teeth slowly disappearing behind her parched lips. 'Lasse spends a lot of time sailing in the Baltic, but I think he's in the North Sea right now. Sometimes he goes out on one ship and comes home on another.'

'It must be a big shipping line. Don't you remember what it's called? Can you describe the company's logo?'

'No, I'm sorry. I'm not so good at things like that.'

Again Carl glanced at the young man; it was obvious he knew what they were talking about. He could probably draw a picture of the damned logo if his mother would let him.

'But it is painted on the van that comes here a couple of times every week,' Assad interjected. That was not well timed. Now the guy's eyes looked uneasy, and the woman drew smoke deep into her lungs. Her face was obscured by a thick cloud when she blew it out again.

'Well, it's not something we're really sure about,' Carl managed to add. 'One of your neighbours thought he'd seen it, but he could be mistaken.' He tugged at Assad's arm. 'Thank you for talking to us today,' he continued. 'Ask your son Lasse to call me when he gets back. Then we can take care of these couple of questions once and for all.'

They headed for the door as the woman rolled after them. 'Push me outside, Hans,' she said to her son. 'I need some fresh air.'

Carl knew that she didn't want to let them out of her sight until they'd left the property. If there had been a car in the courtyard or back here, where they stood, he would have thought she was trying to hide the fact that Lars Henrik Jensen was inside one of the buildings. But Carl's intuition told him otherwise. Her elder son wasn't here; she just wanted to get rid of them.

'It's an impressive group of buildings you have here. Was this a factory at one time?'

The woman was right behind them, puffing on another cigarette as her wheelchair lumbered along the path. Her son was pushing it, hands tightly gripped on the handles. He seemed very agitated inside that ruined face of his.

'My husband had a factory that manufactured sophisticated linings for nuclear reactors. We had just moved here from Køge when he died.'

'Yes, I remember reading about it. I'm very sorry.' Carl pointed to the two low buildings in front of them. 'Was that where the manufacturing was supposed to be done?'

'Yes, there and in the large hall.' She pointed as she spoke. 'The welding shop was there, the pressure testing facility there, and the full assembly was going to take place in the hall. The building I live in was supposed to store the finished containments.'

'Why don't you live in the house? It seems like a nice one,' said Carl as he noticed a row of greyish-black buckets in front of one of the buildings that didn't fit with the rest of the landscape. Maybe they'd been left there by the previous owner. In places like this, time often moved at a snail's pace.

'Oh, I don't know. There are so many things in that house that are from bygone times. And then there's the doorsills; I can't deal with them any more.' She thumped the armrest of her wheelchair.

Carl noticed that Assad was trying to pull him aside. 'Our car is over there, Assad,' he said, nodding in the opposite direction.

'I would just rather go through the hedge there and up to the road,' said Assad, but Carl saw his attention was fixed on the piles of junk that were heaped on top of an abandoned concrete foundation.

'All that rubbish was already here when we arrived,' said the woman, apologetically as if half a container of scrap metal could mar the property's overall dismal impression.

It was nothing but random garbage. On top of the rubbish heap were more of the greyish-black tubs. There were no labels on them, but they looked as if they might once have contained oil or some sort of foodstuffs in large quantities.

Carl would have stopped Assad if he'd known what his assistant had in mind, but before he could react, Assad had already leaped over some metal rods, jumbled piles of ropes and plastic tubing.

'I have to apologize for my partner. He's an incorrigible junk collector. What did you find, Assad?' Carl called out.

But Assad wasn't interested in playing his role at the moment. He was hunting for something. He kicked at the junk, turning it over until he finally stuck in his hand and with some effort pulled out a thin sheet of metal, which turned out to be a sign that was about twenty inches high and at least twelve feet long. He turned it over. It said: 'InterLab A/S'.

Assad looked up at Carl, who nodded in appreciation. It was a hell of a find. InterLab A/S was Daniel Hale's big laboratory, which had now moved to Slangerup. So there was a direct link between the family and Daniel Hale.

'Your husband's company wasn't called InterLab, was it, Mrs Jensen?' asked Carl, smiling at her tightly pressed lips.

'No. That's the company that sold us the property and a couple of the buildings.'

'My brother works at Novo. I seem to remember him mentioning that company.' Carl silently sent an apology to his older brother, who at the moment was probably feeding mink up at the mink farm in Frederikshavn. 'InterLab. Didn't they make enzymes, or something like that?'

'It was a testing laboratory.'

'Hale. Wasn't that his name? Daniel Hale?'

'Yes, the man who sold this place to my husband was named Hale. But not Daniel Hale. He was just a boy back then. The family moved InterLab north, to a different location, and after the old man died, they moved it again. But this is where it started.' She gestured towards the scrap pile. InterLab had certainly made a success of itself if this was how it began.

Carl studied the woman closely as she talked. She seemed to be completely closed off, and yet right now the words were pouring out of her. She didn't seem agitated; on the contrary. She seemed totally poised, all of her nerve endings tautly woven. She was trying to appear normal, and that was precisely what seemed so abnormal.

'Wasn't he the man who was killed not far from here?' Assad suddenly asked.

This time Carl could have kicked him in the shin. They would have to have a talk about these sorts of candid remarks when they got back to the office.

He turned to look at the buildings. They exuded more than the story of a ruined family. The grey-on-grey facades also had other nuances. It was as if the buildings were speaking to him. The acid in his stomach churned even worse when he looked at them.

'Was Hale killed? I don't remember that.' Carl flashed a warning glance at Assad and turned back to the woman.

'I'd really like to see where InterLab started out. It'd be fun to tell my brother about it. He has talked so often about launching his own business. Do you think we could have a look at the other buildings? Unofficially, of course.'

She gave him a much-too-friendly smile, which meant she was feeling just the opposite. She didn't want him here any longer. He should just pack up and leave.

'Oh, I'd be happy to show you, but my son has locked everything up, so I'm not able to let you in. But when you talk to him, you can ask him to show you around. And bring your brother too.'

Assad didn't say a word as they drove past the building with the crash marks on the wall where Daniel Hale had lost his life.

'There was something really off about that place,' said Carl. 'We need to go back with a search warrant.'

But Assad wasn't listening. He just sat and stared into

space as they reached Ishøj with its looming concrete high-rises. He didn't even react when Carl's mobile rang after he'd switched it back on.

'Yeah,' said Carl, expecting to hear a sharp torrent of words from Vigga. He knew why she was calling. Something had gone wrong again. The reception had been moved to today. That damn reception. He could really do without a handful of soggy crisps and a glass of cheap supermarket wine, not to mention that misbegotten soul she'd chosen to join forces with.

'It's me,' said the voice on the line. 'Helle Andersen from Stevns.'

Carl shifted down to a lower gear as he ratcheted up his attention.

'Uffe is here. I'm at Merete's old house, making a home visit, and a few minutes ago a cab brought him here from Klippinge. The driver had driven for Merete and Uffe before, so he recognized Uffe when he saw him poking around in the ditch on the side of the motorway near the exit to Lellinge. He's completely exhausted. He's sitting here in the kitchen, drinking one glass of water after another. What should I do?'

Carl looked at the traffic lights. A breeze of excitement stirred inside him. It was tempting to make a U-turn and floor the accelerator.

'Is he OK?' asked Carl.

She sounded a little worried, displaying less of her countrygal cheerfulness than normal. 'I don't really know. He's filthy and looks like something that's been dragged through the gutter. Uffe's not quite himself.'

'What do you mean?'

'He's sitting here brooding. He keeps looking around the kitchen, as if he doesn't recognize it.'

'That doesn't surprise me.' In his mind Carl pictured the antique dealers' copper pans covering the walls from floor to ceiling. The rows of crystal bowls, the pastel-coloured wallpaper with the exotic fruit print. Of course Uffe wouldn't recognize the place.

'I don't mean the way it's furnished. I can't explain it. He seems scared to be here, but he won't get into the car with me.'

'Where were you planning to take him?'

'To the police station. I'm not going to let him run away again. But he refuses to go with me. Even when the antique dealer asked him nicely.'

'Has he said anything? Made any sort of sound?'

Carl could tell that she was shaking her head. 'No, no sounds. But he's trembling. That's what my oldest son used to do when he couldn't have what he wanted. I remember once at the supermarket –'

'Helle, you need to call Egely. Uffe has been missing for five days now. They need to know that he's OK.' He looked up the number for her. It was the only right thing to do. It would be a bad idea for him to get involved. The tabloids would be rubbing their ink-smeared hands with glee.

Now the small, low buildings began to appear along the old Køge highway. An ice-cream stand from the old days. A former electrician's shop that now housed a couple of buxom girls that the vice squad had had a lot of trouble with.

Carl glanced at Assad and considered whistling to see

if there was still life in him. It wasn't unheard of for people to die in the middle of a sentence, with their eyes wide open.

'Anybody home, Assad?' he asked, not expecting an answer.

Carl reached across him to open the glove compartment and take out a semi-flattened packet of Lucky Strikes.

'Carl, would you mind not smoking? It makes the car stink,' said Assad, sounding surprisingly alert.

If a little smoke was going to bother him, he could walk home.

'Stop over there,' Assad went on. Maybe he'd had the same idea.

Carl shut the glove compartment and found a space to pull over near one of the side roads leading down to the beach.

'This is all wrong, Carl.' Assad turned to look at him, his eyes dark. 'I have thought about what we saw out there. It was all wrong everywhere.'

Carl nodded slowly. There was no fooling this guy.

'There were four televisions inside the old woman's house.'

'Really? I only saw one.'

'There were three next to each other, not very big, over by the end of her bed. They were sort of covered up, but I could see the light from them.'

He must have eyes like an eagle paired with an owl, thought Carl. 'Three TVs that were on, covered by a blanket? Could you really see it from that distance, Assad? It was almost pitch dark in there.'

'They were there then, all the way down by the edge of

the bed, up against the wall. Not very big. Almost like some kind of . . .' He was searching for the word. 'Some kind of . . .'

'Monitors?'

Assad nodded. 'And you know what, Carl? I have been realizing more and more in my head. There were three or four monitors. You could see a weak grey or green light through the blanket. What were they there for? Why were they on? And why were they covered up, like we must not see them?'

Carl looked at the road where trucks were rumbling their way towards town. Those were good questions.

'And now one more thing then, Carl.'

Now it was Carl who wasn't really paying attention. He drummed his thumbs on the steering wheel. If they drove back to police headquarters and went through all the proper procedures, it would be at least two hours before they could be back down there.

Then his mobile rang again. If it was Vigga, he'd just hang up. Why did she think he was at her disposal night and day?

But it was Lis. 'Marcus Jacobsen wants to see you in his office, Carl. Where are you?'

'He'll have to wait, Lis. I'm on my way to do a search. Is it about the newspaper article?'

'I'm not really sure, but it might be. You know how he is. He gets awfully quiet whenever anybody writes something bad about us.'

'Then tell him that Uffe Lynggaard has been found, and he's fine. And tell him that we're working on the case.'

'Which case?'

'The one that will make those damned newspapers write something positive about me and the department for a change.'

Then he swung the car into a U-turn, and considered switching on the flashing blue lights.

'What were you about to say to me before, Assad?'

'About the cigarettes.'

'What do you mean?'

'How long have you smoked the same brand, Carl?'

He frowned. How long had Lucky Strikes existed?

'People do not just change their brands like that, right? And she had ten packs of Prince on the table, Carl. Brand new, unopened packs. And she had such completely yellow fingers. But her son did not.'

'What are you getting at?'

'She smoked Prince with filter tips, and her son didn't smoke. I am pretty sure.'

'So?'

'Why were there then no filters on the cigarettes that were lying almost on top in the ashtray?'

That's when Carl turned on the siren and blue lights.

37

The same day

The work took time because the floor was smooth and she didn't want the steady jolting of her upper body to arouse the suspicions of the people out there who were monitoring her on their screens.

She'd been sitting on the floor in the middle of the room for most of the night with her back to the cameras, sharpening the long piece of plastic stiffener that she'd twisted until she broke it in half the day before. No matter how ironic it might seem, this stiffener from the hood of her jacket was going to be her ticket out of this world.

She put the two pieces on her lap and ran her fingers over them. One would soon have a point like an awl; the other she'd already shaped into a nail file with a knife-sharp edge. That was probably the one she would use when the time came. She was afraid the pointed piece wouldn't make a big enough hole in her artery, and if it didn't happen fast, the blood on the floor would give her away. Not for a moment did she doubt that they'd drop the pressure in the room the second they discovered what she was up to. So her suicide had to be done efficiently and quickly.

She didn't want to die the other way.

When she heard the voices in the loudspeakers from somewhere out in the hall, she stuck the stiffeners in her jacket pocket and hunched over, as if she had dozed off in that position. When she sat like that, Lasse often yelled at her, and she'd refuse to respond, so it was nothing unusual.

She sat there with her legs crossed, staring at the long shadow cast by her body from the floodlights. Up there on the wall was her true self. A sharply delineated silhouette of a human being sinking into decay. Wisps of hair hanging to her shoulders, a worn-out jacket wrapped around nothing. A remnant from the past that would soon disappear when the light was put out. Today was April 4th, 2007. She had forty-one days left to live, but she planned to kill herself five days early, on May 10th. On that day Uffe would turn thirty-four, and she would think about him and send him thoughts of love and tenderness and about how beautiful life could be, as she slit her wrists. His shining face would be the last thing she saw. Uffe, her beloved brother.

'We've got to hurry!' she heard the woman shout through the loudspeakers on the other side of the glass panes. 'Lasse will be here in ten minutes, so we need to get everything ready. Pull yourself together, boy!' She sounded frantic.

Merete heard a clattering sound behind the mirrored panes, and she looked over at the airlock. But no buckets appeared, and her inner clock told her it was too early.

'But we need to have another storage battery in here, Mother!' the gaunt man shouted back in reply. 'There's not enough charge in this one. We can't set off the explosion if we don't change it. That's what Lasse told me a couple of days ago.'

The explosion? An icy wave rushed through Merete's body. Was it going to happen now?

She threw herself on to her knees and tried to think about Uffe as she used all her strength to rub the knife-shaped plastic stiffener against the smooth concrete floor. She might have only ten minutes. If she made the cut deep enough, she could lose consciousness in five. That was the important thing.

She was breathing hard, whimpering as the stiffener slowly changed shape. It was still too dull. She glanced over at the tongs, but the tips had been blunted from digging her message into the concrete floor.

'Ohhh,' she whispered. 'Just one more day and I would have been ready.' Then she wiped the sweat from her brow and held her wrist up to her lips. Maybe she could bite through the artery, if she got a good grip. She nibbled a little at her flesh, but her teeth couldn't hold fast. Then she turned her wrist around and tried to use her incisors, but her arm had grown too thin and fleshless. Her wrist bone was in the way, and her teeth weren't sharp enough.

'What's she doing in there?' the witch yelled in a shrill voice, pressing her face against the pane. Her eyes were wide open, the only thing visible while the rest of her was in shadow, with the blinding floodlights as a backdrop.

'Open the airlock all the way. Do it *now*!' she commanded her son.

Merete looked over at the pocket torch that lay ready next to the hole she'd dug under the bolt of the airlock door. She dropped the stiffener and crawled on all fours to the airlock while the woman jeered at her. Everything inside Merete wept and pleaded for life.

Through the loudspeaker system she could hear the

man rattling the air lock door as she grabbed the torch and shoved it down into the hole in the floor.

There was a clicking sound and then the turning mechanism started moving as she stared at the airlock door, her heart pounding. If the torch and the bolt didn't hold, she was lost. The pressure inside of her body would be released like a grenade; that was how she pictured it.

'Oh, dear God, dear God, don't let that happen,' she sobbed and crawled back to get the stiffener as the bolt began banging against the torch. She turned to watch and saw the torch rock slightly back and forth. Then she heard a sound she'd never heard before. Like a camera's telephoto lens being activated, the hum of a mechanism being precisely released, followed by a quick thump against the airlock door. So now the outer door was open. All the pressure was on the inner door, and the torch was the only thing between her and the most horrifying death she could imagine. But the torch wasn't moving any more. The door perhaps had opened a hundredth of a millimetre, because the hissing sound of air forcing its way out of the chamber grew louder until it was like a shrieking whistle.

She felt it in her body after a few seconds. Suddenly her pulse was beating in her ears and she noticed a slight pressure in her sinuses as if a cold were settling in her head.

'She blocked the door, Mother!' shouted the man.

'So turn it off and try again, you idiot,' the woman snarled.

For a moment the wailing tone fell in pitch. Then she heard the mechanism start up, and again the sound grew louder.

They tried several times in vain to make the inner

airlock door function properly as Merete kept filing the nylon stiffener.

'We need to kill her now and get her out of here. Do you understand?' shouted the she-devil outside. 'Run and get the sledgehammer. It's behind the house.'

Merete stared up at the glass panes. For the last couple of years they had served both as her prison bars and as protection against the monsters outside. If they smashed the glass, she would die instantly. The pressure would equalize in a second. Maybe she wouldn't even have time to feel it before her life was extinguished.

She put her hands in her lap and guided the nylon knife toward her left wrist. She'd studied the artery a thousand times. That was where she needed to make the cut. Now there it lay, so fine and dark and open, in her thin, delicate skin.

Then she clenched her fist and pressed hard as she closed her eyes. The pressure on her artery didn't feel right. It hurt but the skin refused to give way. She looked at the cut she had made. It was wide and long and seemed deep, but it wasn't. There wasn't even any blood. The nylon knife simply wasn't sharp enough.

She tossed it aside and grabbed the pointed stiffener that was lying on the floor. She opened her eyes wide and estimated the exact spot where the skin around the artery seemed thinnest. Then she pressed hard. It didn't hurt as much as she'd expected. The blood instantly coloured the point red, giving her a warm, all-embracing sensation. She watched the blood come trickling out with a sense of peace in her soul.

'You've stabbed yourself, you bitch!' shrieked the woman as she slammed her hand against one of the portholes; the pounding of her fist echoed in the room. But Merete shut her out and felt nothing. Quietly she lay down on the floor, pushed her long hair back from her face, and stared up at the last fluorescent light that still functioned.

'I'm sorry, Uffe,' she whispered. 'I couldn't wait.' She smiled up at the image of him hovering in the room and he smiled back.

The thud of the first blow from the sledgehammer pulverized her dream vision. She looked over at the mirrored pane, which vibrated with every blow. The pounding turned the glass opaque, but otherwise nothing happened. Each blow that the man delivered to the pane was followed by an exhausted groan. Then he tried smashing the other pane, but that one also refused to break. It was clear that his thin arms weren't used to wielding so much weight. The intervals between blows lasted longer and longer.

She smiled and looked down at her body that was lying on the floor in such a relaxed position. So this was how she, Merete Lynggaard, would look when she died. Not long from now her body would be pulverized to dog food, but it didn't bother her to think about. By then her soul would be set free. New times would await her. She had experienced hell on earth, and she had spent most of her life in mourning. People had suffered because of her. It couldn't be any worse in the next life, if there was one. And if there wasn't, then what was there to fear, anyway?

She looked down the side of her body and discovered that the stain on the floor was reddish black, but not much bigger than the palm of her hand. Then she turned her wrist over to look at the puncture wound. The bleeding had practically stopped. A few last drops trickled out, then merged like the hands of twins searching for each other, and slowly congealed.

In the meantime, the pounding on the glass had stopped, so the only thing she heard was the hissing air in the crack of the airlock door and her pulse hammering in her ears. It sounded louder than before, and she noticed that she was getting a headache. At the same time, her body began to ache as if she were coming down with the flu.

Again she picked up the stiffener and pressed it deep into the wound that had just closed up. She filed the flexible stick back and forth and down, to make the hole big enough.

'I'm here now, Mum!' shouted a voice. It was Lasse.

His brother's voice sounded frightened in the loudspeaker. 'I wanted to change the battery, Lasse, but Mother told me to go and get the sledgehammer. I tried to smash the glass, but I couldn't. I did the best I could.'

'You can't break it like that,' Lasse replied. 'It takes more than a sledgehammer. But you haven't damaged the detonators, have you?'

'No, I was careful where I hit the glass,' said his brother. 'I really was careful, Lasse.'

Merete pulled out the stiffener and looked up at the panes now pounded opaque with cracks radiating in all directions. The wound on her wrist was bleeding again, but not very much. Oh God, why wasn't it? Had she punctured a vein instead of an artery?

Then she jabbed at her other wrist. Hard and deep. It bled faster. Thank God.

'We couldn't stop the police from coming on to the property,' the witch said, suddenly.

Merete held her breath. She saw how the blood had found its way to the wound and started pouring out faster. The police? Had they been here?

She bit her lip and felt the headache getting worse, and her heartbeat was slowing down.

'They know that Hale used to own this place,' the woman went on. 'One of them said that he didn't know Daniel Hale had been killed near here, but he was lying, Lasse. I could tell.'

Now the pressure in her ears was beginning. Like when a plane was about to land, only faster and stronger. She tried to yawn but couldn't.

'What did they want with me? Does it have something to do with the one they wrote about in the newspapers? The cop from that new police department?' asked Lasse.

Because her ears were plugged, the voices sounded further away, but she wanted to hear what they were saying. She wanted to hear everything.

The woman almost seemed to be whimpering now. 'I just don't know, Lasse,' she said over and over.

'Why do you think they'll come back here?' he asked. 'You told them I was at sea, didn't you?'

'Yes. But Lasse, they know which shipping line you work for. And they've heard about the van that comes here. The black one let it slip out, and it was obvious that the Danish cop was furious, you could see it. They probably already know that you haven't been to sea for several months now. That you're in the catering division instead. They'll find out, Lasse, I know they will. Also that you send us the leftover food in a company van. All it takes is a phone call, Lasse, and there's nothing you can do about it. Then they'll come back. I think they just went to get a search warrant. They asked if they could take a look around.'

Merete held her breath. The police were coming back? With a search warrant? Is that what they thought? She looked at her bleeding wrist and pressed her thumb hard against the wound. The blood trickled out from underneath and pooled in the folds of her wrist, dripping slowly on to her lap. She wasn't going to let go until she was convinced that the battle was lost. They would probably win, but right now they were feeling cornered. What a wonderful feeling it was.

'What reason did they give for looking around the property?' asked Lasse.

The pressure in Merete's ears grew stronger. She was having trouble counterbalancing it. She tried to yawn as she concentrated on listening to what they were saying. She could also feel a pressure inside her hip now. In her hip and her teeth.

'The Danish detective claimed he had a brother who works for Novo, and he wanted to see the place where a big company like InterLab had started out.'

'What bullshit.'

'That's why I called you.'

'When exactly were they here?'

'Not twenty minutes ago.'

'So we might not even have an hour. We'll also need to shovel up the body and take it away, but there's not enough time. And we'd have to clean up and wash down afterwards. No, we'll have to wait until later. Right now the important thing is to make sure they don't find anything, and then leave us in peace.'

Merete tried to banish the words 'shovel up the body'. Was it really her Lasse was talking about? How could any human being be so loathsome and cynical?

'I hope they come here and get you before you can escape!' she yelled. 'I hope you all rot in prison, like the bastards you are! I hate you. Do you hear me? I hate you all!'

Slowly she stood up as the shadows merged in the smashed panes.

Lasse's voice was ice-cold. 'So maybe you finally understand what hate is! Maybe now you understand, Merete!' he shouted back.

'Lasse, don't you think we should blow up the building now?' the woman broke in.

Merete listened intently.

There was a pause. He must be thinking. It was her life that was at stake. He was figuring out how best to get away with killing her. It was no longer about her – she was done for. It was about saving their own skins.

'No, the way things are, we can't do it. We'll have to wait. They mustn't suspect that anything is wrong. If we blow everything up now, it will ruin our plan. We won't get the insurance money, Mum. We'll be forced to disappear. For good.'

'I'll never manage that, Lasse,' said the woman.

Then die with me, you witch, thought Merete.

Not since the day when she looked into Lasse's eyes at their rendezvous at Café Bankeråt had she heard him

433

speak so gently. 'I know, Mum. I know,' he said. He almost sounded human for a moment, but then came the question that made Merete press even harder on her wounded wrist. 'Did you say that she's blocked the door of the airlock?'

'Yes. Can't you hear it? The pressure is being equalized much too slowly.'

'Then I'm going to set the timer.'

'The timer, Lasse? But it takes twenty minutes before the nozzles will open. Isn't there any other solution? She's stabbed herself, Lasse. Can't we shut off the ventilation system?'

The timer? Hadn't they said that they could release the pressure whenever they liked? That she wouldn't have time to hurt herself before they opened it up? Was that a lie?

Hysteria began rising inside her. Watch out, Merete, she told herself. Don't over-react. Don't retreat inside yourself.

'Shut off the ventilation system? What good would that do?' Lasse was clearly annoyed. 'The air was changed yesterday. It will take at least eight days for her to use up the oxygen. No, I'm going to set the timer.'

'Having problems?' Merete shouted. 'Doesn't your shitty system work after all, Lasse?'

He tried to make it seem he was laughing at her, but she wasn't fooled. It was obvious that her scorn made him furious.

'Don't worry,' he said, controlling himself. 'My father built this system. It was the world's most sophisticated pressure testing system in the world. This is where you got the finest and most thoroughly tested containment linings on earth. Most other places pump water into the containment and pressure-test it from the inside, but my father's company also applied pressure from outside. Everything was done with the utmost precision. The timer controlled the temperature and humidity in the room and set all the parameters, so the pressure couldn't be equalized too fast. Otherwise the containers would crack during quality control. That's why it all takes time, Merete! That's why!'

They were crazy, all of them. 'You really do have problems' she yelled. 'You're all insane. You're finished, just like me.'

'Problems? I'll give you problems!' he raged. She heard some clattering outside and quick steps in the hall. Then a shadow appeared at the edge of the glass, and two deafening bangs came through the loudspeaker system before she saw one of the windowpanes change colour again. Now it was almost totally white and opaque.

'You'd better pulverize this building completely, Lasse, because I've left so many calling cards in here that you won't be able to remove them all. You won't get away.' She laughed. 'You won't get away with it. I've made that impossible for all of you.'

The next minute she heard six more bangs. They were evidently from shots fired in pairs. But both windowpanes held.

A short time later she began feeling pressure in her shoulder. Not too much, but it was still uncomfortable. She also had pressure in her forehead, sinuses and jaw. Her skin felt tight. If this was the effect of the slight equalization caused by the minuscule crack in the door, then what awaited her when they released all the pressure would be absolutely intolerable.

'The police are coming!' she yelled. 'I can feel it.' She looked down at her bleeding arm. The police wouldn't arrive in time; she knew that. Soon she'd be forced to lift her thumb away from the wound. In twenty minutes the nozzles would open.

She felt something warm sliding down her other arm, and saw that the first wound had opened itself menacingly. Lasse's prophecies were going to come true. When the pressure inside her body increased, the blood would come gushing out.

She twisted her body slightly so she could press her other trickling wrist against her knee. For a second she laughed. It felt like some sort of child's game from the distant past.

'I'm activating the timer now, Merete,' he said. 'In twenty minutes the nozzles will open and release the pressure in the room. It will take about another half-hour before the room is back down to one atmosphere. It's true that you have time to kill yourself now, before that happens. I don't doubt that. But I won't be able to watch any more, Merete, understand? I can't see you because the glass is totally opaque. And if I can't see you, nobody else can either. We're going to seal up the pressure chamber, Merete. We have lots of plasterboard out here. So, you're going to die in the meantime, one way or the other.'

She heard the woman laugh.

'Come on, brother, help me with this,' she heard Lasse say. His voice sounded different now. In control.

There was a scraping sound, and slowly the room got darker and darker. Then they turned off the floodlights and more plasterboard was piled against the panes until at last it was pitch dark.

'Good night, Merete,' he said softly out there. 'May you burn in hell for all eternity.' Then he switched off the loudspeaker, and everything went quiet.

38

The same day

The traffic jam on the E20 was much worse than usual. Even though the police siren was about to drive Carl crazy, the people sitting in their cars didn't seem to hear a thing. They were immersed in their own thoughts, with the radio turned up full blast, wishing they were far away.

Assad sat in the passenger seat, pounding the dashboard with impatience. They drove along the verge for the last few kilometres before they reached the exit, while the vehicles ahead of them were forced to squeeze close together to let them pass.

When they finally stopped outside the farm, Assad pointed accross the road. 'Was that car there before?' he asked.

Carl caught sight of it only after scanning the landscape from the gravel road into no-man's-land. The vehicle was hidden behind some shrubbery about a hundred yards away. What they saw was presumably the bonnet of a steel-grey four-wheel-drive.

'I'm not sure,' he said, trying to ignore the ringing of his mobile in his jacket pocket. He pulled the phone out and looked at the number displayed. It was police headquarters.

'Yeah. This is Mørck,' he said as he looked at the farm buildings. Everything seemed the same. No sign of panic or flight.

It was Lis on the line, and she sounded smug. 'It's working again, Carl. All the databases are functioning. It was the interior minister's wife. She finally coughed up the antidote to all the trouble she'd set in motion. And Mrs Sørensen has already entered all the possible CR combinations for Lars Henrik Jensen, as Assad asked her to do. I think it was a lot of work, so you owe her a big bouquet. But she found the man. Two of the digits had been changed, just as Assad assumed. He's registered on Strøhusvej in Greve.' Then she gave him the house number.

Carl looked at some wrought-iron numbers affixed to one of the buildings. Yes, it was the same number. 'Thanks, Lis,' he said, trying to sound enthusiastic. 'And give Mrs Sørensen my thanks too. She did a really great job.'

'Wait, Carl, there's more.'

Carl took a deep breath as he saw Assad's dark eyes scanning the property in front of them. Carl felt it too. There was something really strange about the way these people had set up home here. It was not normal. Not at all.

'Lars Henrik Jensen has no criminal record, and he's a ship's steward by trade,' he heard Lis continue to talk. 'He works for the Merconi shipping company and mostly sails on ships in the Baltic. I just talked to his employer, and Lars Henrik Jensen is responsible for the catering on most of their ships. They said he was a very capable man. And by the way, they all call him Lasse.'

Carl shifted his eyes away from the property. 'Do you have a mobile number for him, Lis?'

'Only a landline.' She rattled it off, but Carl didn't write it down. What good would it do them? Should they call to say that they'd be arriving in two minutes?

'No mobile number?'

'At that address the only one listed is for a Hans Jensen.'

OK. So that was the name of the thin young man. Carl got the number and thanked Lis again.

'What did she say?' asked Assad.

Carl shrugged and took the car's registration certificate out of the glove compartment. 'Nothing we don't already know, Assad. Shall we get going?'

The gaunt young man opened the door as soon as they knocked. He didn't say a word, just let them in, almost as if they'd been expected.

Apparently it was supposed to look as if he and the woman had been eating a meal in peace and quiet, sitting about thirty feet from the door at a table covered with a floral oilcloth. Their meal was presumably a tin of ravioli. But Carl was sure that if he checked, he'd find the food ice-cold. They couldn't fool him. They should save that game for amateurs.

'We've brought a search warrant,' he said, pulling the car registration out of his pocket and briefly holding it up for them to see. The young man flinched at the sight of it.

'May we take a look around?' With a wave of his hand Carl sent Assad over to the monitors.

'That, apparently, was a rhetorical question,' said the woman. She was holding a glass of water in her hand, and she looked worn-out. The obstinate look in her eyes was gone, but she didn't seem scared. Just resigned.

'What are you using those monitors for?' he asked after Assad checked out the bathroom. He pointed at the green light visible through the cloth draped over the screens.

'Oh, that's something that Hans set up,' said the woman. 'We live way out here in the country, and we hear about so

440

many bad things happening these days. We wanted to put up some cameras so we could monitor the area around the house.'

He watched Assad pull off the cloth and shake his head. 'They're blank, Carl. All three of them.'

'May I ask you, Hans, why the screens are on if they're not connected?'

The man looked at his mother.

'They're always on,' she told them. 'The power comes from the junction box.'

'The junction box? I see! And where is that?'

'I don't know. Lasse would know.' She gave Carl a triumphant look. She'd led him into a dead end. There he was, peering up at an insurmountable wall. Or so she thought.

'We heard from the shipping company that Lasse isn't on board a ship at the moment. So where is he?'

She smiled easily. 'When Lasse isn't out sailing, he keeps company with the ladies. It's not something he tells his mother about, nor should he.'

Her smile got bigger. Those yellow teeth of hers were just itching to make a lunge at him.

'Come on, Assad,' said Carl. 'There's nothing for us to do in here. Let's go look at the other buildings.'

He caught a glimpse of the woman as he headed for the door. She was already reaching for her pack of cigarettes, the smile gone from her face. So they were on the right track.

'Keep a close eye on everything, Assad. We'll take that building first,' said Carl, pointing to the one that towered high above all the others. 'Stay right here and let me know if anything happens down by the other buildings. OK, Assad?'

He nodded.

As Carl turned away, he heard a quiet but all too familiar click behind him. He swung around to find Assad with a shiny, four-inch-long switchblade in his hand. Used correctly, it presented serious problems for an opponent; use it incorrectly, and everybody was in trouble.

'What the hell are you doing, Assad? How'd that get here?'

He shrugged. 'It's magic, Carl. I will then make it disappear like magic afterwards. I promise.'

'You'd better do that, damn it.'

Having his mind blown by Assad was apparently turning into a permanent condition. Possession of an illegal weapon? How the hell had he come up with something so stupid?

'We're on duty here, Assad. Do you understand? This is as wrong as it gets. Give me the knife.'

The expertise with which Assad instantly closed up the switchblade was worrisome.

Carl weighed the knife in his hand before he stuck it in his jacket pocket, accompanied by Assad's look of disapproval. Even Carl's big old Scout knife weighed less than this one.

The enormous hall was built on a concrete floor foundation that had been cracked from frost and water that had seeped in. The gaping holes where the windows should have been were black and rotting around the edges, and the laminated beams supporting the ceiling had also suffered from the weather. It was a huge space. Aside from some debris and fifteen or twenty buckets like the ones he'd seen scattered about the grounds, the room was completely empty.

He kicked one of the buckets, which spun round, sending up a putrid stench. By the time it stopped, it had cast off a ring of sludge. Carl leaned down to take a closer look. Were those the remains of toilet paper? He shook his head. The buckets had probably been exposed to all types of weather and then filled up with rain water. Anything would stink and look like this, given enough time.

He looked at the bottom of the bucket and identified the logo of the Merconi shipping company stamped into the plastic. The buckets were probably used for bringing home leftover food from the ships.

He grabbed a solid iron bar from the junk pile and went to get Assad. Together they walked over to the furthest of the three adjacent buildings.

'Stay here,' said Carl as he studied the padlock on the door that supposedly only Lasse had a key to. 'Come and get me, Assad, if you see anything strange,' he added, then stuck the iron bar under the padlock. In his old police car he'd had an entire toolbox that could have sprung something like this lock in a flash. Now he had to clench his teeth and try brute force.

He kept at it for thirty seconds before Assad came over and quietly took the iron bar away from him.

OK, let the young gun give it a try, thought Carl.

It took only a second before the broken lock lay in the gravel at Assad's feet.

A few moments later, Carl stepped inside the building, feeling both defeated and on high alert.

The room was similar to the one where Mrs Jensen lived, but instead of furniture, a row of welding cylinders in various colours stood in the middle of the space, along with maybe a hundred yards of empty steel shelves. In the far corner sheets of stainless-steel had been piled up next to a door. There was not much else. Carl took a closer look at the door. It couldn't lead out of the building or else he would have noticed.

He went over and tried to open it. The brass handle was shiny, and the door was locked. He looked at the Ruko lock; it too was shiny from recent use.

'Assad, come in here,' he shouted. 'And bring that iron bar!'.

'I thought you told me to stay outside,' said Assad as he joined Carl.

Carl pointed to the bar Assad was holding and then to the door. 'Show me what you can do.'

The room they entered was filled with the heavy scent of cologne. A bed, desk, computer, full-size mirror, red Wiltax blanket, an open wardrobe containing suits and two or three blue uniforms, a sink with a glass shelf and plenty of bottles of aftershave. The bed was made, the papers were stacked up neatly. There was nothing to indicate that the person who lived here was unbalanced.

'Why do you think he locked the door, Carl?' asked Assad as he lifted up the desk blotter to glance underneath. Then he knelt down and looked under the bed.

Carl inspected the rest of the room. Assad was right. There didn't seem to be anything to hide, so why lock the door?

'There *is* something, Carl. Or there then would not be a lock.'

Carl nodded and began poking around inside the

wardrobe. The smell of cologne was even stronger. It seemed to be clinging to the clothes. He knocked on the back wall, but nothing seemed out of the ordinary. In the meantime Assad lifted up the carpet. No trapdoor.

They examined the ceiling and the walls and then both of them stared at the mirror, hanging there so alone. The wall around it was painted a dull chalk-white.

Carl knocked on the wall with his knuckles. It seemed solid.

Maybe we can take the mirror off, he thought, but it was fastened securely. Then Assad pressed his cheek against the wall and peered behind the mirror.

'I think it hangs on a hinge on the other side. I can see some kind of lock here.'

He stuck his finger behind the mirror and coaxed the latch out of the lock. Then he grabbed the edge and pulled. The whole room panned past in the mirror as it slid aside to reveal a pitch-black hole in the wall, as tall as a man.

The next time we're out in the field, I'm going to be better prepared, thought Carl. In his mind he saw the pencil-sized pocket torch lying on top of the piles of paper in his desk drawer. He stuck his hand inside the hole in the wall, fumbling for a light switch and longing for his service revolver. The next instant he felt the pressure in his chest.

He took a deep breath and tried to listen. No, damn it, there couldn't be anybody inside. How could they have locked themselves in with a padlock on the outer door? Was it conceivable that Lasse Jensen's brother or mother had been told to lock Lasse in his hiding place if the police came back and started snooping around?

He found the light switch further along the wall and pressed it, ready to jump back if anyone was inside, waiting for them. It took a second for the scene in front of them to stop flickering as the fluorescent lights came on.

And then everything became clear.

They had found the right person. There was no doubt about it.

Carl noticed how Assad slipped silently into the room behind him as he moved closer to the bulletin boards and the worn steel tables along the wall. He stared at the photos of Merete Lynggaard, taken in all sorts of situations. From her first appearance on the speaker's podium to the cosy home setting on the leaf-covered lawn in Stevns. Carefree moments captured by someone who wished to do her harm.

Carl looked down at one of the steel tables and understood at once the systematic way in which this Lasse, aka Lars Henrik Jensen, had worked his way towards his goal.

The first papers were from Godhavn. He lifted up a corner of a few documents and saw the original case files on Lars Henrik Jensen, the files that had disappeared years ago. He'd used some of the sheets of paper to practise, making clumsy attempts at altering his CR number. Along the way he got better at it, and by the top sheet of paper, he'd done a good job. Yes, Lasse had tampered with the documents at Godhavn, and that had won him time.

Assad pointed at the next pile of papers, which contained the correspondence between Lasse and Daniel Hale. Apparently InterLab hadn't yet been paid the balance for the buildings that Lasse's father had taken over so many years ago. In the beginning of 2002, Daniel Hale had sent a fax stating that he intended to file a lawsuit. He was demanding two million kroner. Hale was bringing about his own demise, but he could never have known the determination of his adversary. Maybe Hale's demands had set off the entire chain reaction.

Carl picked up the paper on top. It was a copy of a fax that Lasse Jensen had sent on the very day that Hale was killed. It was a message and an unsigned contract:

> I have the money. We can sign the papers and conclude the deal at my home today. My lawyer will bring the necessary documents; I'm faxing over a draft of the contract. Enter your comments and corrections and then bring the papers with you.

Yes, everything had been carefully planned. If the papers hadn't burned up in the car, Lasse would probably have made sure they disappeared before the police and ambulances arrived. Carl noted the date and time of the proposed meeting. It all fitted together. Hale had been lured to his death. Dennis Knudsen was waiting for him on the Kappelev highway with his foot on the accelerator.

'Look at this, Carl,' said Assad, picking up the paper on top of the next pile. It was an article from the *Fredriksborg Amts* newspaper that mentioned Dennis Knudsen's death at the bottom of the page. 'Death a Result of Drug Abuse' was the curt headline.

The perfect 'cause-of-death' category to be filed under.

Carl looked at the next pages in the pile. There was no doubt that Lasse had offered Dennis a lot of money to cause the car accident. Nor was there any doubt that it was Lasse's brother, Hans, who had stepped out in front of Hale's car, forcing him to veer into the middle of the road. Everything went as planned, except for the fact that Lasse never paid Dennis, as he'd promised, and Dennis got mad.

A surprisingly well-formulated letter from Dennis Knudsen to Lasse presented an ultimatum: either he paid the three hundred thousand kroner or Dennis would obliterate him somewhere out on some road or highway when he least expected it.

Carl thought about Dennis's sister. What a lovely kid brother she was mourning.

He looked up at the bulletin boards and got an overview of the devastating events in the course of Lasse Jensen's life. The car accident, the rebuff from the insurance company. A request for funding from the Lynggaard Foundation denied. The motives accumulated and became much clearer than before.

'Do you think he went good and crazy in the head from all this?' asked Assad, handing something to Carl.

Carl frowned. 'I don't dare think about it, Assad.'

He looked closely at the object that Assad had given him. It was a small, compact Nokia mobile phone. Red and new and shiny. On the back someone had printed in tiny, crooked letters: 'Sanne Jønsson' under a little heart. He wondered what the girl would say when she found out her mobile still existed.

'We've got everything here,' he said to Assad, nodding at the photos on the wall of Lasse's mother sitting in a hospital bed, weeping, of the Godhavn buildings and of a man with the words 'foster-father Satan' written underneath in thick letters. Old newspaper clippings praising

HJ Industries and Lasse Jensen's father for his exceptional pioneering work in the field of high-tech Danish industry. There were at least twenty detailed photos taken on board the *Schleswig-Holstein*, along with sailing schedules and measurements of the distance down to the car deck, as well as the number of steps. There was also a time schedule in two columns. One for Lasse, and one for his brother. So both of them had been involved.

'What does this mean?' asked Assad, pointing at the numbers.

Carl wasn't sure.

'It could mean that they kidnapped her and killed her somewhere. I'm afraid that might be the explanation.'

'And what does this mean then?' Assad went on, pointing at the last steel table, on top of which were several ring binders and a series of technical cross-section diagrams.

Carl picked up the first ring binder. There were section dividers inside, and the first one was labelled 'Handbook for Diving – The Naval Weapons Academy AUG 1985'. He leafed through the pages, reading the headers: diving physiology, valve maintenance, surface decompression tables, oxygen handling tables, Boyle's law, Dalton's law.

It was pure gibberish to Carl.

'Does a first mate need to know about diving then, Carl?' asked Assad.

Carl shook his head. 'Maybe it's just a hobby of his.'

He went through the pile of papers and found a meticulous, handwritten draft for a manual. It was titled 'Instructions for the pressure testing of containments, by Henrik Jensen, HJ Industries, 10 November 1986.'

'Can you read that, Carl?' asked Assad, who apparently couldn't, his eyes glued to the text.

Several diagrams had been drawn on the first page along with surveys of pipe lead-ins. Apparently they had to do with specifications for changes in an existing installation, presumably the one that HJ Industries had taken over from InterLab when the buildings were purchased.

Carl did his best to skim through the handwritten pages, stopping at the words 'pressure chamber' and 'enclosure'.

He raised his head and looked at a close-up photo of Merete Lynggaard that hung above the stack of papers. Once move the words 'pressure chamber' thundered through his mind.

The thought sent shivers down his back. Could it really be true? It was a gruesome, horrifying thought. Horrifying enough to get the sweat trickling.

'What is wrong, Carl?' asked Assad.

'Go outside and keep watch on the place. Do it *now*, Assad.'

His partner was about to repeat his question when Carl turned to look at the last pile of papers. 'Go now, Assad. And be careful. Take this with you.' He handed Assad the iron bar that they'd used to prise open the lock.

He paged quickly through the papers. There were lots of mathematical calculations, mostly written by Henrik Jensen, and also by others. But he found nothing related to what he was looking for.

Again he studied the knife-sharp photo of Merete Lynggaard. It had presumably been taken at close range, but she probably hadn't noticed, since her attention was directed slightly to the side. There was a particular look in

450

her eyes. Something vital and alert that couldn't help affecting the viewer. But Carl was certain that wasn't why Lasse Jensen had hung up this photo in particular. On the contrary. There were lots of holes around its edges. Presumably it had been taken down and put up again, time after time.

One by one Carl pulled out the four pins that held the picture. Then he lifted it off and turned it over.

What was written on the back was the work of a madman.

He read it several times.

These disgusting eyes will pop out of your head. Your ridiculous smile will be drowned in blood. Your hair will shrivel up, and your thoughts will be pulverized. Your teeth will rot. Nobody will remember you for anything other than what you are: a whore, a bitch, a devil, a fucking murderer. Die like that, Merete Lynggaard.

And underneath had been added in block letters:

6/July/2002: 2 ATMOSPHERES
6/July/2003: 3 ATMOSPHERES
6/July/2004: 4 ATMOSPHERES
6/July/2005: 5 ATMOSPHERES
6/July/2006: 6 ATMOSPHERES
15/July/2007: 1 ATMOSPHERE

Carl glanced over his shoulder. It felt as if the walls were closing in around him. He put his hand to his forehead and stood there, thinking hard. They had her here, he was sure of it. She was somewhere close by. It said here they were going to kill her in five weeks, on May 15th, but it was likely they'd already done so. He had a feeling that he and Assad might have provoked the deed, and it had definitely happened somewhere near by.

What do I do? Who would know something? Carl wondered, as he dug through his memory.

He grabbed his mobile and punched in the number of Kurt Hansen, his former colleague who'd ended up as an MP of the Conservative Party.

He paced the room as he listened to the phone ring. Father Time was out there somewhere, laughing at all of them, he could feel it so clearly now.

A second before he was going to put the phone down, he heard Kurt Hansen's distinctive throat-clearing, then his voice.

Carl told him not to speak, just listen and think fast. No questions, just answers.

'You want to know what would happen to a person who was subjected to up to six atmospheres of pressure over a period of five years and then the pressure was released all at once?' Kurt repeated. 'That's a strange question. This is a hypothetical situation, right?'

'Just answer me, Kurt. You're the only one I can think of who knows about these things. I don't know anybody else who has a professional diving certificate, so tell me what would happen.'

'Well, the person would die, of course.'

'Yes, but how fast?'

'I have no idea, but it would be a horrible affair.'

'In what way?'

'Everything would explode from the inside. The alveoli

would burst the lungs. The nitrogen in the bones would shred the tissue. The organs, and everything in the body would expand because there's oxygen everywhere. Blood clots, cerebral haemorrhages, massive bleeding, even –'

Carl stopped him. 'Who could help somebody in this situation?'

Kurt Hansen again cleared his throat. Maybe he didn't know the answer. 'Is this an actual situation, Carl?' he asked.

'I'm seriously afraid that it is, yes.'

'Then you need to call the naval station at Holmen. They have a mobile decompression chamber. A Duocom from Dräger.' He gave Carl the number. Carl thanked him and ended the call.

It took only a moment to explain the situation to the naval officer on duty.

'You've got to hurry. This is incredibly urgent,' said Carl. 'Bring people with pneumatic drills and other equipment, because I don't know what kind of obstacles you're going to encounter. And notify police headquarters. I need reinforcements.'

'I think I understand the situation,' said the voice on the phone.

39

The same day

They approached the last of the buildings with the greatest of caution. They studied the ground carefully to see if any digging had been done recently. They stared at the slippery plastic drums lined up along the wall, as if they might contain a bomb.

This door also had a padlock that Assad broke open with the iron bar – a skill that would soon have to be added to his job description.

They noticed a sweet smell in the hall's entrance. Like a mixture of the cologne from Lasse Jensen's bedroom and the smell of meat that had been left out too long. Or maybe more like the scent of the animal cages at the zoo on a warm, blossoming, spring day.

Lying on the floor were scores of receptacles made from in shiny stainless steel in different lengths. Most of them did not yet have gauges affixed to them, but a few of them did. Endless shelves along one wall indicated that production had been planned on a large scale. But that had never happened.

Carl gestured for Assad to follow him over to the next door, holding his index finger to his lips. Assad nodded and gripped the iron bar so hard that his knuckles turned white. He crouched down a bit, as if to make himself a smaller target. He seemed to do so reflexively.

Carl opened the next door.

There was light in the room. Lamps in reinforced glass fixtures lit up a hallway. On one side, doors opened on to a series of windowless offices; on the other side a door led to yet another corridor. Carl gestured for Assad to search the offices while he started down the long, narrow hallway.

It was unspeakably filthy, as if over time shit or some kind of muck had been smeared on the walls and floor. Very unlike the spirit in which the factory's founder, Henrik Jensen, had wanted to create these surroundings. Carl had a very hard time picturing white-clad engineers in this setting.

At the end of the corridor was a door, which Carl cautiously opened as he clutched the switchblade in his jacket pocket.

He turned on the light and saw what had to be a storage room containing a couple of carts and stacks of plasterboard as well as numerous cylinders of hydrogen and oxygen. He instinctively sniffed at the air. It smelled of cordite. As if a gun had been fired in the room quite recently.

'Nothing in any of the offices,' he heard Assad say quietly behind him.

Carl nodded. There didn't seem to be anything here, either. Except for the same impression of filth as he'd had in the corridor.

Assad came inside and looked around.

'He is not here then, Carl.'

'It's not him we're looking for right now.'

Assad frowned. 'Then who is it?'

'Shhh,' said Carl. 'Do you hear that?'

'What?'

'Listen. It's a very faint whistling sound.'

'Whistling?'

Carl raised his hand to make Assad stop talking and then closed his eyes. It could be a ventilator in the distance. It could be water running through the pipes.

'It is some air saying like that, Carl. Like something that is punctured.'

'Yes, but where is it coming from?' Carl slowly turned around. It was impossible to pinpoint. The room was no more than ten feet wide and fifteen to twenty feet long, but still the sound seemed to be coming from everywhere and nowhere at the same time.

He took a mental snapshot of the room. To his left were four pieces of plasterboard, standing up next to each other in layers that were perhaps five boards deep. Against the far wall was a single piece of plasterboard that leaned crookedly. The wall to his right was bare.

He looked up at the ceiling and saw four panels with tiny holes and in between them bundles of wires and copper pipes leading from the corridor and over behind the piles of plasterboard.

Assad saw it too. 'There must be something behind the boards then, Carl.'

He nodded. Maybe an outside wall, maybe something else.

With every piece of plasterboard they grabbed and carried over to the opposite wall, the sound seemed to come closer.

Finally they were standing before a wall with a big black box up near the ceiling upon which was mounted a number of switches, gauges and buttons. To the side of this control panel an arched door had been set into the wall in two sections that were covered with metal plates. To the other side were two big portholes with armoured, completely milk-white panes. Wires were taped to the glass between a couple of pins that Carl guessed might be detonators. A surveillance camera on a tripod had been set up under each porthole. It wasn't hard to imagine what the cameras had been used for and what the detonators were meant to do.

On the floor under the cameras were several little black pellets. He picked some up and saw that they were buckshot. He felt the glass panes and took a step back. There was no question that shots had been fired at them. So maybe there was something going on here that the people on the farm were unable to control.

He pressed his ear against the wall. The whining sound was coming from somewhere inside. Not from the door, not from the windows. Just from inside. It had to be an extremely high-pitched sound for it to penetrate such a solid enclosure.

'It reads more than four bars, Carl.'

He looked at the pressure gauge that Assad was tapping on. He was right. And four bars was the same as five atmospheres. So the pressure inside the room had already dropped by one atmosphere.

'Assad, I think Merete Lynggaard is inside there.'

His partner stood very still, studying the arched metal door. 'You think so?'

He nodded.

'The pressure is going in a downward direction, Carl.'

He was right. The needle's movement was actually visible.

Carl looked up at all the cables overhead. The thin wires between the detonators dangled to the floor with stripped ends. The plan must have been to fasten a battery or some other explosive device to the wires. Was that what they were going to do on May 15th, when the pressure was supposed to drop to one atmosphere, as had been written on the back of the photo of Merete Lynggaard?

He looked around to try to make sense of it all. The copper pipes led directly into the room. There were maybe ten in all, so how could anyone tell which ones released the pressure and which ones increased it? If they cut through one of the pipes, there was a huge risk they would make matters worse for the person inside the pressure chamber. The same was true if they did anything to the electrical wires.

He stepped over to the airlock door and examined the relay boxes next to it. Here there was no question — everything was printed in black and white on the six buttons: Top door open. Top door closed. Outer airlock door open. Outer airlock door closed. Inner airlock door open. Inner airlock door closed.

And both airlock doors were in the closed position. That was how they would stay.

'What do you think that thing's for?' asked Assad. He was perilously close to turning a little potentiometer from OFF to ON.

Carl wished that Hardy was here to see this. If there was one thing that Hardy could deal with better than anyone else, it was anything to do with buttons or dials.

'That switch was then put in after all the others,' said Assad. 'Otherwise why are the others made of that brown stuff?' He pointed at a square box made of Bakelite. 'And why should that one then be the only one made of plastic, out of all of them?'

It was true. The different types of switches had obviously been fabricated decades apart.

Assad nodded. 'I think that dial might either stop the process, or else it does not mean anything.' What an imprecise but beautiful way of putting it.

Carl took a deep breath. It was almost ten minutes since he'd spoken to the people out at Holmen, and it would still take them a while to arrive. If Merete Lynggaard was inside there, they were going to have to do something drastic.

'Turn it,' he told Assad with a sense of foreboding.

As soon as he did, they could hear the whistling sound slicing through the room at full force. Carl's heart leaped to his throat. For a moment he was convinced that they'd released even more pressure.

Then he looked up and identified the four framed rectangles on the ceiling as loudspeakers. That was how they were able to hear the whistling sounds from inside the room, which had become piercingly enervating.

'What is happening now?' shouted Assad, holding his hands over his ears, making it hard for Carl to answer him.

'I think you've turned on the intercom,' he shouted back, turning to look up at the rectangles on the ceiling. 'Are you inside there, Merete?' he yelled three or four times and then listened intently.

Now he could clearly hear that the sound was air

459

passing through a narrow passage. Like the noise a person makes with his teeth, just as he begins to whistle. And the sound was constant.

He cast a worried glance at the pressure gauge. Now it was almost down to four point five atmospheres. It was dropping fast.

He shouted again, this time at the top of his lungs, and Assad took his hands away from his ears and shouted too. Their combined yelling could wake the dead, thought Carl, sincerely hoping that things hadn't gone that far.

Then he heard a loud thud from the black box up near the ceiling, and for a moment the room was totally silent.

That box up there controls the pressure equalization, he thought, considering whether to run into the other room and get something to stand on so he could open the box.

It was at that instant they heard groans coming from the loudspeakers. Like the sounds uttered by a cornered animal or a human being in deep crisis or grief. A long, monotonic moan of lament.

'Merete, is that you?' Carl shouted.

They stood still and waited. Then they heard a sound they interpreted as a yes.

Carl felt a burning in his throat. Merete Lynggaard was inside there. Imprisoned for over five years in this bleak and disgusting setting. And now she was possibly about to die, and Carl had no idea what to do.

'What can we do, Merete?' he yelled. At the same instant he heard an enormous bang from the plasterboard on the far wall. He knew at once that someone had fired a shot-gun through the plasterboard from behind, scattering buckshot all over the room. He felt a throbbing several places in his body as warm blood began trickling out. He stood paralysed for a tenth of a second that felt like an eternity. Then he threw himself backwards against Assad, who was standing there with one arm bleeding and an expression that matched the situation.

As they lay on the floor, the plasterboard tipped forwards to reveal the person who had fired the shot. It wasn't hard to recognize him. Aside from the lines on his face, which his hard life and tormented soul had produced over the years, Lasse Jensen looked exactly like the boy in the photos they'd seen.

He stepped out of his hiding place, holding the smoking shotgun, inspecting the wounds his shot had made with the same cool indifference as if it had been a flooded basement.

'How did you find me?' he asked, as he cracked the barrel and inserted more shells. He came over to them. There was no question that he would pull the trigger if he felt like it.

'You can still stop this, Lasse,' said Carl, propping himself up so that Assad could get out from under his body. 'If you stop now, you might get off with a few years in prison. Otherwise it's going to be a life sentence for murder.'

The man smiled. It wasn't hard to see why women fell for him. He was a devil in disguise. 'Then there's a lot you don't know,' he said, aiming the gun straight at Assad's temple.

Yeah, that's what you think, thought Carl as he felt Assad's hand feel its way inside his jacket pocket. 'I've called for backup. My colleagues will be here any minute. Give me that shotgun, Lasse, and everything will be OK.'

Lasse shook his head. He didn't believe it. 'I'll kill your partner if you don't give me an answer. How the hell did you find me?'

Considering how much pressure he must be under, Lasse sounded far too controlled. He was obviously raving mad.

'It was Uffe,' Carl told him.

'Uffe?' Now the man's expression changed. That piece of information just didn't fit into the world he was determined to control. 'Bullshit! Uffe Lynggaard doesn't know a thing, 'said Lasse He can't even talk. I've been following the news the past couple of days. He didn't say a word. You're lying.'

Carl could feel that Assad had grabbed the switchblade. To hell with regulations and laws about concealed weapons. He just hoped Assad would have time to use it.

A sound came from the loudspeakers overhead as if the woman in the room wanted to say something.

'Uffe Lynggaard recognized you in a photograph,' said Carl. 'A photo of you and Dennis Knudsen standing next to each other as boys. Do you remember that picture, Atomos?'

The name stung him like a slap in the face. It was obvious that years of suffering were now surfacing inside Lasse Jensen.

He grimaced and nodded. 'So you know about that too! I assume you know everything. Then you also realize that you're going to have to accompany Merete.'

'You won't have time. Help is on the way,' said Carl, leaning forwards a bit so that Assad could pull out the knife and lunge at the man in one movement. The question was whether the psychopath would be able to press the trigger in time. If Lasse fired both barrels simultaneously at such close range, he and Assad were done for.

462

Lasse smiled again. He had already regained his composure. It was the trademark of a psychopath: nothing could touch him.

'Oh, I'll have time. You can be sure of that.'

The jerk in Carl's jacket pocket and the subsequent click of the switchblade coincided with the sound that flesh makes when you stick a knife into it. Sinews being severed, healthy muscles clipped. Carl saw the blood on Lasse's leg just as Assad knocked the shotgun upwards with his bloodied left arm. The boom from the shotgun next to Carl's ears when Lasse fired out of sheer reflex blocked out all other sounds. He saw Lasse silently topple over backwards, and then Assad threw himself at the man, his knife raised to strike.

'No!' yelled Carl, though he could barely hear the sound of his own voice. He tried to get up but now felt the full extent of the shot he'd taken. He looked down underneath himself and saw blood pouring out onto the floor. Then he grabbed his thigh and pressed hard as he stood up.

Assad sat himself down, bleeding, on Lasse's chest with the knife pressed to the man's throat. Carl couldn't hear, but he could see Assad shouting at the man beneath him, and he saw Lasse spitting in Assad's face with every sentence he spoke.

Slowly Carl regained his hearing in one ear. The relay overhead had again begun releasing air from the chamber. This time the whistling sound was a notch higher than before. Or was it his hearing that was playing tricks on him?

'How do we stop this shit? How do we shut off the ventilators? Tell me!' shouted Assad for the umpteenth time, taking another wad of spit in the face. Only now did

Carl notice that each time Lasse spat, the knife was pressed harder against his throat.

'I have cut throats of better men than you!' yelled Assad and made a shallow slice into the skin, deep enough for the blood to trickle down Lasse's neck.

'Even if I knew, I wouldn't tell you,' snarled Lasse. Carl looked down at Lasse's leg, where Assad had stabbed him. It wasn't bleeding very heavily, not like when the big femoral artery in the thigh is severed. But it was still serious enough.

He looked up at the manometer; the pressure was dropping slowly but steadily. Where the hell was the police backup? Hadn't the officer at Holmen called his colleagues, as he'd requested? Carl leaned against the wall and took out his mobile. He punched in the number of the duty officer and was told help would arrive in a matter of minutes. His colleagues and the medics were going to have their hands full.

He didn't feel the blow to his arm; he merely noticed his mobile on the floor and how his arm fell to his side. He jerked his body round and saw the skinny creature standing behind them take aim again and slam the iron bar against Assad's temple. He fell over without a word.

Then Lasse's brother took a step forwards and stomped on Carl's mobile until it was smashed to bits.

'Oh God, is it serious, my boy?' came a voice from behind them. The woman rolled towards them in her wheelchair, all life's woes etched into her face. She paid no attention to the unconscious man lying on the floor. She saw only the blood sieving through her son's trouser leg.

464

Lasse got up with difficulty, giving Carl a furious look. 'It's nothing, Mum,' he said. He took a handkerchief out of his pocket, pulled off his belt, and wrapped both of them tightly around his thigh, assisted by his brother.

She wheeled past them and stared up at the manometer. 'How's it going, you miserable bitch?' she shouted at the windowpane.

Carl looked down at Assad, who was breathing weakly on the floor. So maybe he was going to survive. Carl scanned the floor in hopes of locating the switchblade. It could be underneath Assad, or maybe it would come into view if the gaunt one moved aside.

It was as if Hans was reading Carl's mind. He turned towards Carl with a child's expression on his face, as if Carl were going to steal something from him, or even start hitting him. The look he gave Carl was one that stemmed from the loneliness of childhood. From the taunts of other children who didn't understand how vulnerable a simple-minded individual could be. He raised the iron bar and aimed for Carl's throat.

'Should I kill him, Lasse? Should I? I can do it.'

'You're not doing anything,' said the woman, rolling her wheelchair closer.

'Sit down, you bastard cop,' commanded Lasse as he straightened up to his full height. 'Go get the battery, Hans. We're going to blow this building sky-high. It's the only thing we can do now. Hurry up. In ten minutes we're out of here.'

He reloaded the shotgun, keeping his eyes fixed on Carl, who slid down the wall until he was sitting with his back against the airlock door.

Then Lasse ripped the duct tape off the windowpanes and grabbed the explosive charges. With one swift movement he wrapped the deadly mix of wires and detonators around Carl's neck like a scarf.

'You won't feel anything, so don't be scared. But for her in there things will be different. That's the way it has to be,' said Lasse coldly, dragging the gas cylinders over towards the wall of the pressure chamber behind Carl.

Then his brother came back with the battery and a coil of wire.

'No, we're going to do it in a different way, Hans. We'll take the battery outside with us. You just have to connect it like this,' said Lasse, showing him how the explosives around Carl's neck should be connected to the detonation cords and then to the battery. 'Cut off a really long piece. It has to reach all the way out to the yard.' He laughed and looked straight at Carl. 'We'll connect the current outside, and the explosion will take this fucker's head off and blow up the gas cylinders.'

'But what about before that? What about him?' asked his brother, pointing at Carl. 'He could just tear off the wires.'

'Him?!' Lasse smiled and pulled the battery further away from Carl. 'You're entirely right. In a minute I'm going to let you beat him senseless.'

Then his voice changed, and he turned again to look at Carl, a grave expression on his face. 'How the hell did you find me? You said it was because of Dennis Knudsen and Uffe. But I don't understand. How did you link them to me?'

'You made thousands of mistakes, you clown. That's how!'

466

Lasse backed up a bit with what could only be interpreted as insanity rooted deep in his eyes. He was sure to shoot Carl a moment from now. Just take careful aim and pull the trigger. Then goodbye, Carl. No matter what, Lasse wasn't going to let this cop stop him from blowing up the place. As if Carl didn't know.

With peace in his soul, Carl looked up at Lasse's brother. He was fumbling. Couldn't get the wires to lie properly. They kept curling together as he unrolled them.

At that instant Carl felt Assad's wounded arm trembling against his leg. Maybe he wasn't hurt that badly. Small consolation in this situation, because in a moment they'd both lie dead.

Carl closed his eyes and tried to recall a couple of significant moments in his life. After a few seconds of nothingness, he opened them again. Even that solace was denied him.

Had his life really had so few high points to offer?

'You need to leave the room now, Mother,' he heard Lasse say. 'Go out to the yard, far away from the outer walls. We'll join you in a minute. Then we'll all disappear.'

She nodded, took one last look at the porthole and spat on the glass.

As she passed her sons, she looked down with disdain at Carl and the man lying next to him. She would have kicked them if she could. They had stolen her life, just as others had stolen it before them. She was in a permanent state of bitterness and hatred. No other emotion would be allowed to penetrate the protective glass bubble in which she lived.

There's no room for you to get past, you witch, thought Carl, noticing how awkwardly Assad's leg was stretched out to the side.

When her wheelchair drove into Assad's leg, he uttered a roar. In one movement he leaped to his feet and was standing between the woman and the door. The two men standing next to the windows whirled around. Lasse raised the shotgun as Assad, blood pouring from his temple, crouched down behind the wheelchair, grabbed the woman's bony knees, and stormed towards the men, using the chair as a battering ram. The cacophony of sounds was infernal. Assad roaring, the woman screaming, the whistling from the pressure chamber, and the warning shouts of the two men that was cut off by the chaos caused by the wheelchair as it knocked them down.

The woman lay with her legs in the air as Assad jumped on top of her and threw himself at the shotgun, which Lasse was trying to aim at him. The brother started wailing when Assad got hold of the barrel with one hand and began pounding Lasse's larynx with the other. In a few seconds it was all over.

Assad moved away, holding on to the shotgun. He shoved the wheelchair aside, forced a coughing Lasse to his feet, and stood there for a moment, staring at him.

'Tell us how to stop this shit then!' he shouted as Carl stood up as well.

Carl spied the switchblade over by the wall. He unwrapped the wires and detonators from around his neck and went over to get the knife as Hans tried to pick up his mother.

'Yeah, tell us. Now!' Carl stuck the knife against Lasse's cheek.

They both saw it in Lasse's eyes. He didn't believe them. In his mind, only one thing was important: Merete Lynggaard had to die inside the room behind them. Alone, slowly and painfully. That was Lasse's goal. He would take whatever punishment they gave him afterwards. At that point, what did it matter?

'We will blow up him and his family, Carl,' said Assad, his eyes narrowed. 'Merete Lynggaard is finished soon anyway. We cannot do anything for her more then.' He pointed up at the manometer that now showed well under four atmospheres. 'We do the same to them that they wanted to do to us. And we do Merete a favour.'

Carl looked intently at his partner. Inside those warm, brown eyes he saw a glint of genuine hatred that wouldn't need much coaxing.

Carl shook his head. 'We can't do that, Assad.'

'Yes, Carl, we can,' answered Assad. He reached out and slowly pulled the wires and detonators out of Carl's hand. Then he wrapped them around Lasse's neck.

As Lasse glanced over at his imploring mother and his brother, who was shaking as he stood behind her wheel-chair, Assad gave Carl a look that was unmistakable. They had to press Lasse to the point where he would start to take them seriously. Lasse might not fight to save his own skin, but he would fight to save his mother's and brother's. Assad had seen it in his eyes, and he was right.

Then Carl raised Lasse's arms and attached the stripped ends of the wires to the detonation cords, as Lasse had prescribed.

'Go sit in the corner,' Carl ordered the woman and her younger son. 'Hans, take your mother over there and set her on your lap.'

He looked at Carl with frightened eyes; then he picked up his mother in his arms as if she were a piece of fluff

469

and sat down on the floor with his back against the far wall.

'We're going to blow up all three of you along with Merete Lynggaard, if you don't tell us how to shut off your internal machine,' said Carl as he twisted a detonation cord on to one of the battery terminals.

Lasse turned his gaze away from his mother and looked at Carl. Hatred burned in his eyes. 'I don't know how to stop it,' he said calmly. 'I could find out by reading the manuals, but there's no time for that.'

'That's a lie! You're just stalling for time!' shouted Carl. Out of the corner of his eye he noticed that Assad was considering striking Lasse.

'Believe whatever you like,' said Lasse and turned his head to give Assad a smile.

Carl nodded. The man wasn't lying. He was ice-cold, but he wasn't lying. Years of experience told Carl that. Lasse didn't know how to stop the system without reading the manual. Very bad luck.

He turned to Assad. 'Are you OK?' he asked, placing his hand on the barrel of the shotgun only seconds before Assad would have smashed the butt end into Lasse's face.

Assad nodded angrily. The buckshot in his arm hadn't done any significant damage, nor had the blow to his head. He was made of solid stuff.

Carl carefully took the shotgun out of his hands. 'I can't go that far. I'm taking the gun, Assad, and I want you to run over and get the manual. You saw where it was. The handwritten manual in the inside room. It's in the pile at the very end. On top, I think. Go get it, Assad. And hurry!'

Lasse smiled as soon as Assad left and Carl stuck the

barrel of the shotgun under his chin. Like a gladiator, Lasse was weighing his opponents' strengths to choose the one was matched him best. It was clear he figured Carl was a better choice than Assad. And it was equally clear to Carl that he was wrong.

Lasse began backing towards the door. 'You don't dare shoot me. The other guy would have done it. I'm going now, and you can't stop me.'

'Is that what you think?' Carl stepped forwards and grabbed him hard by the throat. The next time the man made a move, he was going to slam the gun in his face.

Then they heard the police sirens in the distance.

'Run!' screamed Lasse's brother as he abruptly stood up, clutching his mother, and kicked the wheelchair at Carl.

Lasse was gone in a second. Carl wanted to run after him, but he couldn't. He was apparently in worse shape than Lasse; his wounded leg simply refused to obey.

He aimed the gun at the woman and her son as he let the wheelchair roll past and crash into the wall.

'Look!' yelled Hans, pointing at the long cord that Lasse was trailing after him.

They all watched as the cord slid across the floor. Lasse was obviously trying to tear the explosives from his neck as he ran down the corridor. They saw the slack in the cord being taken up as he made his way out of the building, until at last the wires wouldn't reach any further and the battery toppled over and was dragged towards the door. When it reached the corner and ran into the doorframe, the loose wire slipped underneath the battery and touched the other terminal.

They felt the explosion only as a faint tremor, along with a muffled thud in the distance.

*

Merete lay on her back in the dark and listened to the whistling as she tried to arrange the position of her arms so that she could press hard on both wrists at the same time.

It wasn't long before her skin began to itch, but nothing else happened. For a moment she felt as if the greatest possible miracle was going to shine upon her, and she screamed at the nozzles in the ceiling that they weren't going to get her.

But she knew the miracle wasn't going to happen when the first filling began loosening in her mouth. During the next few minutes she considered letting go of her wrists as the headache and joint pains and the pressure on all her internal organs worsened and began to spread. By the time she decided to let go of her wrists, she couldn't even feel her hands.

I need to turn over, she thought and ordered her body to turn on to its side, but her muscles no longer had any strength. She noticed everything getting hazy at the same time as nausea made her retch, almost suffocating her.

She lay on the floor, immobile, and felt the convulsions increase. First in her gluteal muscles, then her abdomen, and up into her chest.

It's going too slow! a voice inside of her cried, as she again tried to release her grip on the arteries in her wrists.

After a few more minutes she slipped into a foggy lethargy. It was impossible to hold on to thoughts of Uffe.

She saw flashes of colour and glints of light and spinning shapes; that was all.

When the first filling burst out of her tooth, she began a prolonged and monotonous moaning. All the energy she had left went into this tortured sound. But she didn't hear herself; the whistling from the nozzles overhead was much too loud.

All of a sudden the seeping out of air stopped, and the sound disappeared. For a moment she imagined that she might be saved. She heard voices outside. They were calling for her, and she stopped her wailing. Then a voice asked if she was Merete. Everything inside her called out: 'Yes, I'm here.' Maybe she said the words out loud. After that she heard them talking about Uffe as if he were a normal boy. She said his name, but it sounded wrong. Then she heard a loud bang, and Lasse's voice was back, slicing through all her hope. She breathed slowly, noticing the clumsy grip of her fingers let go of her wrists. She didn't know if she was still bleeding. She felt neither pain nor relief. Then the whistling in her cage returned.

When the earth shook beneath her, everything turned cold and hot at the same time. For a moment she remembered God and whispered His name to herself. Next she felt a flash inside her head.

A flash of light followed by an enormous roaring and more light streaming in.

And then she let go of herself.

Epilogue

2007

The media coverage was tremendous. In spite of the sad outcome, the investigation and solving of the Lynggaard case was a success story. Piv Vestergård from the Denmark Party was extremely pleased and revelled in the attention, since she was the one who had demanded the formation of Department Q in the first place. At the same time, she took the opportunity to trash everyone who didn't share her view of society.

That was just one of the reasons why Carl finally couldn't take any more.

Three trips to the hospital to have the buckshot dug out of his leg and a single appointment with Mona Ibsen, which he cancelled. That was about all he'd been able to deal with.

Now they were back at their posts in the basement. Two small plastic bags hung from the bulletin board, both filled with buckshot. Twenty-five in Carl's and twelve in Assad's. In the desk drawer lay a knife with a four-inch blade. Eventually the whole kit and caboodle would probably be tossed in the bin.

They took care of each other – Carl and Assad. Carl, by letting his assistant come and go as he pleased, and Assad, by creating a more carefree mood in their basement. After three weeks of stagnation with cigarettes and coffee and Assad's cat-howling music playing in the background,

Carl finally reached over to the stack of case files sitting on the corner of his desk and began leafing through them.

There was more than enough to keep them busy.

'Are you going over to Fælled Park today, Carl?' asked Assad from the doorway.

Carl looked up with an apathetic expression.

'You know. The 1st of May? Lots of people on the streets and drinking and dancing and carrying on? Is that not how you say it?'

Carl nodded. 'Maybe later, Assad. But you go ahead if you want to.' He glanced at his watch. It was noon. In the old days getting half the day off was a human right in most places.

But Assad shook his head. 'It is not for me, Carl. Too many people that I do not want to meet.'

Carl nodded. It was up to him. 'Tomorrow we'll look through this pile of cases,' he said, giving the folders a pat. 'All right with you, Assad?'

Assad smiled so broadly that the bandage on his temple almost came off. 'That's good, Carl!' he said.

Then the phone rang. It was Lis with the usual request. The homicide chief wanted to see him up in his office.

He pulled open the bottom desk drawer and took out a thin plastic folder. He had a feeling that this time he was going to need it.

'How are things going, Carl?' This was the third time in a week that Marcus Jacobsen had had occasion to ask that question.

Carl shrugged.

'Which case are you working on now?'

He shrugged again.

Jacobsen took off his reading glasses and set them on top of the paper massacre in front of him. 'Today the prosecutor agreed on a plea bargain with the lawyers representing Ulla Jensen and her son.'

'Is that so?'

'Eight years for the mother, and three years for the son.'

Carl nodded. Only to be expected.

'Ulla Jensen will most likely end up in a psychiatric institution.'

Again Carl nodded. No doubt her son would soon land in the same place. That poor guy would never survive a prison sentence in one piece.

Jacobsen lowered his eyes. 'Is there any news about Merete Lynggaard?'

Carl shook his head. 'They're still keeping her in a coma, but there's little hope. Apparently her brain was permanently damaged from all the blood clots.'

Marcus nodded. 'You and the diving experts from the Holmen naval station did everything you could, Carl.'

He tossed a newspaper over to Carl. 'It's a Norwegian publication for divers. Take a look at page four.'

Carl opened the paper and glanced at the photographs. An old photo of Merete Lynggaard. A picture of the pressure container that the divers had attached to the airlock door so the rescuer could move the woman out of her prison and into the mobile pressure chamber. Underneath was a brief article about the rescuer's role and the preparations that were made inside the mobile unit. About how it was attached, about the pressure-chamber system, and about how initially the pressure in the chamber had to be raised slightly, partly to stop the bleeding from the woman's wrists. The article was illustrated with a blueprint of the building and a cross-section drawing of the Dräger Duocom unit with the rescuer inside, giving the woman oxygen and first aid. There were also photos of the doctors standing before the National Hospital's huge pressure chamber and of Senior Sergeant Mikael Overgaard, who tended to the patient, – gravely ill with the bends – inside the chamber. Finally, there was a grainy photo of Carl and Assad on their way out to the ambulances.

In big type it said in Norwegian: 'Excellent coordinated efforts between naval diving experts and a newly established police division resolves Denmark's most controversial missing-persons case in decades.'

'Well,' said Marcus, putting on his most charming smile. 'Thanks to that article, we've been contacted by the Oslo police department. They'd like to know more about your work, Carl. In the autumn they want to send a delegation to Denmark, and I'd like you to meet with them.'

Carl could feel his mouth turn down at the corners. 'I don't have time for that,' he objected. He'd be damned if he was going to have a bunch of Norwegians running around downstairs. 'Keep in mind that there are only two of us in the department. And exactly how much did you say our budget was, boss?'

Marcus nimbly evaded the question. 'Now that you've recovered and returned to work, it's time for you to sign this, Carl.' He handed Carl the same stupid application for the so-called 'qualification courses'.

Carl made no move to pick it up. 'I'm not doing it, chief.'

'But you have to, Carl. Why don't you want to?'

Right now both of us are thinking about having a smoke, thought Carl. 'There are plenty of reasons,' he said. 'Just think about the welfare reform. Before long the retirement age will be seventy, depending on rank, and I have no desire to be some doddering old cop, and I don't want to end up a desk jockey, either. I don't want lots of employees. I don't want to do homework, and I don't want to take exams. I'm too old for that. I don't want to have a new business card, and I don't want to be promoted. That's why.'

Jacobsen looked tired. 'A lot of the things you just mentioned aren't going to happen. It's all guesswork, Carl. But if you want to be head of Department Q, you have to take the courses.'

He shook his head. 'No, Marcus. No more books for me; I can't be bothered. It's bad enough that I have to help my stepson with his maths homework. And he's going to fail anyway. I say that from now on the head of Department Q should be a detective inspector. And yes, I'm still using the old title. Period.' Carl raised his hand and held the plastic folder in the air.

'Do you see this, Marcus?' he went on, taking the paper out of the folder. 'This is the operations budget for Department Q, exactly as it was approved by the Folketing.'

He heard a deep sigh from the other side of the desk.

Carl pointed to the bottom line. It said five million

kroner per year. 'According to my calculations, there's a difference of more than four million between this number and what my department actually costs. Don't you think that's about right?'

The homicide chief rubbed his forehead. 'What's your point, Carl?' he asked, obviously annoyed.

'You want me to forget all about these figures, and I want you to forget all about the course requirements.'

Jacobsen's face visibly changed colour. 'That's blackmail, Carl,' he said in a carefully controlled tone of voice. 'We don't use those kinds of tactics here.'

'Exactly, boss,' said Carl, taking a lighter out of his pocket and holding it to the corner of the budget sheet. Figure by figure the flame swallowed up the whole document. Carl dumped the ashes on top of a brochure advertising office chairs. Then he handed the lighter to Marcus Jacobsen.

When Carl returned to the basement he found Assad kneeling on his rug, deep in prayer, so he wrote a note and placed it on the floor just outside Assad's door. It said: 'See you tomorrow.'

On his way out to Hornbæk, Carl brooded over what to tell Hardy about the Amager case. The question was whether he should say anything at all. During the past few weeks, Hardy had not been doing well. His saliva secretion was down, and he had difficulty talking. They said it wasn't permanent; on the other hand, that's what Hardy's depression had become.

Therefore they had moved him to a better room. He

was lying on his side and presumably could just catch a glimpse of the convoys of ships out there in the sound.

A year ago the two of them had been sitting in a restaurant in the Bakken amusement park, eating huge portions of roast pork with parsley sauce as Carl griped about Vigga. Now he was sitting there, on the edge of Hardy's bed and couldn't permit himself to gripe about anything at all.

'The police in Sorø had to let the man in the checked shirt go, Hardy,' he said, deciding not to beat around the bush.

'Who?' asked Hardy hoarsely, not moving his head a millimetre.

'He had an alibi. But everybody is convinced he's the right man. The man who shot you and me and Anker and committed the murders in Sorø. But they still had to let him go. I'm sorry to tell you this, Hardy.'

'I don't give a shit.' Hardy coughed and then cleared his throat as Carl went over to the other side of the bed and wet a paper towel under the tap. 'What good would it do me if they caught him?' said Hardy with saliva in the corners of his mouth.

'We'll catch him and the others who did it, Hardy,' said Carl, wiping his colleague's mouth and chin. 'I can tell that I'm going to have to get involved soon. Those shits aren't going to get away with this; no fucking way.'

'Have fun,' said Hardy, and then swallowed, as if preparing to say something else. Then it came: 'Anker's widow was here yesterday. It wasn't nice, Carl.'

Carl remembered the bitter expression on Elisabeth Høyer's face. He hadn't spoken to her since Anker's death. She hadn't said a word to him even at the funeral. From the second they informed her about her husband's death, she had directed all her reproaches at Carl.

'Did she say anything about me?'

Hardy didn't answer. He just lay there for a while, slowly blinking his eyes. As if the ships out there had taken him on a long voyage.

'And you still won't help me die, Carl?' he asked finally. Carl stroked his friend's cheek. 'If only I could, Hardy. But I can't.'

'Then you have to help me go home. Will you promise me that? I don't want to be here any more.'

'What does your wife say, Hardy?'

'She doesn't know yet, Carl. I just decided.'

Carl pictured Minna Henningsen in his mind. She and Hardy had met when they were both very young. By now their son had moved out, and she still looked young. At this point in her life, she probably had enough to attend to.

'Go and talk to her today, Carl. You'd be doing me an awfully big favour.'

Carl looked at the ships in the distance.

The realities of life would probably make Hardy regret that particular request.

After only a few seconds, Carl could see that he'd been right.

Minna Henningsen opened the door to reveal a group of jovial, laughing women. It was a scene that couldn't possibly fit in with Hardy's hopes. Six women wearing colourful outfits and pert hats who were making wild plans for the rest of the day.

481

'It's the first of May, Carl. This is what we girls in the club always do today. Don't you remember?' He nodded to a couple of them as she led him out to the kitchen.

It didn't take Carl long to explain the situation to her, and ten minutes later he was once again out on the street. She had taken his hand and told him how difficult things were for her, and how much she missed her former life. Then she put her head on his shoulder and cried a bit as she tried to explain why she didn't have the strength to take care of Hardy.

After she dried her eyes, she'd asked him with a timid smile if he might want to come over and have dinner with her sometime. She needed to talk to somebody, she said, but the intent behind her words was as blatant and direct as could be.

Standing on Strand Boulevard, he took in the noise coming from over in Fælled Park. The festivities were in full swing, so maybe the people were once again waking up.

He considered going over to the park for a while and having a beer, for old times' sake, but he changed his mind and got back in the car.

If I wasn't so crazy about Mona Ibsen, that stupid psychologist, and if Minna wasn't married to my paralysed friend Hardy, I might take her up on her invitation, he thought to himself. Then his mobile rang.

It was Assad, and he sounded excited.

Hey, hey, slow down, Assad. Are you still at work? Tell me again. What is it you're trying to say?'

'They just called from the National Hospital to talk to

the homicide boss. I just found out from Lis. Merete Lynggaard has been brought out of her coma.'

Carl's eyes slid out of focus. 'When did it happen?'

'This morning. I thought you would like to know then.'

Carl thanked him, put down the phone, and stared out at the vitality of the trees towering overhead, their light green, trembling branches flush with spring. Deep down he ought to be happy, but he wasn't. Merete could wind up a vegetable for the rest of her life. Nothing in this world was straightforward. Not even springtime lasted; that was the most painful thing about reliving it every year. Soon the days will start getting shorter again, he thought, hating himself for his pessimistic outlook.

Once more he glanced over at Fælled Park and the grey colossus of the National Hospital looming in the distance.

Then for the second time he put the parking timer on his dashboard, then headed for the park and the hospital. 'Restart Denmark' was this year's May Day slogan. People were sitting on the grass with their bottles of beer as a big screen projected Folketing politician Jytte Andersen's farewell speech all the way to the Freemason Lodge.

A lot of good that was going to do.

Back when Carl and his friends were young, they had sat here in T-shirts, looking like daddy-long-legs. Today the collective corpulence was twenty times greater. Now it was an excessively self-satisfied populace that came out to protest. The government had given them their opium: cheap cigarettes, cheap booze, and all kinds of other shit. If these people sitting on the grass disagreed with the government, the problem was only temporary. Their average lifespan was decreasing fast, and soon there wouldn't be anybody left to get upset over having to watch healthier people's sporting feats on Danish TV.

Oh yes, the situation was well under control.

A pack of journalists was already on the scene in the corridor.

When they saw Carl come out of the lift, they pushed and shoved at each other to make their questions heard.

'Carl Mørck!' shouted a reporter in front. 'What do the doctors say about the brain damage sustained by Merete Lynggaard? Do you know?'

'Has the detective inspector visited Merete Lynggaard before?' asked another.

'Hey, Mørck! What do you think about the job you did? Are you proud of yourself?'

Carl turned towards the voice and looked right into the red-rimmed piggy eyes of Pelle Hyttested, while the other reporters stared daggers at the man, as if he were unworthy of their profession.

Which he was.

Carl answered a couple of the questions and then turned his attention inwards as the pressure in his chest got worse. No one had asked him why he was there. He didn't even know himself.

Maybe he'd expected to see a bigger group of visitors on the ward, but aside from the nurse from Egely, who was sitting on a chair next to Uffe, there were no faces that he recognized. Merete Lynggaard was good material for the media, but as a human being she was just another patient case file. First, two weeks of intensive care provided by decompression doctors in the pressure chamber, followed by a week in the trauma centre. Then intensive care in the neurosurgical department, and now here in the neurology ward.

Waking her out of the coma was an experiment, said the ward's head nurse when he asked. She admitted that she knew who Carl was. He was the one who had found Merete Lynggaard. If he'd been anyone else, she would have thrown him out.

Carl slowly approached the two seated figures that were drinking water from plastic cups. Uffe was using both hands.

Carl nodded to the nurse from Egely, not expecting anything in return, but she stood up and shook his hand. She seemed moved to see him, but didn't say a word. She just sat down again and stared towards the door of the hospital room, her hand on Uffe's arm.

There was obviously a lot of activity going on inside. Several doctors nodded to them as they strode back and forth, and after an hour a nurse came out to ask if they'd like some coffee.

Carl was in no hurry. Morten's barbecue parties were always the same, anyway.

He took a sip of coffee and looked at Uffe's profile as he sat quietly, watching the door. Occasionally a nurse would go by, blocking his view, but each time Uffe again fixed his eyes on the door. Not for a moment did he let it out of his sight.

Carl caught the eye of the Egely nurse and pointed at Uffe, asking her in silent pantomime how he was doing. She gave him a smile in return and shook her head slightly, which probably meant not bad but not good either.

It took a few minutes for the coffee to have an effect, and when Carl came back from the toilet, the chairs out in the hall were empty.

He went over to the door and opened it a crack.

It was completely quiet in the room. Uffe was standing at the end of the bed with the Egely nurse's hand on his shoulder while the hospital nurse wrote down figures that were displayed on the digital instruments.

Merete Lynggaard was almost invisible as she lay there with the sheet pulled up to her chin and bandages around her head.

She seemed peaceful; her lips were parted, and her eyelids quivered faintly. The blood suffusion in her face was apparently starting to fade, but the overall impression was still worrisome. For one who had once looked so vital and healthy, she now seemed fragile and under threat. Her skin was a snowy white and paper thin, and there were deep hollows under her eyes.

'It's all right to go closer,' said the nurse as she stuck her ballpoint pen in her breast pocket. 'I'm going to wake her up again, but she might not react. It's not just because of the brain damage and the time she's spent in a coma; there are a lot of other factors. Her vision is still very poor in both eyes, and the blood clots have caused some paralysis and presumably major brain injuries as well. But it's not as hopeless as it may seem at the moment. We believe that one day she'll regain mobility; the big question is how much she'll be able to communicate. The blood clots are gone now, but she still hasn't spoken. Most likely the aphasia has permanently robbed her of the ability to speak. I think that's something we all need to prepare ourselves

486

for.' She nodded to herself. 'We don't know what she's thinking inside that head, but we can always hope.'

Then she went over to her patient and adjusted one of the many IV drips hanging over the bed. 'All right. I think she'll be with us in a moment. Just pull the cord if there's anything you need.' And then she left with her clogs clopping on the floor as she moved on to the next of many tasks.

All three of them stood silently looking down at Merete. Uffe's face was utterly expressionless; the Egely nurse had a mournful look in her eyes. Maybe it would have been better for everyone if Carl had never got involved in this case.

A minute passed and then Merete very slowly opened her eyes, clearly bothered by the light from outside. The whites of her eyes were a reddish-brown network of veins, and yet the sight of her awake was enough to take Carl's breath away. She blinked several times, as if trying to focus, but apparently without success. Then she closed her eyes again.

'Go on, Uffe,' said the nurse from Egely. 'Why don't you sit a while with your sister?'

He seemed to understand, because he went to get a chair and placed it next to the bed with his face so close to Merete's that her breathing caused his blond fringe to flutter.

After he'd sat there watching her for a while, he lifted up a corner of the sheet so her arm was visible. Then he took her hand and sat there, his gaze quietly wandering over her face.

Carl took a couple of steps forward and stood next to the Egely nurse at the foot of the bed.

The sight of the silent Uffe holding his sister's hand, face resting against her cheek, was very touching. At that moment he seemed like a lost puppy who, after restless searching had finally found his way back to the warmth and security of the other puppies in the litter.

Then Uffe moved his face slightly back, stared intently at Merete again, laid his lips against her cheek and kissed her.

Carl saw Merete's body tremble slightly under the sheet, and how the display of her heart rhythm rose slightly on the ECG apparatus. He glanced at the next instrument. Yes, her pulse had also increased a bit. Then she uttered a deep sigh and opened her eyes. This time Uffe's face shielded her from the light, and the first thing she saw was her brother, who sat there smiling at her.

Carl could feel his own eyes opening wide as Merete's expression became more and more conscious. Her lips opened. Then they quivered. But there was a tension between the two siblings that simply wouldn't allow contact. This became apparent as Uffe's face grew darker and darker, as if he were holding his breath. Then he began rocking back and forth as whimpers formed in his throat. He opened his mouth; he seemed confused and under strain. He squeezed his eyes shut and let go of his sister's hand as he raised his hands to his throat. No words came out, but it was clear that he was thinking them.

Then he let all the air out of his body and seemed about to fall back in his chair, having failed in what he wanted to accomplish. But then the sounds in his throat started up again, and this time they were not as gutteral.

'Mmmmmmmmm,' he said, panting hard with the effort. Then came 'Mmmmmeme.' Merete was now staring hard at her brother. There was no doubt that she knew who was sitting in front of her. Tears filled her eyes.

Carl gasped. The nurse standing next to him put her hands up to her mouth.

'Mmmmeerete,' finally burst out of Uffe after an enormous effort.

Even Uffe was shocked by the outpouring of sound. He was breathing hard, and for a moment his mouth fell open as the woman standing next to Carl began to sob and her hand sought his shoulder.

Then Uffe again reached for Merete's hand.

He gripped it hard and kissed it. He was shaking all over, as if he'd just been pulled out of a hole in the ice.

All of a sudden Merete tipped back her head, her eyes wide and body tensed; and the fingers of her free hand curled into her palm as if in a cramp. Even Uffe recognized this change as something ominous, and the Egely nurse immediately pulled the cord to summon help.

A deep, dark moan issued from Merete's lips, and then her whole body relaxed. Her eyes were still open, and she was looking at her brother. Another hollow sound came from her, almost as if she were breathing onto a cold windowpane. Now she was smiling. She seemed almost amused by the sounds she was making.

Behind them the door opened, and the nurse rushed in followed by a young doctor with a concerned expression. They stopped in front of the bed to watch Merete, who looked relaxed as she held her brother's hand.

The doctor and nurse glanced inquiringly at all the

instruments but apparently found nothing alarming, so they turned to the Egely nurse. They were just about to ask her a question when sound came out of Merete's mouth again.

Uffe placed his ear close to his sister's lips, but everyone in the room could hear it.

'Thank you, Uffe,' she said quietly, and looked up at Carl. And Carl felt the pressure in his chest slowly fade.

Acknowledgements

A big thanks to Hanne Adler-Olsen, Henning Kure, Elsebeth Wæhrens, Søren Schou, Freddy Milton, Eddie Kiran, Hanne Petersen, Micha Schmalstieg and Karsten D. D. for their invaluable and thorough critiques. Thanks to Gitte and Peter Q. Rannes and the Danish Centre for Writers and Translators at Hald for providing the peace and quiet I needed during crucial periods while writing this book. Thanks to Peter H. Olesen and Jørn Pedersen for inspiration. Thanks to Jørgen N. Larsen for research, to Michael Needergaard for factual information about the effects of pressure chambers, and my thanks to K. Olsen and Police Commissioner Leif Christensen for correcting issues in the book related to police matters. Finally, a big thanks to my Danish editor, Anne Christine Andersen, for an exceptional collaboration.

Read on for an extract from the next novel in the
Department Q series . . .

Disgrace

Jussi Adler-Olsen
Translated from the Danish
by K. E. Semmel

Available in Penguin Books

Prologue

Yet another shot echoed over the treetops.

The shouts of the beaters were much clearer now. His pulse hammered against his eardrums, the damp air forced so fast and hard into his lungs that it hurt.

Run, run, don't trip. I'll never get up again if I fall. Fuck, fuck, why can't I get my hands free? Run, damn it, run. Shhh . . . can't let them hear me. Did they hear me? Is this it? Is this really how my life is going to end?

Branches slapped against his face, drawing streaks of blood, the blood mixing with sweat.

The men could be heard shouting all around him. Now the fear of death really seized hold.

A few more shots. Bullets whistled through the chill air, so close that the sweat poured out of him, settling like a compress under his clothes.

In a minute or two they'd catch him. His hands bound behind his back refused to obey. How could the tape be so damn strong?

With a flutter of wings, startled birds flew off over the crowns of the trees. The dancing shadows beyond the dense row of firs were even clearer now. Maybe only a hundred yards below. Everything was getting clearer. The voices. The bloodthirsty rage of the hunters.

How would they do it? A single shot, a single bolt from a crossbow, and it would be over? Was that it?

No, no, why would they settle for that? They'd never show any mercy, those bastards. That's not how they were. They had their rifles and their filthy knives. He'd seen how effective their crossbows could be.

Where can I hide? Is there any place to hide? Can I make it back in time? Can I?

His eyes searched the forest floor, back and forth. Eyes almost blinded by the tape, but his legs kept up their stumbling pace.

Now I'm going to find out for myself what it feels like to be in their power. They won't make an exception for me. That's how they get their kicks. It's the only way.

His heart was pounding so hard that it hurt.

I

She was practically walking a tightrope as she ventured along the pedestrian street called Strøget. With her face half-hidden by a mud-green shawl, she slipped past the glaring shop windows, her alert eyes scanning the street scene. It was a matter of recognizing people without being recognized herself. Being able to live with her demons in peace and leave everything else to the people rushing past. Leave the rest to those fucking bastards who wanted to harm her, and to those who shied away with a dead look in their eyes.

Kimmie glanced up at the street lamps that were sending an ice-cold sheen over Vesterbrogade. Her nostrils flared. Soon the nights would grow chilly. She had to get ready for winter hibernation.

She was standing near the crossing with a cluster of frozen people emerging from Tivoli, looking towards the main train station, when she noticed the woman in the tweed coat next to her. A pair of squinting eyes looked her up and down, then the woman wrinkled her nose and took a step away. Only an inch or two, but that was enough.

'Don't, Kimmie,' a warning signal pulsed in the back of her head as the fury tried to take hold.

Her eyes moved down the woman's body until they

reached the calves of her legs – her stockings gleaming, her ankles taut in the high-heeled shoes. Kimmie noticed a treacherous smile curling the woman's lips. With a good kick she could snap those heels in half. The woman would topple over backwards. She'd find out that even a Christian Lacroix suit would get dirty on a wet pavement. That would teach the bitch to mind her own business.

Kimmie looked up, right into the woman's face. Heavy eyeliner, powdered nose, her hair meticulously cut, one strand at a time. Her expression rigid and dismissive. Oh yes, she knew the type better than most people did. She'd been there herself at one time. Among those arrogant, upper-class snobs with the gaping emptiness inside. That's what her so-called women friends were like back then. That's what her stepmother was like.

She despised them.

'So do something,' whispered the voices inside her head. 'You don't have to put up with this. Show her who you are. Come on!'

Kimmie stared at a group of dark-skinned boys across the street. If it hadn't been for their roving eyes, she would have given the woman a shove just as the number 47 bus roared past. She pictured it so clearly: what a glorious bloodstain the bus would leave behind. What a shock wave the snooty woman's smashed body would transmit through the crowd. What a delicious sense of justice.

But Kimmie didn't push her. There was always a vigilant eye in a crowd of people, and there was also something inside holding her back. That terrible echo from long, long ago.

She held her sleeve up to her face and took in a deep

breath. It was true, what the woman next to her had noticed. A horrible stench came from her clothes.

When the light turned green, she stepped on to the crossing with her suitcase bumping along behind on its crooked wheels. This was going to be its last trip because it was time to get rid of the old rags.

It was time to change her skin.

In the middle of the main hall of the train station a sign was posted in front of the Danish Railways kiosk displaying the day's newspaper headlines and making life bitter for those who were in a hurry or blind. She'd seen the newspaper placards several times on her way through the city, and they made her sick with disgust.

'That sonofabitch,' she muttered as she passed the signs, keeping her eyes focused straight ahead. But then she did turn her head and caught a glimpse of the face on the *BT* tabloid placard.

The mere sight of that man made her shake all over.

Under the PR photo it said: 'Ditlev Pram buying up private hospitals in Poland for 12 billion kroner.' She spat on the tile floor and paused for a moment until her body's reaction subsided. She hated Ditlev Pram. Him and Torsten and Ulrik. But one day she'd show them. Sooner or later there'd be hell to pay. Just wait.

She laughed out loud, making a passer-by smile. Yet another naive idiot who thought he knew what went on inside other people's heads.

Then she stopped abruptly.

Up ahead she saw Ratty Tina in her usual spot. Bent over and rocking slightly, with filthy hands and drooping eyelids, spaced out, one arm extended, trusting that somewhere in this swarming anthill at least one person would be willing to give up a ten-krone coin. Only drug addicts could get themselves to stand in one place like that, hour after hour. Miserable wretches.

Kimmie slipped past behind her and headed straight for the stairs down to Reventlowsgade, but Tina saw her.

'Hi! Hey, Kimmie! Wait up, damn it!' she heard Tina snuffle behind her in a flash of lucidity. But Kimmie didn't respond. In that huge open space, Ratty Tina wasn't any good. It was only when they sat on a bench together that her brain managed to function at all.

On the other hand, she was the only person that Kimmie would even tolerate.

The wind whistling through the streets on that day was inexplicably cold, so everyone was hurrying home. That was why there were still five black Mercedes with their engines running in the queue of taxis on Istedgade outside the steps to the train station. She thought there was bound to be one left when she needed it. That was all she wanted to know.

She dragged her suitcase across the street to the basement Thai shop and set it next to the window. Only once had she had a suitcase stolen when she'd left it here. But she was sure it wouldn't get stolen in this weather, when even the thieves were staying indoors. Besides, it really didn't matter. There was nothing important inside.

She waited a scant ten minutes at Banegårdspladsen in front of the train station before she saw her pigeon. An extravagantly beautiful woman wearing a mink coat, her agile body not much bigger than a size 10, was removing a suitcase on solid rubber wheels from the boot of a hired car. Previously Kimmie had always looked for women who were a size 12, but that was years ago now. Living on the streets as a homeless person never made anyone fat.

Kimmie stole the suitcase while the woman was standing next to a ticket machine and getting her bearings in the entrance hall.

Then she strode towards the rear exit and was outside among the taxis on Reventlowsgade in no time.

Practice makes perfect.

There she loaded the stolen suitcase into the boot of the first taxi in the queue and asked the driver to take her for a little ride.

She pulled a thick bundle of hundred-krone bills out of her coat pocket. 'I'll give you another couple of hundred if you do what I say,' she told him, ignoring his suspicious glance and quivering nostrils.

In about an hour they'd be back to get her old suitcase. By then she'd be dressed in new clothes, with another woman's scent on her body.

And the taxi driver's nostrils would be quivering for a whole different reason.

Ditlev Pram was a handsome man, and he knew it. In the business-class section of any aeroplane there was always a good array of women who had no objections to hearing about his Lamborghini and how fast it could drive out to his domicile in the fashionable suburb of Rungsted.

This time he'd set his sights on a woman with soft hair gathered at the nape of her neck and glasses with heavy black frames that made her look unapproachable. He found that titillating.

He'd already spoken to her, though without any luck. Offered her a copy of *The Economist* with a photo of a backlit nuclear reactor on the cover, but received only a dismissive wave of her hand in reply. He'd ordered her a drink, which she hadn't touched. And by the time the plane from Stettin landed punctually at Kastrup Airport, he'd wasted a total of ninety precious minutes.

That was the sort of thing that brought out his aggressive side.

He started down the glass corridors of Terminal 3 and found his mark just before he reached the moving walkway. A man headed in the same direction was having trouble walking.

Ditlev picked up his pace so he arrived at exactly the moment when the old man set foot on the walkway. Ditlev pictured it so clearly: a carefully aimed kick would make the crippled body fall hard against the Plexiglas so that the old man's face, with his glasses askew, would slide along the side as he frantically tried to get back on his feet.

Ditlev would have loved to put his thoughts into action. That was the sort of person he was. He and the others in the group had all been raised that way. It was neither exhilarating nor shameful. If he'd actually done what he was thinking, it would have been that bitch who was to blame. She could have just gone home with him. In an hour's time they'd be lying in his bed.

It was her own damn fault.

His mobile rang as Strandmølle Inn slid past in the rear-view mirror and the dazzling waters of the Sound again rose up in front of him. 'Yes?' he said, glancing at the display. It was Ulrik.

'I know someone who saw her a couple of days ago,' he said. 'At the crossing outside the main train station on Bernstorffsgade.'

Ditlev turned off his MP3 Player. 'OK. When exactly?'

'Last Monday. The tenth of September. Around nine p.m.'

'What have you done about it?'

'Torsten and I went to have a look around. We didn't find her.'

'Torsten went with you?'

'Yes. You know how he is. He wasn't any help.'

'Who have you put on the job?'

'Aalbæk.'

'Good. And how did she look?'

'She was dressed OK, from what I heard. Thinner than before. But she reeked.'

'She reeked?'

'Yes, of piss and sweat.'

Ditlev nodded. That was the worst thing about Kim-mie. Not merely the fact that she could disappear for months or years at a time, but that they never knew who she was. Invisible and then suddenly alarmingly visible. She was the most dangerous element in their lives. The only person who could truly threaten them.

'We're going to get her this time, do you hear me, Ulrik?'

'Why the hell do you think I phoned?'

read more   (P)

JUSSI ALDER-OLSEN

REDEMPTION

Two young brothers wake bound and gagged in a boathouse by the sea. Their kidnapper has gone, but they know that he will soon return. Their bonds are inescapable. But there is a bottle and tar to seal it. Paper and a splinter of wood for writing. Blood for ink.

In Copenhagen's cold cases division Detective Inspector Carl Mørck has received a bottle. It holds an old and decayed message, written in blood. It is a cry for help from two boys. Is it real? Who are they and why weren't they reported missing? Can they possibly still be alive?

Though the investigation initially appears hopeless, soon Carl and his team find themselves on the trail of not just these missing children – but others. Boys and girls taken – never to be seen again.

And a cold-hearted killer unable to stop . . .

'The new "It" boy of Nordic Noir' *The Times*

'Engrossing' *Sunday Express*

'Adler-Olsen's fascination with abnormal psychology once again pays off' *Sunday Times*

JUSSI ADLER-OLSEN

DISGRACE

Kimmie's home is on the streets of Copenhagen. To live, she must steal. She has learned to avoid the police and never to stay in one place for long. But now others are trying to find her. And they won't rest until she has stopped moving – for good.

Detective Carl Mørck of Department Q, the cold cases division, has received a file concerning the brutal murder of a brother and sister twenty years earlier. A group of boarding-school students were the suspects at the time – until one of their number confessed and was convicted. So why is the file of a closed case on Carl's desk? Who put it there? Who believes the case is not solved?

Carl wants to talk to Kimmie, but someone else is also asking questions about her. They know she carries secrets certain powerful people want to stay buried deep. But Kimmie has one of her own. It's the biggest secret of them all.

And she can't wait to share it . . .

Disgrace is the terrifying new episode in the Department Q series. The first, *Mercy*, was a No. 1 international bestseller.

'The new "It" boy of Nordic Noir' *The Times*

'Gripping story-telling' *Guardian*